PENGUIN BOOKS

HIS *Greatest* TREASURE

GREATEST LOVE SERIES BOOK 4

About The Author

Hannah is a twenty-something-year-old indie author from Canada. Obsessed with swoon-worthy romance, she decided to take a leap and try her hand at creating stories that will have you fanning your face and giggling in the most embarrassing way possible. Hopefully, that's exactly what her stories have done!

Hannah loves to hear from her readers and can be reached on any of her social media accounts.

Join Hannah's reader's group for bonus content and group-only giveaways! Hannah's Hotties

Subscribe to my newsletter to be kept up to date on all things Hannah Cowan!
www.hannahcowanauthor.com

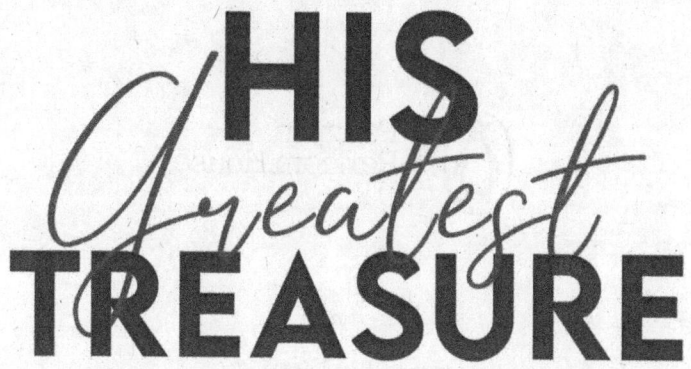

GREATEST LOVE SERIES BOOK 4

HANNAH COWAN

PENGUIN BOOKS

PENGUIN BOOKS

UK | USA | Canada | Ireland | Australia
India | New Zealand | South Africa

Penguin Books, Penguin Random House UK,
One Embassy Gardens, 8 Viaduct Gardens, London SW11 7BW

penguin.co.uk
global.penguinrandomhouse.com

First published 2024
002

Copyright © Hannah Cowan, 2024

The moral right of the author has been asserted

Penguin Random House values and supports copyright. Copyright fuels creativity, encourages diverse voices, promotes freedom of expression and supports a vibrant culture. Thank you for purchasing an authorized edition of this book and for respecting intellectual property laws by not reproducing, scanning or distributing any part of it by any means without permission. You are supporting authors and enabling Penguin Random House to continue to publish books for everyone. No part of this book may be used or reproduced in any manner for the purpose of training artificial intelligence technologies or systems. In accordance with Article 4(3) of the DSM Directive 2019/790, Penguin Random House expressly reserves this work from the text and data mining exception

Typeset by Jouve (UK), Milton Keynes
Printed and bound in Great Britain by Clays Ltd, Elcograf S.p.A.

The authorized representative in the EEA is Penguin Random House Ireland,
Morrison Chambers, 32 Nassau Street, Dublin D02 YH68

A CIP catalogue record for this book is available from the British Library

ISBN: 978-1-405-97877-4

www.greenpenguin.co.uk

Penguin Random House is committed to a sustainable future for our business, our readers and our planet. This book is made from Forest Stewardship Council® certified paper.

Author's Note

Hi, everyone! I wanted to make sure that before anyone jumps into this story that you know His Greatest Treasure is the fourth installment in a second-generation series. This means that there will be a heavy helping of characters involved in this story, both new and from the previous stories.

Keeping that in mind, I have written this to be read as a complete standalone.

If I am a new author to you and you are interested in reading the books prior to this one, I have included a recommended reading list on the next page. If not, I have also added a family tree.

Reading Order

Even though all of my books can be read on their own, they all exist in the same world—regardless of series—so for reader clarity, I have included a recommended reading order to give you the ultimate experience possible.

This is also a timeline-accurate list.

Lucky Hit (Oakley and Ava) Swift Hat-Trick trilogy #1

Between Periods (5 POV Novella) Swift Hat-Trick trilogy #1.5

Blissful Hook (Tyler and Gracie) Swift Hat-Trick trilogy #2

Craving the Player (Braden and Sierra) Amateurs in Love series #1

Taming the Player (Braden and Sierra) Amateurs in Love series #2

Vital Blindside (Adam and Scarlett) Swift Hat-Trick trilogy #3

Her Greatest Mistake (Maddox and Braxton) Greatest Love #1

Her Greatest Adventure (Adalyn and Cooper) Greatest Love #2

His Greatest Muse (Noah and Tinsley) Greatest Love #3

Family Trees
CHARACTER ORIGINS

SWIFT HAT-TRICK TRILOGY

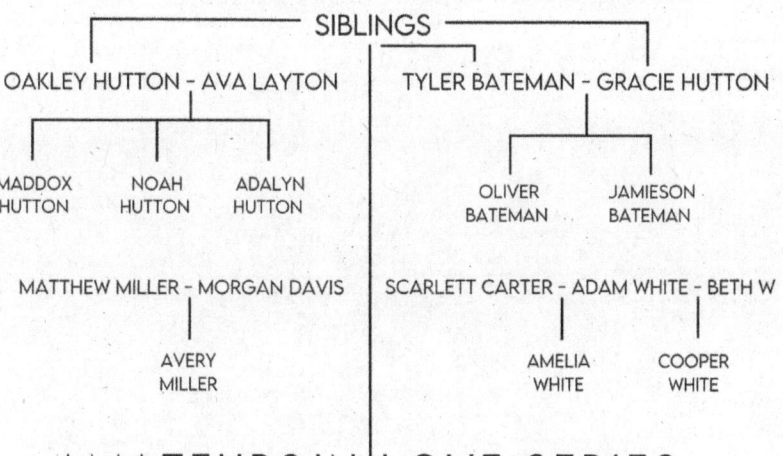

── SIBLINGS ──

OAKLEY HUTTON - AVA LAYTON
- MADDOX HUTTON
- NOAH HUTTON
- ADALYN HUTTON

TYLER BATEMAN - GRACIE HUTTON
- OLIVER BATEMAN
- JAMIESON BATEMAN

MATTHEW MILLER - MORGAN DAVIS
- AVERY MILLER

SCARLETT CARTER - ADAM WHITE - BETH W
- AMELIA WHITE
- COOPER WHITE

AMATEURS IN LOVE SERIES

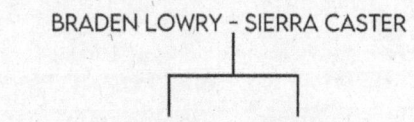

BRADEN LOWRY - SIERRA CASTER
- TINSLEY LOWRY
- EASTON LOWRY

I Think He Knows — Taylor Swift ★	2:53
Close To You — Grace Abrams	3:46
Love Me Like You Mean It — Kelsea Ballerini	3:00
Unwell — Matchbox Twenty	3:49
Numb — Linkin Park	3:08
Short Skirt Weather — Kane Brown	3:14
When She Comes Home Tonight — Riley Green ★	4:10
Always You — Louis Tomlinson	3:07
Black Butterflies and Deja Vu — The Maine	3:23
How Do I Do This — Kelsea Ballerini	2:51
I love You, I'm Sorry — Grace Abrams	2:37
You're Gonna Go Far — Noah Kahan	4:46
Mess It Up — Grace Abrams	2:51
stranger — Olivia Rodrigo	3:13
After All The Bars Are Closed — Thomas Rhett	3:12
Holy Smokes — Bailey Zimmerman ★	3:15

Dedicated to anyone who's ever been told they expect too much or that they should lower their expectations. Fuck. That.

You are worthy of receiving love and support. Those who put a limit on what they can give you have no place in your life. Know what you want and accept nothing less. Always.

1

Oliver

I'VE ALWAYS WONDERED IF IT WAS ACCEPTABLE TO show up to family gatherings with earplugs in.

While I'm used to even louder and far more crowded dinners, the ones I spend with just my parents and younger brother seem to put those to shame in the volume department. Maybe it's my brother, Jamieson's, brute tone or my father's gruff one, but for some reason, their every comment bounces off the walls and makes my ears ring.

My mom is the gentle one, her voice soft and soothing in that typical motherly way. It's the reason I'd always insist on her reading me books before bed and my father being the one to attend my sports events, knowing he'd make the opposing teams nervous with his pissed-off shouts.

"I've got the rest of the season tickets for you guys," Jamie says between bites of pasta. His lips are covered in Alfredo sauce when he slurps a noodle into his mouth and adds, "You too, Ollie. I expect you to at least show up for a handful of games this season."

I twirl my fork in the saucy pasta and grimace at his lack of table manners. "Sorry, I couldn't make out what you were saying over your mouthful of food."

"Just tell me you'll come this season."

"I came last season too."

It was his first in the CFL after being drafted out of college. He's one of the youngest on the BC Pythons' team at only twenty-two.

Jamie huffs, stabbing more noodles with the prongs of his fork before bringing them to his mouth and tapping his lips. "You came to two games."

"I worked a lot last year. My job is unpredictable," I say past the guilt clogging my throat.

Mom eyes me across the table. "Leave your brother alone, Jamie."

Our mother is a dainty woman with blonde hair that should have grayed with age but hasn't and sharp blue eyes. She's the smallest one of all of us, and we always pick on her for it. Dad used to bench-press her in the backyard gym when we were kids because Jamie and I thought it was the funniest thing in the world. Now, I think she'd swat him hard enough to bruise if he tried it.

Small in size, but not bravery or attitude. Somehow, she puts the three of us in our places with ease. Dad might have the towering size and scowl to intimidate any living soul he comes into contact with, but against her, he doesn't stand a chance. He'd never attempt to intimidate her, though. They're as in love as two people can be.

Jamie swaps his fork for a beer, taking a quick sip from it. His glare is weak when it lands on me. "A little old to have mommy fighting your battles, aren't you?"

"Old enough to beat your smug ass with ease too," I mutter.

"That never ends well for you."

"Or you, if I remember correctly."

"Christ alive. Just when I think you've both grown old enough to move past the beating each other up phase, you go and prove me wrong," Dad says.

Mom smiles at him amusingly. He curls his arm around the back of her chair and leans into her space.

"I'll never be too old to beat Ollie's ass," Jamie boasts.

"Your coach would put out a hit on me for injuring you during the season. Don't tempt me to risk it."

"Maybe I'd put the hit out myself."

"I'll run you over with the fire truck when I know the ambulance is out on a call," I deadpan.

He sucks a breath through his teeth. "Fuck, you're a dark son of a bitch, Oliver."

Dad's loud laugh cuts through the room, and just like that, we let the fighting go. Sure, Jamie and I like to give each other a hard time—mostly because he's got the personality of a golden retriever puppy while I'm more like a Rottweiler—but I love the guy. We're close, only four years apart in age at twenty-six and twenty-two. We've given each other a few bruises over the years, but it's mostly all talk.

"You're on shift tomorrow until when, Oliver?" Mom asks while swirling a chunk of garlic bread in a puddle of sauce.

"Four on, four off. I'll be free in time for your game Saturday." I kick Jamie's foot, and he grins wide, happy with the news.

"Do you own my jersey, big bro?"

I swallow a laugh. "I was thinking of wearing one of Dad's old ones."

Jamie's scowl is deeply etched, and the urge to laugh grows at how ridiculous he looks when he's annoyed. "You're not wearing a hockey jersey to my football game, asshole."

"Why not?"

"Oliver," Dad warns, but there's no heat behind it.

Our father, Tyler Bateman, was one of the best defensemen on the Vancouver Warriors NHL team back in the day. He played there for a long damn time before retiring in his forties. I use his career to bug Jamie more often than I probably should.

We all expected him to follow in Dad's footsteps when he was a kid playing both hockey and football, but when he was forced to choose once he got older, he chose football without a second thought.

Myself, on the other hand, I played hockey until I was eighteen, but it was more just to give myself something to do after school and over the weekends. I never loved the sport and didn't have it in me to give any others a try. Being a firefighter is my passion, and my entire family has always supported that.

"I obviously own your jersey, Jamieson," I tell him.

His scowl disappears in a blink. "Damn right you do."

"You'll have an entire row of people wearing number seventy-seven, sweetheart," Mom soothes.

I finish off my glass of water and push my plate up the table so I have room to lean my elbows against it. Steepling my fist beneath my chin, I meet my mom's stare. "Was there a reason you were asking about my schedule?"

She hums, nodding. "Yes. Registration is closing soon for fall dance classes, and I wanted to see if you'd be able to be there for the last day. I'm expecting a few stragglers to come in, and you always sell the place so well."

"You don't need anyone to sell the studio, Mom. It sells itself at this point," I say.

"That's sweet of you, honey."

"Suck-up," Jamie mutters beneath his breath.

I kick his shin, shutting him up. "I've got Sunday open. I can come by then."

Dad tips his chin approvingly at me. "Good man."

"I bet you'd sell the studio better if you had Jamie and the team set up outside. They could host a shirtless car wash," I suggest with a smug smile.

Jamie considers me for a moment before smacking the table with his palm. "That's actually not a bad idea. It's scorching outside this summer. I could chat with Sarah about it."

"You boys are too good to me," Mom sighs, her eyes beginning to glisten. My skin tightens over my bones uncomfortably as the tears begin to fall. "Oh, fucking hell. Here I go."

Jamie laughs at her foul mouth. We heard every curse word

under the sun all throughout our lives. Dad's never been able to censor himself.

I've never been good with tears, maybe because I saw them so rarely growing up. The moment I do, I lock up tight, and my protective instincts scream in outrage.

Dad's quick to rub her arm, his mouth grazing her cheek while he swipes her tears away. "They aren't too good to you. They're doing what you deserve, Gray."

The shortened version of my mom's name, Gracie, has always been used more often than not by everyone but Jamie and me. She's just Mom to us.

"We've got your back, Mom," Jamie promises with a shove of his hand over his floppy blond hair that's so similar to hers.

The movement makes him look just as boyish as his personality is to match. Fitted with the same steel-blue eyes as her, they share a resemblance that's hard to miss. So opposite of my resemblance to my father's black hair and brown eyes.

"Yeah, we do," I say in agreement.

Mom sniffles and straightens, pushing back the swell of emotion that had tugged her under. "Thank you. I know that the studio has taken up a lot of our time over the years, but it seems I can't let it go just yet."

Dad frowns. "You don't have to let it go ever if you don't want to."

I grunt. "It's your legacy. Keep it forever."

The studio has been open since before I was born. It's a space for families who can't afford the expensive cost of regular dance studios. Every year, Mom takes in as many applicants as she can and helps dozens of kids learn to dance the way she loves to. The studio covers everything from the lessons themselves to the competition costs, ballet shoes, uniforms, and costumes.

It's been nearly three decades of love, blood, and a whole lot of sweat from an entire team of people to make the studio what it is now. Yeah, she might delegate a lot more now that both she and Dad are officially retired, but my guess is that she'll be ninety years old and still helping out if she has her way. And I want her to have her way. She deserves it.

Mom's blue eyes meet my hazel ones as she tilts her mouth into a warm smile. "I'll certainly try, love."

"Just let us know whatever you need from us whenever you need it, and we'll take care of it," I promise gruffly.

Jamie pats my back harder than necessary. "Damn right we will."

"Oh, we got lucky with you two. I feared because of what a little shit your father was when we met that you'd be his karma, but that couldn't be further from it."

Dad scoffs in mock offense. "A little shit? I've never been little."

"A big shit, then. Better?" she asks, batting her lashes up at him.

He pinches her cheek and laughs when she swats at him. "It's more appropriate."

"Oliver's a big shit too. He just hides it all behind his gruff exterior," Jamie says, smirking at me. "Isn't that right, Olliepop?"

My childhood nickname—the one I despise more than anything else—grates against my nerves the way he knew it would.

"I'll tie you up by your fucking old man briefs if you don't stop poking me," I threaten.

He pouts. "But I love it so much. Your anger is such a warm comfort at the dinner table."

"If you're going to throw punches, please do it in the backyard," Mom begs.

Dad stands and starts to clean up the dirty dishes from the dining table, his grin subtle enough to make me believe he's trying to keep it from stretching into a full-out grin.

"It's your turn to scrub the dishes," Jamie tells me, no longer pouting. "Am I remembering correctly, Dad?"

I snap my eyes up at my father and glare when he nods, suddenly placing the stack of plates in front of me. The mess of food he's piled on the top one makes my stomach roll.

"Why so green?" Jamie asks, knowing damn fucking well why.

Mixed food like this... isn't for me. I've always had a sensitive stomach, and the sight of Alfredo-slicked noodles mixed with soggy bread and cut-up lettuce from the Caesar salad has me swallowing repeatedly to keep from throwing up right here.

"Stop being an ass to your brother, Jamie, or I'll have you cleaning the dishes with your tongue," Dad muses.

My brother pats his stomach like a heathen. "I'm still starving, so I'm up for the challenge."

"You're repulsive," I mutter before standing and clasping the dishes in my hands.

Without breathing through my nose and risking smelling the mix of food, I suck in air through my mouth and slip into the kitchen. Soft footsteps follow me, and a second after I've placed the dishes on the counter to be rinsed off, Mom settles beside me. Rubbing a hand over the middle of my back, she leans her cheek against my arm.

"Thank you for helping Sunday, sweetheart. I know you feel it's your responsibility, but it still means a lot to me."

I drop my arm to her shoulders and squeeze. "Anything for you, Ma. I mean it."

"Want some help with the dishes? I can clear the plates, and you can wash them?"

"Go sit down and relax. I've got the dishes."

The stainless-steel dishwasher a few feet away taunts me, but we never use it during family dinners. Even if I wish we did.

With a nod, Mom leans up on her toes to kiss my cheek before leaving me in the kitchen. It isn't even three minutes later that Jamie appears and brushes me aside to take over the washing so I don't have to stick my hands in the water and risk touching the bits of food missed with a rinse.

We wash the dishes in silence, but for the millionth time in my life, I'm reminded exactly why I love my family as fiercely as I do, loud to the point of ear pain or not.

2

Oliver

Shaking out of my turnouts, I take a deep breath and swipe away the thin layer of soot from my forehead. Exhaustion makes my bones heavy, the back-to-back-to-back calls the past two days making my sleep heavy but short. Even if we weren't called to the barn fire this morning, I still wouldn't have been recuperated. Not with the adrenaline racing through me from the call before it.

The sun has started to break over the horizon and sneaks beneath the bay door before it shuts, blocking us from the early morning. With a yawn, I grab my turnouts and dump them in the bin that'll be wheeled in for the next shift to wash.

Brent Adams, one of the longest-standing squad members, bumps into me from behind, and I'm too tired to keep from swaying on my feet. "You coming for a drink, Lieutenant?"

"No. Going right home."

"Thank fuck for that! You need a nap, old man!" Hart, a rookie fresh from the academy, shouts, her expression far too lively for the end of a four-day shift.

"Not everyone is old because they're older than you, new blood," Adams says.

He tosses an arm around my shoulder, and while he's a couple of inches shorter than me, he's jacked. His biceps bulge obnoxiously against my neck when he tightens his hold and tugs me closer.

While a handful of years older than me, he's young at heart. His spirit is impossible to crush, and that's a feat in our line of work.

"I hate when you call me that," Hart hisses.

I glance across the garage and cock my head when I see her standing around with her hands on her hips instead of heading in for a shower. Even when trying to appear intimidating, she looks like an innocent puppy in a house full of wolves. As the first of only two women in the station, I admire her for carrying her own, and I'll admit to testing her a bit more than I do the others.

She can handle it, and I know that her continuing to succeed in tough situations has grown the respect the others have for her. If they didn't respect her, they wouldn't speak with her so freely and would have probably stuck to calling her by her first name, Rebecca, or Rookie, instead of by her last name.

"Go shower, Hart," I tell her, jutting my chin to the exit. "Good work today."

The other members of our squad are already gone, most ready to get the fuck out of here and back home to their families. Four days is a long time to be away from them, only home in time to fall into bed. Something I haven't had to worry about thus far in my life.

"Yes, sir. Whatever you say, sir," she retorts before ducking out and disappearing.

Brent leads us after her, his arm still wrapped around my neck. I shrug it off and step to the side as we duck through the doorway and into the fire station entrance. It's already loud and full as the shifts switch and the fresh squad tumbles in.

A few familiar faces pass us, and I use the minuscule bit of energy I have left to greet them with nods on my way to the locker room.

"You sure you don't want to come out with us? You don't

have to stay for long. Just one drink," Brent says, trying too hard to convince me.

"The only thing I want is to sleep."

"You're a bore, Bateman."

"Don't you have a wife to get home to?"

I head directly for my locker once we step into the room and tug it open to grab my duffle bag and the change of clothes I keep inside of it.

Brent does the same but wastes time slapping the backs of the guys around us like he always does. "Yeah. Doesn't mean I can't slip out for a drink before coming home to her. She'll be sleeping by the time I get home, so I can just slip into bed with her and crash before having to find it in me to chat about the week. Don't worry your pretty head about it."

"Okay," I relent, not in the mood to push. His marriage isn't my problem.

He blows air between his teeth. "Okay, he says. "Shit, you're the one that asked."

"I asked, and you answered."

"Don't even think about judging me, Bateman. Not when you're the one who refuses to so much as spend even one night with a woman."

"I'm not judging you. I'm dog-fucking-tired. End of discussion."

He tightens his stare on me for a beat before letting it go with a nod. "I'm a bit touchy. You know how things have been."

I do. Not because I've asked to be brought into the drama with his wife but because he's a talker, and all of his problems become the station's problems. We're a family here, yeah, but shit. His marriage has been on the rocks for years now, and he hasn't done much to fix it. Not as far as I know. But again, it's not my business.

"Yeah. I know."

With a pile of clean clothes tucked beneath my arm and my toiletry bag in my hand, I leave the conversation and duck into the showers, finding the closest available stall before stripping out of my tee and blue uniform pants. Steam fills the space soon after I crank the dial as hot as it'll go and step into the water.

My neck aches when I drop it and let the pulsing stream of water massage the tight muscles. I'm only twenty-six, but some days, I feel older. Weathered and weighed down. It's this career, but even still, I don't think I'd change it for anything.

Being a firefighter gives me a purpose. Something I always felt I lacked in comparison to everyone else in my family. I didn't grow up with a dozen talents and a head for schoolwork like Jamie did. My grades sucked, and when it came to university, there were no scholarships waiting or a football coach going to boot for me. But I didn't let that stop me from searching for a passion outside of the normal secondary school route. The moment I found firefighting, I latched onto it and didn't let go.

Now, seven years out of the academy, I'm one of two lieutenants in our station. A respected member of the team and the entirety of Vancouver Fire. It's a good life, if not sometimes a harsh and lonely one.

If I have to continue the long stretches of sleepless nights and the overworking of my body in order to continue living the life I have, then that's what I'm going to do. I've never been easily distracted, and I'm content with that.

I don't see my life changing anytime soon.

I SHOOT UP IN BED, my eyes wide and searching my surroundings for the culprit of the bang that woke me. It's hard to make out anything in the blackness, but as the cloud of sleep starts to drift from my mind, I remember where I am.

The blackout curtains hung over my bedroom window block almost all the light from outside, but as the air-conditioned air blows up from the vent beneath them, they sway, exposing tiny bursts of sun.

Fuck, I'm tired. Throbbing pain between my brows makes me wince. There's no way I slept as long as I wanted or needed to. I've become accustomed to sleeping like shit most of the time, yet with how tired I am right now...

Another loud bang accompanied by a rattling noise makes the pain in my head worsen. My body lags as I stand from the bed and grow dizzy for a second before slumping my way to the window. Parting the curtains, I curse at the blinding sun and squeeze my eyes shut.

"Definitely early morning, then," I mutter.

Slowly, I open one eye at a time and blink to focus them. The street is relatively full of vehicles, with most people still at home getting ready to leave for work or, like me, *sleeping*. Nothing I see is out of the ordinary.

I live in a quiet, family-friendly neighbourhood, and over the four years that I've been here, I've never been woken up by the noises on the street, even while sleeping during the day. Nothing I can see would be the reason for the banging—

I narrow my stare when I spot a potential culprit. The moving van parked in front of the house beside mine with the wide-open back door that swings in the wind, its chain whipping at the sides.

A breath gets stuck in my windpipe when a woman jumps out from inside of it, a pair of black shorts riding up beneath a round ass and a tank top with the bottom tucked under itself, exposing the entire lower half of her back. Her pink Converse sneakers touch the road a second before she reaches inside the truck and collects a cardboard box with the top open.

A long braid of dirty-blonde hair has slipped over her shoulder and lies along her spine as she carries the box up the sidewalk before disappearing from view. I spin and round my bed in search of my phone. It's plugged into the charger, but I rip the cord out when I check the time and see that it's just after seven *in the morning*.

I've only been home for twelve hours, and now I'm more than annoyed at the disruption. I'm pissed off. Both the exhaustion and throbbing in my head create a terrible concoction of intense irritability.

After finding a pair of sweatpants on the ground, I tug them up my legs and storm out of the room. The porch scrapes against the bottoms of my feet due to the fact I didn't bother with shoes, but I ignore that as I rush down the stairs and along the sidewalk.

The woman is heading back outside when I abandon the sidewalk and cut across the lawn we share. Her eyes widen, and she takes a step back when she notices me, a surprised sound escaping her. I move another few steps before stopping, now close enough to stare at her mouth and the way her lips shine in the sun, as if she's just freshly applied lip gloss. It's odd, considering her face looks otherwise bare of makeup.

Without the window and a large number of yards between us, I notice far more than just her shiny lips. The long braid at her back is messy, with stray strands falling and framing her full cheeks and narrowed chin. Her eyes are round as she watches me and as blue as the sky above us. The freckles splattered over her nose and forehead are a stark contrast to the paleness of her skin. With her clothing choice today, I hope she at least put sunscreen on, or she's going to be burnt to a crisp.

Speaking of clothes . . . she's missing some from what I gathered during my earlier look. My jaw tightens when I force myself to keep my eyes above her shoulders and not examine the expanse of exposed paleness.

"Do you know what time it is?" I snap. It comes out gruff and really fucking rude.

She blinks slowly, her lips rolling before parting. "What?"

"Do you. Know. What time. It is?"

Her throat jumps with a swallow, and I don't miss the downward glide of her eyes. They fall to my chest, and I follow them before realizing I only grabbed pants and not a shirt. An unmistakable sensation of smugness hits me when she continues to stare at my abdomen.

I clear my throat pointedly, and she flinches, snapping her gaze upward and taking a second step back. A splotchy shade of red crawls up her neck before swallowing her cheeks and ears.

"I don't know the time. Is—is that—is that why you came out here?" she stammers, something soft and almost expectant in her eyes that has me stiffening. I pick up on an almost familiar accent that hangs on to her words.

Crossing my arms, I stare down at her with obvious annoyance, not bothering to hide it. She's medium height but still far shorter than me.

"No."

"Okay, so?"

"So?"

"So, why are you asking me what time it is, then?"

I look at the moving truck and then back at her. "It's seven in the morning on a *Saturday*. Why are you being so goddamn loud? You're going to wake the entire neighbourhood with all your banging and clanging."

"I wasn't under the impression there's a certain time I'm allowed to make noise."

"And you need to be told not to slam shit around at this time? I assumed it was common courtesy."

She arches a brow at that, eyes flaring with anger, that soft emotion long gone. "I don't have to explain myself or my reasons for moving at this time of day to you."

"Look," I begin, trying to level my tone. "You just bought the place, right? The house wasn't on the market for very long, but the old owners were nice people."

"And you assume I'm not a nice person because I've started moving in too early?"

"Should I assume differently?"

"Yeah, actually." She scoffs, darting her eyes to the door of her place. "If you're done yelling at me now, I want to finish hauling my stuff inside."

I rake my fingers through my hair, my head pulsing harder than minutes ago. "Can you wait?"

She tilts her head at me, looking at me a bit too closely. "Why?"

"Because it's never a good idea to make enemies of your neighbours on your first day in a new place?"

"And that's what I've become? An enemy all because I needed to unpack my things this morning?"

"Glad we cleared that up."

Hurt flickers in the blue of her eyes before she blinks it away. Surely, I haven't been *that* rude. I can't have hurt her feelings. Annoy and anger her, yeah. But hurt? I narrow my stare and try to dig inside her head to figure out what's going on.

She jams her hands onto her sloped hips and glares at me. "The only thing we cleared up is that you're an *ass*."

"Just keep the noise down. Some of us are trying to sleep," I grit out before spinning on my heels and leaving her on the lawn.

I don't want to hear another word. Silence sounds like fucking bliss right now. So does a solid eight hours of sleep. It's what I would have gotten before I was woken early.

Maybe then I'll wake up with no pain in my head and a calmness that I'm severely lacking. One can hope, anyway. If not, my brother is going to regret asking me to come to his game.

3

Avery

I'VE LOVED FLOWERS SINCE I WAS A LITTLE GIRL growing up in Sweden.

The majority of my childhood was spent lying in the meadow behind the house that bloomed with smörblomma. Tall buttercups are what they call them in North America, and the name is fitting. I'd collect bundles of the bright and glossy yellow flowers and keep them in my room. They didn't last awfully long, but by the time they were drooping, I was replacing them with more.

That's where my fascination started. It's only grown over the years, and as I step into Linnea and Lillies, an overwhelming sensation of comfort washes over me. With a long inhale, I ignore the scent of mildew and focus on the hint of flowers from the lone bouquet that sits on the counter.

This place is far from being ready to open, but I'm not in a rush. It was always a dream of mine to open my own flower shop, and after spending nine years back in Canada getting my life together to the point it became a reality, I want it to be perfect no matter the timeline.

"It stinks in here, Mom. Like Dad's sweaty socks."

I roll my lips to keep from laughing and turn to face my daughter. Her button nose is scrunched, thin blondish-white brows tugged together as she strolls through the place like she owns it. With a dainty finger pointed, she drags it over the shelf on the wall and inspects it for dust.

"It's dirty too."

"It's going to be dirty, honey. Nobody has cleaned it in forever, I'm sure."

"*Behöver jag göra det?*" she asks, disgusted enough with the idea of cleaning the place that she asks the question in Swedish.

"No, Nova. You don't have to clean it. But keep up the attitude, and maybe that will change."

She shakes her head, tight blonde curls swishing around her face. "What attitude?"

"You forget that speaking in Swedish to hide your real words only works if you're around someone who doesn't also speak it." I wink and set my purse on the counter.

The surface of it is dirty too. But it's sturdy and shines in the sunlight poking through the filthy windows. A little bit of surface cleaner and it'll be as good as new. Hopefully.

The same can thankfully be said for the rest of the shop. The front of it, at least. I've only ventured to the back once before I put a bid on the building, but one look into the bathroom had me wanting to demolish it instead of cleaning it.

If it weren't for the beautiful black-framed windows on the front side of the shop, the pale blue herringbone tile flooring, and the large walk-in cooler, I'd have passed on the place. It was expensive—too expensive for the size and location—but after one look inside, I couldn't pass it up.

"When do we get to go home? I want to unpack my room."

"We've been here for five minutes."

"I'm bored."

Planting my hands on my hips, I cock a brow. "I can always change my mind and get you started on the cleaning today."

"No, thank you."

"Then just stay bored for a couple more minutes. I have to do something really quick, and then we can leave."

She huffs, all four feet of her bubbling with a disturbing amount of attitude. Even for a seven-year-old. "Fine."

In all honesty, we didn't need to come here today. The electrician I called in to take a look at the place isn't coming until tomorrow, and I'm too tired from hauling all of our boxes into our new house this morning to tackle cleaning any form of mess right now.

I just needed to get away from the house for a while. The conversation I had this morning with our next-door neighbour has lingered in my head all day, and I've grown angry now that I've stewed on it for hours.

Oliver Bateman clearly doesn't remember me, but I remember him. I'd have to swap my brain out for another to forget him and all of the childhood memories I have that include him and his sulky presence.

He's the son of one set of my parents' lifelong friends. Tyler and Gracie Bateman went to university with my mom and dad. My dad and Oliver's even played on the same junior hockey team for a while. That was before my parents moved to Sweden so Dad could play hockey there, but that didn't stop us from visiting them.

It was only once a year, but I saw the Batemans multiple times over the course of my early life. We were young the last time I was around Oliver, though. Ten years ago, he was only sixteen, and I was twenty. I hate to admit it, but it's not that surprising he doesn't remember me.

I've changed a lot since then, as has he. No longer the scrawny, pimple-faced teen that used to sit and sulk in corners by himself with a book in hand, he's a man. One with a wide, sharp jaw and thick, rippling muscles that I had a hard time not ogling when he was barking at me in my front yard wearing nothing but sweatpants.

My face flushes as images of his chest pulsing with angry breaths and his huge, veiny hands and long fingers running through his messy black hair flash behind my eyes. He was tall to the point that if I were closer to him, I'd have had to tip my head all the way back just to keep eye contact.

He was all grumpy, brutal man with an axe to grind with me, and I felt small and fragile in his presence, two traits that I never use to describe myself. It was like I was waiting for him to finish snapping at me, only to pick me up by the back of my shirt and flick me across the neighbourhood.

The only thing more mortifying than remembering our conversation clearly enough to recount it in my mind is knowing that he noticed the way I checked him out and was so disgusted by it that he grew even grumpier. As if I offended him by growing flushed at the sight of a half-naked, unfairly attractive man.

He can step barefoot on a pile of pine needles and thistle bushes for all I care. Clearly, while he's grown physically, he's stayed the same mentally, choosing to be a grumpy asshole all his life.

"Why are you glaring at the wall, Mom?" Nova asks, forcing me to reel myself back in.

I swallow to ease the dryness in my throat and force a smile on my face for my daughter. "You know what? Forget it. Why don't we go out for dinner tonight before we head back?"

Her blue eyes twinkle at the suggestion as she jumps and claps her hands together. "Yes! Lucy's?"

"As if we'd go anywhere else. Just let me lock up first."

LUCY'S DINER IS A STAPLE. It was a staple in my parents' lives, and from how much Nova loves it here, it'll be one in hers.

Every time we came back to visit Vancouver when I was a kid, we would wind up here. It's never changed, and I don't think it ever will. The teal-blue-and-white retro diner with the light-up *Open 24 Hours* sign on the windows and door and the jukebox that's played more music on a Friday night than any radio ever has are a comfort that I don't ever want to give up.

I feel like a kid again as we slide into a booth against the front window, and Nova beams at the elderly woman who sets our menus on the table before leaving us alone.

"I know what I want. I don't need a menu," Nova declares, her chin resting on her clasped hands.

"Grilled cheese, add bacon, and sweet potato fries on the side?"

"And?"

I laugh softly. "And a strawberry milkshake with extra whipped cream on top with three cherries."

She nods proudly. "Yep."

"What am I having?"

"Turkey sandwich and fries with gravy. And a Diet Coke," she says without hesitation.

I glance around the diner, taking in the familiar hustle and bustle that I've missed over the past few weeks. "Maybe we go here too often."

"No! We didn't come lots when we lived with Dad. I like it here."

"We still came once every couple of weeks," I point out.

Sure, the forty-minute drive sucked and kept us from coming as often as I'd like, but I still made a point to take the trip in. Even if we did only stay for a short time.

My smarty-pants of a daughter leans back, arms crossed. "Yeah, but now we can come once a week. Remember? You promised."

"Yeah, I did. And we will."

Her grin is dimpled, her slightly crooked front tooth flashing. "Good."

The elderly waitress comes to our table and takes our order before patting the top of Nova's head and sliding to the next table. My seven-year-old frowns while patting down her hair.

"Why do old people do things without asking? I didn't want my hair ruffled."

I laugh, reaching across the table to tuck a loose curl behind her ear. "I don't know, sweetheart."

"Rules are rules. Even if you're old, you still have to be nice," she grumbles.

"You're right."

"Mormor said that they should have to retake their driving tests too once they get old."

"Your mormor should have retaken her test years ago, and not just because she's getting old."

Nova's grandmother, or Mormor, as she calls her sometimes, is the worst driver I've ever met. She's not reckless, but she has road rage unlike anyone I've ever seen before. It's why she hardly drives, and Dad made it his mission to turn the both of us into passenger princesses.

I'm ashamed to admit that she passed the bad driving genes onto me.

"She's a funny driver."

"No, she's not. She's lucky nobody's ever rammed into the back of her car from how often she slams on the brakes in front of people."

"It's because they're on her ass, Mom."

"Nova!" I scold despite the laugh building in my throat.

She smiles overly sweetly and bats her blonde lashes. "What?"

"Does your dad let you swear like that when you're at his house?"

"Sometimes," she admits.

I inhale through my nose and settle back in the booth. My ex and Nova's father, Chris, is an alright guy, but he doesn't have a single parental bone in his body. He allows her to do whatever she wants when she visits every second weekend, and while she enjoys it now, she won't later when it starts to affect her more. It's been like this since she was born and was inevitably what broke us apart.

Suffering with postpartum depression while being the only active parent of a colicky newborn was where my resentment of him started. It grew with every year I struggled to carry the weight of being a single parent while not actually being single.

When Nova was small, it was cute when she swore, and it made everyone laugh. But now that she's older, it gets her in trouble at school more often than not. She's seven but has the vulgar vocabulary of a seventeen-year-old.

With a frown and pink cheeks, she adds, "Don't tell him I said that. He doesn't *really* let me swear."

"No? You just said he did."

"I was kidding," she says, but it's more like a question than a statement.

"I won't tell him you told me."

The last thing I need is a fight to break out between them over something like this. With the move and the new distance put between them because of it, I don't want to make anything worse.

It's taken a lot of hard work to be cordial with Chris after our breakup four years ago, but the real struggle has been allowing him even the two weekends a month he gets her. I don't trust him with her, but for Nova, we've somehow managed to make it work. That's not to say we're a perfectly oiled machine, though.

And with this new start to our lives, I can't be too careful. This is a chance for us to flourish, but in order for that to happen, I have to make all the right choices. Starting with treating my girl to dinner at our favourite spot and unpacking our things so we can make our new house a home.

4

Oliver

I've been at Illumina Dance Studio for four hours now. The steady stream of parents and young kids has been never-ending. I've grown tired of reciting the same welcome speech with every new set of faces that approaches the table I'm stuck sitting behind.

I love helping my mom out in the place because she deserves the support. That doesn't mean I don't want to pluck my fingernails off one at a time as I'm forced to smile and pretend I'm interested in knowing about Mrs. Clark's new poodle or the latest HOA decision for a neighbourhood I don't even live in.

The two phone numbers I've been handed—one from a woman with enough kids to outfit an entire baseball team and another shoved beneath my nose by an old lady wanting me to take her granddaughter out—are hidden beneath my empty coffee cup. Out of sight and mind.

I tug at the collar of my shirt and shift in the hard plastic chair in an attempt to get comfortable. My ass is half-numb, but if I stand, I'll lose the safety barrier the table gives me.

Dad picked Mom up an hour ago, insisting that I've kept her from him too long. In reality, she was only here for two before that, but my dad is a selfish bastard when it comes to her time. It's a miracle he let us have as much time with her growing up as we did. I'm sure it just *killed* him.

I stretch my legs beneath the table and drop my chin to my chest. My hands are clasped and rest on my stomach as I close my eyes and push the chair back to balance on two legs.

"Don't tell me you teach ballet."

The snarky voice has me snapping my hands out to grip the edge of the table to avoid falling backward. I glare at the woman in front of the table before noticing the smaller version of her standing beside her and inwardly wincing.

The girl is short. *Dainty*, Mom would call her. She has wide blue eyes that stare at me with a slight murderous glint that would scare me if she were older and bigger. Blonde hair that's brighter and has fewer brown streaks than her mother's has been parted down the centre of her head and braided neatly. They have the same narrow nose and soft bone structure, making their relation that much more obvious.

Mother and daughter, if I had to bet.

I look from the girl back to the woman. "What are you doing here?"

"You know, at this rate, you'd be better off writing me a list of things I'm not allowed to do and places I'm not allowed to visit," my new neighbour snarks.

"Would you listen if I did?"

A laugh builds in her throat but doesn't escape fully. "Not a chance. I'd light it on fire."

"I'm Nova. This is my mom," the girl says, taking a step toward the table. She shoots her hand out in front of her and lets it hover over the stacks of papers and pens. The murderous glint in her eyes has dulled, now more curious than anything else. "It's nice to meet you."

I clear my throat and try to even out my expression so I'm not shooting daggers at a little girl. Her hand is swallowed in mine as we shake quickly. "Oliver."

"This is where we sign up for ballet, right?" she asks.

Her mom's eyes are a brand on my face as she glowers at me. I'm pretty sure she's wishing she'll be able to light me on fire with them. Clearly, she didn't want to see me again as much as I didn't want to see her, and she doesn't bother with trying to pretend otherwise.

"Yes," I grunt.

I search through the stacks of already completed registration forms before finding the blank ones. Snagging a pen from beside them, I offer them both to her mother.

"Fill it out completely, and then leave it with me . . ." I trail off, still not knowing her name.

She hesitates for a moment before saying, "Ary."

"Right. Fill out the forms from start to finish. If you have any questions, just ask. Try not to leave anything blank, *Ary*."

She's so stiff she'd crack right down the middle if I blew on her. "Do I have to fill them out here?"

"I suppose not. But you'll have to bring it back to me today either way. Last couple hours to register."

"Right."

"You do know this is for those who can't afford regular classes, right?" I ask before I can think better of spouting off the jackass question.

Shit, my mom would ream my ass out here and now for speaking to a woman like that.

Ary's peach-tinted lips part, the pillowy look of them hard to ignore even as she curls the top one back. Fury heats her cheeks.

"And just what do you know of my financial status?"

I should apologize. It's the nice, respectful thing to do. But fuck me, my tongue is loose, and my own frustration with her has me doing all the wrong things today.

"I know that the house you just bought wasn't cheap."

"Do you have any hobbies that don't involve being a—" She cuts herself off with a glance at her daughter before clearing her throat. "We'll fill the papers out and leave. It seems we've already overstayed our welcome."

"Look, Mom, empty chairs. We can do it here," Nova says, jabbing her finger to the plastic chairs we've set up by the entrance.

At least she's naïve to the tension between her mother and me. Fuck's sake.

"Great," Ary says on a breath before clenching the pen and papers and striding to the makeshift waiting area.

I watch her go, my eyes drawn to the graceful way her body moves with each step. It's like she's floating on goddamn air, even in a pair of wedges that give her a couple more inches in height. Shit, they do more than just make her taller. The bare expanse of her tanned legs leading up to a pair of cut-off jean shorts appear even longer than they did yesterday morning. The tiny shorts, in addition to the oversized white tee that hangs off her left shoulder, make her look like something out of one of a younger me's wet dream.

Gritting my teeth, I glare at the messy table in front of me and start cleaning it up. Every pen I drop in the plastic cup seems to annoy me more and more, until soon enough, I'm crumpling the edge of each registration form instead of stacking them neatly.

There's something about that woman that unnerves me. Maybe it's her scowl that somehow rivals mine or the way she still hasn't apologized for being rude yesterday—as if she needs to with how fucking terrible I've been to her. I can't put my finger on what it is that's riling me so badly, and that's the most aggravating thing of all.

I sit and stew for a few more minutes before she slams the stack of papers on the table, leaving her fingers splayed over the top one until I bring my gaze to hers.

Hunched over the table, she breathes fire, her cheeks as red as the trucks at the station. "Here. Try not to lose them."

The rapid rise and fall of her chest is hard to ignore, but when my cock twitches in my jeans, I make damn fucking sure I don't let my eyes stray.

"How did you hear about this place?"

"That's not your business."

I lean forward, my elbows digging into the table. "It is considering this is my family's business."

"Worried someone's been blabbing about you to those undeserving?"

"I never said you were undeserving."

"Close enough to it."

"A lot of people try and take advantage of this place. I'm doing my job."

She blows out a disbelieving breath. "You don't work here."

"I'm here, aren't I?"

With a flick of her eyes, she looks at the words written on the corner of my T-shirt. "Vancouver Fire Department. Lieutenant Bateman. Are you trying to brag?"

"Why? Are you impressed?"

The flirtatious question confuses me. I stiffen and lean back, putting more distance between us. She straightens, doing the same.

Her next words are pointed, aimed to kill. "Nothing you could do would impress me. I'm not interested in arrogant, selfish assholes."

"Mom!" Nova gasps, appearing out of nowhere. She gawks at her mom with a devilish grin. "See, it isn't only Dad that says those words. *Now* can I?"

At the mention of her dad, I'm searching Ary's left hand for a ring. If there was a man in her life, why was she moving boxes that probably weighed as much as she does into her house on her own? I don't have to like her to think she should have had help.

Asshole I may be, but I still wouldn't have had my woman carrying shit all if it were me. Alone or otherwise.

Ary grimaces and drops her hand to Nova's shoulder. "No. You can't. I shouldn't have either."

"Ugh. Whatever."

She closes her eyes for the slightest moment before opening them again. "It's time to go, Nova. Leave it at that."

"We're coming back soon, right?"

"Classes start in a little over two weeks. You'll come back a few days before that to pick up your shoes and uniform and meet the instructors. Your mom will get an email with the specifics before pickup day," I explain.

She nods eagerly and grabs her mom's hand, linking their fingers. "Okay!"

Ary's expression is blank as she looks at me a final time and then turns on her heel, tugging her daughter along with her out of the studio. Nova skips beside her despite her mother's current mood, and it almost makes me smile.

Jamie was like that as a kid. Hell, he's still like that now. Alive and carefree, happy despite how shitty life can be at times. He's my opposite, and apparently, so is the little girl whose mother can't stand me.

Luckily, it's hard to be offended when the feeling is mutual.

5

Avery

BETWEEN BACK-TO-SCHOOL SHOPPING, UNPACKING years of our lives into a new home, preparing to open a business, and trying like hell to ignore the side-eye Oliver gives me every time we see each other outside, it's been a long week.

By the time the weekend rolled around, I was both clutching Nova's hand to keep her from going with Chris and reminding myself that I should appreciate the break. Seven years after having my daughter and I still haven't beat it into my brain that it's okay to need a moment to yourself. The guilt that comes with leaving her with her father never fails to make me feel like the world's worst mother.

I spent last night curled up on the couch, nursing a glass of cheap white wine and watching the first DVD I found in one of the living room boxes until I fell asleep. It was a quiet Saturday night. Nothing special in the slightest.

The familiar ring of an incoming FaceTime call has me sitting up in my patio chair, a sheen of sweat sticking to my skin as I reach for my phone. It's mid-afternoon on a scorcher of a Sunday, and I'm lounging in my backyard beneath the sun, hoping to tan my pasty skin. I wasn't expecting a call from my mom, but from the name on my phone screen, that's what I'm getting today.

At least I didn't attempt to tan in the nude like I contemplated until remembering my grumpy neighbour would certainly have had a problem with that if he saw.

Maybe that should have given me all the more reason to do it, but I'm mature enough not to try and piss him off. *For now.*

Mom's face appears on the screen the moment I accept the call. Her grin could melt snowcaps with how warm it is. I wish I got her dimples, but she only shared her hair colour and terrible driving skills with me.

"*Hej, min älskade,*" she sings before blowing a kiss at the camera.

"Hi, Mom."

"Hi, Mom? That's all I get?"

I lift a hand to shield my eyes from the sun. "*Du är dramatiskt igen.*"

"That's better, even if it is an insult. 'Hey, Mom' is so boring," she says on a sigh.

"I didn't know you were going to call today."

Her eyes narrow suspiciously, and if I didn't know better, I'd think she was trying to look around me to notice whether I'm alone or not. "Did you not want me to call?"

"I always want to talk to you, Mamma. I just wasn't expecting it, is all."

"Well, I missed you today. I couldn't wait until Nova got back to call you."

I smile softly, fully understanding how she's feeling. "I miss you too. Where's Dad?"

"Oh, he's around here somewhere. Probably tinkering around with someone that doesn't need to be tinkered with."

"Is he that bored?"

"Your father is always bored now. Old age is supposed to make a man settle, but not him. He would rather be on the ice risking breaking his brittle bones than snuggling with me on the couch."

I bite the inside of my cheek and shake my head. My parents

have always been ones to bicker in a way that would seem tedious but is just their love language. My dad is young at heart despite his age being in the fifties, and if he had it his way, he never would have retired. Unfortunately, regardless of whether he believes it or not, his time as a goalie is over.

"I know you're not talking shit about me, Morgan. I'll have you know that I'm not brittle at fucking all."

My cheeks burn from the smile that splits my mouth at the sound of his voice. When he ducks into the view of the camera, he's scowling, but it's weak and disappears the moment he sees me, replaced with a grin.

The lack of wrinkles on his face should be studied, but the grey hairs streaked through the brown give away his age, even if he has perfect skin. His eyes twinkle as he looks at the camera, and my heart swells.

"*Mitt hjärta*," he murmurs, calling me his heart for the millionth time in my life. "I missed your face."

After thirty years of living in Sweden, my parents are both fluent in the native language and, more often than not, speak in Swedish as opposed to English.

While they're both from Vancouver, I was born and raised in Malmö, Sweden, after they moved there while Mom was pregnant with me. I grew up speaking both languages and learning about two countries that each hold a significant piece of me. Our vacations to Canada were the only time I got to see where my parents grew up, but I clung to it like I'd always shared my life between both places.

Once I turned twenty-one, I made the decision to move to Canada. It wasn't supposed to be a permanent thing, but once I met Chris and had Nova . . . it became one. I miss Sweden more than words, but I'm also happy here. I feel at peace where I am while also knowing that could change at any time.

"Hi, Dad," I say, tucking my feet beneath me on the chair. "Mom was telling me about how you won't sit and watch movies with her?"

He sits beside Mom on the couch now, one arm slinging over her shoulders. His eyes find hers as he smirks. "Is that so?"

"Apparently, you'd rather fix things that aren't broken," I add.

"Avery!" Mom scolds half-heartedly. "You tattletale."

"It's payback for all the times you did it when I was a kid." I shrug.

Dad tips his chin at the phone, where Mom holds it extended in front of them both. "That's my girl."

"When are you coming to visit? It's been too long since I've held you and my precious Nova," Mom says.

"I don't know. Fall break, maybe? School starts next week, and the shop is still a work in progress."

Her lips press together as she nods, her features tugging in a way that makes me feel terrible for not being able to come right this moment. "Now I know how my parents felt when we moved here."

"I'm sorry. I didn't move here to hurt you."

It's still hard being away. I think it always will be.

"Oh, don't apologize to us. We know. It's only fair for you to get to experience what we had growing up. Canada is a part of you," Dad soothes.

"I'll try to come as soon as I can. I've got to save—"

"*Not a chance*," Mom interrupts me. "We'll pay for you. Don't be silly."

I frown. "I'm thirty, Mom. I can pay for my own trips."

"Not when I'm the one begging you to come. Enough of that nonsense. We'll talk about this later."

"We can consider it a birthday present, hmm?" Dad offers.

Knowing better than to continue arguing about it, I let the topic go. "I'm supposed to pick up Nova in a couple of hours and still have a few things to do first. We'll call you tomorrow morning, okay?"

"Okay, *mitt hjärta*," Dad says before Mom has a chance to jump in. "We'll talk later. Love you."

Mom brings the phone closer to her until it's only her face in the camera. "I love you, Avery."

"I love you both. I'll call soon."

Ending the call, I release a tight breath and stand, my legs stiff. I let the phone fall to the empty chair and stretch my back before heading for the blow-up pool we put up a couple of days ago.

It's only a small one that doesn't even come up to my hips, but with a couple of weeks left of this obscenely hot weather, it'll do.

The water is cold when I step into it and drop to my ass, not caring much about the sudden drop in temperature. I smell like sunscreen and the anti-algae chemicals I dumped into the water earlier as I try to relax, my head so full it could explode.

The silence is damn loud without Nova here. If she were, she'd be splashing me in the face or shooting me with a water gun, and while I'd shoo her away, saying I want time to soak peacefully, I'd give in and pick up a water gun to join her.

My entire life revolves around her, and while that isn't a bad thing in the slightest, sometimes I do wish that I had . . . more for myself. Sure, I have flowers, but they won't keep me company either. They won't wrap me in muscled arms or distract me from overthinking with warm breath on my neck . . .

I jolt out of my thoughts when a door slams. Shifting, I stare at the house beside mine and wait for another sound to follow.

Oliver's house is nicer than mine, but only slightly. The yard is bigger, with a massive shed and grass decorated with criss-crossing lines from a mower. Mine is overgrown and infested with dandelions. I'd be embarrassed that he must have seen the state of it already if I gave a shit about him and his opinion. Which I *do not*. Obviously.

The moment his back door swings open and he steps outside in little more than a pair of gym shorts and a towel thrown over his shoulder, I know I should look away. He'll bitch me out the moment he catches me staring, but Christ. First, he comes and yells at me for moving in wearing a pair of sinful grey sweatpants and nothing else, and now this? I've never seen so many abs outside of gym rat videos or TV.

At least there are only a couple more weeks of summer left. Then he'll have no choice but to layer up with clothes to keep warm.

He lifts his hand and squirts water from a bottle into his mouth before proceeding to soak his bare chest in it. I almost laugh at how porny it looks, but I can't because he's also so fucking sexy, all glistening and wet in the sun.

His hair is messy and already damp, and his cheeks are red, his chest puffing with every breath he takes. I swallow the excess moisture in my mouth and curl my fingers in the pool water when he heads toward the rack of weights beside his shed and starts to pick two up.

"You've got to be fucking kidding me," I mutter.

He's really going to work out in the backyard right now. In the heat while dripping in water and what I think is sweat from whatever other activity he was doing before now. I tip my head back and force my eyes shut before he catches me looking.

With my fingers still curled, I get to my feet, the water swishing and splashing around me as I nearly slip on a slick spot of whatever the hell this pool is made of. I grow tense, freezing when something drops to the ground in the direction of where Oliver stands.

"Pool's a bit small, isn't it?" he asks, that gruff voice of his falling like a sledgehammer between us.

"Wish I could say the same about your ego," I reply stiffly.

Why didn't I buy a house with a real fence instead of a pathetic wire one that doesn't give me a single inch of privacy?

"You don't know a damn thing about my ego, princess."

I glare harshly at him and grip my waist. "I wish that were true. The last thing I want is for you to take up an inch of my brain space."

His brown eyes narrow right back as he stays rooted to his spot in the grass. It aggravates me even more than his presence does when he doesn't drop his gaze for even one second to take in the skimpy bikini I'm wearing. Yeah, it's probably stupid to want a man to ogle me, but considering I've just done it to him, it's only fair.

I'm too curious to learn if he's as impressed with what he sees as I am to be modest. For God's sake, it's not like he can't tell that I'm in a bathing suit that does little to cover my tits, considering it's neon yellow. Still, he doesn't budge.

"Are you sure I'm not already?" he asks, a smirk twisting his mouth.

I'd love to punch it off.

"I hope you drop one of those weights on your foot, *butternalle*," I toss back before heading inside, my steps more stomped than they should be.

His voice carries on the breeze, reaching me just before I get to the door. "What was that?"

"Nothing."

The corner of my mouth tips up as I go inside, leaving him wondering. Only once I've closed every set of blinds in this place and stepped into a cold shower do I forget about Oliver Bateman again.

6

Oliver

I DUNK MY HEAD INTO THE SINK FULL OF COLD WATER and open my eyes, hoping that the water will wash the image of Ary out of them.

My exhale makes the water bubble before I pull my head back and inhale. A neon yellow bikini still stains my vision, even as I stare at myself in the mirror of the medicine cabinet. Fuck my life, she shouldn't look as good as she does.

It's a cruel joke.

I've managed to avoid her well over the past week, but this? This is my winning streak coming to a whopping end. If she's going to lounge around every day in a bikini with pink skin glistening with water and suntan lotion, I'm going to go out of my goddamn mind. I can't spend every day for the rest of the summer with a hard dick and anger-flushed skin. I'll have to avoid my backyard like the plague or maybe build a new fence. One high enough to block her out...

The worst part about what just happened isn't even that we were bickering like two immature teenagers but that I *liked* it. The back and forth filled me with excitement. I wanted to keep going, so I'm glad she put a stop to it when she did.

The muscles along the underside of my arm ache when I reach

up and run wet fingers through my hair. Lifting weights wasn't my plan at all for today. I had only just got home from a two-hour run when I stepped into the backyard, not expecting to find my neighbour tanning almost naked in a kiddy pool.

The choice to add weights to my workout surged into my subconscious when I noticed the way she was watching me. Like she was *impressed*. It was a brute decision that I'm paying for with my sore and overworked muscles.

Leaving the bathroom, I rub my shoulder to try and soothe some of the pain there. The house is quiet like usual, maybe too quiet, if I'm being honest. I forced myself to be okay with the quiet once I moved out of my parents' house and got my own place, but I grew up around noise. A lot of it.

My family is massive, made up of both blood relatives and friends that I'm just as close with. There was never a single weekend spent in silence or a holiday that wasn't cluttered and so loud my ears would feel bloody by the end of the night.

I used to tell myself that once I got older, I'd spend my weekends in silence as much as possible, but those were wants of a kid who took what he had for granted because he was a stubborn shit. I don't want that anymore. Maybe that's why I'm always at my parents' house or bothering my cousins whenever possible.

A heavy feeling grows in my chest as the silence really sinks in. It's an overload of emotions that I try to push down but can't seem to. I'm lonely, and I wouldn't be surprised if that's half the reason why I enjoy bickering with Ary so much.

The kitchen is bright without the lights on as I step inside and head right for the fridge. The clink of beer bottles fills the kitchen when I pull one out and twist off the cap. It's cool on my throat, the first swallow soothing some of my tension.

I could call one of twenty numbers of people who would come keep me company if I asked, but it feels desperate. My family has grown in size over the past few years with babies and marriages. I'm the third oldest of all the kids, only behind my non-blood-related cousin, Cooper, and my blood cousin from my mom's side Maddox. Both of whom have families of their own. I should be next in line, but everyone knows that in reality, I won't be.

"Fuck, you're one depressing bastard," I grunt.

The BC Pythons game is still playing on the TV in the living room from when I turned it on right after getting back from my run, so I flop down on the couch in front of it to watch. My brother's team is playing today, and now I'm wishing I had taken the tickets he offered me.

Last weekend's game was good. His team won, and he was phenomenal, the way he always is. The experience should have convinced me to go again today, but I couldn't bring myself to join my parents.

The silence is hard, but sometimes, the noise is harder.

Crowds and tens of thousands of watching people keep me from going as often as I should. It's selfish, but it's the way I've always been. With my family and my team of firefighters, it's different. Strangers make my skin crawl.

With a slow exhale, I set my beer down on the floor and maneuver myself into a lying position. It's half-uncomfortable with my ankles hanging off the armrest, but when my eyes start to droop, I don't give them or my feelings another thought.

I just sleep.

It's dark when I wake up. Through blurry eyes, I see that the game is over and a poker match has replaced it. Fumbling for the remote, I find it on my chest. I turn the TV off, not wanting to die of boredom from having to watch poker, and stand.

I wobble for a beat before gaining control of my legs and forcing myself up the stairs. My sleep schedule has grown so messed up over the past couple years, but I'm hoping with my new two on two off shift, I can fix it up a bit.

My bedroom is brighter than the living room, and I grow confused as to what time it actually is when I step inside and stare out the window beside my bed. The sun is still setting and peeking up from the horizon, making it... nine, maybe.

I go to pull the blinds down when I freeze, muscles locking up. The pain in my muscles is worse now than hours ago, and as I tense up, it only grows more intense. I stop caring about that in an instant.

Ary always has her blinds closed over the window straight across from mine, probably because she thinks I'm a fucking creep who will stare into it all the time, but tonight, they're still up. And thank God for that because the tendrils of smoke curling in the air from whatever lies beneath the window have me taking off out of my room.

I storm down the stairs, my focus zeroed in on that smoke as alarms ring in my head. Somehow, I manage to grab my fire extinguisher before leaving. My front door is left open as I hurry across the yard and jump onto her front porch.

"Ary, open the door!" I shout, banging my fist on the wood over and over again. "Ary!"

Footsteps sound on the other side of the door, but I continue hitting it until it swings open. Wide blue eyes meet mine as I shoulder past her and walk inside, not waiting for an invitation.

"Oliver? What are you doing?" she asks, her voice higher-pitched than normal. "It's not socially acceptable to just storm into other people's houses!"

"Stay here," I demand before leaving her behind, taking the stairs two at a time.

My chest pounds, adrenaline already creating a fog over my mind. Years of training keep me focused on the task at hand and nothing else. Get the fire out before it grows, and make sure everyone is safe.

"You can't go in my room! Oliver!"

"Is Nova here?"

"No, she's—"

Her answer good enough for me, I stop listening and inhale, smelling the telltale scent of something burning. It's not a fire yet, but it will be soon if I don't get it under control.

"You're an absolute lunatic!" she shouts behind me, following at a quick pace to keep up with my long strides.

"Did you leave something on in your bedroom? A curling iron or something?" I ask, my voice dangerously low in an attempt to keep from shouting at her.

"What are you talking about?"

I stop, and she nearly runs into my chest when I spin to face her. The fire extinguisher in my hands rests between us, and when she stares at it, I take a second to look at her.

She's done her makeup and hair tonight, and her tiny body is wrapped in a shimmery fabric that stops above her knees—

I swallow a growl and leave her there before searching for the room across from mine. Getting distracted is not a part of the plan.

Wanting to avoid speaking to her again, I take a guess that her place has the same layout as mine when I see the same number of doors and head for where my bedroom would be. When I step into the room and see the smoke coming from the towel below a curling iron that's still plugged into the wall, I drop the extinguisher on the ground.

"Christ, woman," I snap while tugging the cord from the wall and pulling the curling iron off the towel.

The towel is what's smoking, so I take it off the vanity and leave the room in search of the bathroom. When I find it, I drop it in the sink and turn the tap to cold, letting it soak the cotton.

Ary is behind me in the doorway when I look over my shoulder. Her face is pale, fingers dancing anxiously at her sides.

"How long have you had this plugged in for and sitting on that towel?" I ask, gripping the handle of the curling iron too hard as I hold it up.

"I don't know. Not long. I always keep it on that towel, and it's never smoked like that before," she rambles.

I blow out a tense breath and tip my head back before looking back at her. "You can't leave a hot tool on a towel unattended. You shouldn't even do it attended, but at least you'd know to take it off if you were watching it. If the towel had started on fire—"

"Yeah, I got it."

"Do you? Because if I hadn't seen the smoke—"

Her eyes tighten at the corners as she takes a step forward, crossing her arms and cutting me off for the second time. "What were you doing looking in my window anyway?"

"Are you being serious right now?"

"What were you doing?" she presses, full-blown glaring at me now.

I want to drop the curling iron I'm still holding, but it's so hot that I don't know where to put it yet. Choosing to shut the tap off instead, I meet her glare with one of equal power.

"I wasn't looking in your window. I was going to shut my blinds and then saw the smoke."

She twists her lips. "If you say so."

"Why were your blinds open in the first place? Were you looking in *my* window?"

"As if. There isn't anything I want to see in there."

"Likewise."

"Great."

"Fan-fucking-tastic." I jab the curling iron in her direction and wait for her to take it from me before squeezing through the non-existent space in the doorway. "I'll be going, then."

Her huff is loud enough that the neighbours on her other side probably heard it. "Thank you."

I stop in my tracks and twist to look back, only having made it a couple of steps from her. She rolls her eyes at my surprise and jabs a finger in my direction.

"Don't be a jackass about it. Just say 'you're welcome' and leave."

"You're welcome, Ary. Just be more aware of your surroundings. Especially considering you were leaving?"

"I was only going for dinner. And I don't need you to lecture me."

I laugh tightly. "That wasn't a lecture. I don't want your house to burn down. Do you have a fire extinguisher?"

From the quick perusal of her bedroom I managed while sorting out the almost fire, there wasn't one there, and something tells me that if I searched this place from top to bottom, I still wouldn't find one.

"No," she admits, her cheeks filling with colour.

"Does your boyfriend? Husband? Nova's father?"

Surprise makes her eyes flare, but I don't know if it's because of the bluntness of my question or if it has something to do with her daughter.

I won't deny that I've been curious about her daughter's father. He hasn't been around while I've been home—not that I've been looking—and there was no secondary phone number or name on the registration forms she filled out at the studio.

She avoids my eyes. "While it's none of your business, Nova's father isn't my boyfriend. And even if he were, he's less likely to have a fire extinguisher than I am. He's less likely to do a damn thing anytime. The *latmask*. And just because I can tell you're wondering, sometimes women enjoy going out for dinner on their *own*, thank you very much."

The bit of information gets stored deep in my mind along with the second name I've heard her speak in that other language. She's dressed up for herself tonight, not anyone else. I shouldn't care about that.

"Keep the one I brought, then. And enjoy your dinner."

"I'll buy my own extinguisher."

"Well, I'm not taking mine back with me, so you'll only have two in that case. The more, the better." I shrug a shoulder and head back down the stairs before she has the chance to argue further.

A soft set of footsteps follows after me. "You're an impossible man."

"Yeah, heard that before. Now, no more towel fires, please."

I didn't even take my shoes off when I got here, but I don't have it in me to feel guilty about the mess they might have left in my hurry. She can ream my ass out about it another day.

"If I do have another one, I'll make sure to keep my blinds closed," she mutters when I reach for the door.

Something hot prods in my chest as I huff a breath and cross the distance between us. "Is your phone on you?"

"Yes," she says suspiciously.

"Give it here."

"A please would be appreciated."

I grind my teeth. "Please."

She leaves the entry for a moment before reappearing with a small purse in her hands. With a dip of her hand inside of her, she pulls out her phone and then quickly unlocks it.

I take it from her and open her contacts before adding mine and sending myself a text so I have her number.

Handing it back, I say, "Keep the blinds closed if you want to, but you call me if you so much as smell something funny in here. I don't play around with this shit, Ary. Got it?"

She sobers slightly, losing some of her stubbornness. "Yeah, I got it."

After a final glance at her darkly lined eyes, red lips, and slim-figured body in that tight-as-fuck red dress, I leave.

This time when I get back inside my place, I don't just dunk my face in cold water. I bathe in it.

7

Avery

"I don't want to go to ballet, Mom," Nova moans, kicking her feet in the back seat.

"You wanted to go every day for the last two months. If you've changed your mind now, I'm sorry to say it's too late."

I turn into the parking lot of Illumina and turn the radio down, muting the twelfth consecutive song request from Nova. With school starting this upcoming Monday, I know she's feeling nervous. It's why I've let her play all of the Nickelback songs she wanted on the way here. An introduction to a new ballet studio and other girls her age is bound to be intimidating, even if she's never been afraid of social events.

Nova thrives in crowds, but like me, new faces can intimidate her. She just doesn't show it.

"Fine. But nobody better not pick on me." She cracks her knuckles and snaps her teeth like an animal. "I watched *Kung Fu Panda* a lot, right, Mom?"

"Oh, only about a hundred thousand times. I'm sure you've picked up quite a few skills from that panda. Let's just try not to beat up the other ballerinas, okay?"

"We'll see."

"Behave, *älskling*."

"What?" she asks, blinking innocently.

I blow out a laugh and meet her stare in the rear-view mirror. "Behave, *sweetheart*. And stop pretending you don't know your Swedish, or I'll have to ship you back and have you stay with Uncle Oskar and Aunt Klara."

She sticks out her bottom lip and scrunches her nose as she thinks about it. "They have cute dogs."

Oskar and Klara wouldn't let me live it down if they knew Nova would willingly go back just to spend time with them and their dogs. Friends of my parents, the two of them have been around since I was born. Oskar played on the same team as my dad, but their bond grew deep enough to last long after they both retired.

"You'd leave me for a couple of dogs?" I ask, unbuckling my seat belt.

"Not totally."

"Hmm."

"And I miss her food," she adds.

I twist in my seat, mouth gaping in offense. "Is there something wrong with my food?"

"You don't know how to make *stuvade makaroner* like her."

"I'm sure I could try. I didn't know I made it so . . . poorly."

She cocks her head. "It's a little wet."

"Oh."

"It's okay to be a bad cook, Mom."

With a quick flick of her wrist, she has her seat belt unbuckled and her door open. I yank the keys from the ignition and grab my purse before stumbling out of the car after her.

"You're not getting away that easily, Nova. Why didn't you tell me before that you wanted *stuvade makaroner*? How long have you been wanting it? I don't want to keep you from remembering your heritage, and I know we haven't been there to visit in a while, but—"

A small hand grabs my wrist as she cuts me off. "I don't want it that bad. I like the Gifflar and chocolates grandma sends us."

I know I should believe her, but instead, I feel guilty. With my shoulders tight, I drop a hand to her head and run it over her slicked-back hair, heart heavy in my chest.

"I can tell her to send you some more. Or I can try and make cinnamon buns for you myself instead."

Her grin is instant, melting some of the tension from my muscles. "Okay!"

"Now, your mormor told us to come to this studio of all the ones in Vancouver. So, promise to keep an open mind?"

She nods in agreement, and I take her hand before we head to the building. My mom wanted us to come to this studio because it belongs to Gracie Bateman. I know about it from all the times we visited Vancouver, which is why I fought her on us attending when she first brought it up.

The studio is meant for low-income families, not for family friends to receive special treatment. But I was promised that Nova's spot wouldn't take one from anyone else more deserving of it. It was the only way I agreed to sign her up.

Other than Oliver, I haven't seen another member of the Bateman family in nearly a decade. Not because of any sort of drama or bad blood but because I was always the odd one out when it came to my parents' friends and their kids.

It's nobody's fault that I feel like that. It was hard to be close to all the childhood friends I should have had when I lived across the world from them. I never had the chance to become best friends with Adalyn Hutton or Tinsley Lowry the way I used to wish I could.

It was hard on me to have to watch everyone grow closer and closer as the years passed through social media and second-hand information from my parents.

We all grew up together ... except we didn't. Not really.

Maybe that played a part in why I was so hesitant to take Nova to Illumina. Bringing her into this studio opens a million doors that I don't know if I'm ready to walk through yet.

Unfortunately, I don't think I have a choice. Considering that out of every single person in Vancouver, my next-door neighbour *had* to turn out to be one of those childhood friends. It's only a matter of time before everyone else learns that I'm no longer in Surrey and instead have come right to the centre of it all, no longer able to hide in plain sight the way I have been since I moved to Canada.

"Mom?" Nova tugs at my hand, and I jerk my head to look down at her. "I said I'll behave."

"Thank you, honey."

We're in front of the doors, and I blow out a breath when a tall, pastel purple-haired woman pulls one open for us. She smiles at me, and I'm struck stupid for a second at how effortless the act appears, like smiling is her default setting.

Realization hits me a second later when I drop my eyes to the hand she has holding the door open. The tattooed black ring on her left hand is one that I've seen a dozen times on her social media. Her entire presence is one that's hard to forget, but apparently, no matter how many times I stalked her online, I wasn't prepared to see her in person. Not after ten years.

"You guys head in! I'm just waiting for my husband to park the car. He's such a perfectionist I'm sure he's been trying to get as straight as possible," she says, her voice hitting me right in the gut.

The lack of recognition that appears as she stares at me is just as bad as when I saw it on Oliver's face.

The backs of my eyes burn, and I jerk my chin before urging Nova inside quickly. A deep ache of homesickness grows as I step inside and get greeted by another sucker punch to the chest.

Gracie Bateman is standing directly in front of me, her platinum hair pin straight and her blue eyes still electric. Tall and lean, she doesn't look her age in the slightest.

"Avery! Oh my God! Look at you," she shouts, not caring for the curious people watching. Even in a pair of wedges, she moves quickly through the crowd until we're close enough she can set her hands on my shoulders.

"Hi, Gray," I murmur.

Her eyes water as she stares at me for a beat longer before looking down at Nova, a sheen of wonder flashing across them. Bottom lip wobbling, she drops to a crouch in front of her and offers her hands for Nova to take.

"I'm Gracie Bateman, Nova. It's so, so good to finally meet you. Your mormor has told me so much about you."

If I wasn't so in my head, I'd have laughed at how she pronounces the Swedish term. Her heart is so golden that I'd bet she knows how terrible it sounded but doesn't care about looking silly.

"Hi. You're one of my mormor's friends, right?" Nova asks, offering her hand for a shake.

Gracie giggles at her and takes her hand in a soft shake. "Yes I am. And I've known your mom for a very long time."

"That's cool. I've known her longer." She puffs her chest out.

"Is that so? Well, I guess that makes you pretty lucky."

"It does."

Gracie glances up at me before standing and flashing me a wobbly smile. "I'm so glad you're here. You've grown up so beautifully, Avery."

My appreciation is sincere enough to have my eyes watering now. "Thank you. And you don't look like you've aged at all."

"Oh, please. Where did you get your sweetness from? Because I know it wasn't from your mother. She told me just last week that my hair looked dehydrated like silver streamers."

"She's ever the sweet talker," I muse. "I had to have gotten it from my dad."

A voice comes from behind me, accompanied by the clip of heels on the floor. "No way you're doing introductions without me, Auntie! You're absolutely no fun."

"You snooze, you lose, Addie," Gracie says with a smirk.

Nova turns beside me, her features calm. "There's a lot of people here. When did you make so many friends, Mom?"

Adalyn Hutton stops in her tracks a few feet from us, and one glance at her shows that she's stricken by my daughter's voice.

"Yeah, I guess I do, sweetheart. Do you want to meet them?" I ask.

She jerks a shoulder nonchalantly. "Sure."

"Alright," I say.

Adalyn continues toward us after getting permission. The man at her side takes me an embarrassing amount of time to recognize. Cooper White, her husband, is the son of another of my parents' friends but is the oldest of everyone, myself included.

Tall and built in a slimmer way than Oliver is, he's not as intimidating as I expected. There's something warm about his features despite their sharpness. Ten years older than his wife, he carries himself with a maturity that I can't help but resonate with. Addie has always been the liveliest person at the party, and even now, watching as she almost skips over to us, Cooper keeps a steady, calm hand on her back.

I never saw their marriage coming, but watching their relationship on social media has made it hard to believe that they're not sickeningly in love with each other.

Addie's purple curls bounce when she stops in front of us and surprises me by pulling me into her arms. I expected a hug from her aunt, but getting one from her ... it has the burn returning to my eyes.

"I missed you, Avery. It's been so damn long since I've seen you. I tried to text and message the last few years, but you never responded," she whispers while we're hugging.

I swallow, blinking away tears. "I'm sorry. It's been a busy few years. I didn't even think you'd recognize me after all this time."

She shakes her head on my shoulder. "Don't apologize. Of course I did. I just didn't want to scare you by swarming you out there. I've kept up with you on social media, even if you don't post, like, *ever*, so I've had a good idea of what you looked like now. We'll have lots of time to talk soon. I'm just glad you're here."

Relief fills me from bottom to top. The last time I saw her, she was twelve... yet she still recognized me upon first glance.

Unlike her dickish cousin.

"So am I."

Stepping back, I take another look at her and how grown-up she's become before sliding my eyes to Cooper. He's two years older than me and has matured more than I expected. His body has filled out, age strengthening his features. It's hard to imagine him as the kid I remember. We were never *that* close growing up, if you don't count weekly how-are-you texts, but he's a nice guy. A really, really nice guy and a good friend.

"You look old," I tell him, keeping my tone light.

He smiles, brown eyes crinkling at the corners. "Addie tells me that all the time. It's nice to see you again, Avery."

"You too." I mean it more than I thought I would. Resting my hand on Nova's shoulder, I say, "This is my daughter, Nova. Nova, this is Adalyn and Cooper."

Addie beams, her model features every inch as beautiful as they look online and on magazine covers. "Hi, pretty girl."

"It's nice to meet you, Nova," Cooper says.

Nova blushes, her cheeks and neck flushing a deep red. "Hi."

"You're here for ballet, right? I promise that Aunt Gray only hires the best of the best. You'll be in fantastic hands here," Adalyn tells her.

Gracie nods. "You have my word. We'll get you all set up today, and then next week, you can come and start dancing."

"Okay. So, I get my tutu today?" Nova asks.

"Yep. Your tutu, bodysuit, and pointe shoes. I have plenty of helpers here today, but I'd like to be the one to get you set up if that's okay?"

Her words have me searching the space for Oliver. It's been a week since he stormed into my house and saved me from lighting my house on fire with my curling iron, but luckily, he's been gone during the days, so I haven't seen him since. I'm sure he's just as happy about that as I am.

When I don't find him lurking around the studio like a pest, I relax. Even as the text he sent me two days ago flutters into my consciousness.

Oliver: *Your lawn needs to be mowed.*

Asshole. He didn't offer to mow it either. As if I would have accepted his help.

"Sure. You can help me," Nova says.

She offers Gracie her hand and looks up at me, waiting for permission to go with her. I give it easily, trusting Gracie without a doubt.

The two of them leave, and then Addie is shifting. She stares at me with a sense of hope so thick it could suffocate me if I let it.

"Can we find a seat and talk? Catch up? I know it's been a long time, but I'd love to get to know who you are now, if you're up for it."

She doesn't know it, but the begging isn't necessary. I'd have tried to sit down with her even if she hadn't cared about me being here.

8

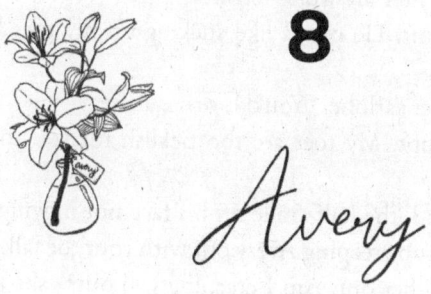

Avery

"So, you're married now," I say in a terrible attempt to break the ice.

Addie sits on the chair to my left while Cooper takes the one beside her. It's not exactly quiet in here with all the excited voices and chit-chat, but it's better than silence.

"We got married twice, really. The first wasn't on purpose nor legitimate," she explains with a wink at her husband.

Rubbing the thick black band of the tattooed ring on his finger, he keeps his eyes on Addie, the warmth in them enough to make me jealous. Not of her but of the love they so obviously share.

It's palpable, and I've never felt love that strong before in any of my past relationships. I thought I was close with Chris, but I know now that I was wrong.

I fold my hands in my lap and look away from them. "Did you go to Vegas and get Punk'd by an Elvis impersonator?"

Cooper chuckles. "Something like that. We were drunk in Ireland but got Punk'd nonetheless."

"So, you came home and got married for real?"

"Not right away, but soon enough. Cooper's too obsessed

with me not to be my husband. He has a fetish for telling everyone I'm his wife," Addie teases.

I snort a laugh. "There are worse fetishes."

"You've got a point. He could like sucking on my toes like lollipops or something."

Cooper tugs on her earlobe. "You'd love me anyway."

"Maybe. Maybe not. My toes are too ticklish for you to be macking on them."

He shakes his head, the half-smile on his face not moving an inch. "Alright, love. Stop creeping Avery out with your toe talk."

"I'm not creeping her out. Am I creeping you out?" she asks me, flustered.

"You're not creeping me out, but toes do."

She winces, smiling apologetically. "Right. Okay, well, tell me about you. How have the last ten years been? You look incredible, but I do miss the black hair. When did you get rid of the nose ring? And O-M-G, your little girl! Tell me all about her. How old is she? Is her father here somewhere? I didn't see him when you arrived, but I had to drag Cooper here, so I wouldn't blame him for not—"

"Breathe, Addie. One question at a time," Cooper murmurs, his hand steady against her back.

Addie sucks in a long inhale and slows her roll a bit. "I'm sorry. I'm just . . . I'm just really excited. I feel like I know you so well but also like I don't know you at all. Does that make sense?"

"Yes. It makes a lot of sense." I unclasp my hands and slide them over my thighs. "I wasn't sure what you guys knew about me, if anything at all. It's not like I've been around to ask."

"We know some. Little bits and pieces that trickled down from our parents. We knew you were in BC but not where until your mom called mine and Aunt Gray to tell them you were going to be bringing your daughter to the studio. I think everyone just thought that you didn't want us to know much. When you didn't answer any of my messages . . ." She trails off, biting down on her lip.

"You thought I was cutting you out," I finish for her.

"Yeah."

"Life is hard on everyone, Avery. We understood that. You didn't grow up here like we did. There was nothing forcing you to keep in contact with us," Cooper says.

I know he means well with his words, but the honesty in them only makes me feel worse. These people were my family, and I just cut them out.

"That doesn't mean I still shouldn't have. I did want to keep in contact with you, but it was hard being so far away all the time. Everyone was so close to one another, and once we got old enough, I felt like a hang-around most of the time. When I decided to move to Canada, I didn't know if it would be awkward to pop up out of nowhere and hope that you still wanted me around, so I never reached out. I'd always felt like the odd one out, and I think I just got so used to expecting you guys to forget about me that I convinced myself it was easier to just . . . let it go," I admit, relief following soon after.

Keeping my feelings inside has never benefited me, yet I tend to lean into the habit. It's easier than baring your insecurities to someone in hopes they don't take advantage of it and hurt you deeper than before.

Adalyn reaches her hands out for mine, and I give them to her. With gentle squeezes, she parts her lips on a sincere smile and leans forward, our shoulders touching.

"You were never a hang-around. I always wished we were closer in age because then we would have had a real chance at becoming good friends back then, but I'm up for it now, if you'll have me."

"You're family regardless of where you grew up or how often we saw one another, Avery," Cooper adds gently.

I grip Addie's hands tighter and look between the two of them. "Then I'd love to get to know you guys again. Nova and I are in Vancouver now."

"This is so exciting. I'm going to be all over you all the time now," Addie gushes.

I grow warm both inside and out. "Is everyone else still here?"

"Well, Maddox and Braxton are in Ottawa, Noah and Tinsley live in Toronto, and Addie, me, and the Bateman family are still here," Cooper answers.

"I remember hearing about Maddox signing with the Ottawa Beavertails. But Noah and Tinsley? He moved over there with her?"

Maddox, Noah, and Adalyn are all Huttons, while Tinsley is a Lowry and Cooper's a White. It's one hell of a complicated, extravagant group of friends around here, but after a while, it grows less confusing.

"Yeah, he left the Vancouver Warriors and found a good home in Ottawa. He loves it there," Addie starts before her eyes take on a haunted appearance. "And Noah, well, it wasn't a surprise when he went after Tinsley. You remember how attached those two were back when we were kids, right?"

Noah Hutton may very well be more famous than his NHL star brother. His name is all over the news and radio stations as one of the biggest up-and-coming names in rock music. It wasn't surprising to hear about, considering how attached he always was to music, but I wasn't expecting such an explosion of talent. Maddox might be one of the most well-known NHL players in the world, but he's no rock star.

Tinsley Lowry is a pro boxer and has been Noah's best friend since the moment they both popped out into the world. She, like me, didn't grow up in Vancouver with the rest of them. Her family is from Toronto, and now, apparently, Noah's there too.

"Oh, I remember. He's on tour now, right? I thought I heard about it on the radio," I say.

Addie swallows hard enough for it to be audible. Concern sizzles in my gut as I watch Cooper scoot closer to her, his arm folding around her back.

I tighten my hold on her hands, not wanting her to tug them free. "What's wrong?"

"Noah was hurt pretty badly a few weeks ago. Everyone's still a little on edge about it," Cooper explains.

Queasiness fills me. "I didn't hear about anything happening to him."

Addie sniffles, thick lashes batting with quick blinks. "We did everything we could to keep it out of the media. He's okay now. Both he and Tinsley will be at the house tomorrow. You should come and reintroduce yourself to everyone."

"Are you sure? I don't want to intrude."

"You won't be intruding. You're family, remember?" Cooper asks.

Adalyn nods in agreement, her eyes clearing a bit. "Please come. We do these family dinners every weekend, and I know everyone would love to see you."

I push past my immediate want to refuse their kind gesture. It's an olive branch. One I've been ignoring for years and probably don't deserve at this point.

"Alright. Just tell me when and where, and we'll be there."

Both Adalyn and Cooper look pleased with my answer, and I let that settle me a bit. I search the front of the studio for Nova and Gracie, finding them a beat later. Nova's nodding along with every word Gracie says as she shows her the massive corkboard hung on the wall and all the tacked photos scattered across it. Years of ballet performances and ballerinas are displayed with pride.

I remember Gracie loving ballet. It's one of my core memories of her. Seeing her passion put to use this way is special. A full-circle moment.

Nova notices me watching and cracks a grin as she waves wildly. A couple of the girls close by watch her, looks of interest on their young features. There's a boy hovering, his ears tipped with red and olive eyes wide. His arms are full of dance attire, but he doesn't pay any of it half as much attention as he does my daughter.

"Ah, shit. She's already snagged a boy's attention. Poor Momma Bear," Addie teases, knocking her shoulder against mine.

I scowl. "She's only seven. There will be no crushes yet."

"Isn't it adorable, though? Look!"

The boy has shuffled closer while slipping a hand out from beneath his pile of things just long enough to push his curly brown hair from his eyes. Nova has spotted him now and has her head cocked while staring bluntly, curiously.

"She'll tell him to leave her alone," I say to myself.

But she doesn't. Mortified, I watch as my daughter smiles in encouragement and brings him into her conversation with Gracie. I should be proud of her for being friendly, but why does she have to be friendly with a boy?

I'm going to age at least twenty years over the next several months.

"It's cute, isn't it? She's already making friends," Cooper says, his tone hopeful.

"You won't think it's cute when your daughter is accosted by a young boy," I warn him.

He brushes me off. "Easy fix. We won't have a girl."

I smirk, shaking my head. "Yeah, okay."

"What if I want a girl," Addie says. "Then what?"

I laugh when he visibly glitches, too busy thinking about the right answer to keep his brave face. He's in for a surprise when and if he and Adalyn have children. Just because I don't like Nova making friends with a boy who looks at her like he just saw heaven for the first time doesn't mean that I'll do anything to stop it.

One of the first lessons I learned as a parent was that our children always come first. You have to put aside your own wants and needs when it comes to them. Your own opinions on their choices don't matter when they bring them happiness. They need to experience life to the fullest. Have to forge their own path no matter what.

Nova may only be seven, but she's been her own person for a

long time now. I'm not sure me telling her not to converse with boys would even register anyway. Controlling isn't the type of mother I want to be.

Cooper presses a kiss to Addie's cheek and whispers something in her ear that turns her red. An answer to her question that I don't want to hear.

"I better go introduce myself to this boy," I say, standing from the chair. "Tomorrow, right? You'll text me the information?"

Addie looks up, cheeks still flushed. "Tomorrow! Do you want my number first?"

"Oh. Right," I mutter before handing my phone over.

We exchange numbers quickly, and after a tight hug, I leave them and head over to my daughter. She notices me when I step behind her and set a hand on her shoulder. Her closeness settles me, the mom in me happy with knowing she's safe.

"Hi, Mom. I made a friend," she gushes, lips spread in a wide grin.

"I see that. Will you introduce us?"

Gracie squeezes my bicep and steps aside to greet another family, leaving us alone for a minute.

The boy tips his head back to look at me, nervousness in his gaze. I try to make myself look as unintimidating as possible.

"I'm Jacob," he stammers.

Nova tugs at my wrist. "He likes Jake better."

"It's nice to meet you, Jake. I'm Avery."

His hand shoots out, and with a soft laugh, I shake it. Wetting his lips, he points to the woman walking toward us, her hair tied back in a neat bun and classy outfit, looking as though she must have come here straight from work.

"You sure know how to make yourself scarce in a crowd, Jake," she says once we're only a few steps apart.

I turn to her, keeping my expression light. "You must be Jake's mom. I'm Avery Miller, and this is my daughter, Nova."

"Tasha Rogers. It's nice to meet you."

Jake settles into her side, and his cheeks lose some of their redness. Tasha is a short woman with the deepest brown eyes I've ever seen and a gentle aura about her that draws me in. I don't want to scream in frustration at her company, so that already makes her better than Oliver.

Fuck, I have to stop thinking about him.

Nova interrupts my thoughts. "Me and Jake are friends now."

"Is that right? Well, that's great. My Jakey doesn't make friends all that easily," Tasha says.

I laugh at that. "Nova makes them a bit too easily."

"Can we go for ice cream together, Mom?" Nova pokes at my side.

"What about next time? We've got to stop by the shop tonight."

"My mom sells flowers," Nova tells Jake and his mom.

My skin heats at the blunt info drop. "I *will* sell flowers. The shop is still under renovations."

Jake gasps up at Tasha. "You love flowers, Mom!"

"You do?" I ask, interest piqued.

She waves off the question. "I like gardening. I'm not so sure it's the same as owning a flower shop."

"It can be. If you love flowers, then you love flowers. You should stop by sometimes. It's a mess right now, but it has good bones."

"I'd like that," she says softly.

I make the offer to exchange numbers and inwardly laugh at how often I've done the same thing over the past couple of weeks. Before we moved to Vancouver, I don't think I gave anyone my number in months.

Things are already changing so quickly, but I think I like it. A fresh start might have been what we were needing all along.

9

Oliver

> Me: The weeds in your grass are hideous.

> Ary: Are you offering to pluck them for me, or do you just enjoy pissing me off?

> Me: If you mowed the lawn, the weeds would disappear.

> Ary: Bye, jackass.

I SCOWL AT MY PHONE, THIS MORNING'S CONVERSATION with my neighbour not appeasing me by any means. Yeah, my messages could be construed as rude, but it's impossible not to give in to the urge to piss her off every chance I get. She doesn't care about her yard, but I do. Only because if hers looks like shit, it makes mine look like shit. Yeah, that's it.

I'd mow it for her if she asked, which is what I was hoping she'd do. I thought my offer was clear when I texted her telling her how terrible her lawn looked the other day. Instead, she left me on Read.

> Me: I'll mow it next time I do mine.

I send the text and immediately want to unsend it. But there's no time. As if she's been sitting there waiting for me to reply, hers comes a beat later.

> Ary: No thanks. I'd prefer you pick the weeds by hand.

"What's your problem, Olliepop?" my cousin Tinsley asks.

The nickname grates, but I ignore it. "If you were a single mom with no support, can you tell me why you wouldn't want to accept help from someone who has offered multiple times? Are all women so damn stubborn?"

Okay, the *multiple times* is a stretch, but oh fucking well. I'm guessing about the no-support part yet feel it in my gut that I'm right. Her small rant about her daughter's father was enough of a giveaway to put together that she's raising her almost completely on her own.

Tinsley's best friend, Noah, dips his fingers into the waistband of her shorts, tugging her close to him. The dark possessiveness in his eyes as he tries to flay me open with them would scare me shitless if I hadn't grown up with the psychopath.

"She'll never be a single mother. What the fuck kind of question is that?"

I roll my eyes, shrugging off his words. He's a scary fuck, but he's family. Even decked out in head-to-toe tattoos, including one that spans the entire expanse of his throat and makes it appear as though it's been photographed in an X-ray machine, he doesn't scare me.

"I'm not talking about Tinsley, you brute."

Jamie shares the same way of thinking I do. "Are we not going to talk about how Noah clearly made his move on her, though?"

"Am I supposed to be shocked or something?" I ask, blinking at the obvious display Noah's been putting on with Tinsley since they stepped inside his parents' house.

He's been pining after her since he was a kid. It's about damn time he stopped pussyfooting around.

"You're so boring," Jamie mutters.

"And the two of you are headache inducing," Dad says, offering Tinsley a tight, apologetic expression. "Good for you and Noah. You look good together. Always have."

From Mom's spot on the arm of Dad's chair, she slots into the conversation. "He's right. I love the two of you together so much."

"I should have taken Maddox up on that bet when we were teens," Jamie says.

Adalyn comes bouncing into the living room, her purple hair bright. Cooper is following behind, staring at her like it would pain him to look away.

"You should have because you just lost four hundred bucks," she says to Jamie.

The rest of the family tumbles into the living room, and I stand, too annoyed with Ary to sit and listen to the flurry of conversations that are about to take place. When Maddox and Braxton's son, Liam, pushes his way through Addie's legs and runs into Noah's arms, I use the distraction to slip out.

The Hutton house is the closest thing to a mansion I've ever seen. I grew up in a big place, but it was nothing compared to this one. Mom used to bug her brother, Oakley, all the time about it, calling him a show-off every chance she got.

In reality, he's the furthest thing from it. The house might be massive, but it's still warm. The generous expanse of land it sits on has seen more Sunday game days than a football stadium, and more than a few of my best memories were made here.

Stepping out onto the front porch, I breathe in the clean air and stare at the tree house standing across the driveway. Jamie and I didn't climb up there too often—it was more Maddox and Braxton's thing—but we did every few visits.

The sound of a car engine has me looking down the driveway,

squinting to see better through the bright sun. It's a small car, not one that any of my family members drive.

No, it's the car that's been parked in front of Ary's house for weeks now. The deep blue Ford Focus with the *Hot Girls Hit Curbs* sticker on the bumper above a deep dent decorated with yellow paint and all four tires curb rashed to utter shit.

My stomach tightens to the point of discomfort. There's not much room for her to park with everyone else here, but she manages to squeeze in between my Tahoe and Jamie's Jeep. She's crooked as all hell, and when she swings her door open, there's hardly enough room for her to squeeze out without hitting my door with hers.

She takes a look at her park job and winces, worrying her lip before rounding the trunk and helping her daughter out of the back seat.

"Oh," Nova says, her head swivelling in every direction. "This house is really big."

Ary steers her down the driveway with a hand on her back. "Yeah, it is."

"Why is it so big?"

"Because they wanted a big house."

"Yeah, but why? Don't they get lost?"

"I'm sure they know where they're going, honey."

"How? A map?"

"You'll flatter the Huttons if you tell them their house should have a map made for it," I say, my voice cutting through the air.

Nova's the first to look at me, her head cocked, mouth twisted innocently. I can't say I expected to see her here. Either of them. Their surprise presence doesn't make sense. I'm immediately on the defensive.

Ary reads my expression quickly, a warning flashing in her stare. "I had a terrible feeling you'd be here today."

"This is my uncle's house, after all."

"Is it?" she asks, her tone dripping with enough sarcasm to confuse me. "I had no idea."

I suck back my irritation with a glance at Nova. "Who invited you here?"

"Why, scared I followed you?"

"Unlikely. I'd have noticed your terrible driving if you were behind me. Probably have a piece of your front bumper attached to my SUV."

"My mom is a good driver. She's better than my mormor," Nova says sternly.

The term is unfamiliar to me, and it must show.

Ary ruffles Nova's hair and says, "Her grandmother."

"Right."

Nova tips her chin back and stares me down. "She's in Sweden."

"Sweden?" Something tingles in my brain. A thought I can't quite latch onto. "Is she visiting?"

Ary starts ushering Nova up to the steps, and I furrow my brows, trying to dissect the look on her face. Annoyed and nervous. A weird mix.

Nova stares at me the entire time up the porch steps, almost daring me to be the one to break the staring contest first.

"No. My mormor lives in Sweden. So did my mom," she explains.

That tingle grows and grows, becoming impossible to ignore. My eyes bulge when a fragment of a memory slips loose.

"No way she gives you even a double look, Olliepop. She's way out of your league," Maddox says with a deep laugh.

We're sitting on the hood of Cooper's car, the moon high and sky clear of clouds. It's summer break for me, but Maddox and Cooper have already graduated high school. At least they still hang out with me, even if I am only sixteen and they're twenty and twenty-two.

"Not to mention, you're not even eighteen yet. She's dating men, Oliver, not teenage boys," Cooper adds.

I shrug off their concern. "I'm a man. Don't patronize me. I've got big plans for my life. Impressive ones that she won't be able to dismiss."

"Damn right you've got big plans. That's fucking great, man. But she's twenty. Not to mention, her father would beat you to a bloody pulp if you got involved with his daughter," Maddox says.

Their doubt was expected. They've known about my crush on Avery since I first started having one the last time she visited Vancouver. She was eighteen, and I was fourteen. I'd kept it to myself then, not daring to tell her about it. But now, I'm sixteen. I've grown a lot these past two years. I'm ready for her to know that I want her now. Plus, her father's already threatened to beat me up for looking at her too much, so I have nothing to lose now.

Two years is a long time to not see her even once face to face. But she lives in Sweden, and her family has visited less and less over the past few years. Now might be my last chance to tell her how I feel. I can only stalk her social media accounts and send boring texts so many times without being considered a creep.

Cooper pats my back and hands me a bottle of Coke. The two of them still won't let me drink. Pricks.

"Well, my dad said they get here tomorrow. Are you going to do it right away?"

I nod. "The sooner, the better."

"It's your funeral," Maddox says.

I remember that night and the next as clear as day. Avery and her family showed up at Cooper's father's house with her Swedish boyfriend in tow. His presence was a very unwelcome one. It only took one look at him for my crush on Avery to shrivel and die.

It was easy enough to block her on social media and pretend she didn't exist after she went back to Sweden and, as far as I knew, stayed there for good. Nobody brought her whereabouts up, knowing I didn't want to hear a word about anything involving her, and I never asked, content on not knowing.

Obviously, I missed something very crucial, considering she's now standing right in front of me, no longer the quiet girl with box-dyed black hair and too much eyeliner that used to make the blue in her eyes bright enough to blind. She doesn't have the bull ring in her nose or the ball piercing at the end of her tongue. Her face has slimmed out as she's aged, along with her entire figure.

I feel like an outright idiot to have bought the name she fed me and not caught the small birthmark on her left eyelid. She's grown up, matured in a way that's halted my ability to recognize her.

"Are you going to be sick?" Nova asks, poking me hard in the stomach.

Avery—*not* Ary—ushers her daughter toward the door, sweeping her gaze over me, a hint of sadness there and gone in a flash. "If he is, we best get a move on so we aren't in the splash zone."

"Yeah, that would be gross."

I stare at the daughter I never knew Avery had as something hot and unforgiving flares in my chest. Regret is a brutal bastard that makes me feel like the world's biggest douchebag for not recognizing one of my childhood friends on sight. Or at all.

This family dinner just got a lot more awkward.

10

Avery

It's about damn time.

Watching the colour leach from Oliver's cheeks as he finally realized who I am was just as satisfying as I hoped it would be. Selfishly, I hoped it would happen in front of more people, but a win is a win.

Turns out that he was the only one who didn't remember me, a fact that made my heart grow a half dozen sizes while simultaneously shrivelling up. From the moment Nova and I walked inside the house, it was a flurry of hugs and tears as I was tossed around from family to family.

Nova hasn't stopped smiling since Ava Hutton ushered her into the kitchen and poured her the biggest glass of pink lemonade with a matching pink swirly straw.

I didn't know what to expect coming here today, but the reception we received was beyond my wildest dreams. It's like we didn't leave, which sounds as crazy as it feels.

The endless swarm of people has also made it easy to ignore Oliver. Another bonus.

He's done a great job of avoiding us thus far, but as everyone lines up along the white marble island in the Huttons' monstrous kitchen, he pops up as expectantly as a pimple on prom night.

I clench the plate in my hands and try to ignore him as he waits behind me. The endless array of prepared food spread in front of us is a bit overwhelming, but I start with the bowl of pasta salad that I won't eat, but I know Nova will.

"My mom's taking care of Nova," Oliver mutters, suddenly beside me and jerking his chin to the end of the island, where Gracie's helping Nova plate her food.

"How do you know I'm not plating my own food?"

He eyes the pasta salad. "Call it intuition."

"Yeah, right. I didn't ask her to help Nova. I've been serving my daughter just fine on my own for seven years now."

"Never said you haven't been. My mom loves doing stuff like this. You didn't have to ask her."

It almost makes me smile. It's been a long time since I haven't had to make Nova a plate before thinking about myself. Having been around Chris' family as often as I was for years, I'm used to accepting the scraps left by the time I'm done making sure she gets enough to eat. He certainly wasn't going to make sure I was plated up before he was.

"Might want to hurry up, though. I'm starving," Oliver adds.

I cock a brow and grab the tongs buried in the bowl of garden salad, leaving it there, not moving. "Should have lined up before me, then."

He shifts his big body into my space and reaches across my arm to grab the pasta salad spoon that I abandoned. I get a waft of his cologne and grit my jaw at how good it smells.

My annoyance grows tenfold when he drops a whopping scoop of the salad on my plate and reaches for the roasted carrots next, adding them to the growing pile of food.

The chunks of hard-boiled eggs in the pasta salad make my stomach curdle, and at the first whiff of them, I'm suddenly wishing for another smell of his cologne.

"What's with the face?" he asks, and one glance up exposes his humour with the situation.

This guy didn't even remember me when he saw me; there's no damn way he remembers how much I hate eggs. Not after this long.

Yet that's the only explanation I can come up with as to why he's smirking and watching me try not to throw up all over the island.

I part my lips on a wide grin and push the nausea down. "Nothing. I just really, really love eggs."

With a scroll of my eyes over all the food, I spot the one I need and lean forward on my toes to snag the spoon set inside its container. I'm still grinning sweetly when I dump the cheese-sauce-covered brussels sprouts on his plate and reach for the mashed potatoes, adding them so close that they touch.

"You said you were hungry. I just want to make sure you get enough food," I say.

His eyes are wide as he stares at the cheese sauce pooling on and around the potatoes. I look away from him long enough to put the garden salad I wanted on my plate before moving along the island and adding a grilled chicken breast to it.

I'm unprepared for the wallop of orange potatoes that smothers my chicken and salad. I crinkle my nose and whip my head to the side. Oliver pushes the serving spoon back into the sweet potato mash as slowly as possible, holding my stare. "Your plate was missing a starch" is all he says.

My steel will keeps my smile in place as I grab the gravy boat. "Thank you. I forget my food groups sometimes."

"You're wel—"

His words die when I begin to cover his plate in gravy. The thick brown sauce seeps into his potatoes and soaks his brussels sprouts. A dinner roll he must have grabbed in the past few seconds grows soggy before I set the boat back down and shuffle forward along the island.

He's silent as I make to grab a fork and knife, but he's not done. I jerk to the side when he takes a container of grated

Parmesan cheese and dumps some all over my food. The smell is immediate, and I gag, turning my head to the side to try and avoid it as much as possible.

"So, you can remember all of the foods that make me want to vomit, but you couldn't actually *recognize* me?" I hiss beneath my breath.

He blinks, as if he's surprised by my angry question. "I recognize you now."

"Too little, too late."

I snatch a fork and go to leave before fingers wrap around my wrist, their hold strong but not painful. One shake and I guarantee I'd be set free.

"You don't look like you did ten years ago," he defends.

"The key words there are 'ten years ago,' Oliver. I'm not the girl I was back then." *And you're not the guy you were either.*

The sixteen-year-old boy who ignored me like he was trying to score first place in some imaginary avoid-Avery contest. I didn't pay much attention to his actions then, and I can't say that I wanted to think about them much afterward. He was young. We both were. But the lack of communication that followed my family's departure back to Sweden that last time . . . I'll never forget that.

"So don't hold it against me that I didn't recognize you. Last time I saw you, you had black hair and piercings and liked dark makeup."

His words are growing in volume, drawing the attention of others around us. Not everyone looks at us, though, and I can only imagine that it's because they've been already watching us for a while now. Long enough to have seen why both of our plates look like the one everyone uses to scrape scraps onto after a meal.

My cheeks grow warm at the attention. It makes it easier to shake my wrist free and leave Oliver standing there, his excuses not meaning a damn thing to me.

It's fine that he didn't recognize me. Clearly, he decided

during my last visit here ten years ago that I wasn't worth remembering. It's totally fine. Not hurtful at all. I don't even care.

I most definitely didn't stalk him on social media for years, drooling over his photos and checking every day for a follow back.

I'm far too old to be concerned over that sort of thing. Again, it doesn't matter.

Pissing him off constantly now has given me more enjoyment than a follow back years ago would have. And I don't plan on stopping that particular action either. Not when seeing his scowl is so soothing to my wounded pride.

And scowl does he ever. Sitting beside Nova as we eat, I chit-chat with Gracie, Ava, and Tinsley and watch Oliver across the kitchen. He sits at a smaller table and forces the food from his plate into his mouth and swallows, his throat straining as he tries not to retch.

Jamie is sitting on his left with his dad on his right, both of them staring at him. His dad is more subtle with his entertainment, but Jamie is loud, poking fun at him for everyone to hear.

"Eat a brussels sprout next, Ollie," he begs, egging him on.

When Oliver slides one into his mouth and gags, unable to keep the noise in, Maddox slides up behind him and pats his back.

He waves a hand over his plate. "What's with your dinner? You hate literally all of this. Is it a bet? If so, I want in."

Jamie's laugh is loud but warm. "Nah, no bet. Go have a look at Avery's plate."

I glare at him with the heat of a thousand suns. Maddox heads my way, and I have to crane my head back to meet his eyes. He's even bigger than Oliver but not as aggravating, so I don't mind him.

He sets a hand on his mom's shoulder and eyes my plate. "Can't say I've ever seen you eat a hard-boiled egg."

"What do you mean? They're one of my favourite foods."

"She hates eggs. They smell like farts," Nova pipes up, grinning like a menace.

Maddox winks at her. "Yeah, they sure do."

"I've grown to love them in the past few minutes, actually," I say stubbornly.

Jamie blurts out, "The two of them were flirting at the island or something and ended up with two nasty plates."

I balk. "We weren't flirting."

"Oh, it was foreplay if I've ever seen it."

"Don't talk about foreplay at the table, Jamieson," Gracie scolds. "There are kids around."

"My bad. Sorry."

"I'm sad I missed the entertainment," Maddox says with an indecipherable look at Oliver.

I ignore it and continue scraping the sweet potato mash from my chicken. Whatever "bro" moment they're having, I don't want any part in it.

"Your mom was telling me about your flower shop the other day," Ava says, changing the subject. I smile appreciatively at her. The last thing I want is for everyone to think I'm even slightly interested in Oliver. "We'd love to come by and help get it ready. I imagine it's been quite a feat."

"I'd appreciate that. It's a really nice space, but it needs some TLC. I'm hoping to open up in a couple of months. Definitely before winter."

"I wouldn't let Ava anywhere near your flowers. She's got the blackest thumb of all black thumbs. They'll die if she so much as breathes on them," Gracie says.

Ava gives her a shove. "Ouch, Gray."

I cut a piece of chicken with the edge of my fork. "My mom's the same way. I was the one taking care of the plants back home. Dad, too, sometimes."

"Maybe you can teach me how to keep them alive. Just me. Not Gracie," Ava says.

Gracie meets my eyes and winks. "It'll be our secret."

"For real, I'd really appreciate your help. Nova starts school tomorrow, and then I'll be at the shop pretty much all the time," I tell them, hoping I don't sound desperate.

The two women just nod and smile, happy with my offer. We continue eating in comfortable silence, and only once I've managed to slip every piece of egg from my salad onto Nova's plate do I risk a look at the smaller table. Oliver's no longer there, and for some ridiculous reason, I wish that he were.

11

Oliver

Adjusting my headset, I keep my focus on the house up ahead and the flames swallowing its left side. The fire engine plows through the street with Adams behind the wheel. Sirens blare, and the neighbourhood residents watch as we pass, their fear potent.

It's early morning, and while this is the start of our day, it's also the start of everyone else's.

The moment we pull up in front of the scene, I'm the first off the truck. My turnouts are a welcome weight as I find station 8 already on scene and slap my helmet on.

I'm assessing the scene in an instant, noticing a family huddled off to the side, their frames bundled beneath blankets and oxygen masks on their faces. A set of EMTs speak to them in low voices, attempting to soothe the couple but not succeeding.

"Don't leave him in there!"

"I couldn't find him!"

My stomach swoops, knowing we have to execute a search and rescue. The smoke billowing from the second-storey windows isn't comforting.

Lieutenant Holloway from station 8 rushes toward me and

gives a rundown of the fire and their current plan of action before I reach up to my shoulder and turn my radio on.

"Engine 3, we have a two-storey residential structure with heavy smoke and flames tearing through the left side of the building. All occupants are reportedly out, but there's a pet still inside. Prepare for a primary search and attack."

The family cries out at my order, but I put them to the back of my mind for now. "Hart and Jacobs, you're on fire attack with me. Adams and Lerman, start on the first floor and find that damn dog. Patel, I want a water supply now!"

They don't hesitate. My team moves on fast-forward, and after fitting my mask on and waiting for a quick confirmation from Patel regarding the water supply, I'm leading the charge into the house, the hose line in my hands.

"As soon as I create a break in the flames, fan out and bring that dog to its family. They're five minutes away from tearing inside and attempting to find it on their own," I shout into the radio, the flames loud and hot in front of me.

They flare out before I open the hose line and start knocking them down. Search and rescue take off down the hall, their shouts impossible to hear this close to the flames.

Bit by bit, we force the flames back toward the ignition point. I'm not surprised to find our path leading to the kitchen. I drop my head and grab my radio with one hand. "Adams, what's your status?"

My radio crackles on my shoulder.

"Advancing to the second floor. Visibility is poor, but the fire hasn't spread from the first floor yet."

"Proceed with caution."

Hart falls behind me, the second hose line pulsing in her hands as we tag team the flames. Engine 8 continues spraying the fire from the outside, but the heat doesn't die down. Sweat trickles down my forehead and off my nose, and I sniffle in my mask.

After what feels like hours later, Adams' voice comes from the radio.

"We have the dog, Lieutenant. Exiting now."

"Copy that. Fire is contained to the back left quadrant, but stay cautious in case of sudden spread."

"Copy."

Hart advances, and I follow, antsy to finish this. By the time the last of the fire is put out inside, my arms ache from the weight of the hose. I tighten my hold and take a long sweep of the kitchen before pulling my team out.

Station 8's captain is outside when we exit. She directs her team to head back inside for another sweep of the controlled fire, and I roll my eyes. I wouldn't have pulled my team out without finishing the job, but when it comes to the other stations, they don't share the same trust in me that my team does.

I hand off the hose to Jacobs and rip my mask and helmet off before rounding up my team and giving them all pats on the back. We head back to the station soon after, and it takes everything in me not to let my eyes drift shut.

We've moved onto a two-on-two-off shift, and I'm grateful for the break from the hell that was four on four. The first week of September is here, and with it, fall has teased its company.

The heat isn't as scalding, but it's nowhere near cool yet. And I'm grateful for that, considering the massive pool I have arriving today. It'll take up the majority of my backyard, but the look on Avery's face when she sees that I've purchased it just to one-up her will be so, so worth it.

By the time I make it out of the station, my shift is long over. Paperwork has been filed, I've showered, and the sun is bright despite it being the late afternoon. The drive home is long, exhaustion wearing heavily on me like normal. It's more common to be half-awake at this point than it is to be well rested.

I pull the SUV up my driveway today instead of leaving it on the street and sigh while tugging the keys free. My muscles resemble noodles as I slip out and grab my bag from the back seat before starting up the sidewalk.

A moment of weakness has me glancing to the street in front of Avery's house in search of her car. It's there, and I drag my tired eyes to the front door as if I'll be able to see through it.

From everything I picked up from the Hutton house this past weekend, I know that Nova started school on Monday, but she's done at three thirty every day.

I toss the keys in my hand and catch them before stalling as I go to unlock my front door. An itch grows on the back of my neck, an inkling that something isn't right.

One look at the grass in my front yard and I'm tossing my head back, laughter bolting out of me.

The perfectly patterned lines in my lawn have been decorated with two that are cut so low to the dirt you'd think I'm regrowing the grass. They spread from the edge of her lawn right across to the sidewalk that separates my front yard. It smells like fresh-cut grass still, meaning she couldn't have done it that long ago.

Laughing again at the sight, I stare at how perfectly cut her front lawn is. It's almost like she did it on purpose to spite me. Fuck, she definitely did. There's not a goddamn weed in sight either.

This is her attempt at payback for me not recognizing her, and I'll give her the kudos she deserves. Attacking my yard was fair game, but now the score is even.

I adjust my bag and bring it higher up my shoulder before unlocking my door and stepping inside.

She may think she has the upper hand here now, but I'm about to rain on her parade.

IT TAKES two hours to get my pool set up in the backyard. Thankfully, I know a guy who did me a favour and brought a water truck over to get it filled quicker than it would have taken with the hose alone.

Avery left shortly after I got home and hasn't gotten back yet. I've wasted the entire rest of the afternoon that I should have been using to relax, but there was no way I was going to relax enough to do that with the ideas running through my head.

The terrible excuse of a fence between our backyards was easy enough to climb, but the real struggle was finding enough Jell-O cups to fill her kiddy pool. I bought out three stores' worth before I had enough, and the scooping of each one? I'm never doing that shit again.

It's easy to keep myself busy as I wait for her to get home. I inflate the pool floaties I ordered and toss them in the pool before slipping on my swim trunks and grabbing a beer on my way back out.

The sun is hot on my skin as I climb into the water and hop onto the inflatable green lounge chair. I've finished off my beer by the time two car doors shut out front.

"Can we go to the spray park?" Nova asks loudly enough for the entire neighbourhood to hear.

Avery's voice follows. "No. If you want to play in the water, we have a pool. We're going to have dinner soon."

I'd feel guilty for ruining pool time for Nova if I didn't have a plan for that as well. I've thought of everything and even surprised myself with all of it, considering how half out of my mind I am with the need to shut my eyes and sleep for a week.

A handful of minutes later and their back door is sliding open. I keep my eyes pointed up at the sky and smirk when the anticipation in my chest gets to be too much to ignore.

"Are you coming in the pool with me, Mom?"

"Unless you don't want me to, then yes."

My heartbeat stutters at those words and the image they paint in my mind. One made of neon yellow and pale skin. Fuck.

"Uh, what's wrong with the water?" Nova asks.

"What do you—Oliver!"

I bite my tongue to keep from laughing as Avery's shout rips through the neighbourhood. The birds that were eating from the feeder on the back fence fly away out of fear. If I were smart, I'd follow suit.

"It's Jell-O!" Nova sounds more excited than anything else.

"Don't eat it, Nova!" Avery shrieks. Nova groans at the order.

The chain rattles along the fence, and finally, I look away from the sky to find Avery glaring at me from her side of it.

"Tell me you didn't fill my pool with Jell-O," she spits.

"I can't."

Oh, fuck, is she ever mad. Colour fills her cheeks, and I drop my gaze to her chest as it rises and falls at an alarming rate. Her bathing suit isn't yellow today. It's a hot pink one-piece with a cut-out in the middle, right above her lower stomach and belly button. It's impossible to keep from following the line of the suit to the high-cut bottom in the shape of a V.

"My eyes are up here," she snips.

I blink and meet said eyes. "Do you not like Jell-O?"

She parts her lips but doesn't speak. I drop a hand in my pool and swirl it around in the water, her glare dripping with poison.

"Did you think I was going to let you get away with ruining my yard?" I ask calmly.

"I didn't ruin your yard. I gave it character."

I huff a laugh. "Then I did the same to your pool."

"Did you buy yours before or after you ruined mine?"

"Oh, this thing?" I dip my toes in the water. "I've had this pool forever."

"You're an ass."

"I won't deny that."

"Are you going to come help me get rid of the Jell-O?"

"Will you help seed the stripes in my yard?"

She shoves an angry hand through her hair and pulls it over her shoulder. "No."

"Then you have your answer."

"I only wanted to give you something to remember me by this time around."

"That isn't why you did it. You did it because you're pissed."

"Rightfully so!" she shouts, leaning closer to the fence. "You deserved it."

I crane my neck to stare past her at Nova, who's drawing on the cement pad that counts as their back patio with chalk. She doesn't seem concerned over the pool, and I'm relieved. This fight is between her mom and me, and I don't want her to get stuck in the crosshairs. She seems like a nice enough kid.

"Do you want me to apologize to you, Avery?" I ask tightly.

Her eyes flare with bewilderment. "No. It wouldn't mean a thing now if you did."

"Nobody told me you were in Canada, let alone Vancouver. If they did . . ." I don't finish my sentence.

Would it have made a difference if anyone had told me? I still wouldn't have sought her out. There were too many answers to questions that I didn't want to know.

"If they did, then what?"

I shake my head. "Nothing."

"Nova, we're going back inside," she orders, turning her back to me.

The little girl looks up from her drawing and frowns. "Do we have to, Mom?"

"Yes. I have to empty the pool and clean it out before we can use it again."

No. I'm not going to feel guilty for this. It was deserved. Right?

My jaw tightens as I stare at the blue sky and curl my fingers in the water. With a long inhale through my nose, I slide off the pool floatie and hop out of the pool. Avery looks at me when I grip the metal fence an inch from where she holds it and then haul myself over it the way I did earlier.

"What are you doing? You're not welcome in our yard!"

I ignore her and crouch in front of the pool. The strong smell of the jiggling substance inside of it isn't a good addition to my guilt-lined stomach.

It's too heavy to lift in one go, so I shove my hands into the Jell-O and start pulling it all to one side in preparation for emptying the pool.

"Stop," Avery blurts out, moving to my side, so damn close I can feel the heat from her legs against my arms. "Just leave it, and I'll get rid of it later."

"I've got it," I grunt.

"I said to stop."

"And I said that I've got it."

"Can I help?" Nova asks, padding with bare feet to my other side.

"Yeah," I tell her.

"No," Avery says at the same time.

Nova takes my approval as permission despite her mother's frustration and digs her tiny hands into the mess. I watch her smile, excitement making her eyes glitter. The sight is nice.

I'm too busy watching Nova play in the Jell-O to prepare myself for Avery's next move. The splat of gelatine on my neck and chest is a jolt to my system. In disbelief, I lose my balance and fall back onto my ass, the grass cushioning my fall.

"I said to stop, Oliver."

With a swipe of my hand, I clear the mess from my skin and pin her in place with a heated gaze. She blanches, losing her bravado and slowly creeping backward.

My fists are full of Jell-O in an instant. I pull my arm back and then throw the first fistful at her. It hits her dead smack on the chest, and the gelatine slithers down and between her tits before dropping to the ground.

Nova gasps, but it's an excited sound. A beat later, she's tossing a fistful of her own at her and squealing, a high-pitched laugh following after. It's a sound that reminds me of my childhood, and I release a laugh of my own.

Avery watches me carefully, dissecting my every action. I

throw another batch of it at her to keep her distracted from her own thoughts. It hits lower this time, sticking to her exposed belly.

"You're in trouble now," she warns.

"Uh-oh!" Nova shrieks while grappling for more Jell-O.

I fill my hands and toss some at Nova, her head falling back with a dimpled grin before she's stalking toward her mom. Avery's eyes bulge when she notices me, and then she's darting away, running around the yard.

When I start to chase after her, Nova joins in, and the easy laugh that escapes her makes me stumble. It's a sound I haven't heard in ten years but somehow is even better now.

I let it fill the yard and chase her again and again for what feels like hours, not stopping out of fear of losing her laugh again.

12

Avery

WE'RE ALL RED AND STICKY BY THE TIME WE'VE SPREAD the Jello-O all over the yard. There are clumps in the grass, on my tanning chair beneath the pool umbrella, and even stuck inside the holes in the chain-link fence.

Nova hasn't stopped giggling since Oliver threw the first fistful, and it's made things all the more complicated. How am I supposed to be angry about the mess and my ruined pool when she's so happy? Especially after the stressful first two days she's had at school.

The nerves of starting a new school in a new place have made my daughter more closed off at school than she's ever been. She shied away from the kids in her class when I dropped her off and picked her up, and that's just not like her.

Maybe it's just first-week jitters...

"Can Oliver stay for dinner, Mom?"

I shrink into myself a bit at the question, my gut reaction being to say no. An hour of laughter with me and my daughter doesn't erase everything prior. But damn it all to hell, when Nova grips my sticky hands and bats her lashes at me, there's only ever one correct answer.

"I'll ask him if he wants to join us. He might be busy," I tell her.

I don't want to look over to where I know Oliver's back on his side of the fence, wiping his neck and chest with a towel. One that he stole from the back of my lounge chair before he scuttered from my yard like a rat. Shit. I look anyway.

The thick ridges of his abdomen ripple as he leans the slightest bit backward and drags the towel along them, spending way too much time cleaning in between each one. His hair is a mess, strands sticking up left and right with clumps of red gelatine. The waistband of his swim trunks hangs low on his hips and ride up high on his thighs, at least a couple of inches above his knees. And they're tighter than they should be. I'd prefer if he wore full-length loose pants instead.

I half expected to see him sporting a farmer's tan, but no. He's golden all over. Sun-kissed like a swimwear model straight from Cali.

Tilting my head to the side, I jab my thumb along the ridge of my bottom lip to make sure I'm not drooling before asking, "Do you have dinner plans?"

When he whips his head toward us with both his brows up in surprise, I contemplate begging the earth to swallow me whole. I can only imagine what he's thinking right now.

"No," he answers, curiosity thick in his tone.

"Do you want some?"

His body shifts until we're standing face to face, only the chains of the fence between us. "Will my food be poisoned?"

"That's a risk you'll have to take."

There's a minuscule twitch of his lip as he lifts the towel to the back of his neck and wipes it clean. "Dinner would be nice."

"Okay," I say, beyond awkward.

Truthfully, I blame this all on my freakish obsession with online stalking him. That's the only reason why I can't stop finding myself in such compromising positions like this. I was enamoured with him for so many years that it must have caused my brain to misfire.

"I'll shower first."

"Oh, yeah, that's probably a good idea," I rush out.

"Is this a truce?"

"For tonight. I'm not letting the pool go unanswered."

He turns away from me, and a second later, his back shakes, almost as if he's laughing? The silent type that he doesn't want me to see.

"When do you want me to come?" he asks a tad breathlessly.

"Half an hour?"

"Alright."

I wait for him to look at us again, but he just goes inside without a word, my pink-and-yellow towel looped around his neck. A sigh puffs out of me. Alright then. It's good to know that he doesn't feel any different after our Jell-O fight either. He's still the same old grumpy Oliver Bateman.

Nova wraps her small arms around me from the side and squeezes. "Thanks, Mom."

"For inviting him for dinner?"

A jerky, excited nod. "He's cool. I like him."

"I'm glad you think so, kiddo. Let's go get cleaned up, okay? Then I'll put in an order for pizza."

"Pizza? Can I get ham and pineapple?"

"Sure." Even if just the smell of the fruit on the pizza will make me want to retch. "Anything else?"

"Chicken wings!"

"Deal. How about you go inside and hop in the shower while we wait?"

She doesn't argue. My girl loves showers and baths. She has an entire basket in the bathroom full of bubble baths and shower gels. Pampered already, she's my twin in far more than just one way.

Once we're inside and she's ducked into the bathroom, I put

the order in for pizza and start anxious cleaning. The vacuum hums loudly as I run it over the exact same spot in the living room carpet ten times, needing it to be as clean as possible. Hell, we're not even dirty people to begin with. I keep a tidy, dust- and crumble-free house at all times. But as I spiral, I find invisible dust on the coffee table and a make-believe stain on the grey couch cushion that I cover with a throw pillow.

I wasn't expecting Oliver the day he stormed up my stairs and helped himself to a view of my bedroom, but he wasn't looking then. Tonight, I just know he will be. That smirking, Jell-O-tossing douche will be holding a damn magnifying glass over every inch of this place in the hopes of finding something to call me out for.

He isn't going to have the chance. Magnifying glass or not.

By the time Nova cracks open the bathroom door and steps out in her tiger-striped robe and her hair wrapped in a loose towel, I'm already waiting to take my turn scrubbing clean.

"You got between your fingers and behind your ears, right?" I ask before she pads into her room.

"Yes."

"Okay. I'll be out in a couple of minutes. If you need me—"

"Tell you. I know, Mom."

"Yes, tell me." I blow out a breath and nod to myself before slipping inside the hot room and shutting the door behind me.

Ten minutes later, I'm tugging a sweatshirt down over my stomach when the doorbell rings. I don't remember the last time I could spend more than ten minutes showering and getting dressed without worrying about Nova. Actually, I can.

She wasn't born yet.

Seven used to sound like such a blessed number when I was struggling with a newborn and a toddler, but I still worry too much. Drive myself out of my mind, more like. So much could go wrong in ten minutes when I'm not around. Showers are loud, and I don't trust myself to hear her over the pelt of water as much as I should.

It's all worth it in the end. Every time I see her smile or feel her arms around me in a tight Nova hug, all the stress and fear fades to the background. The love I have for her isn't something made on this earth. It comes from somewhere else. A place pure and bright.

"Can I get the door?" she asks, sneaking past me, moving like her ass is on fire.

I laugh lightly. "It looks like you're already going to."

Feet tucked into a pair of fuzzy frog slippers, she slides the rest of the way down the hall with her hands held out like she's mid-yoga pose. As she fumbles for the doorknob to gain balance, her excitement is potent.

"Hello!" she shouts after the door is opened to reveal Oliver.

I take one look at him and curse the way my lower stomach tightens. Is it common practice for men to show up to a woman's house with damp, messy hair and black joggers that cup their tree-trunk thighs? Even though his shirt is baggy, it doesn't do me any favours. I've seen him bare-chested and therefore know *exactly* what he's hiding beneath the moss-green material. Row upon row of abs that deserve to be photographed instead of hidden away.

My eyes could cross with pleasure at the sight of his biceps cording and straining in the shirt sleeves, as if even sizing up in shirts is still not enough to house those beasts. He could pick me up and toss me over those girthy shoulders, and I'd purr, *Thank you, Lieutenant.*

Lieutenant. Fuck's sake. The overconfident ass with his *does it impress you* shit. Yeah, actually. It does. But I'll never admit it. Not even having my teeth yanked out one at a time would reveal the secrets I have that involve him. I'll take them to the grave if I have to if it means saving myself that embarrassment.

"Do you know how to wrap your hair in a towel?" Nova asks, her voice cutting through the fog of my bitter arousal.

I lick my dry lips and slowly move toward them. "I'm sure he does."

"How do you wrap it?" He surprises me with the genuine curiosity in his tone.

Nova's eyes glitter. "Oh! I can show you."

"Later, sweetheart. We don't need hair wraps tonight. Dinner will be here any minute."

She pouts but doesn't argue. Her tiny nod makes me feel guilty, and I take a bated breath.

"Your mom is right. Next time," Oliver says.

My heart skips like a horny bitch at his support, but I don't focus on it. Instead, I scold the damned organ and set a hand on Nova's shoulder to guide her away from the door.

"Come inside. I don't want bugs in the house," I mutter.

"She makes me kill them," Nova says, the traitor.

Oliver smirks at that, one brow pulling upward. "Even the spiders?"

"Especially the spiders. But I like doing it."

"Not all the time," I defend myself. With both of them out of the doorway, I'm quick to shut it and twist the lock. "It's either that or leave them trapped in a cup just so they can escape later when I forget about them."

"Just squash them with a shoe."

"That's what I do!" Nova squeals, preening under the smile he flashes her way.

"Smart girl."

I huff at their bonding. It's too sudden. He hasn't even had to work to earn Nova's affection, and she's already handing it to him like she shares her snacks with other kids on the playground. I should be proud of her for being so kind and open, but when it comes to Oliver, I don't want him to gain her friendship too quickly only to hurt her later on when he grows tired of whatever kind of game it is he's playing with us.

My momma bear instincts rear up as I fix him with a tight look and wait for him to notice. He slips out of his shoes, and finally, his hazel eyes dart to me.

"Drink?" I ask, voice short and sharp.

"Water's good."

"Great." Spinning on my heel, I leave him in the kitchen, knowing Nova will show him around on my behalf.

My seven-year-old daughter is proving to be more mature than me right now. More accepting and kind. I'm behaving like an immature asshole, but my natural stubbornness makes it hard to change that. Not yet, without knowing that he's worth the effort.

13

Avery

I KEEP AN EAR OPEN SO I CAN HEAR OLIVER AND NOVA talk as I take two glasses from the cupboard and fill them with the jug of filtered water from the fridge. Dew collects along the edges of the glasses, leaving my hands wet when I carry them out to the dining table. I get one of Nova's juice boxes next—the kind with so much sugar she only gets them on nights like tonight—and set it beside the waters.

"Do you like being a firefighter?" Nova asks when I join them again, seemingly walking into their already sparking conversation.

"Yes."

"Are you strong?"

"I think so."

She hums, and I imagine she's tapping her chin in thought. "Can you carry a person?"

"Yes."

"Four?" Nova gasps.

Oliver's chuckle is low, almost non-existent, but it makes me shiver. *Fuck.* "Two, maybe. Not four."

"My dad can carry *me*."

The pride in her voice makes my eyes prickle, any shivering

non-existent now. Chris would lose his shit if he knew Oliver was here right now. He'd be pounding on my door in half the normal time it takes to drive from Surrey with a scowl and orders for Oliver to leave.

It wouldn't matter if it was a harmless meal. Not to my insecure, selfish ex. When it comes to Nova and me, we're possessions. Two trophies that he likes kept on his shelf, close enough for others to stare at but never for him to truly care for. In his eyes, we both belong to him regardless of our relationship status.

I struggled with that realization for years, thinking that I could somehow change him. Bring out the thought and care that I wished lived inside of him. But, surprise, just like every single time a woman has told herself that she's the chosen one who can change a man who fundamentally doesn't know how to give us what we want, I was let down epically.

A person can only take so many years of being pushed aside, left to struggle on her own, before she grows tired of it and rebels. For me, that was four years ago. Five too late.

"Avery?"

I clench my fingers around nothing and whip to face Oliver. No longer in the living room with Nova, he's in the doorway separating the kitchen from the main living area. The space isn't huge, but it still isn't small. Yet with him crowding the doorway, suddenly, the kitchen is the size of a shoebox.

"Is the pizza here?" I ask tightly.

"No."

I dust my palms down my thighs. "Should be soon."

"You mad at me about the pool still?"

Good. He thinks my mood is from earlier. "Yeah. My entire backyard is soaked in gelatine."

"You can use mine. I'm off the next two days, but it's yours if you want it."

"That won't be necessary."

He reaches to scratch the back of his neck. "There are blow-ups. A frog for Nova."

I pause, getting the weirdest urge to rub at my chest. "Why a frog?"

"I noticed her shirt at the Huttons'. Frogs all over it."

"They're her favourite. Frogs and lizards. She's been asking me to get her own for months."

The info dump bubbles out of me. I'm not sure why I'm sharing details, but once I start, I don't want to stop. The only people who've wanted to hear them for a long time now are my parents.

Oliver leans a hip against the door, his arms folded across his intimidatingly huge chest. "Are you going to get her one?"

"I should. But I can't."

"You don't like reptiles," he states.

"Never have."

"Her dad?" he asks so simply, as if it's nothing but a fleeting question.

I stiffen, my walls rebuilding brick by brick until I don't fear him jumping headfirst into my thoughts. "Her dad doesn't have the ability to care for her and a pet."

He can barely take care of himself.

"Is that why you aren't together anymore?"

"It's one reason in a long list of others."

Before Oliver can reply, the doorbell rings, and I'm rushing out of the room, not giving a shit about how ridiculous I must look for hightailing it out of there. God, I'm a mess.

"Pizza's here, Mom!" Nova squeals, nose smooshed to the front window.

"Want to pick a movie for us to watch?" I ask her.

She's quick to agree, diving from the couch to the small rack of DVDs beneath the television. "Yep!"

The pizza delivery boy is waiting on the other side of the door when I whip it open and snag the boxes from his hands. He tells me the total for all the food, and I leave him there while I drop the boxes on the coffee table and grab my wallet. Oliver's voice stalls my movements.

"Have a good night. Thanks."

The door clicks shut, and I glare the entire way back to it. Oliver turns the lock on the door the way I did when he arrived and shakes his head as I stop in front of him.

"I'll eat most of the food. It's not a big deal," he grumbles.

"I didn't need you to pay for that."

"You didn't. I paid anyway."

My neck hurts from craning it back so much to meet his stare, but I'm trying to prove a point, so I tip it back even more, narrow my eyes further, and tug at the hem of my sweatshirt to keep from shoving him out the door after the delivery boy.

"This isn't a date," I argue.

A muscle above his eye twitches. "I'm well aware of that."

"So don't do that again. Next time, I'll pay."

I realize after I speak that I just insinuated there would be a second time, but it's already out there, and I can't take it back. Not without stumbling over my words.

"Fine," he says, not mentioning my mess-up before brushing past me, the heat from his body scorching my arm.

The pizza boxes on the table don't stay there long. He lifts them with little effort and carries them to the kitchen. Then I hear the cupboards opening one by one.

I let my shoulders fall forward slightly and follow him, tossing a glance at Nova as she continues to pick between two movies. *Lady and the Tramp* and *Cars*, the same two she's debated on every night since we moved here.

"The plates are to your left," I say, stepping into the kitchen. At least I've unpacked most of the kitchen by now.

Oliver looks at me over his shoulder for a brief second and then opens the right cupboard. He grabs three plates and carries them to the table, setting them beside the two boxes and white container with chicken wings inside.

"One is Hawaiian, Nova's choice, and the other is three meat. I didn't know if you still liked the same pizza after all these years, but I forgot to ask earlier," I admit, feeling almost nervous.

"I do." His throat bobs as he surveys the boxes. "I still like the same, I mean."

A burst of warmth surges through me that I try to ignore. "Well, help yourself. Nova's picking a movie. Our cable hasn't been hooked up yet, so we're stuck watching one of the few disks we own."

"Why isn't your cable set up?"

I peel open the top box, thankful it's the ham and pineapple as I take a slice for Nova. "It's been a struggle to get the company out. They've cancelled a few times so far."

When he scowls, I duck into the living room and get Nova set up on her beanbag chair. She's already got the DVD in the ancient-looking player I found at the thrift shop, and as the opening credits pop up onscreen, I hand her her plate.

Turning from her to head back to grab my own, I stumble at the sight of Oliver behind me, one plate in each hand. My mouth runs dry when he extends the one with three pieces of pizza, all meat.

"No pineapple, right?" he asks.

"No pineapple." I take the plate from him and sit on the couch. "Thank you."

He grunts in response, his eyes taking in the space in a way that shows he hadn't really before. The boxes lined up against the walls have me feeling a bit self-conscious, but I've been knocking out as much unpacking as possible in whatever free time I have. The place feels cluttered and unorganized, but I remind myself it'll be better soon.

For now, the furniture, empty shelves, and full boxes will have to do.

"What company are you using for cable?" he asks after I swallow my first bite of pizza.

Nova glides greasy fingers over the DVD remote and chooses

the Play option on the TV. The *Cars* opening scene fills the screen, and Lightning McQueen's mantra floats through the speaker before I mutter off the name of the cable company to Oliver.

He hasn't taken a bite of his food. If it were a person, it'd have shrivelled at his glare. "Did they say why they couldn't come out sooner?"

"No. Just that every time they're set out to come, something's come up."

It's bullshit. But the only thing fighting them on it will do is piss them off enough they *never* come. There are a few different ones in Vancouver, but this one's the cheapest. Maybe that's for a reason.

Oliver grunts. I take it as an answer, considering how often he does it.

"I miss my cartoons," Nova says between bites of her pizza. "We don't have lots of movies. And Mom can't watch her show now."

Oliver gives Nova his full attention. "What's your mom's show?"

"*Survivor*."

Discomfort twists my insides, growing worse with every bit of my life Oliver gets exposed to. "You'll get your cartoons back soon, *mitt hjärta*. Promise."

"What does that name mean?" Oliver asks.

I busy myself with picking off a piece of crumbled bacon from my pizza to keep from looking at him. "My heart."

He doesn't need to know that I call Nova my heart because my dad's been calling me that for as long as I can remember. My past isn't his concern.

"And the name you called me the other day?"

"I didn't call you a name," I lie.

He turns his attention to my daughter. "Nova?"

"What name?"

That's my girl.

Surprisingly, he lets it go. "You have an accent. I couldn't figure out what it was before."

"Yeah, that happens when you grow up in Sweden. I've had one my entire life. Including the last time I was here."

Awkward tension vibrates in the room at the reminder of the last time we saw one another. It was so, so long ago, but I remember it like it was yesterday. Maddox's hockey drama, Jamie's broken ankle, Cooper's art shows, Tinsley's boxing classes.

Oliver everywhere but where I was.

"I didn't notice it much back then," he admits bluntly.

It burns when it shouldn't. "Why would you have? We weren't close."

"I wasn't outgoing then. Didn't make a lot of conversation with anyone but Cooper, Maddox, and Jamie."

"How is Jamie doing? We watch his games, but it's not the same as talking in person. I didn't grab a moment with him at dinner." I change the subject, abandoning the prior one.

He shifts, knees spreading half an inch. I don't dare look away from the TV. "Jamie's good. Lively. Enjoying the game still. That hasn't changed. He hasn't."

"Is he seeing anyone?"

"Why are you asking?" he asks a bit harshly.

I cock my head and raise a brow. "Everyone seems to have someone now. That's why I'm asking."

"I don't," he bites out.

I stumble over what to say back, coming up blank. Then a question just . . . tumbles free. "Are you mad about that? Do you want someone too?"

My eyes go wide when he jolts off the couch and rubs a hand over his scruffy jaw. The veins that bulge beneath his skin are provocative as they flex and pulse, and I stare at them for a moment too long.

"I have to go to the washroom," he mutters before stepping into the kitchen, his plate clattering on the countertop.

It doesn't matter that he didn't answer my question. The answer is obvious with his speedy takeoff. If he does want something with someone, it certainly isn't me, and that's good.

We wouldn't work anyway.

14

Oliver

I'M NOT GOING TO DRIVE BY HER HOUSE.

I'm not. Going. To drive. By. Her. House.

I didn't demand Adams turn the truck down our street on the way back to the station from a small apartment fire. And I sure as hell am not leaning my cheek against the window so that I can get a closer look.

That would be pathetic. Embarrassing. *Total simp behaviour*, as Addie would say.

But yet here I am with my squad sending me half-cocked, humoured looks that I ignore while not risking dragging my eyes from the street for even a moment. Just in case I catch a glimpse of Avery and Nova in my yard. Playing in *my* pool.

The past two days have been non-stop calls with little sleep in between. We got halfway through making lunch yesterday when one came in. By the time we got back to the station, everything was ruined. Stale, cold, and undercooked.

We've all been running on fumes, but that's the normal for us. We love the job, so we suck it up. Seeing the relief and tears in the old woman's eyes that we saved from her bathroom while her apartment burned to a crisp was more than worth the ruined meal.

Despite the exhaustion and hunger, I made us take a detour. I've never been one to get so shaken up on a call that simple before, but I haven't been able to shake the worry that's plagued me since busting into that woman's apartment. The array of children's toys on the ground had my mind running at three times speed. It was only the woman there, but we didn't know that at the time.

My mind went to Nova at the sight of the stuffed frog on the couch, and that was that. I've never rescued a civilian that fast in my life. But now I'm left on edge, my leg bouncing and heart thrashing with worry. It's a mix of leftover adrenaline and genuine concern.

It's unnerving. I know Nova's okay. It wasn't her grandmother's apartment. She wasn't anywhere close to the building, but that information doesn't seem to mean shit to my erratic thoughts.

"Since when do we head to your house after calls, Lieutenant?" Adams asks, his deep voice coming through loud in the headphones cupping my ears. "I'll be tossing you beneath the bus when Captain asks why we took so long."

I ignore him. My squad is otherwise silent. If I looked back, I'm sure I'd find them dozing in their seats by now, no longer concerned with me.

My throat grows sticky when we come up on my house, the street busy, crowded with kids playing basketball on driveways and dogs barking. It's after four on a Friday afternoon, the sun shining bright and hot without a cloud in the sky. Those who work normal jobs are either off for the weekend or planning on leaving work as soon as possible.

I've watched Avery more than I should. I'm well aware of that and even pissed a bit about it too. But it's how I knew that she'd be home with Nova right now. It's a wild hope to think that she'd take me up on my offer for them to use my pool while I'm working, but fuck, for some stupid reason that doesn't make sense to me, I want them to.

I only bought it to get a rise out of Avery, and now that I have, they should get to reap the benefits of it.

Adams slows the truck a couple of kilometres as we drive by, and I don't think about how overeager I must look when I turn to face the door and focus on the glimpse of my backyard.

The splashing water and frog floatie cause my heart to stall, only thumping again when I see Avery lounging in the flower tube I blew up for her last night.

She'd probably have punctured it with a knife if she knew I bought it especially for her.

It's Patel's voice that cuts through my intense staring, making me slump back in my seat. "Are you renting out your pool or something?"

"If you are, I want a turn. I've been stuck inside all summer and could use some fun in the sun," Hart adds.

"Not renting my pool," I grunt.

Hart pushes. "Can you?"

"No."

"He needs a nap and a meal before you can convince him to share shit with you, rookie. Don't push it," Adams says.

I need a lot more than a nap, but I keep my mouth shut instead of exposing myself. We might be a big family, but there's nothing worth mentioning to them right now.

We pass down the street too quickly. Once Adams turns back onto the street that'll take us straight to the station, I stare at the side mirror, desperate for another glance at Avery and Nova that I never get.

My mood drops even further, but at least my worry is sated. They're fine. Having fun.

I remind myself of that for the rest of the day.

SHOVELLING another forkful of piping hot spaghetti past my lips, I ignore the voices around the table in an effort to convince myself I'm sleeping while eating.

I've been hunched over the dining table for the past ten minutes, my empty stomach continuing to rage regardless of how quickly I eat. We've been call-less since we got back an hour ago. The squad split off half and half, the ones not pulling extra hours off to sleep in their beds while the rest of us prepare for the final hours of our shift.

"Breathe, Bateman," Captain says gruffly.

I'm half animal as I inhale through the food in my mouth. I swallow before speaking, hearing my mother's chastising tone in the back of my head.

"I'll breathe when I'm full."

"You'll be dead by then."

"At least I won't be hungry," I mutter before filling my mouth again.

My fork scrapes the edges of the bowl as I twirl the last bit of pasta onto it and stab a chunk of beef. Captain Gallagher shakes his head at me and leans back against the kitchen island with a tablet in his hands.

Half the chairs at the table are full, but it's quiet. We're all concerned with eating as fast as we can out of fear of being forced back out with empty stomachs again.

"I'm pretty sure you'd be left hungry in hell, Bateman. I doubt the devil'll be feeding you caviar," Adams puts in from his spot across the table.

I fit him with a narrowed gaze. "Who said anything about hell? And I'm not a caviar guy."

"There's no way you're winding up at the pearly gates with your potty mouth. So unless you've got a third option . . ." he drones.

Captain keeps his eyes on the tablet but scratches at his silver-streaked beard with one finger. "Just let him eat, Adams. We'll all be better off then."

"You make me sound like an asshole, Captain."

"One of the nicest I've ever known," he retorts.

"I think that was redundant. Bateman doesn't need compliments." Adams finishes off his food and brings his bowl to the sink. "Now, who's on cleanup?"

"You are," I say after swallowing my last bite.

Adams looks at Captain with a helpless expression. Cap flashes him a *too bad* look before meeting my eyes. "Try to get your incident report from the apartment fire on my desk before next call. Only a few more hours to go."

"Can't complain about a forty-eight after how long last rotation was. I'd do this shift over any other," Adams says.

He has a valid point. I'd prefer never to pull another four-day shift.

"Do the dishes, then" are Captain's last words before he slips from the kitchen.

"Better scrub 'em good. I'll be checking," I warn Adams.

"No you won't."

"At the risk of another four-day shift? I'd do just about anything to avoid that."

"Alright, fine. You win. Now, are you going to come out with us tomorrow? You've avoided after-shift drinks for a long damn time."

He plugs the kitchen sink and squirts soap into it before turning on the faucet. With a hip against the counter as the basin fills, he watches me stand and carry my bowl over.

"All I want is to finish and go home to bed, Brent. Drinks don't appeal to me."

"This have anything to do with the drive-by today? Or the woman and kid that were in your yard?"

"It's got to do with how tired I am."

It's not the whole truth but not a full lie either. With my stomach full, my exhaustion is that much tougher to ignore. Brent is an important part of our squad and a good friend, but he wants answers to questions I don't have yet.

I'm not the most open person to begin with, and this bro-to-bro shit he wants to happen right now isn't my favourite. I deal with it when it comes to my brother and my two closest friends, but they're different. I've never had another choice but to share, and we were doing it since we were old enough to talk in the first place.

Adams raises his hands in surrender before shoving the stack of waiting dishes into the bubbled sink, the water splashing a bit. "Alright. Keep it to yourself for now. But next time—"

"Won't be a next time."

"Good. Don't flash personal things in front of us if you don't want us asking about them."

I stretch my neck, feeling the strain in the muscles. To anyone but my team, I wouldn't have been flashing anything with that quick drive down my street. Brent only feels that way because he knows where I live, as most of everyone here has been over on the occasional moral building night.

"You won't even let us know her name?" he asks after a beat, clearly not content with his own words. "Just give me something. If it really was nothing, then say it and mean it."

I'd tell him to get fucked if I wasn't already speaking despite my best efforts. "Her name's Avery."

"Pretty." He smirks.

I glare. "Don't fucking smirk like that."

"Like what?"

"Like you're thinking about her. Get her out of your head," I demand.

His laugh is loud and pisses me off. "You got it, Lieutenant. But for the record, I think you've got bigger problems than me if you're acting like this because of a woman."

"Noted."

I drop the bowl in the sink and leave him alone to clean the dinner mess, his laugh nipping at my heels the entire way to the bunkroom.

Only once I'm falling into an open bed and closing my eyes

do I stop hearing him. Instead, I'm haunted by images of Jell-O, eating pizza on the couch, and two girls filling my yard with more laughter than there's ever been.

15

Avery

Boots stomp on my pretty tile flooring, leaving dirty prints as the air-conditioning technician leaves the shop for the millionth time this morning. It's still hot and sticky in here over an hour after he arrived, warm air flowing through the vents instead of cold.

I puff out a breath and bundle my hair into my fist before tying it up and off my warm neck. My shorts and loose tee should have kept me cool in theory, but I doubt anything less than walking around stark naked would help at this point.

The smell of fresh paint and wood fills the shop. The weak, quivering muscles in my arms are the aftermath of a full day of painting. It's still not done, but if I think about coming back tomorrow to finish, I'll collapse and never get up again.

I plan to spend the entire weekend at the shop, hoping and praying that sooner rather than later, I'll be able to open instead of continuing to piss money like I've got an endless supply of it. The reality is so much more depressing.

Nova doesn't love it here because it's boring in its current state, but I've kept her busy today with painting the cooler room walls while we wait for Chris to show up. I gave her full creative freedom, knowing she needed it to keep distracted from her father's tardiness.

Does six hours late even still count as simple tardiness? Fuck, probably not. But to a seven-year-old, that's what I'll downplay it as so he doesn't hurt her feelings.

Anger sizzles beneath my skin. You'd have thought only getting to spend every second weekend with your daughter would light a fire beneath your ass and have you actually excited to spend quality time with her, but Chris has proven once again that he's such a sorry excuse—

"Has Dad called yet?" Nova asks, peeking her head out from inside the backroom.

With pink cheeks and hopeful eyes, she gazes up at me, her hands pressed to her stomach. I blink past the sudden prickle in my eyes and try to smile. It's heavy and so, so tired.

"I'm going to step out to give him a ring, okay? Maybe he lost his phone."

My daughter's too smart for someone her age, and while it usually makes me so proud, right now, I wish she weren't. Some naivety would have been appreciated for once.

"Okay," she whispers before going back into the cooler room, shoulders sagging.

I wait until she's gone and then turn, pressing the heel of my hand hard against my sternum. Three inhales and exhales, and then I'm pushing the door open and stepping onto the street. I don't pay attention to the white AC van parked directly out front or the line of cars on either side of it.

The location of the shop is alright, right in the centre of a little shopping centre with a farmer's market every Tuesday afternoon.

They're all fleeting thoughts. Nothing matters right now besides fixing this situation for my daughter.

Calling Chris, I listen to the line ring six times before he picks up.

"I know I'm late, Avery," he snaps, no hello or sliver of an apology.

"We've passed late. Now you're only hurting Nova."

"She's tough."

"She *seven* and doesn't need to be tough. Are you coming or not?"

"Yeah, I'm coming. I just got tied up at work."

It's a bald-faced lie and one I call him out on. "Since when is the shop open on Saturday afternoons? That many people needing oil changes?"

"Since fucking now. Drop it. This wouldn't have even been a problem at all if you hadn't moved to Vancouver and taken my daughter away."

He's spewing the same shit I've heard since I told him we were moving. It's always big talk, but we both know the only reason he wants us close is so he can keep an eye on us. Not to spend time with Nova and definitely not to speak with me.

"You getting caught up at work wouldn't have happened if I hadn't moved? Right. Don't put this on me. Please, I'm exhausted. Nova just wants to spend the weekend with you." I'm half pleading, but for Nova, I'd drop to my knees and downright beg.

"Have her ready and waiting at the house after dinner, and I'll pick her up."

Emotion clogs my throat. A raw sense of guilt at the reminder that this is the man who gets the title of Nova's father. Someone who sounds resigned to spend his two weekends a month with her. Tipping my head back, I inhale through my nose to keep the tears at bay.

"If you don't want to take her, then I'd rather you didn't. She's not a burden, Chris. Don't speak about her in a way that makes me think that's what you believe."

"I've already moved my plans so that I can. You'll pick her up first thing Monday morning?"

A tear drips, slithering down my cheek. "Yes, I'll pick her up the moment your two days are up."

"Don't say it like that, Avery. Don't guilt me."

"I'm not . . ." I trail off when two familiar people step onto the sidewalk from the street and head my way. "I've got to go. Text me before you head to the house, and I'll make sure she's waiting."

Oliver Bateman keeps his mom's arm tucked in his as he stares at me with laser focus. The closer he gets to me and the shop, the closer his brows tug together. His jaw pulses, eyes slipping to the wetness I feel on my cheek.

With my hand still gripping my phone, I use the back of it to hastily wipe the tear away. I'm embarrassed to be caught like this, especially by him, and I can feel myself beginning to burn with it.

"Why are you crying? What's wrong?" The low timbre of his voice makes me jump, but not out of fear.

I swallow and straighten my posture, refusing to look weak in front of anyone, let alone Oliver. Gracie sets a hand on my arm and tilts her pink-painted lips in a soft smile. I try to replicate it, but I fear it's more of a grimace.

"Hi. What are you guys doing here?" I ask softly.

"Avery? Who's that?" Chris barks, his voice muffled with the distance between the phone and my ear but still loud enough for everyone to hear.

Oliver's glare darkens at the rough male voice, his head tilting slightly as if he's sizing up an invisible enemy. Not ready to dig into that right now, I ignore his reaction as much as I can and put the phone back to my ear, turning to the side.

"Text me before you come. I'll only keep her up until nine. If you're not there by then, I'm locking the door and tucking her into bed."

"No. Forget it. I'm coming now. Have her ready," he demands, piercing my ears with his words before the call ends.

I press the phone to my stomach and lick my dry lips, completely fucking mortified that there were witnesses to that exchange. This isn't the first time he's spoken to me like that—far from it—and it won't be the last. He's forever a figure in my life, regardless of how he speaks to me because Nova deserves to know her father. I'll suck it up until my last day, keeping my tongue pinched between my teeth. My first priority will always be Nova, and she loves him deeply.

I'm not sure I have the strength to care for anyone but her. Myself included.

"Are you okay, honey?" Gracie asks, swaying toward me half a step.

My smile is fake. Every inch of it. "Yeah, it's just been a long week."

I can feel Oliver's eyes on me. The weight of them is sharp, like daggers digging into my skull an inch at a time, hoping to sink into my brain.

"Anything we can help you with? I was hoping to swing by and offer, but if now isn't a good time, we can come back! I should have called beforehand," Gracie says.

I dare a look at Oliver, unable to help myself. His deep brown eyes are waiting and latch onto mine, keeping them locked there.

"Isn't today your first day off?" I ask, my tongue pissed that I held it with Chris and now wanting to lash out.

"Keeping track of my schedule?"

I'm already flushed, but another rush of heat crawls up my neck. "It's hard not to when you flaunt it."

"Did you use the pool while I was working?"

"No," I say, flashes of the past two afternoons Nova and I spent swimming and tanning in his massive pool invading my thoughts.

He hums deep in his throat. "You're lying."

"How would you know that?"

"You've always been a terrible liar," he admits.

It's a casual mention of our history. Maybe small and meaningless to him, but to me, it's another reminder that we shouldn't be strangers.

"I think I've missed a few things," Gracie puts in. She's looking between Oliver and me with a devilish curiosity. "How often do the two of you see each other?"

"We're neighbours," Oliver replies.

She sucks in a dramatic breath. "You're neighbours? You're neighbours with Avery, and you didn't tell your own mother?"

"She could have told you too," he states.

I roll my eyes at him before glancing at the door to the store behind him. The reality of the situation outside of this conversation is too shitty to ignore.

Tensing up at the idea of pushing them aside when they've come to help me, I push forward and say, "Nova's father is coming to pick her up. He . . . he's late, so she's a bit upset. I've got to get everything put away for when he arrives and make sure she's ready to go. I'm sorry."

"Oh! Don't apologize. We can get out of your hair. Can I give her a quick hug before she goes?" Gracie asks, her voice so damn kind it wraps around my sore feelings, soothing their burn.

"Of course you can. She's painting in the backroom. I'm sure she'd love a hug."

Gracie strokes my arm before dashing inside, leaving me alone on the sidewalk with her son.

His closeness screws with me. Despite my best efforts, I've begun to grow comfortable around him. He's kept to himself since dinner the other night, but I'm learning that that isn't unusual for him. Every time I ask something a little too deep or personal, he pulls back as if he's scared I'll bite.

I wouldn't unless he provoked me to.

His inability to open up is a sign as obvious as any. I'm not in the place to be prying apart the brick wall he's laid around his heart, but like a fool, I'm interested enough to try.

Nodding to the shop, I say, "You can say hi to her too. If you want."

"Does her father talk to you like that often?" he asks, replacing my question with his own.

"Would it matter?"

"Yeah, princess. It would matter," he grunts, features tightening with frustration.

"Don't start with the princess, Oliver. I'm far from it."

"We'll stay here and help you until he arrives, *princess*." He sounds almost playful when he says it, so I let it go.

"There's not much to do. And I prefer to stay busy once she's gone."

"She's with him every second weekend?"

I smile slightly. "Now who's keeping track of whose schedule?"

"I'll admit it when you do."

"So . . . never?"

"Never works."

I tug at the tie in my hair and shuffle to the side when the technician rounds his van and stomps back into the shop. Oliver tracks his every move, only looking back at me once he's out of view.

"I'm getting the air conditioning fixed," I tell him before he can ask.

"He's tracking mud inside."

"You should see the mess on the tiles."

His throat bobs as he stares at me, swallowing my body with the intense glimmer in his eyes. "I'm not leaving until he's gone and Nova's father's shown up."

"Why? We don't need a babysitter."

"I don't want to babysit you, Avery. You just don't have to be alone all the time. Let us help you."

"We did use your pool," I admit on a limb, wanting or maybe needing to say something honest after that. "Nova loved the frog. She told me to ask if she could be the only one to use it, but I told her she had to ask you."

"It's hers. Only hers."

My heart flutters. "Thank you."

One step and he's right in front of me, no more than a foot

away. His cologne swirls between us, combining with the heat to make my head swim. I want to say something snarky just to poke at him and see if he'll come even closer.

"You don't like asking for help, and that's fine. But I'm going to give it anyway. It would make both of our lives easier if you just accepted that."

"Why do you want to help me so badly?" I blurt.

He balances a hand between us, fingers strained and curled as if he's fighting to keep from touching me. I'm devious enough to contemplate grabbing it myself, but I don't.

"I'm making up for lost time. I couldn't stop if I wanted to."

16

Oliver

I'VE NEVER BEEN ONE TO CARE ABOUT FLOWERS OR plants in general, but Avery's shop is nice. It will be better once it's finished, but she's got a good, solid foundation.

There's plenty of space and natural light. It has a break room, bathroom, and a big cooler that would rival one at a restaurant. The messy writing and flowers painted on the cold walls make it unique, and Nova's proud of her work in a loud way.

"Your air con should be good to go now. If you have any questions or concerns, give me a call, and I'll come back out," the technician tells Avery, a small card extended toward her.

I stare at him, my shoulders squaring of their own accord as she takes his card. He ignores me the way he has since I arrived, only offering Avery a final nod before leaving, a large bag jostling around on his arm.

Mom has Nova in the backroom under the pretense of saying goodbye, but they're giggling like nuts back there, and if I had to guess, I'd say Mom's filling the girl full of the candy she keeps in her purse while showing her photos of all of us as kids. She hasn't stopped talking about Nova since she met her, and I know she's trying to make up for all the years she's missed. If Avery let her, I know she'd love to do the same with her.

She's not the only one.

I ignore that thought and close the door after the technician. With a quick glance up and down along the street, I search for the man we're all waiting for. It feels wrong as hell to let him take Nova from Avery, even if it is only for a couple of nights, but it's not my business.

It's. Not. My. Business.

Maybe if I repeat it enough, I'll finally get it through my thick fucking skull.

"You and your mom don't have to stay," Avery murmurs, leaning over the counter with her hands steepled beneath her chin.

"We're staying."

The corner of her mouth curls. "Alright."

Her hair is loose in its ponytail, stray hairs falling around her face to frame her jaw. She doesn't pay them any attention, leaving them there to sway in the breeze from the cool air pumping through the vents. A glass bottle of grape pop sits in front of her, dew dripping from the sides before she wraps long fingers around it and lifts it to her lips.

Blue eyes drifting shut, she gulps down the fizzy drink, the column of her dainty throat straining with each swallow. Mine closes in at how regal she makes it look. It's fucking weird to draw that relation, but I can't think of anything more fitting.

Avery is beautiful. She has the kind of beauty that stops you on the street and has you contemplating how on earth you'll manage to start up a conversation with her. Like a siren singing to sailors at sea, you're powerless to her draw, damn near ready to bend over backward just to see her smile at you.

I've felt that draw for years. Tried to forget about it but didn't succeed. Even with her halfway across the world, I wished for another shot to tell her those same thoughts.

I very well might have ruined my chance, though, considering I didn't recognize her when she was dropped right in front of me and, because of that, treated her shit and started this war of wills between us.

If she was out of my league before, she's not even in the same universe as me now.

"Is Chris always late?" I ask stiffly.

I've had this guy on my mind for weeks, and not a single thing about him has given me a good impression. The way he spoke to her on the phone had me wishing he were here to pummel.

Avery sets the bottle down and licks her lips clean. She picks at the wet, peeling label. "More late than he is on time."

"When did you decide on every second weekend?"

"After we split. It was the first suggestion I gave. He didn't even fight me on it. I haven't been able to decide if that was a good thing or a horrendously bad one. It saved me on lawyer fees not having to get it taken care of in court, but at the same time, he didn't even fight for her."

I'm tense as I stare across the shop at where she leans, waiting for her to tear her attention away from the bottle. "He's a fool."

"He is. Nova deserves better."

"She's not the only one."

Our gazes catch when she looks up. I take two steps forward, that draw between us demanding I get closer. She blinks slowly, lashes fluttering over tired, pale blue eyes.

"I haven't thought about what I deserve in a long time. I'm not sure now is the best time for it," she admits on a soft exhale.

"If not now, then when? When she's grown and you've been alone for years?"

"If that's what it takes."

"That's not fair to you, princess."

"Parenthood's hardly ever fair."

Her shoulders drop, and the sight of it has me moving to the counter. My hips dig into the edge as I stand opposite her and set my hands on it. She watches me move without speaking a word, and I risk taking that as an invitation.

"When's the last time someone took care of you?" I ask, voice low and rough.

"I don't remember."

My chest strains. The words sound wrong coming from her lips. *Painful*. My head is a mess of half-baked plans and ideas on how to fill the place in her life that is so hauntingly empty. It takes everything in me to shove them down before I blurt out something reckless.

I swallow once, twice, three times before grappling with something safe to say, but nothing comes out. The sad smile that appears in front of me is not what I wanted to see. The shutters slam shut so quickly it's startling, the window into her heart she'd granted me disappearing, leaving nothing but false normalcy.

"I've got to find Nova's backpack," she says before pushing from the counter and disappearing into the backroom.

I grip the edge of the counter in tight fists and blow out a tight breath. Moment ruined by my inability to be even mildly open and honest, I drop my head.

The shop door opens fast enough for a rip of wind to slash at my back. I know who it is without having to turn around, but when I do, the sight of his anger-stricken face intensifies my shit mood.

"Where's my daughter?" he snaps, taking large steps toward me.

By the time he stops, he's close enough for me to smell the coffee on his breath and perfume on the collar of his oil-streaked shirt. With green eyes the opposite of his daughter's blue ones, he glares hard, puffing his chest.

He jabs a finger into my chest. "And who the fuck are you?"

"You need to calm down and step back before I tell you shit. Your daughter is close enough she could hear you right now," I say calmly.

The reminder of Nova doesn't embarrass him like I hoped it would. He doesn't drop his finger or back up either.

"If you're hanging around my daughter and Avery, I need to know who you are."

"Drop your hand and take a step back, then I'll tell you."

He curls his lip but does as I say this time.

I smooth a hand over my chest where his finger leaves a burn in my skin. "Oliver Bateman. Friend of the family."

"Not that close of a friend, considering I haven't heard of you. Stay the fuck away from *my* family."

Footsteps sound behind me, and then Chris' eyes dart over my shoulder. He doesn't smile or relax, only looks back at me with a silent demand for me to fuck off.

Not a chance.

"Chris, this is Gracie Bateman, Oliver's mom. I grew up around their family, which I've mentioned a few times," Avery explains, her voice overly soothing in the way I'd expect to hear while she's talking Nova down from a tantrum.

"Dad! You're here!"

Nova runs at Chris, his lateness forgiven in the blink of an eye. She burrows her face into his chest and winds her tiny arms around him as he lifts her in a hug.

Something gnaws on my ribs as I watch them, an emotion I refuse to admit to myself.

I look away and shift my stance, focusing on Avery instead. Her eyes glisten with unshed tears that I can't distinguish between happy or sad, and I swear I'm going to break. The shop is suddenly too small, a shoebox I've been shoved into with the lid taped shut.

"Mom. Time to go," I say, hoping to fucking God she can read me well enough by now to know I'm not kidding.

One look at me and she's nodding before hugging Avery and standing beside me. I pulse my jaw to keep focused and head for the door.

"Oliver—" Avery starts, a single footstep following my name. "Thank you."

"No worries."

I step onto the street, and Mom slips her arm through mine as the door shuts behind us. Counting the seconds, I wait for her to speak, knowing she has something to say.

"He seems like a piece of work."

"Yeah. But he's Nova's dad."

"Dad or not, he's still an ass," Mom huffs.

Slipping my keys out of my pocket, I unlock my SUV doors. "You should stop by again and help her once the flowers arrive."

"I will. Nova's first ballet lesson is Wednesday. I'll talk to Avery about it then."

"Good."

"Will you be there too?"

I turn my head, brows furrowed. "Why would I be there?"

"You're not working, are you?" she asks, the picture of innocence.

With a shake of my head, I open the passenger door for her and wait for her to slip into the SUV before answering, "I don't know shit about ballet other than what you've told me."

"No, but you seem to know quite a lot about Avery. Much more than I expected after so long apart."

I pin her with an expression that I hope portrays how little I want to talk about this and shut the door when she pouts up at me. The second I slide into the driver's seat and slip the keys into the ignition, she's cranking the AC and fiddling with the music.

"Does she know you had a crush on her growing up?" she asks a beat later.

I freeze, holding my breath. "You knew about that?"

She nods firmly. "I'm your mother. I know everything."

"You never said anything."

"If I had, you would have done everything in your power to hide your feelings from me. Once you stopped asking about her, I figured you'd outgrown it. Was I wrong?"

I spread my hands over the steering wheel before holding it tight. "I was young. She had a boyfriend and never came back to visit again. Of course I outgrew it."

"Mm, you're sure about that?"

"She had a daughter with another man."

"And? If you're about to say something about not being interested in her because of that, I'll smack you upside the head, Oliver Bateman. There is nothing wrong with her being separated from her daughter's father."

"Jesus, Mom. I wasn't going to say that." I release a breath and, with a glance at the shop from the rear-view window, pull away from the curb. "I don't know why I mentioned that at all."

She stares at me across the cab before reaching across the console to pat my bicep. "Yes you do. You said it because it upset you to see them all together. I saw the way you stared at Nova and Chris back there. Like you—"

"Like I *nothing*. I don't want to talk about this anymore."

"Oh, my love. Okay, I'll leave it alone," she murmurs. "But if you change your mind, I'm here."

I won't, but I don't bother saying that. There's no reason to. She wouldn't believe me anyway.

And she's not the only one.

17

I DON'T GET HOME UNTIL PAST DINNERTIME. ONCE Nova was buckled into the back seat of Chris' car and out of sight, that familiar sense of overhanging loneliness hit, and I buried it beneath hours of manual labour.

My back and arms ache as I step onto the curb outside my house and lock my car doors behind me. The small weight of the beaded key chains Nova's made me over the years feel too heavy in my hand, even compared to the bottle of wine red in my other one. I need a long bath and to sift through the takeout menus in my junk drawer until I find something I can drown my sorrows in.

If I called and asked Adalyn, she might be up for joining me, but then again, she has a family of her own now. Tinsley is back in Toronto with Noah, and Maddox's wife, Braxton, and I have never been all that close. The women in our giant found family are slim in numbers compared to the men. It's never felt more unfair than right now.

Inside my empty, silent home, I kick off my shoes and head straight for bed, takeout be damned. The TV I bought for my room leans against the wall opposite the bed and beside the wall mount I've been meaning to hang. It would probably help if I had a drill or something, but I don't know shit about tools. Not unless they come in the shape of a man.

I sneak a peek at the window that looks into Oliver's bedroom to make sure the blinds are down before tossing the wine bottle onto my mattress and beginning to strip.

Naked, I sniff my armpit as if needing proof that I do, in fact, stink like sweat and then hop in the shower. I stay beneath the hot water for longer than I do when Nova's home and lean my forehead against the cool tiles, my eyes drifting shut.

Surely it would be pathetic for a thirty-year-old woman to call her mom and beg her to watch a movie with her over Skype, right?

I tried the whole taking myself out for dinner thing a couple of weeks ago, and all it did was make me feel shittier about my lack of friends.

"Fuck," I groan before turning the water off and stepping out of the tub.

Ten minutes later, I've slipped on a pair of sleep shorts and a tank top, brushed through my hair, and applied enough anti-wrinkle cream to cover the faces of at least five different women.

Once I've popped the bottle of wine in the kitchen and grabbed my extra-large glass from the cupboard, there's a knock on the door. It's a loud, pounding one that has me immediately on edge, knowing damn well who's responsible for it.

I leave the wine on the counter and then tug the bottom of my tank top as I go to the door. A second round of knocking starts when I'm two steps from answering. My glare is already fixed in place as I twist the deadbolt and swing open the door.

"You're incredibly impatient," I say, getting an eyeful of Oliver's back.

He spins at the sound of my voice, his hand dropping from where he was gripping the back of his neck. The flush to his cheeks has to be from the heat . . .

"Sorry. Didn't know if you could hear it or not."

"I was only in the kitchen."

He jerks his head in a nod and swallows before blinking four times in quick succession. When his eyes fall to take in my outfit, I'm the one flushing all the way down to the soles of my feet. Pupils swelling in the sea of deep brown, he checks me out blatantly, maybe completely unaware that he's doing so. Weeks ago, I might have been offended by this type of attention, but now, his interest in my physical appearance makes me ache in a way I haven't in a long, long time.

Dropping a hand to my jutted hip, I wait for him to look up again, my tongue too twisted to tell him to stop ogling my tits and the inward curve of my waist where my blue silk top is too cropped to cover. By the time he's basking my naked thighs in the heat from his intense stare, I'm helpless to the draw of squeezing them together in hopes of soothing the intense pulsing in my core.

He notices my fidgeting. Fuck me, his lips part on a long, tight exhale before he grips the edge of the door in a hold tight enough for the veins on the back of his hand to strain and snaps his eyes up to mine.

"Do you always answer the door dressed like this?" he asks, and so help me, I think my nipples bead from the gruff words alone.

I nip at the inside of my cheek hard enough to bring me out of my lustful haze. "Maybe. What does it matter to you?"

"Nothing. Just isn't safe."

Unable to help myself, I raise a brow and ask, "Am I in danger right now, Oliver?"

It takes him a minute to answer, those long, strong fingers tightening on the door. "No, princess. I'm not a danger to you."

I hear every word he doesn't speak aloud. *I'm not in danger yet, but I might be if I keep poking the bear.*

"What did you need, *butternalle*?" I ask, attempting to sound bored.

His eyes spark at the nickname, but he leaves it be. "Have you eaten?"

"Dinner?"

"Yes. Dinner. Have you eaten dinner?" he asks, frustration leaking from the words.

"No. I was going to have a liquid dinner of red wine and then order something for dessert."

He inhales and exhales twice before speaking again. "I accidentally made too much food for just me. Do you want—are you hungry?"

"What did you make?"

I'm already going to say yes, regardless of what he made. I don't know why or how, but one simple offer from him and a blast of warmth sends my loneliness abandoning ship, disappearing.

"I grilled a couple steaks. There's a salad too..."

"How do you accidentally cook two steaks instead of one?"

He shifts on his feet, lips twitching. "It fell onto the grill, and I couldn't waste it."

"Right," I muse, fighting back a smile of my own. "Do you like wine?"

"It's not my drink of choice, but I don't hate it."

"I'll bring the bottle I was going to drink on my own, then. Give me a sec," I say before leaving him in the doorway to grab the bottle.

"Do you want to change first?" He raises his voice so it reaches me, and I shiver at the power in it.

I grip the bottle hard and head back toward the door. "No. I like what I'm wearing now. It's comfortable."

And I know you like it.

He coughs, and I reach him just in time to watch as he adjusts the front of his jeans and grips the bulge...

My temperature spikes, eyes glued onto the stiff movements of his hand before he releases himself and shifts.

"Ready to go?" he asks tightly.

I bounce my eyes back up to his and tip my chin, snagging my keys from the hook on the wall. "Lead the way. I've just got to lock up."

He swipes my keys and ushers me around his body with a hot hand burning the skin of my lower back. "I've got it."

"I'm capable of locking my own door."

"I know. You're capable of anything."

My tongue swells in my mouth. I don't know how I'm able to form a coherent sentence, but I manage somehow.

"You're being nice tonight. Why?"

He tucks my keys into the pocket of his jeans, and I make a mental note to take them back before the end of the night.

Walking across our front lawns side by side instead of across from one another after a prank showdown is a completely different experience. I haven't been inside of Oliver's house before, and my palms are sweating now that it's happening.

"I can be nice, Avery," he grunts.

"Are you going to prank me the moment I step in your front door? Is that it?"

"Keep pushing me and maybe I will."

My laugh is short but loud. "I'm serious."

"I'm not going to prank you. I figured you'd be hungry, and with Nova gone, I wasn't sure if you'd make a meal for yourself big enough to restore all the energy you spent at the store today."

I roll my lips inward, staring down at my feet smooshing his grass when the urge to smile starts to eat at me. "So, you didn't accidentally drop a steak, then."

"No, princess. I didn't."

The confirmation that he cooked dinner for me because he was worried . . . I stop keeping the three inches of distance between us and cautiously move closer.

He either doesn't notice my sudden closeness or finds it okay because he doesn't move away. Even when we climb the front steps, he stays beside me, our shoulders knocking on the way to the top.

A key ring that doesn't resemble mine in the slightest with the lack of bright, handmade accessories slips over his thumb before he unlocks his front door and ushers us inside.

"Our layouts are pretty similar. I replaced the flooring on both levels last year and updated the kitchen a bit. Took out the old sink and put in a new one, then painted the cabinets," he says, holding the door open with his arm for me to head in first.

I survey the space and grow jealous of the dark wood floors that put my scratched orangey-brown ones to shame. The upgrade is obvious, and I'm a second from asking—begging—him to help me with mine when he interrupts my train of thought.

"Come and eat. I don't want the food to get too cold."

"Did you do any more renovations other than the floors and the kitchen?" I ask, too curious not to.

"Yes. There were two extra bedrooms upstairs, so I turned one into a gym. And the basement wasn't finished when I bought the place, so I hung the drywall, painted, and carried the hardwood down there. The bathroom is still a work in progress."

"So, you're a real-life Bob the Builder, then."

"I watch a lot of YouTube tutorials," he says, his palm skimming my back again, this time swiping up my spine. "The kitchen, Avery. I'll show you all of the renovations after you eat."

Refusing to purr like a cat at the affectionate touch, I let him guide me down the hall and through the archway that opens into the kitchen. The floor plan is identical to my house, just a lot brighter due to the lack of brown walls.

His kitchen sink is a white farmhouse one instead of the double steel kind, and the cabinets are a deep green that's emphasized by the marble countertops and white tile backsplash.

"You did a good job," I tell him sincerely, watching as he shifts away from me to grab two plates from the corner cabinet.

Setting them beside the one already on the counter with two thick steaks on it, he says, "Thanks. My dad helped a lot."

"How often do you see your family?"

"A few times a week and a big dinner every Sunday." He starts dishing up our plates and piles a heaping serving of pasta salad on my plate next to the steak. "There's no eggs in it."

"Really? You didn't want to take the opportunity to make me eat them again?"

"No. Once was enough."

I don't reply, and a comfortable silence settles over us while he digs utensils out of a drawer and then hands me my food.

"I won't be able to eat all of this," I gasp at the mountain of food.

He jostles a shoulder. "Try. I think I remembered how you liked it cooked. Brown with a little pink, right?"

"Yes." My heart bangs around in my chest when I realize he's cut the steak into bite-sized pieces already.

"If you tell me that you're capable of cutting your own steak, I'll hand feed it to you."

"I wasn't going to say that."

"Good. Do you want to eat on the couch?"

He carries his plate over to me and stands close, searching my face as he waits for an answer. The piles of food on my plate don't come close to what's on his. It's not surprising, considering how massive he is and what he does for a living, but it takes me aback anyway.

"If you have cable, I'd love to sit on the couch."

"You still don't have any?"

"No. I'm going to start calling a couple of other companies this week."

He nods, and we step into the living room. His TV is mounted on the wall above a long, slim table with a gaming system and two controllers on it. The L-shaped couch takes up the majority of the room but doesn't make it feel too small. It's a warm cream colour, with cushions that look thick and comfortable and a few deep green throw pillows that match the kitchen cabinets.

"Do you ever spill on the couch? That colour would never last in my house. Nova spills anything and everything on ours."

He glances at the couch, inspecting it. "I have one of those little green fabric-cleaning machines. Maddox's son has spilled a number of foods on it so far."

"Do you watch his son here often?"

"No. They're in Ottawa most of the year. I've hosted dinner here a couple of times. Jamie's made a mess more than Liam, I'm sure."

I nod, looking around the rest of the room. A man like Oliver doesn't scream book enthusiast, but the stacked bookshelf against the wall that separates the living space from the front hall has me rethinking that. I don't recognize any of the thick titles, but they look mostly non-fiction.

Three books at the end of the bottom shelf have me setting my plate down and dropping to a crouch, leaning in for a closer look. Recognition sparks at the children's book titles.

"Nova had these when she was a toddler. She loved them," I say softly, tracing the spines of each one.

He moves behind me and leans over my head, his presence heavy and *comforting*. I fight back a flush and stay focused on the books.

"Once Liam's a bit older, I'm sure the two of them will get along well," he says. "I can give you a tour of the rest of the house *after* you eat."

"Who said I was staying long enough to get a tour once I'm finished?"

He drops a hand to my shoulder, and my muscles quiver beneath his fingers—*not* a fucking exaggeration either. I stare directly ahead at the books and focus on my breathing when he sweeps his palm along my arm and gently holds my elbow. Using the hold to pull me onto my feet, he turns me so we're face to face.

I stare at the swooped neckline of his shirt and fidget, more nervous than I've been in a long time. They aren't bad nerves, necessarily, just . . . ones I'm not used to feeling. The jittery variety that reminds me of high school crushes and giggling at lame jokes beneath the football field bleachers.

He stretches an arm past me and then brings my plate back in front of my chest. I take it quickly, seizing the chance to busy my hands.

"I recorded *Survivor* for you," he says.

My eyes jump to his. "You did?"

Maybe he doesn't notice the excitement in my tone because he doesn't say anything about it as he releases my arm and moves to the couch, sitting on the middle cushion. "Couldn't get access to the ones that have already played on TV, so I recorded the newest one and bought the earlier ones. Where were you before you lost your cable?"

"I only saw the premiere," I mutter loosely, too surprised to speak any other way.

"Episode two, then."

He loads up the episodes he's purchased on the TV and waits for me to sit before starting the second one. I peel my feet from where they've stuck to the floor and join him.

My fingers cramp as I release them from their iron grip on the plate and set it on my lap. The lack of distance I've kept between us when I sat on the cushion beside him was natural. I want to be close to him. I'd have moved closer even if I hadn't wanted to spook the both of us.

The familiar intro song plays on the speakers he has hung on the wall on either side of the TV, and I take my first bite of the food in front of me. A mix of flavours attacks my taste buds as the steak melts on my tongue, and my stomach growls.

I snap my head to the side to see if he heard it, and when he looks at me with a smirk, I laugh. It feels good and sounds even better. A light feeling floats through me then, and I take another bite, turning my attention back to the screen.

Maybe Oliver isn't *all* that bad.

He does make a killer steak, after all.

18

Oliver

WITH A WINEGLASS RESTING OVER THE KNEES SHE HAS tucked into her chest, Avery watches the show with intense focus beside me. She's the type of show watcher who doesn't like to speak outside of commercial breaks. Focused on the current competition happening onscreen, she hasn't looked away in minutes.

I have the opposite problem.

Every two minutes, I'm sneaking looks at her, enthralled by her love of the show. I've never been able to get into reality TV like this or any at all, really, but if it means time with her . . . I'll have to start liking them.

We're on episode four now, but it doesn't feel like we've been sitting on the couch for three hours. Dinner is cleaned up and put away, and the bottle of wine is nearly empty on the coffee table. It's comfortable. I'm relaxed, my muscles loose and pulse steady.

Avery looks beyond beautiful right now. Happy and calm, her emotions open and loud. Maybe that's why I can't seem to look away. It's been years since I've gotten the chance to see her this way, and I'm downright feasting on it.

Her hair was dripping wet when I arrived at her house, but it's dried completely now, the long length of it curled at the bottom and frizzy at the top. Still dressed in those nearly see-through silk pajamas, her long legs are exposed, thigh muscles taut when she tucks one closer into her chest and rests her chin atop it.

I stare and stare, knowing I need to look away but not able to bring myself to do just that. Every flutter of her light brown lashes brings my focus to the pale blue colouring of the thin skin beneath her eyes. I get the overwhelming urge to tell her to sleep so the skin returns to its normal colour.

"Do you want more wine?" she asks with a turn of her head in my direction.

I look at the TV, finding an advertisement for deodorant playing. "No. I'm good, thanks. You can finish it."

"Trying to get me drunk?"

"If it would help you get some sleep tonight, then sure."

She stares at me for a minute, no doubt trying to make sense of my comment. "I sleep fine."

"Alright."

"Do I not look like I sleep fine? Should I be offended?"

"Would it be such a bad thing if I just cared about your well-being?"

"Maybe. Depending on why you suddenly give a shit."

She turns back to the TV, leaving the wine bottle where it is. I lean my head against the back of the couch and sigh. My inability to not piss her off at every turn has made me question whether or not I've been single for so long is because I can't word my sentences for shit.

"I've always given a shit, Avery. I just . . ."

I place my glass beside the bottle on the table and run a hand over my head before sitting back. Shifting my body toward hers, I risk it and cup her shin. The skin is so soft and smooth I almost choke on nothing.

She speaks before I do, her eyes dropping to focus on where I touch her. I wait for her to shove my hand away, but she doesn't. Instead, she covers my fingers with hers and leaves them there, not squeezing, just holding.

"You have a hard time showing it?" She finishes my statement for me.

"Yeah."

"Me too. The only person I know how to show affection or care toward are my parents and Nova. Maybe I'm too guarded, or I've just been hurt too many times," she admits, frowning.

"Nova's dad the one who hurt you?"

Her laugh is nothing more than an angry huff. "Probably. Or I was already damaged goods long before he showed up."

"Don't call yourself damaged goods. You're not damaged," I grit out, my fingers flexing over her leg, drifting to brush her calf. "There's nothing wrong with not keeping your heart on your sleeve."

She shrugs a shoulder. "I want to put all the blame on him, but I also teach Nova about personal accountability. It would be hypocritical to not take some of the blame for how I am now. Back when I was a kid, it didn't matter who you were, I would have showered you in hugs and attention."

"Then take accountability for some of it, but don't let him off the hook. Don't dismiss the way he hurt you because you want to be a good mom. You're already one of those. And people are allowed to change. Don't punish yourself for that."

"Is that an order, Lieutenant?" she asks softly, almost teasingly.

"Yeah, it's an order," I confirm.

Her eyes sink their hooks into mine and keep them there, forcing us to miss the recap of the show now echoing through the speakers. I'd ignore the entire thing if it meant I could keep looking at her like this. Like the last thing I want to do is blink and lose this connection.

I'm falling right back into the feelings I had when I was a teenager, except now, they're swelling and growing into the kind that would have terrified me back then.

Right person, wrong time...

I sound like my mother.

"What did he do to you, Avery?" I ask despite knowing the risks that come with the question.

The chance that she could shut down and lock up the fortress of her mind that I've gotten a peek inside of tonight.

She surprises me when she lets me continue looking. "Other than the constant belittling and lack of support, I'm sure he was a fine boyfriend. Unfortunately, I was too hurt by all of the bad to make light of any of the good. If it was ever there in the first place."

I wet my lips and glide my palm up over her knee and to the bottom of her thigh, leaving it there. She keeps her hand on mine, but her fingers curl over it now, like she doesn't want to accidentally let go.

"How long were you together before . . ."

"Six months. It was a broken condom that he never told me about that led to me missing my period and taking a test. Full transparency, I expected him to leave after I told him, but he surprised me by staying. He made this big deal out of it too, as if staying to father his own child was worthy of a damn Nobel Prize or something. My dad would never admit it, but I think he threatened him to make him stay. Sure, we were still getting to know each other when I got pregnant, but Chris was very clear that he didn't want kids. He didn't tell me about the broken condom because he was hoping it wouldn't have mattered. I doubt he thought the one time would lead to a kid."

My distaste for the guy turns into a hatred that sears me from the inside out. "Why didn't you go back home? Your parents would have helped you, right?"

"They asked me the same thing. Both my mom and dad wanted me to go home and raise Nova in Sweden with them. But Chris wouldn't come, and I understood his decision because I know firsthand how hard it is to move that far away from the place you were raised. I wanted Nova to grow up with a father figure, and he's given her that."

"And what has he given you, Avery? Other than your daughter."

She diverts her eyes, staring at the TV as her hold on my hand grows tighter. The fog that slips over her gaze isn't something I'd ever like to see again.

"Nothing worth mentioning," she whispers.

"How long have you been alone, princess? How long has it been since you were someone's priority?"

Her admission sears through me. "I don't know."

I want to scold her for not reaching out to me when she was struggling. For not coming to me for help when she was stuck picking up the scraps that Chris left behind for her, but I keep quiet. Blaming her for what she went through is a bad move that even someone as lacking in conversation skills as me can recognize.

"That's over now. You have family here now. Mom, Aunt Ava, Addie. If you need anything, you ask for it, and they'll give it without question," I declare.

She turns her head slowly, and our eyes clash. "Are you included in that family? I don't want to expect anything, but Nova likes you, and—"

I slide my hand out from under hers and fight back a wince at the rejection that sparks in her stare. I'm quick to move again, desperate to help clear it all up for her.

Dropping my arm so it curls over her shoulder, I pull her close. She melts into me, not fighting the new position as I swirl my fingertips along her bare skin, drawing soothing circles.

"I'm not tucking myself into the same category as everyone else. I don't want to only be called when you need help with Nova. Yeah, you let me know when you need me for that, but you deserve to be someone's priority, and I've made you mine. That means you call me or bring yourself here to my front door anytime Avery the woman needs something, and not just Avery the mom. That clear?"

"I'm always Avery the mom, Oliver. Sometimes there isn't a

divide," she murmurs, her legs stretching out before she goes limp against me.

"What about right now? Who have you been tonight?"

"Right now... right now, I'm just me."

I brush my mouth over the top of her head, taking my fill of the moment. "Not *just* you. That word doesn't belong in that statement. You're you, Avery the woman."

And I make a promise to myself that I'll do everything I can to keep her here with me. Even if that means opening myself up in a way that should have me running in the opposite direction.

19

Oliver

I PEEL MY EYES OPEN AND BLINK OVER AND OVER AGAIN until I can make out the shapes on the TV. It's silent, the screen too bright in the darkness of the ... living room. I'm in the living room. And it's hot despite the fact I know I had the AC on earlier.

With my left arm, I swipe a hand over the couch cushion beside me and find the TV remote. I turn off the screen and stop squinting when the blinding light disappears, and my eyes stop burning.

I swallow to wet my throat and try to spread my legs before freezing, feeling a weight on them that wasn't there earlier. Or I don't think it was. Fuck, I don't remember anything after the fifth episode of *Survivor*.

My heart stalls in my chest when I look down at my lap. Avery's head rests over my thighs, her blonde hair splayed over my jeans, the colour light enough to be obvious in the dark.

My hand rests on her hip. *Her bare hip.* The thin pajama top has ridden up high, leaving her stomach exposed. It's too dark to see too much, but she's hot to the touch, the heat from her body making my neck slick with sweat.

"Avery?" I whisper, needing to know if she's asleep or awake and too scared to move. She doesn't answer, so I try again. "Princess?"

Silence.

I drop my head back and flex my fingers, straining to keep myself from touching any more of her. She's asleep, and I shouldn't even be touching her hip without her permission. But Christ, I don't want to pull my hand away.

We can't stay here like this, but the thought of waking her unsettles me. She needs to sleep. I don't know if she has problems doing so at home, and I don't care to know for sure. All I do know is that she has bags under her eyes that tell me she needs the rest, and I'm going to make sure she gets it, even if she wakes in the morning and kicks my ass for what I'm about to do.

With my breath stuck in my throat, I slip out from beneath her and wait for her head to touch the cushions before dropping to a crouch along the edge of the couch.

Peaceful is the term that comes to mind when I look at her, seeing her face for the first time since we fell asleep. Her lips are parted slightly as her eyes remain closed, features completely relaxed. For now, she's free of the heavy load of responsibilities that will weigh her down come morning.

It's easy to scoop her up and carry her up the stairs. She's light in my arms, her head resting against my chest and legs swinging in the air with every step I take. Climbing every stair carefully, I manage not to trip in the dark. I carry her into my bedroom and gently set her on the mattress, making sure there's a pillow beneath her head.

The comforter is tucked beneath the pillows, so I leave it and grab a spare blanket from the linen closet in the hallway instead. She doesn't move a muscle as I drape it over her and tuck it beneath her feet before hovering at the edge of the bed, unable to walk away.

I know she'd call me out on being a creep for the way I'm watching her, like she's something I want to protect from the world. I wouldn't disagree with her either. It is creepy, but I don't care.

Leaning down, I tuck a strand of hair behind her ear before brushing a few others from her forehead. The worry lines that tend to crinkle between her brows are gone, and I brush my thumb over the smooth skin there before dropping my hand.

She moans a beat later, burrowing her cheek into the pillow before cracking an eyelid open. When she sees me, she doesn't freak out like I expected. A second eye opens as her hand reaches out, and she grips my wrist, tugging at it.

"Did you carry me to your bed?" she whispers.

With a jerk of my head, I say, "I was leaving. You're safe here."

"I know." Her eyes close, but her fingers remain locked around my wrist. "Sleep beside me."

"I'll sleep on the pullout in the spare room."

She cracks an eye open again just long enough to get another group of words out. "Sleep in the bed with me. It's been a long time since I've slept beside someone."

"Me too."

"Don't think about it so much. Just get in."

Don't think about it so much? Fuck, this woman is going to drive me to an early grave.

"Are you sure? I didn't take you up here for this. I'm fine on the—"

"Don't make me get up and shove you into bed. *Lägg dig ner med mig, butternalle.*"

"What does that mean?"

She pushes her hand beneath the pillow. "Please, Oliver."

"One day, you'll tell me what you've been calling me."

I leave her there and move to the opposite side of the bed before pulling my shirt off and stepping out of my jeans. She stays on her side, facing away from me as I lie on the bed, tucking my arm beneath my head and staring at the ceiling.

"Have you slept in bed with a woman before, or are you

always just this awkward?" she asks when I remain rigidly on my back.

"I have. Sorry."

She blows out a breath. "I shouldn't have pushed you into sleeping in bed with me. I'm sorry. Go if you want to."

I should face palm myself. "I could have asked whether you wanted me to just carry you home instead of putting you in my bed in the first place."

"I like it here," she admits, turning onto her back. The corner of the blanket lifts at the same time she looks at me. "Like you said, I'm safe."

"You are."

"So get under the blanket with me."

I don't make her ask twice. Moving closer, I rest my head on the edge of my pillow and cover myself with the spare blanket. She sighs and tucks it beneath her chin, shutting her eyes again.

"Good night, Oliver."

Leaving the blanket beneath my pecs, I close my eyes. The heat from her skin warms me better than the blanket does as she reaches out and touches my hip.

I grab her fingers and hold them tight. "Good night, Avery."

THE NEXT MORNING, I push down the top of my coffee machine and hit the Start button while Avery uses a spatula to flip a pancake on the stove.

"You were always a little pyromaniac when you were a kid. I'm not surprised you chose to become a firefighter."

"I didn't like starting fires," I grunt, watching the coffee start to fill the mug beneath the nozzle.

"No? So that time Maddox's dad let you light the burn pile on fire, you didn't dump an entire jerry can of gasoline on it just to see how high the flames could go?"

"He told me to add gas to it."

She snorts a laugh and flips another pancake. "Not the entire thing!"

"He should have made that clearer. I was ten. Of course I was going to dump the whole thing on it."

"Alright. You win."

Changing the topic from myself, I pull the full mug of coffee to the side and say, "I don't remember you loving flowers enough to open up your own store to sell them when you were younger."

Dressed in proper clothes now after running home to change before we started breakfast, Avery turns from the stove to face me. The yellow shirt she's wearing is baggy over the high-waisted leggings and hides the bare strip of skin along her stomach that I've grown used to seeing since last night.

She tucks her hair behind her ears and leans a hip to the counter. "I've always loved flowers. They're prettier in Sweden, though, and I never spoke about them much around you and all the guys. Maybe that's why you never knew."

"I should have asked."

"Why? Did you care about flowers in your younger years? I doubt you and Maddox discussed them much in your free time between hockey practices."

I dig out the used coffee pod and replace it with a new one before sliding another mug in place beneath the spout. "You remember those?"

She turns back to the stove. "I never got to see many of your games, but I remember hearing about them all the time. Hockey was Maddox's entire personality, and football was Jamie's. You never really cared much for either, did you?"

"No. I just played to kill time."

"I get it. My parents tried to get me to play hockey, but much to my dad's disappointment, I can barely skate without gripping the boards."

"No shit?"

She slides two pancakes onto the plate beside her and sprays the pan with oil before pouring two more thick circles of batter onto it. "No shit. My dad got over it fast. Being an only child has its perks."

"Did you ever want another sibling?"

"No. I had all of you when I was younger, and then my friends back home kept me busy. Now I have Nova, and she's enough for me."

"Jamie was a lot growing up."

She nods, looking at me over her shoulder. "He kept you on your toes. The two of you would argue constantly."

"We still do. Drives Mom nuts."

"It's just sibling banter, though, right? You two get along well?"

"Yeah. We're close. He's just a lot. Loud and hyper half the time."

"And you're the opposite. Quiet and broody and grumpy," she teases with a wink before focusing on the pancakes again.

"The best three qualities in a man."

"Agree to disagree on that one."

I pull the second mug of coffee to the side before moving to the fridge. Grabbing the creamer from inside of it, I ask, "Why's that?"

"Well, for starters, men like that love to fill your pool with Jell-O, make you eat food you hate, and don't follow you back on Instagram."

"Fuck, I thought I was being unique. You're saying those are common actions from a guy like me?" I close the fridge and move back to the coffees. "And how do I follow someone back that doesn't follow me in the first place?"

"I've followed you since I was here last," she says, ignoring everything else I said.

"No you haven't."

"Watch the pancakes for a minute," she orders before taking off out of the kitchen.

I shake my head and pour the creamer into my coffee, stopping when it goes from black to a dark brown before mixing it with a spoon.

There's no way she's followed me all this time. Why would she have wanted to keep up with my life after going back home? It's not like I post online often. My entire feed is just photos of my family and the occasional one of my backyard or the sky with some lame quote Jamie encouraged me to caption it with.

I made an effort not to look her up online, but if she's been doing the opposite this entire time, I'm going to feel like a colossal douchebag even more so than I already do.

Taking over the pancake flipping, I finish the last ones on the pan and turn off the stove. Breakfast was my idea after we woke up and she didn't run like hell out of my house. It was a shameless seizing of an opportunity to spend more time with her that I don't regret.

"Get ready to eat your words, Oliver Bateman," she calls from the hallway.

A second later, she's swooping into the room with her phone in her hand, the screen lit up with the proof that she wasn't lying. I stare at the screen for too long with an obvious winced expression.

"So, what do I get for being right?" she asks while locking her phone.

I grab my coffee and gulp half of it down, not caring that it burns my throat. "Bragging rights aren't enough?"

"I suppose they can be."

"I didn't know," I blurt.

"It's fine. Not a big deal or anything."

I let it go because I'm not sure how to soothe the sting without telling her the reason I made sure not to search her up in the first place.

"I'm not sure how you take your coffee, so I left the creamer beside it."

"Coffee with a dash of creamer, usually," she says before fixing her coffee the same way I did mine. "How do you—"

The ringing of her phone cuts her off, whatever it was she was going to ask me lost in the sound. She moves quickly, answering the call without hesitation.

"Chris? Is everything okay?"

Her concern morphs into anger in the blink of an eye. I take a step toward her, abandoning my coffee on the counter.

"What do you mean you're dropping her off early? This isn't just early—it's ridiculous. You've had her for less than twenty-four hours!" With her fingers pinching the bridge of her nose, she speaks again. "Too fucking late now. Yeah, I'm home . . . No, I'm not going to lie to her for you. If you're content with cutting your time short with her, then that's your loss and your problem. I'm not going to try and make light of it on your behalf. That's your job . . . See you soon, then. Bye."

She drops her phone on the counter beside the coffee machine and laughs. It's loud and dark and swirling with a million emotions. I don't move despite wanting to comfort her.

"He's bringing Nova home?" I ask.

"Yep. One night and he's done with her. Just like that. Fucking pathetic asshole."

"When will she be here?"

"Forty-five minutes, give or take a few. I have to go."

"Yeah, you do. Bring breakfast over with you so you don't have to cook again. Has she eaten?"

I'm already grabbing a takeout container and filling it with the pancakes we made when I feel her hand on my back.

"Bring it all. Come over and eat with us."

"Nova will want to spend time with her mom. Not me."

"I wouldn't be so sure of that. She was the one who convinced me to invite you for dinner after the pool incident."

I look at her over my shoulder, trying not to get my hopes up. "Are you sure?"

"Yes. She'll be happy to see you. Especially because we made pancakes. I have whipped cream and sprinkles at my house too, so consider that an incentive."

"Let's go, then."

20

Avery

VIOLENCE HAS NEVER BEEN MY FIRST REACTION. I might get angry enough to shout and curse someone out from time to time, but I've never physically injured someone because of something they've done to me.

I'm debating breaking my celibacy when Chris ushers Nova up my sidewalk almost an hour after calling.

The pain in her eyes shatters something inside of me as she slumps along, bottom lip wobbling. Something comes over me, and before I can think twice, I'm pulling Nova away from Chris and lunging at him, my palm an inch from his cheek when a set of fingers wraps around my wrist.

The tingles diving deep beneath my skin where I'm touched tell me the fingers belong to Oliver, but I still tug my hand away without a care who's touching me. Chris takes advantage of my pause and steps out of reach before I can make contact with his good-for-nothing skin.

Fucker.

"You're a piece of shit, Chris," I spit, looking down my nose at him despite him having a couple of inches on me.

He rolls his eyes. "You were about to slap me in front of our daughter. Who's really the piece of shit?"

"Excuse me?" Oliver says, tone so hard that I almost flinch. "Say that again."

Chris disregards him and stays focused on me, eyes brimming with more annoyance than anything else. It's such typical behaviour from him that it doesn't shock me to see it now.

"Call off the guard dog, Avery. We're not going to fight in front of our daughter. She's seen enough with that little fit of yours just now."

"My fit?" I echo incredulously. "You're really going to turn this on me, huh? Well, you're nothing if not predictable, Christopher. You can leave now. I've got my daughter."

The front door slams behind me, and I wince. Shame sinks in right alongside years of unresolved anger and resentment until I'm overflowing with too many negative emotions to think straight. I take a stunted step back and push my hair out of my face.

Every good moment from last night and this morning is spoiled by Chris. The man who has taken so many happy memories from me that I've lost count. He's ruined more than a handful of days, but these ones . . . it bites harder than usual.

Oliver moves into my space, completely obliterating any distance between us while palming my back, fingers drifting slowly back and forth. Despite my efforts, I melt a little at his touch.

Hot breath sears my ear when he whispers, "Go see Nova. I've got Chris."

I stare up at him, and I know there's doubt there. He curls his fingers in the back of my shirt and shifts closer somehow.

"I won't bloody him up. I'll leave that to you next time. Your daughter needs you, and I can handle this. Let me help."

The sincerity in his gaze is enough for me to force myself to agree, taking a risk with my trust for the first time in too long.

With a final glare at Chris, I say, "Go home. You have two weeks to get your life together because if this happens again, we'll be renegotiating our current custody agreement, and this time, it will be written in stone."

He sucks in a breath, surprised by the threat, but I'm stalking off before he has a chance to argue with me about it.

Two days every fourteen. That's it. And it's still too many.

My heart aches as I step inside the house and go straight for Nova's room. The door is shut, her backpack left outside in the hall. The sound of angry cries is enough to crack my heart clean down the middle.

Pushing the door open, I sneak inside and sit beside her hunched-over body on the bed. She's got the pillow pressed to her face and her knees curled into her stomach.

"I'm sorry you had to come back early," I murmur, smoothing her hair. "What do you need from me?"

She shakes her head, face still hidden in her pink pillow. I keep smoothing her hair and kiss the sliver of the right cheek she has exposed.

"I'll leave you alone, okay? Just come get me when you're ready to talk, and I'll be here to listen," I tell her softly before pushing to my feet and leaving the room.

After closing her door behind me, I go back to the front of the house and steal a glance at the two men who are still on the sidewalk from the front window.

Chris is in Oliver's face, spouting shit that I'm glad I can't hear while Oliver stands there and takes it, his hands steady on his hips. His calmness is sexy, and a devilish part of me wants to see just how long he could keep that same calm exposure in a more personal, intimate setting...

A car door slams, and I flinch while focusing back on the window. Chris is pulling away from the curb in his car, and Oliver's climbing the front steps, swinging the door open a beat later.

"Do I want to know what he was saying out there?" I ask the minute he's in front of me.

"He doesn't want me near either of you."

"So, the obvious stuff, then," I mutter with a grind of my jaw. "What did you see in him?"

I turn away from him, fidgeting with my hands. I'm so used to keeping things to myself that I've been dumping information on Oliver in loads, and now is no different.

"I was young and stupid. Starved for male attention after being so sheltered growing up. My dad made it impossible to date, and the one time I did, it was with someone he wanted me with. Someone with an NHL career in their future and an ego to match."

"The guy you brought with you on vacation. You introduced him to everyone." His tone is darker now, colder.

Curiosity has me turning back around. His tense expression and crossed arms aren't what I was expecting to see.

"I didn't think you even noticed. You didn't speak to me once that trip."

"You were busy. Didn't want to interrupt you," he says.

There's a tingle in the back of my mind, like there's a memory I've forgotten over the years and can't seem to bring back.

"Either way, yes, I brought him, and he met everyone, and it was fine. But I wasn't about to marry him or anything. I convinced my dad that he wasn't the guy for me, and he let it go. Fast-forward to when I moved here, and it was the first time in my life I had complete freedom. I dated often and made a million mistakes in only a few months on my own, but when I met Chris, he was everything I thought I was wanting.

"Outgoing, loud, friendly. He loved to show me off, and I enjoyed being introduced as his girlfriend just as much. I had blinders on, and once the honeymoon period disappeared, it was easier to see the guy he hid behind the persona I was always shown. Arrogant, proud, possessive. He was suddenly everything I knew I'd never wanted. Then, I got pregnant, and you know what happened after that."

"He's not worthy of either of you. Not of your time, attention, or concern," Oliver grunts.

"I know that now. I've known it for years. But it's too late to kick him to the curb. We're tied together for life. Nova deserves a family, and I already feel bad enough that it's a broken one," I admit, regret lining my stomach.

"Fuck that," he says, moving toward me with long strides. I tip my head back to keep eye contact and swallow. "Nova doesn't have a broken home. She has a mother who loves her more than anything and will do everything she can to make her happy."

"How long will that be enough? How long will *I* be enough for her?" My words drift to whispers when my voice cracks, exposing my hurt.

I tear my eyes away and drop my head, but he's there with a finger beneath my chin, tipping it right back up.

"You will *always* be enough for the people who love you."

"Fuck. You're supposed to be a grumpy asshole," I say with a weak smile, hoping to downplay the effect his words have on me.

"I have moments of wisdom hidden beneath the rudeness. They come out every once in a while."

"If you let them out more often, you'd have women swarming you."

"That isn't what I want."

"Oh."

He lifts the corner of his mouth into a tiny smile and slowly curls his finger over the edge of my jaw before gliding it along the underside. I shiver and lean closer, feeling the subtle touch all the way down in my toes.

"Is Nova going to be okay?"

I manage to tip my chin enough for it to be construed as a nod. "She's strong."

"Gets it from her mom."

"Now you're just trying to suck up," I tease faintly.

"If that makes it easier for you to accept the compliment, then sure, princess. I'm sucking up."

"The last time I tried to dive into your head, you ran off. I'm just trying to avoid that happening again."

"I've had enough running from you, I think," he says.

"What do you mean?"

"Mom? Can I have a hug now?" Nova asks.

Oliver steps back before I can make myself do it, and I shoot him a grateful smile. Nova doesn't look surprised to find him in our living room, and her lack of reaction speaks volumes.

I rush toward her and pull her into my arms. "You can have a million hugs if you want, baby."

"Can we do something fun today?" she whispers into my shoulder.

"Sure. What do you want to do?"

Pulling back, she peeks over my shoulder and asks, "Are you still a firefighter?"

I twist in time to see Oliver grin at my daughter, and I think I black out for a second as my ovaries pop and sizzle.

He's not put out by the childish question. Instead, he leans into it with an openness that means the world to me.

"Yeah, peanut. I'm a firefighter. Have you ever seen a fire truck up close before?"

"No!"

"Do you want to?"

"Can I? Mom, can I?" she asks, gripping my arms tight while batting her lashes. "Please?"

Her excitement has me turning to Oliver, my heart thumping in my ears at what a day spent together with all three of us could mean.

Something that we have to talk about soon. Before the feelings I'm growing for him become any more overwhelming.

"Is that allowed?" I ask him, tone cautious and heavy with a double meaning.

"It's encouraged."

For now, that has to be enough.

I rub Nova's back. "How about you get changed out of your PJs, and I'll braid your hair for you before we have breakfast. I'll even do that fancy inside-out one you like."

"This is awesome! I'll be right back!"

I watch her run toward her bedroom and focus on Oliver, wishing he wasn't so far away. *Another dangerous thought.*

"Are you sure about this?" I ask, needing to be sure.

He moves toward me with confidence, returning to the spot he was in before Nova joined us. There's no face touching this time, just a strong, male hand taking my smaller, feminine one and holding it between us.

"She'll have fun. But if you'd rather me not be around right now, just tell me, and I'll go. It's completely up to you."

"I don't want you to go."

"We'll finish that conversation from earlier once you're ready. Nova's the priority."

He's saying all the right things. Every single word I wished Chris would say just once the entire time we were together and now, years later. It feels too good to be true, and I'm pessimistic enough lately to believe it.

It's a flaw that I've struggled with for most of my life, but I've never been more frustrated with it than I am right now.

"Okay," I agree.

His brows tug inward, but he doesn't say anything else. We both clearly have problems and things we wish we knew how to express but don't.

It's going to be a battle to get to where I'm growing to want to be, but I also have a feeling that he might be worth the effort.

21

Oliver

I'VE NEVER INVITED ANYONE TO THE FIREHOUSE. NOT my parents, my friends, or cousins. I'm positive there's a rule written somewhere that once you bring someone here, there's no going back from it.

My squad is my second family. The trust and friendship we've built over the past seven years together is as strong as steel. They trust me to have their backs, and I trust them to do the same. We're bound in blood, sweat, and tears.

The moment I introduce my squad to Avery and Nova, they're as good as mine. The two of them will be welcomed into our family with open arms with no take backs allowed.

I know all of that, and I've made peace with it.

Today will be a test of sorts since my squad is on days off like I am, and my girls will be meeting the second unit instead. Better to dip their toe in and test the water before I throw them in headfirst without life jackets.

While I may not be the warm and fuzzy guy, I know my emotions well enough to tell when I'm interested in someone. And fuck, what I'm feeling toward Avery isn't simply interest. It's something gentle hidden beneath rough words and quiet in volume but loud in action. If there's a word to describe all that somewhere, it isn't in my vocabulary just yet.

I'm borderline obsessed with the idea of taking care of her. *Of both of them.* They don't need me, but I want to prove to them that they can. There's something fulfilling about making sure Avery eats a real meal and gets a full night's sleep, even if I'm not offered the spot beside her that I hope could one day be mine. The toothy grins that Nova flashes every time I do something to make her happy—whether it's buying a pool floatie shaped like a frog or sneaking her extra sprinkles for her pancakes after her mom's turned away—make my heart soar so fiercely I'm surprised it hasn't flown away.

I feel stupid to have thought that I could ignore the familiar feelings that rose to the surface at my first glance at Avery the day she moved in. Convincing myself that she was nothing more than a nuisance was the second worst mistake I've ever made. The only one above it is having ignored her all of these years when I could have been here, caring for her and her daughter.

"Can I ride in the fire truck?" Nova asks from the back seat of the SUV.

She's swinging her legs in the air, her seat belt wrapped around her front and buckled in over the booster seat I snagged from Avery's car. The bright yellow shirt with the cartoon frog sticking his tongue out and saying "peace" stands out like a sore thumb amongst the cream leather seats. I like it.

"If the truck's there, I'll make sure you get at least a tour of the inside. That work for you?"

"Yes!"

Avery's eyes dart across the console, a small smile brimming beneath them. "You're sure we're allowed to come? I don't want to pop up and be a distraction."

"Family comes all the time. It's good for morale," I say.

I'd kill to be distracted by her during a long shift.

"Alright then. Good. I've never been inside a fire station before."

"With any luck, we'll be interrupting lunch. St. Clair is on shift today, and he's always tossed in the kitchen for meals. Best cook in all of Vancouver."

"Really? Can he make PB&J shaped like horses?" Nova asks.

I look at her in the rear-view mirror and nod. "If I tell him to, he will."

"Which is something you're not going to do," Avery chides.

"Then I'll do it myself."

"Yay!" Nova cheers, and I wink at Avery, taking in every inch of her playful eye roll.

"You're a suck-up," she says softly so her daughter doesn't hear.

"I am."

"She has plenty of people who spoil her already."

"Doesn't matter. None of them are me."

"Will you still say that once she's grown attached to you?"

I look at her, keeping my expression as serious as I can without coming off as abrasive. "I've grown attached to *her* already."

Her cheeks pinken, her eyes bouncing around the SUV. "Oh."

"If you're surprised by that, I've done a shit job of showing it," I grunt.

"You haven't. I just didn't want to assume anything. You haven't known her very long. Me either, really."

"Is there anything else you're trying not to assume? 'Cause I thought I knew you pretty well."

"No, there isn't."

"You sure?" Releasing the steering wheel from my right hand, I reach low and grip her thigh, right above her knee. "I'm attached to you too, princess. Real attached."

"Same," she says on a breath, peering across the console at me.

The single syllable is enough to send my pulse raging. Heat fills my chest as I pull the SUV into the fire station parking lot and refuse to remove my hand from her leg just yet.

Now isn't the right moment to pull her over onto my lap and kiss her senseless, but fuck, I'm contemplating it.

"We're here!" Nova squeals, the click of her unbuckling her seat belt following soon after.

Avery appears as reluctant to move as I feel, but she's gone in a blink, leaving my palm searing hot and hovering over where her thigh just was.

Nova pokes the back of my neck through the space beneath the headrest. "Let's go, Ollie!"

For the first time in my entire life, I don't mind the nickname.

My hand hovers over Avery's back as I hold open the door for her and Nova to step inside the fire station. The little girl dives beneath my arm first, eyes wide and frantically looking around.

"So cool!" she gasps, staring through the windows behind the front desk that look into the engine bay.

The truck is there, doors shut and paint glistening. With the bay seemingly void of the squad on call, I contemplate risking taking them for a ride before I'm shutting the idea down. If I were on call, I'd find a way to make it happen, but asking the captain on shift for permission would be a huge use of time today.

"Lieutenant Bateman? What are you doing here?"

The rookie on desk duty stares up at me from his seat, his Vancouver FD shirt at least one size too small and gripping at the base of his throat in a way that makes me cringe. I've met him once or twice, I'm sure, but he's not one of mine. If he were, I'd have made sure he weren't suffocating every day in his own clothes.

"Giving a tour. Pretend I'm not here," I mutter, forcing his eyes back to me when they wander to Avery with awed interest. "Pretend *none of us* are here."

He gulps, dropping his attention to the phone on the desk.

"Captain's out, but I'll let him know you're here once he gets back."

"Sure." It doesn't matter to me if he knows.

Nova sets her hands on the lifted edge of the desk and peers over it at the rookie, expression open and curious. Sweet too.

"Is your name really Proby? That's a weird name."

I choke on an unexpected laugh and wait for him to answer her, feeling Avery's stare hot on my cheek.

"Uh, no. My name's Jake," the rookie answers.

Nova spins toward me and tugs at my hand. "His name tag is wrong, Ollie."

The name tag is a patch stitched into his shirt, no doubt done by one of the old guys on the squad. The name is given to all the rookies, but I've never thought about stitching it onto any shirts before. Maybe I should.

"Jake's nickname is Proby. It's a joke his friends have played on him," I explain.

She cocks her head. "Like how you call me peanut?"

"Like peanut, peanut. He likes the nickname. Don't you, Proby?" I ask, narrowing my eyes on him in a silent warning to agree with me.

"Yup! I love it," he rambles.

Nova accepts the answer but doesn't let it go. "It's kind of weird."

"Nova, don't call people weird," Avery chastises.

"I didn't! His *nickname* is weird."

Avery sighs. "Apologize, please."

"Really?" Nova pouts, arms folding over her chest.

"Yes, really. We don't call people or their nicknames weird. It isn't nice."

I keep my mouth shut and watch Avery speak with such dominance and warning. Fuck me, she makes my cock stiffen in my jeans at the worst possible times. She's being a stern momma bear, and I'm learning quickly that I'm very, *very* into that side of her.

"I'm sorry for calling your nickname weird," Nova says quietly.

The rookie looks confused as to what to say, so I glare at him again, hoping he gets it.

He gulps again. "It's okay. All good, kid."

"Great. We'll be going. I want to show them the engine bay," I say before gesturing to the door behind him. "Ready, peanut?"

"Yes! My friends are going to be so jealous."

Pride fills me. "Come on. I'll take a picture of you in front of the engine."

Fifteen minutes later, Nova's still gushing over the truck when I lead them toward the pole I've caught Avery staring at every so often.

I crouch in front of Nova while sneaking a glance at her mom where she watches beside the truck. "Do you want to slide down the pole?"

She gasps, hands coming up to her mouth as she spins to ask Avery, "Can I, Mom?"

"As long as Oliver's there to catch you."

"I've got her," I promise, something sharp but comforting spiking in my chest at her trust in me. "And then you're next, princess."

"I'm not going down that thing," she argues, shaking her head too quickly.

I smirk. "Yeah, you are."

"Not happening."

"We'll see."

Nova's bouncing in place when I meet her beside the pole and lead her out of the engine bay to the stairs leading to the second floor of the station.

"Do you want to go down on your own?" I ask, keeping my tone soft.

She hums, rubbing her chin. "Can you go down with me the first time?"

"Sure can."

Her smile is beaming and innocent. Free in the way a child's should be. "You promise not to drop me?"

"I promise. I've got you."

"Can you go down with my mom too? She looked scared to try."

"You think she'd feel safer with me?"

"Yes," she says with an easy shrug.

One word said so simply, but that slams into me at full force. I trip over my feet and catch myself with a whispered curse before my face hits the carpet.

"I'll go down with you both," I promise before clearing my throat and stopping in front of the pole. "Just wrap your body around me like a monkey, and don't let go until we're on the ground."

"Okay."

The fall is only one storey high, but the thought of dropping her makes me want to cling tighter.

Avery's already waiting beneath us, her hands on her hips, fingers tapping. I've never gone down the pole with a second person before, but with Nova, it'll be easy enough. She's tiny, and as I pick her up, I'm pretty sure she weighs less than my turnouts do.

"Ready?" I ask once she's clinging to me tight.

Readjusting my arms when she doesn't reply, I slide her onto my hip more than my chest and grip the pole with a single hand. Wrapping one leg around the pole, I ask again, "Ready, Nova?"

She nods, chin bouncing against my shoulder. "Yep!"

I tighten my hold on her even more before hooking my second leg around the pole and sliding down. The drop is slower than normal, and my bicep strains with use as I control how fast we go. Nova giggles and cheers the entire way down, and I can't help but smile at her excitement.

"Mom! Mom! Look at me!" she shouts before my feet hit the ground. "Did you see?"

Avery grins, eyes soft and warm. "I did, *älskling*. You looked like a real firefighter."

"It's your turn now!" Nova says as I lower her to her feet. She shoots toward her mom and grabs her hands, tugging her toward me. "Oliver said he'll keep you safe."

"Did he now?"

Our eyes meet, and my smile is natural. "I did."

"Then I guess I have no choice but to listen."

"Best plan I've heard in a while."

"Hurry, hurry!" Nova says, giving Avery a push from behind.

Avery tugs at one of Nova's braids and watches me expectantly. "Lead the way, Lieutenant."

"Stay close to the pole, Nova, okay?" I reach for Avery's hand but, at the last second, drop mine back to my side.

I'm not about to do anything in front of Nova that I don't know if Avery wants her to see. As much as I'd love to take her hand and hold her close, we're not dating. To Nova, I'm just her mom's friend and their neighbour.

I shove my hand into my pocket and lead Avery down the same path I took Nova. She trails behind me, and once the door to the engine bay closes and we're alone in the stairway, I'm fighting every instinct that tells me to keep her in here with me for as long as possible.

"Thank you for doing this for her, Oliver," she murmurs, her voice caressing my back.

"It's nothing."

"It's not nothing. You've made her day. Helped bring some light back in her eyes after what happened this morning. It means a lot to me."

"When I said I was here for both of you, I meant it. I'm not the guy to give out false promises. It's not worth the effort."

She snags my hand the moment I pull it from my pocket. "I know."

Frozen in my tracks, I glance back at her, mouth going dry. Alone in the stairway, it takes everything in me not to pull her into my arms. This intense need to be as close to her as possible is alarming, but I don't focus on that right now.

"I . . ." She bites down on her lip, hesitating. "Everything is so much more complicated with a child. I have things I want to say to you, but I don't know how to get them out properly yet."

"You don't have to say anything right now," I reassure her.

"I want to, though. I'm frustrated because in a different life, I'd have taken this opportunity to tell you to kiss me."

A shiver climbs up my spine, pressure building in my groin as I lean against the wall, fingers twitching. We're only three steps apart, but it feels like miles.

"Avery," I warn. "I'm hanging on by a thread here. Don't tell me that."

She inhales, holding it in for a long moment before letting it out. "Things need to move slow. For Nova's sake."

"For Nova," I agree, dropping a step closer.

Another step disappears between us when she moves. "I don't know what you want in the future. What you see your life like in ten years."

"I haven't spent a lot of time planning that far ahead."

"Why not?"

"There's been no reason to. Nobody who wanted to know."

"Before now," she whispers, eyes falling to the last step separating us.

It's a game of wills. Who will be the one to close the distance—

A knock on the door at the bottom of the stairs has me jumping back up the steps.

"Hello? Did you fall, Mom?"

Avery frowns, flicking her eyes to the door. "No, sweetie. We'll be coming down the pole in a second!"

"Okay!"

"I'm sorry—"

"My ability to be patient is one of my best assets. Don't apologize. Let's go and make your daughter smile," I say before she can give in to the guilt so obviously written on her face.

Reluctantly, she lets it go, and we reach the pole without another word spoken. I wait until she's checked on Nova before crouching and lifting her into my arms.

"Oh!" she gasps, pawing at my shoulders.

"Wrap your legs around my waist and hold on tight, or I'm going to drop us both on our asses," I instruct, holding the pole.

"This feels incredibly dangerous. I don't think you're supposed to carry a full-sized person in your arms while doing this. Let me go, and I'll slide down on my own."

I tighten my arm around her back and keep her held against me. "No. I like you here."

A lot. It feels right to hold her like this. She fits against me like she's supposed to be in my arms.

"I've got you," I add, splaying my fingers out over her back until the ends of her hair brush over them. "Don't get down yet."

She keeps her arms looped around my neck and rests her chin against my shoulder. "Okay."

"Come down, come down," Nova chants, clapping enthusiastically.

"Ready?" I whisper.

The ghost of warm lips along the side of my throat has me seeing stars. "Ready."

With one step, we're falling.

22

Avery

I WAKE MONDAY WITH A MIGRAINE AND A TERRIBLE attitude.

It's the ultimate kick in the cooter after the high of a weekend I never wanted to end. Nova was sulky all morning, hardly eating and complaining every spare second she could find. We left the house with a bowl of soggy cereal sitting on the table and a bagged lunch with a KD cup and an apple in her backpack alongside her unfinished homework.

I'm sure I failed some hypothetical mom test this weekend, and this terrible morning is my karma.

Nova wanted nothing to do with me when she jumped out of the car and headed inside her school, and I tried not to take offense to her attitude, but it still bit. I've been running through a handful of different reasons for her behaviour, and almost all of them come back to something I've done.

Did I push her into hanging around another man after being so disappointed by her father? Is she mad at me for what happened with Chris? Was I not supportive enough when she was upset? Did I just miss something?

I bury my head in my hands and groan. Motherhood is the

greatest gift that can be given to anyone, but it's not always sunshine and daisies.

Sometimes, it's locking yourself away when you're on the verge of screaming the house down, fearing that every choice you make is the wrong one and you're going to screw your kid up without knowing it, and bottling your pain so you can be a pillar of strength.

It doesn't matter that seven years have gone by. I still have no damn clue what to do half the time. Raising a child is a guessing game where every option is probably wrong in one way or another. There's never one right answer, and learning that lesson on my own was torturous.

They say to find a support system for a reason. Between hormones, stress, and fear, raising a child is a test of will. And doing it alone tested me more than I anticipated.

Peeling my face from my palms, I let my arms fall to my sides. The new cash register rests on the counter in front of me beside the monitor that cost far too much of my budget. I'm sure it will be worth it in the long run, but as of now, all it is is a paperweight.

The grout between the floor tiles has gotten dirtier as the days have passed, and with only half the shop painted . . . I try as hard as I can not to get discouraged.

This was never going to be easy or quick, and it won't suddenly be just because I'm tired and want it finished. A few more weeks and I'll be surrounded by the smell of fresh flowers and chatting with husbands who need advice on what type of arrangement to order their wives to apologize for a stupid fight.

I swipe at the screen and start the process of connecting the monitor to the store's Wi-Fi, getting it taken care of quickly before powering on the handheld card reader.

It only takes a few minutes to get everything set up, and when I check the time, I'm relieved to find there are only a few more minutes before I have to pick up Nova. Maybe I'll stop and grab her an ice cream on the way. With any luck, it will win me back some po—

A crash fills the street, the sound of metal hitting metal so loud I cover my ears and curl behind the counter out of fear. My skin flushes cold as I round the counter a heartbeat later and tumble out the door.

The commotion along the curb is almost as shocking as the crumpled car in the exact same spot mine was parked all day. I blink, ears hot. The crumpled car *is* mine.

Or it was.

I lift a hand to my mouth and gawk at the smooshed hood of a truck that's pressed against the driver's door of my car. Smoke leaks from beneath the truck as I clear the sidewalk, racing to where a man runs shaking fingers through his hair and rambles curse after curse.

"Did you hit my car?" I shriek, jabbing a finger at him.

Whipping my head to the side, I gape at the damage the entire left side of my car took. It's completely crumpled, the frame shoved inward, glass shattered and spread all over the pavement. The fuzzy dice hanging on my rear-view mirror are still intact, so that's a win.

"I didn't mean to!" the man shouts.

"No shit! You just don't know how to drive." The shop is at the end of one street with another running horizontally past it. "Where did you think you were going? It's a flower shop, not a McDonald's drive-through! Did you completely miss the stop sign, or did you ignore it?"

He breathes quickly, continuing to make a mess of his hair. Glasses slipping down his nose, he makes no move to push them back up.

"I don't know! It just happened. Do you think that I wanted to ruin my truck? I still have three years of payments on this thing!"

"I'm calling the police," I hiss, patting my pants for my phone before remembering it's inside. "I have to go back inside, but don't you dare move! I swear to God that I'll hunt you down and hit you over the head with a brick if you do."

"I'm not running."

I don't trust him in the slightest, but I leave him anyway, knowing I'm fucked out of any real choice. The first thing I have to do is call the police. Then I can properly freak out. Because what. The. Fuck!

There's no time for this. No money, no second vehicle I can use while I get mine towed to a junkyard! Oh, my God. Nova. School. Pickup time.

My phone is still on the counter beside the register, and before I can talk myself out of it, I'm dialling the first person that comes to mind.

"Come on," I whisper, tapping my foot on the tile.

The line rings and rings until it catches on his voicemail. A gruff, blunt greeting reaches me before I end the call and try him again.

Oliver's at work. I know it, and I still call him a second time. Every ring in my ear is a shove further into the pit of embarrassment I can feel my heels sinking into. I shouldn't be bothering him at all, let alone when he's working. It's needy, but still, I can't hang up. Can't call someone else. Don't want to.

"Avery?"

My eyes water immediately, throat tightening up. "Hi."

"What's wrong?"

"Nova—"

"Bateman? You good, Lieutenant?" a man whose voice I don't recognize asks, voice deep and cutting. It's a shock to my mess of a system right now.

Oliver seems to move away from the man because a second later, a door slams, and then he's asking, "Something happen to Nova, princess? I'm leaving the station right now. Just tell me where to go."

Something hot pierces my chest, right between the ribs. "Nova's okay. She's at school, and I need someone to pick her up. Something's come up, and I'm going to call the school so they hold her in the classroom for a few minutes after the bell, but I still won't be able to get there in time."

"Why not? Did something happen?"

"My car—" I cut myself off, deciding to keep the accident to myself. "I'm stuck at the shop. I should have called your mom or Addie, but I just... I didn't."

"You always call me, Avery. Always. Doesn't matter what I'm doing, okay? I'll pick up your girl."

"Thank you," I whisper.

There's rustling in the background and a few mumbled voices around him. They're muffled as if he's put the speaker to his chest before suddenly pulling it away. "Do you want me to bring her to the shop after?"

"No!" I shout, wincing. "I mean, I'll call your mom and see if she's home to watch her for a couple of hours."

"How about I bring her back here? That okay with you? My squad's been asking about her all morning. About both of you."

I lean against the shop door and watch the driver of the truck speak on the phone, still standing on the road. "You're working. I've already interrupted your day badly enough with this."

"You're the best type of interruption, Avery. I wouldn't have asked if I wasn't sure I could swing it."

Gnawing on my lip, I exhale and say, "She'd love to go to the station again."

"Alright. Can you send me the address of the school and the classroom number? I'll leave now and text you when I've got her."

"Yes, I'll do that."

"You did good by calling me. Don't get tied up in your head telling yourself otherwise. I told you that I'm here and that I want you to call when you need me."

"Do you promise that it's really okay?"

"I'll promise you a million times if it makes a difference. You don't have to do everything on your own anymore," he declares, and for the first time in a long time, I believe those words.

"Thank you. You've really saved me today."

"You can thank me by explaining what happened when I see you later. I'm sending someone to the shop right now, and we'll talk later. Her name is Rebecca Hart, and she's a rookie but a good one. You need anything, you tell her."

I furrow my brows and grip the door handle. "I don't need you to send anyone. I'm good."

"Then she won't be there long. Just humour me, princess."

"Fine. Okay."

"Keep giving me attitude about it and we'll be having a different conversation when I see you," he warns, the sheer amount of heat in his words encouraging me to squeeze my thighs together.

"I didn't give you anything."

He hums low and deep. "I'm leaving the station right now. Send me that address."

"Thank you, Oliver."

"You're welcome. See you soon, beautiful."

I miss his voice the minute it disappears. Sending off the text with all Nova's school info feels good, knowing that it's Oliver who's going to take care of her.

The thought of going back onto the street to speak with the car rammer again is a trigger for my migraine. Soon, the police will arrive, and it'll only get worse.

Inhaling a big fucking breath, I straighten my shoulders and make the call to Nova's school, knowing that I need to get this taken care of as soon as I can.

23

Oliver

Rushing into Nova's elementary school, I smooth down the front of my shirt and try to steady my breathing. I got lucky finding a parking spot in the lot out front, but I don't even remember if I locked the doors before jogging up the steps and through the door.

It's my first time at this school. Oliver and I went to a different one a few minutes west of here that smelled like BO. The classroom number and teacher's name I've kept up on my phone don't lead me in a specific direction, so I dive into the front office like Avery instructed me to.

The woman behind the desk glances up at me in surprise behind her round glasses and offers me a soft smile. "You look a little lost. Are you here to pick up a student?"

I laugh on a quick exhale. "Yeah. Nova Hayes. Her mother, Avery Miller, said she called?"

Nova's last name behind Chris' makes my skin flush hot with anger, but I push that shit down. Not the time.

"Yes! Oliver Bateman? Do you have ID?" she asks, eying the name stitched onto the corner of my shirt. "School policy."

"You won't hear me complaining about you protecting my girl."

Their policy is a damn good one. I tug my wallet from my back pocket and flash her my license. She nods and smiles again.

"Turn right outside the office door, and then take another right. Mrs. Kerby's class is the fourth door on the left," she says.

"Thank you."

"Have a good day!"

I wave over my shoulder and follow her directions before coming to a sudden stop in front of the classroom doorway. Nova's backpack is still hung on the rack on the wall beside a couple of others, so I grab it and slip it up my arm before knocking on the door.

The older woman at the front of the class is perched behind her desk, a pair of glasses slipping down the bridge of her nose before she looks up and fixes them. Nova's sitting at a collection of four desks that have been turned to face one another in a square, colouring in a thick book with an array of coloured markers.

"Ollie!" she shouts when she spots me, picture abandoned.

I smile, taking a step inside. "Ready to go, peanut?"

"You must be the Oliver that Nova's been talking about. I'm Mrs. Kirby, her teacher," the older woman says, approaching me now.

"Nice to meet you."

"He's a firefighter, Mrs. Kirby," Nova sings as she stands, chin up and shoulders straight. "A lieutenant."

"That's right. My apologies, Lieutenant," Mrs. Kirby teases with a quick wink.

Nova nods in approval and starts to collect her things from the desk. I watch her, an obvious lightness in my chest.

"Is everything okay?" Mrs. Kirby asks now that Nova isn't listening.

"Avery got held up at work."

She tips her chin. "So, I shouldn't expect you to be the one picking Nova up after today?"

"It'll be either one of us from now on."

There's a sparkle in her eyes when I look away from Nova and toward her. "Alright. I'll make note of that."

"I'll try to make sure we're on time from now on."

"I love my job, Oliver. And Nova is a sweet girl. It's hardly a punishment."

"That's all Avery. She's done an incredible job raising her."

"Ollie, can we go now? Where's Mom?" Nova asks, stepping into the conversation with her colouring book and markers in her arms.

I take them from her and drop the backpack from my shoulder to put them inside. "Yeah, let's go. You're coming to the station with me for a little while."

"Really?" she shrieks, eyes wild with excitement.

"Really. You can meet my squad this time."

"This is so awesome!"

"Glad you think so," I say with a pat to her back. "Come on, we've gotta make a stop on our way back."

Nova takes my hand and tugs me toward the door. "Okay. Goodbye, Mrs. Kirby."

"See you tomorrow, Nova. And I hope to see your lieutenant again as well," Mrs. Kirby replies with a grin.

We step out of the classroom, and Nova takes charge, leading me down the hallway and explaining which teachers teach in the rooms we pass and what grades painted the murals on the walls.

I listen to every word she says, enamoured with the way she switches between Swedish and English with ease, almost as if it's happening without her knowing it. I've ordered a beginner's guide to learning Swedish, but there's no way I'll be able to learn it without help.

"Why didn't my mom pick me up today?" Nova asks once we've left the school.

"She got busy at the store and asked me to help."

"Okay. Cool."

"Do you like donuts?"

"With sprinkles and jam. Those are the best."

"We're going to pick some up for the station. You can pick all the flavours if you want."

She punches the air. "Nice."

The donuts are absolutely a bribe for my squad, considering I left moments before everyone dived into their chores and opted into giving Adams my laundry duty.

Hart didn't have much to do, so sending her to Avery was an easy choice. It helped that she's a woman, and without having introduced Avery to any of the guys on the squad, I don't want them around her without me. Not until I can threaten them with death if they try and flirt with her.

I open the back seat for Nova and watch with a small smile as she hops into the vehicle and onto the booster seat I stole from the extras pile at the station. She buckles herself in and gives me a thumbs-up before I head to the front seat.

"Do you have a favourite type of music, peanut?" I ask.

"Mom calls it *dad rock*."

I keep my lips closed as I laugh to try and keep it silent. "Does she? I love dad rock. Do you have a favourite band?"

"Linkin Park and Matchbox Twenty. Nickelback too."

I turn to stare at her, not having expected those answers. "Does your mom like that music too?"

"She loves it. Like me."

Scrolling on my phone for a song, I find a playlist I made years ago and play it. I turn up the volume and put the SUV in drive before stealing a look at her in the rear-view.

"Numb" by Linkin Park wasn't what I pictured Nova banging her head to, but as she starts singing the lyrics and tapping her thighs with the beat in my back seat, I think she crawls further into my heart, making a home for herself there.

"You're cheating," Nova accuses Patel, his latest match of cards pinched in her fingers.

Patel shakes his head, black hair flying. "I'm not cheating. How would I cheat at Go Fish anyway?"

"By peeking at my cards."

Nova tucks her four cards against her chest, and I flick Patel's arm, scowling. "Don't look at her cards."

"I wasn't!"

"He was!"

"I think you're the one cheating and trying to blame me," Patel says.

Nova glares adorably. "It's naughty to lie."

"But I'm not lying!"

"Patel, give her your matches," I order.

He gapes at me. "No way."

"You can't disobey your lieutenant's orders."

"Yeah!" Nova drawls, sticking her tongue out at him.

"This is harassment in the workplace," he argues.

I roll my eyes. "Better take the loss, then."

"No way." Patel tosses his three sets of matches to Nova, and she beams at me before pulling them toward her like they're treasure. "Now we're even. No more cheating from you, fox."

"I'm not a fox," she protests.

"You're sneaky like one," he says.

Nova twists her mouth. "Okay, I guess."

I glower at my squad member, but he ignores me. I'm the only one allowed to give her a nickname, and now I'll have to smack him upside the head later.

The lack of calls today has been a blessing. Other than a small restaurant fire this morning, it's been quiet. Captain was eager to busy himself and took my spot so I could stay here with Nova, and I owe him big time for it. I don't want to leave her here without me, even if I know she'll be well taken care of.

Patel asks Nova if she has any fours while I check my phone

for an update from Hart. The only one there is from shortly after I got Nova back here.

> Hart: She's all good.

> Me: And? What else?

> Hart: I'll update you later.

Avery sent me the same messages, but there's a feeling in my gut that tells me there's more to it than I'm being told. They're hiding something, and I want to know what it is.

"I'll be right back. Try not to get into a fist fight with a seven-year-old girl," I warn before standing and stepping into the gym.

Texting Avery, I try not to glare at the phone.

> Me: Nova is cheating in go fish. Did you teach her how to do that?

Her reply comes back too quickly to ease the suspicion in my gut.

> Princess: It's a life skill. Of course I did.

> Me: Are you okay?

> Princess: Almost done. Thank you for sending Rebecca. I'll come by the station in a few to get Nova.

> Me: Take your time.

It's almost dinnertime, but after eating half a box of donuts, I don't think she'll be wanting real food anytime soon. My bad.

"I win! I win!" Nova shouts, voice piercing when I open the gym door and head back to them.

"Only because you took all of my matches and I had to start over!" Patel mutters.

"Don't be a sad loser," I tell him gruffly, taking my seat again. "Your mom is coming to get you in a few minutes, peanut. Do you have one more game in you?"

"Can it be just you and me this time?"

I glance at Patel and wait for him to notice before saying, "Did Adams finish laundry?"

"I'll go check. Thanks for the game, Nova," he says.

She smiles at him and starts gathering all the cards into one pile. We're left alone as she attempts to shuffle the deck but ends up flinging cards all over the table.

I stack them all back into a pile before separating it into two. "Here, watch me."

Bending the two decks, I show her how to use your fingers to move the cards until they're flipping into one pile. She watches and then tries again, coming closer to doing it this time.

"I couldn't shuffle cards until I was fifteen."

"That's old."

"You're already way ahead of me. A few more times and you'll have it down pat."

"Thank you, Ollie." She grins at me, and I smile back.

"One more game, and then we'll get all our stuff together for your mom."

"Okay." Her grin falls, and her eyes dim.

Alarm steals my breath. "What's wrong?"

"I was mean to her before school. Is that why she didn't pick me up?"

"What? No, Nova. She'd never leave you at school because of that. Your mom loves you."

"I didn't try to be mean."

"I know. It's never nice to be mean to someone, but sometimes we do it on accident. We just have to try not to make a habit of it," I try to explain.

I'm severely lacking in the teaching life lessons skill, and it's more obvious now than ever. With no practice, I don't think I'm ever going to be any help in these situations.

That stings. If I want a chance with Avery, I have to prove that I'm someone she can count on. It has to be more than picking up her daughter when she can't. I've got to prove to her in other ways that I can be someone she trusts to have in her and her daughter's life.

"I don't mean to be mean to her," Nova whispers, bottom lip quivering.

"She knows. It takes practice to handle emotions. My brother, Jamie, used to get so hyper he would work himself up so badly that he hated being told no. He'd shout and throw fits, but he learned that instead of acting out, it would be easier to use his words to explain why he was upset. Once he started talking things through, everyone knew how to help him. If you tell your mom why you were upset and apologize, she'll understand why you acted the way you did."

She blinks up at me. "Really?"

"Really."

Shoving her chair back, she smiles despite the two tears on her cheeks. I don't have time to open my arms before she jumps at my chest and hugs me. She presses her face into my shirt, and I pull my arms out from between us and hug her back.

"I like you, Ollie. You're nice."

A harsh wave of emotion clogs my throat. "I like you too, Nova."

24

Avery

Oliver's backup arrives while I'm finishing up my statement for the police. The tall, red-headed woman storms toward me and the officer, chin to the sky and hands tucked into the pockets of her navy blue pants. I meet her deep green stare head-on, feeling her out.

The officer speaking to me—Richards, he said his name was—lifts a brow at Rebecca's sudden appearance and flips his notepad closed. There were only a handful of notes, considering I wasn't here to witness the hit, but he made sure to write them all down anyway.

"There was no second fire engine called," he says, eyeing the firefighter.

Right. Second, because the first was here for all of three minutes before disappearing. All their presence did was remind me of Oliver and, in turn, had me feeling all the more guilty for not telling him the truth about what happened.

"No need to make a call. I'm here." Rebecca stares down the officer for a beat, putting on a show of dominance before turning her attention to me. "Avery, I assume? I'm Rebecca Hart."

I nod. "Oliver mentioned you."

"Oliver Bateman? What's station 3's business in this collision?" the officer asks, eyes flicking between Rebecca and me.

The former shrugs a shoulder and turns to face my car as it gets hooked onto the back of a tow truck. The whine of metal makes me flinch.

"Family involvement."

"Bateman family?" Richards asks.

I flush at the question, nipping at the inside of my cheek. Rebecca answers for me.

"You could say that."

The officer relaxes. "Everything's been done by the book. Information swapped for insurance claims, statements taken. Ms. Miller's car was hit on the driver's side head-on from there—" He shifts to point at the end of the street across from the shop. "Driver of a Ram-1500 blew through a stop sign and has been issued a ticket accordingly. He's been taken to the hospital for a suspected concussion and whiplash. Station 8 was here and put out a small engine fire beneath the Ram's hood. They cleared out fast afterward."

"And you have no injuries?" Rebecca asks me, doing her own silent inspection.

"No. I was inside when it happened."

"Okay. So, she's done here, then?"

The officer tucks his notepad into a pocket of his vest and does another sweep of the scene. "Yeah, you can take her."

"There's glass all over the street," I blurt out. "I need to get it taken care of."

"The officers will get it cleaned up," Rebecca says pointedly. Extending an arm to me, she hooks it through mine and starts leading me toward a small blue car parked up the street.

I glance over my shoulder and shout, "Thank you, Officer!"

He salutes me and goes back to the other officer he arrived with earlier. Rebecca snorts and unlocks her car with a fob. I locked the shop up once the officers arrived, and it bothers me that I never got a chance to finish up what I was doing before all this.

"They'll contact you if they need anything else. I suggest you reach out to the insurance company ASAP. Is the tow taking your car to a shop?"

"There's no point, but yeah. For now. It's totalled."

"Keep it there until you've gotten an answer from your insurance. Which shop is it?"

"Uh, some small place on Third Avenue. I wrote the name in my phone."

"Send it to Oliver, and he'll make sure it's kept without charge."

"Oliver doesn't know about this, and I still don't know if I want him to. I'll talk to the shop myself."

"No offense, but you're crazy if you think he won't find out. If your name was known amongst stations, he'd already have been contacted."

"Well, it's not. And he doesn't."

She releases a quiet laugh. "Alright, didn't mean to push."

"How many people in this city know him, anyway?"

"Enough. He's been a firefighter for seven years. Jumped the ranks quicker than usual and made friends all over. You'd be surprised how many people we come into contact with on the job. Those cops back there are only two at that specific station that I guarantee he knows on a first-name basis."

She unhooks her arm and gets in the driver's side of the car. I get in the other and wait for her to start the engine before answering.

"Do you think Officer Richards will call him?"

"No. I'd bet he assumes he already knows, considering he sent me. So, where am I taking you now? The station?"

I pause, and she's too focused on me to ignore it.

"Or we could get coffee first? Bateman's already going to be scrubbing turnouts for sending me on a personal mission today, so might as well make it worth his while," she offers.

"I'd like that."

Twenty minutes later, we pull into the station lot. I've got a cardboard holder full of four drinks on my lap and another four buckled into the back seat. Apparently, coffee runs involve everyone in the station, and I couldn't argue with that. They're one big family here, and I've always admired relationships like that.

"If you need a ride anywhere until you get your wheels figured out, just give me a call," she says while we're unloading the coffees into our arms.

"Thank you, Becca. I appreciate the help today."

She smiles softly. "Anytime. You're a cool chick. I can see why the lieutenant sent me."

"Why's that?"

"As if you don't know," she teases, a snort following. "You've got a leash around his neck. I'd bet he barks when you ask him to."

The image is more funny than sexy, but where Oliver's involved, anything can be at least a little sexy. I don't think he'd ever bark on command, though.

"I'm family."

"You're also stubborn as fuck."

My smile is genuine, easy. While I may not have wanted Rebecca to show up in the first place, I'm happy she did. I think we could be easy friends.

"Not the first time I've heard that one," I reply.

Following behind her to the station doors, I let her step inside first. She sets the coffees on the desk at the front and then takes the ones from me to do the same.

"Just grab yours, and everyone else can come get their own," she instructs, snagging Nova's strawberry banana smoothie and her large vanilla drink.

I take my almost black coffee and reach for the second on instinct. "Lead the way, Hart."

"*Funny*. It's Becca to you."

"Hart, that you?" a deep voice shouts from the top of the stairs we're climbing.

"Yep. Found a straggler too."

At the top of the stairs, I whirl around in search of Nova, finding her not even a heartbeat later. My throat and mouth dry at the sight of her and Oliver at the table.

She's scooted her chair as close to his as possible but keeps the cards in her hands hidden from him. He has an arm resting along the back of her chair, his long fingers tapping a silent beat on the edge of it. Her favourite brand of juice box is in front of them, two matching boxes crumpled in the middle like they both squished them once they were empty.

"Juice boxes and donuts? You went all out on babysitting duty, Lieutenant," Becca says.

The duo turns at the same time, but it's Nova who stands first and runs toward me, her dimpled grin shooting straight for my heart. "Mom! Mom!"

"Hey, baby," I murmur, raising my hands so I don't spill coffee on her.

"I missed you," she says into my chest.

"I missed you right back."

The coffees are taken from my hands. Oliver watches me with a soft expression, but his eyes are lined with worry. Our coffee cups are in front of his chest, gripped in hands that I've begun to dream about holding me.

"Hey, princess."

My pulse quickens. "Thank you for watching her."

"She was great."

It's relieving to hear that. I've raised her to be a good girl, but you never know how a child will behave in front of someone else.

Nova steps out of my arms and waves at a man at the table with deep brown skin and long black hair swept out of his face. He waves back and tips his head at me.

"Thank you for playing cards with me, Patty," Nova says.

He points at her and waggles his finger. "Next time, there won't be any cheating on your side, fox."

"Don't start," Oliver scolds him.

Rubbing Nova's back, I ask, "Were you cheating at cards again?"

"Again!" Patel shouts. "I knew it."

"Mom!" Nova glares at me. "Tattletale."

Oliver's laugh is loud, and I swear I can almost feel the vibration from it in my chest. The warm, happy sound stops me in my tracks, and I find myself stuck staring at him, following the circle of black around the warm brown in his eyes.

The sound trickles off when he notices me staring, and I go hot, embarrassed at being caught.

"Do you have time to talk before you go?" he asks.

I clear my throat. "Yeah, sure."

"How about you show me how you cheat at cards while they talk for a minute, hmm?" Becca asks Nova, offering her the smoothie.

"Sure."

I leave the two of them there and follow Oliver to a room a few steps away from the kitchen. He swings the door open and holds it for me to enter first. It's a gym. A big one fit with several types of equipment I'd have no idea how to use.

The door clicks behind me, sealing us in together. Alone.

A wall of floor-to-ceiling mirrors is across the room, and I stare at the reflection of the two of us. Me, with my muscles tense and lip trapped between my teeth, and Oliver, with his stance open and height towering. He's not looking at the mirror but at me instead.

Arousal makes my knees tremble, tension shrinking the room until I'm sure that our reflections are lying and he's breathing down my neck instead of a handful of feet away.

"Thank you again for watching Nova today. I'm sorry for calling while you were at work. I won't make a habit of it. I just didn't feel comfortable asking anyone else yet."

I might as well have not spoken. The words disappear into thin air.

Oliver moves quickly. I watch in the mirror, waiting for the moment the heat from his body caresses mine. I close my eyes and let my muscles go loose. There's a soothing voice in my head that tells me I'm safe here. With him.

"What happened today?"

I can't lie. "My car was hit outside the shop."

Hot, strong hands close around my arms as he spins me, and I open my eyes, latching onto the ones waiting. Panic rips across his face before his hands drift down my arms and over my shoulders.

"Why didn't you tell me that? I'd have been there in an instant. Fuck, are you okay? Hurt? Were you checked out?"

I shake my head once. "I wasn't in the car."

I'm tucked into his chest, and I don't fight his hold. It relaxes me further, my legs melting into jelly.

"If anything like that happens again, *I'm* the one who comes to you. *I* make sure you're taken care of. You can drive my SUV home and use it for as long as you need to."

"I can get a rental, Oliver. I can take care of myself well enough. I've been doing it for a long time," I whisper.

He exhales and threads his fingers through the hair at the base of my skull, using the grip to pull me closer. When he starts to massage my scalp, I wind my arms around his waist, breath steadying.

"I know you can. But I'm not going to stop asking you to let me help until you finally let me. You don't have to let go of control, just let me in. Let me take some of it from your shoulders. At least let me ask my mom to drive you home tonight, and once I'm done with this shift, my SUV is yours to use."

The idea of continuing to fight him on all of this isn't appealing anymore. "Okay."

"Okay?" he asks, his surprise evident.

"I'll start letting you help take care of me and my problems, including using your car to get around, but under one condition."

"Anything."

I drift my hands up his back, exploring the feel of his strong lines of muscle beneath my fingers for the first time. My next exhale is shaky, liquid fire sizzling between my legs.

He moves his mouth to my ear, hot breath coating my skin. One hand still buried in my hair, he lowers the other to my hip, subtly shifting me closer.

"Whatever you want, Avery. Ask me for anything. Everything."

Tipping my head back, I slide my eyes up the strong column of his throat, wide jaw, and parted pink lips.

"Kiss me, Oliver."

25

Oliver

IT'S A MOMENT I'VE THOUGHT ABOUT COUNTLESSLY over the years.

Her taste, the touch of her lips on mine, how soft they'd be. Would she be gentle and follow or assertive and in control of every moment? Every lash of tongues and gasp of air from one mouth to another.

I was a kid when I first imagined holding her like this. I preened under her attention back then, even when there wasn't much more than a timid, friendly smile tossed in my direction. She was completely unavailable to me, but that didn't mean shit to an overeager teenage boy.

I still held out hope that once our age gap wasn't so daunting, she would realize that she could be into me if she gave herself that chance. Obviously, that didn't happen. My hopes crashed and burned, and I shut those feelings down hard immediately after. I was too young, too inexperienced and naïve, and she was mature and had better things to do than slum it with an underage guy. But I'd have still done anything for her. That's only become more evident now.

I'm lost to her. A total fucking sucker for the woman in my

arms who's telling me to kiss her like she hasn't just walked back into my life and shook it all up.

Fuck the pranks and the beating around the bush. I'm not losing her again. This is a redemption as obvious as ever. My second chance to seize the life I dreamed up ten years ago.

It's a bit different than I imagined back then, but even wishing she'd never gotten with Chris doesn't sit well. Not when he gave her Nova and, in turn, brought her into my life.

Blocking out thoughts of the man who got to spend the past few years with my Avery, I inhale another breath of her scent and slip my hand from her hair to hold her face.

She's waiting, every blink of her lashes antsy. I nearly give in and kiss her, but this isn't where I want it to happen.

"I'm a picky bastard when it comes to you, princess. Our kiss isn't happening in the station's gym with my squad members outside the door. And not when you're using it as a bargaining chip."

"What?"

The rejection in her eyes is a blade to the gut. It's the last thing I want to see, but fucking hell, I've waited long enough for this, I'm going to make sure it's perfect.

"When I kiss you, it's going to be when we're alone and you're ready for what it means for me to taste you on my lips. I'm not going to do it just for fun," I explain as softly as possible.

She shakes my hand from her face and takes a generous yet reluctant step back. My stubborn girl lets her claws out, anger turning her chest and neck red. "I'm glad it's all up to you."

"I'll always make sure your thoughts, wants, and feelings are heard, Avery, but this one thing isn't up for negotiation."

"Because *you* say so? Yeah, that's not going to work for me. I don't want to play games, Oliver, and I don't allow anyone to make decisions for me. If that's what you're doing, then you're right about us not taking that step."

Her statement shouldn't make me hard, but I'm painfully so,

my jeans suddenly a size too tight in the crotch. "I'm not playing games."

She glares at me, filling the gap between our bodies with invisible spears that I'd bet she's hoping I'll impale myself on.

"I'm not some young girl who's been saving her kiss for a movie-worthy moment. I want spontaneous and emotion. It doesn't matter if we're on the top of the Eiffel Tower or in a dark alley behind some grungy bar. If I say I want to be kissed, then I damn well want to be kissed—"

One long stride and I'm eagerly throwing myself onto those spears of hers. Her cheeks are hot beneath my palms, but her lips are hotter. The first brush of them against mine yanks a groan from deep in my chest, desire swelling from the pit inside of me that's been buried for years.

She leans up into me, eyes shut and mouth eager. There's more to her kiss than desire or interest. It's acceptance, a release of the tight grip she's kept on her emotions for years. Since she became a mother, no doubt.

She gives in to me, and I move my mouth against hers with a million silent promises. Care, affection, service. Anything she wants, I'd give her. There's no point in beating around the bush about it.

Avery Miller didn't stumble back into my life; she was shoved by something bigger than us.

For a guy that's never given much of a shit about that kind of thing before, it feels pretty fucking significant to do so now.

"You're used to calling all the shots. Making the decisions and bearing the consequences of the ones that aren't always appreciated. But this right here . . ." I exhale against her mouth. "You've just given me permission to step in to share those responsibilities of yours. I tried to give you the chance to think about it, but you chose to be a brat instead."

Her pupils widen, the blue around them sparkling. "A brat, hmm?"

"A beautiful one that has me all out of sorts." I nip her bottom lip almost in punishment. "Do you know how long you'll be without a car?"

"Not yet. Really, I can just use an Uber until I've got everything figured out. You don't have to loan me your SUV."

I kiss her before she can add to that answer with something that won't help her case. Dipping my hand to cup her waist, I tuck her against my front, beyond pleased with how well she curves into me. A perfect fit.

"My SUV is far better than an Uber. For tonight, I'm sure my mom will love to see Nova before her first ballet class Wednesday."

"She's not busy with other things? I don't mind taking an Uber."

"Did you get Nova's booster seat from your car?"

She stares behind me, frowning. "No. I didn't think about it. Shit, how did I *not* think about that? It should have been the one thing I made sure to grab."

"I've got one in mine. If you're okay with my mom coming to get the two of you, I'll load it in her car before you leave."

She pinches her brows together. "Did you go out and buy one? Tell me how much it was—"

Her words die off when I press my thumb to her lower lip and curl my pointer finger below her chin, tipping her head back slightly. "You're going to drive me mad."

"Is that a surprise to you?" she breathes out.

"Not at all."

A tentative hand slips between our bodies and presses over my sternum. Her throat bobs. "You're serious about this, right?"

"What is 'this,' exactly?"

She huffs an exhale. "Us, Oliver. You and me. Because with Nova involved, you can't just decide in a couple of days or weeks that you change your mind. If you let her get close to you, she'll be heartbroken if you leave."

"You really need to ask me that?"

Her fingers curl in my shirt, clutching onto it. "Just answer."

I tap the underside of her chin and hold her stare, hoping to fuck she can see my sincerity.

"You're not the type of woman to believe words. You need to see action in addition to spoken promises, and I'm more than up for the task of proving myself to you. All I need is the chance to do that."

"How do you know me so well already?"

I almost laugh. "I've had a long time to learn."

"You keep saying those things but not explaining. If I didn't know better, I'd assume you used to have a crush on me when we were kids."

A cough gets stuck in my throat, and I retreat a step with my fist thumping my chest. Heat burns the skin of my neck and chest, but I don't blush. Fuck me, I haven't done that shit in years. Not until Avery came back into my life.

"Oliver?" She looks like she's holding in one hell of a laugh, and I scowl back at her. Realization hits when I don't deny her accusation. "Wait, did you have a crush on me?"

"Does it really matter now?"

"Yes! Are you kidding me? How long? When?"

"I'm not getting into that story here."

I've never wanted a call to come in so fucking bad. I'm not even picky on what the call is as long as I can get out of here before she forces me to divulge all of my secrets.

"Don't close up on me now! I had no idea—"

A knock at the door cuts her off, and while it's not a call, it does the job. Avery frowns at the interruption, but I seize it, rushing toward the door and opening it before she can stop me.

Adams is waiting, arms crossed and expression eager. He leans to the side and smiles at Avery over my shoulder before shoving me out of the way and stepping through the doorway.

"Avery, I assume? It's a pleasure to meet you. I'd have been here to welcome you to the station, but I was on a call," he says, extending his hand for her to shake.

I loom over them like a statue, keeping my eyes sharp and

focused on Adams. The guy's a good friend, but he loves to get a rise out of me. Pulling the moves on Avery despite his shitty marriage to do so isn't a line he wouldn't cross.

Avery takes his hand. "It's nice to meet you too..."

"Brent Adams. Bateman's best friend," he says.

"Not my best friend, and watch it."

I tug on his wrist until he releases Avery's hand.

He grins like a crazy person, clutching his wrist to his chest. "If the lieutenant here ever gets to be too much, I'm only one locker away."

"I'd love to meet your wife sometime," Avery replies, tone sharp, smile saccharine. "Does she come around here often?"

Adams blows out a long, loud breath. "Damn, girl. I don't know why Oliver's been having us drive past your house after calls. I think you're a woman who can take care of herself."

"Brave of you to assume anything about me so soon," she says, but it's me she's looking at.

Instead of being annoyed with my overprotective ways, she looks pleased. Flattered, even. Fuck, my throat tightens at that expression.

"Gonna continue to do it, princess," I say.

"A text would work the same," she teases.

"No it wouldn't." Not even close.

Adams tosses an arm around my shoulder, the bulky bicep weighing me down. "I did interrupt for a reason other than meeting your girl, Lieutenant. Captain's wondering where you are. Wants to have a chat with you."

"Thanks."

I shrug off his arm and take Avery's hand before looking down at her one last time in this room.

"Call my mom and take Nova home. I'm off again starting Wednesday morning."

She tips her chin, giving my hand a squeeze. "Thank you for taking care of Nova."

"Anytime, Avery. And I mean that."

"I know." The corner of her mouth lifts before she's slipping out of the room and crouching beside her daughter at the kitchen table.

"That's the one, huh?" Adams asks, standing beside me now, staring at the same scene I am.

"Yeah, that's the one."

26

Avery

ADALYN SITS ON THE COUCH CUSHION BESIDE ME WITH Nova on the floor between her legs. She weaves another strand of my daughter's hair into a sophisticated braid and repeats her steps to me as if I've got a single goddamn clue what she's doing.

"Yeah, I'm already lost," I admit.

Addie giggles, running another section of Nova's silky hair through her fingers. "This is one of the most complicated ones. I had to teach it to myself because my mom couldn't get it either."

"Did you always do your own hair? I don't think I saw you often without your hair done up, even when you were a little girl."

"I convinced Maddox to try a couple tutorials with me, but he was even worse than Mom. And Dad, well . . . he's not to touch anyone's hair but his own," she says.

Nova twists to look at the both of us, and Addie grips onto her hair to keep from losing it. "Grandpa once cut my mom's bangs."

"He did?" Addie asks squeakily.

"Did the whole grab, twist, and cut method. They were less than an inch long and stuck straight out." I shiver at the memory, sinking into the cushions.

"That's rough," Addie notes, offering a sympathetic smile before turning Nova back around. "My dad didn't cut my hair or anything, but he did help me box dye my hair the first time and missed an entire section at the back of my scalp."

"What colour?"

"Hot pink."

I chuckle before stopping myself. Nova's silent, shoulders slouching forward. Tugging at my lip, I look to Addie, and she's already watching me, waiting.

She mouths an "I'm sorry," but I shake my head. There's no need for her to apologize. Nova's sudden silence is because of Chris, I'm sure of it.

"Do you want to dye your hair, *mitt hjärta*?" I blurt out.

"No, thank you," she says too softly.

Addie smooths a hand over the frizzy hairs on the top of Nova's head. "Do you want to cut it? I'm a pro with some scissors."

"Will I have funny stories to tell about Dad, Mom?"

There's a near audible crack in my chest as I fumble for an answer. "Of course, baby. You're only seven. You'll have a million stories to tell by the time you're our age."

She tugs her legs into her body and leans forward, clutching her ankles. In a blink, I'm on the floor beside her, my hand on hers.

"You know, Nova, I've been keeping a secret for a while now, and I think I want you to be the first to know," Addie says, abandoning the braid.

When she leans close to Nova's ear and whispers, Nova grins so wide, all thoughts of Chris abandoned. My appreciation for Adalyn triples in size.

"Really?" she shrieks, turning to stare at Adalyn's stomach in awe.

My eyes bulge as I gawk at Addie, my question obvious in the way she giggles and nods.

"I'm pregnant," she tells us, patting her belly. "Seven weeks along."

My sight grows blurry. I push to my feet and throw myself onto the couch before pulling her into my arms. "Oh, Addie. I'm so happy for you."

"Is it a girl like me?" Nova asks, joining our hug.

"It's still too early to tell, but I'd love a girl."

Cooper was meant to be a girl dad, but I keep that to myself for now, not wanting to remind Nova of what she's just forgotten about.

"And we're the first to know?" I ask instead.

Addie huffs and sits back, slowly peeling herself from Nova's grip. "I've been leaving clues all over the house for a week, but Cooper's always too focused on me to pay attention to them. I've decided that I'm going to paint the walls tonight with terrible pictures of baby things until he gets the idea."

"Men can be so obtuse," I say.

Nova sits on my lap, cuddling close. "What is obtuse?"

"Dumb," Addie answers. "Men can be really dumb sometimes."

"But we shouldn't call them that. We shouldn't call anyone names," I add, staring pointedly at Addie.

She hides a smile. "Your mom's right. No name-calling."

"Oliver isn't obtuse. Right? You said he was kind."

The words are a shock to Adalyn, and I can understand why. The last time we saw her, Oliver and I were at each other's throats, and the last thing I would have called him was kind. Gracie had a similar expression when she picked us up from the station yesterday and Oliver made sure to tell her to drive safer than she normally does. Or, well, more like threatened her. *His own mother.*

She didn't pry in the car, but I could tell she wanted to. Yesterday was probably my only pass when it comes to her and the thousands of questions she's thought of since.

"Your mom said Oliver was kind?" Addie asks slowly, expression slack.

"Yes. Last night. He watched me at the fire station. I played Go Fish with his friends!"

"They're his colleagues, Nova," I correct pointlessly.

"Okay, hold on. Give me a second here. Oliver, as in Oliver Bateman, the resident grump of the Bateman family, watched you at the fire station? Why did he do that?" Addie asks, her eyes slowly sliding to me. "And why were you giving him compliments? I feel like I've missed a chapter here."

A car door shuts outside, and Nova's jumping up immediately, eyes wide and excited. She climbs onto the couch and leans over the back of it to stare out the window at the street.

"Ollie!"

I swallow, ignoring Adalyn's even stronger sense of surprise and following my daughter's stare. Seeing Oliver for the first time since leaving the station yesterday does something to my stomach. It flutters, *hard*. I fight to ignore it while he grabs a duffle bag from the back seat and throws it over his shoulder. Before shutting the door, he reaches back inside to grab a rectangular box.

Even from all the way over here, I can see how exhausted he is. I'd be lying if I said I hadn't been checking my phone every single hour since waking this morning, waiting for him to get home. Every time I checked and he wasn't back, I let my mind run in circles for a few minutes before busying myself with something else.

I got in the car I rented last night and drove to the shop before scrubbing the floor spotless. It took me all day, but by the time I picked Nova up from school, brought her home to meet with Adalyn, and fed them supper, I wasn't obsessing over where he was and why he wasn't home yet.

I know his job is dangerous and busy. We got lucky yesterday to have so much of his time and attention, but I don't have any experience dating someone who works outside of a dirty mechanics shop every day. I never thought I'd be here.

Nova knocks her knuckles against the window once Oliver starts up the sidewalk, and he squints at us. I expect him to wave and head to his house, but it's our sidewalk he takes, not his.

"He's coming over!" Nova shouts, scrambling off the couch to open the door for him.

Adalyn grabs my arm and blinks at me, lips parted. "You've been holding out on me all afternoon."

"You never asked."

"I didn't think there was anything to ask about!"

I smile apologetically. "My bad."

"Ollie! Ollie! You're home!"

"Hey, peanut."

His voice makes me inhale a sharp breath, suddenly aware of just how much I've missed him. I should have texted. Done something.

"Can you come to ballet tonight?" Nova asks.

I jerk out of Addie's hold and join the two of them, an apology already on my tongue for Nova's question, not wanting him to feel pressured. It disappears into thin air when Oliver toes his boots off and smiles at her, one hand already ruffling her hair.

"Hi." It escapes me in a whisper.

He focuses on me, eyes simmering with words unspoken. The tiny curl of his lips sets my skin on fire. Fuck, he's good-looking. The five o'clock shadow he's rocking makes my toes curl into my socks.

"Hi, princess."

"You're home later than usual."

A cock of his brow. "Were you waiting for me?"

"She was," Nova says, earning herself a glare.

I cross my arms, leaning back on my left foot. "I just didn't know when your shift was over."

"Should have been about five. We didn't get back from the last call until an hour ago." He hands the box in his hand that I can now see is from Nova's favourite cookie place to her. "Want to take this to the kitchen for me?"

She nods and snatches it from his hands before disappearing down the hall. Shuffling forward a step, I ask him, "Are you okay?"

"Yeah. Just a bad call."

I search his face for any hint of a lie but don't find anything but exhaustion and a heaviness that I'm not used to seeing on him. It has me saying fuck it and going to him the way I've been forcing myself not to since I first saw him on the street.

He takes me into his arms the moment I move toward him, securing me to him as I slip mine around his middle. The scent of smoke lingers in his clothes, but it doesn't stop me from continuing to breathe him in, searching for the regular scent of his cologne.

He blows out a long, weighted breath over the top of my head and then presses his cheek against it. "I'm sorry I didn't text you. I planned on helping you at the shop before Nova went to bed."

I move my head side to side as best I can. "You're busy. But you should go home and eat. Go to bed early too."

"Nova asked me to go to ballet."

"She'll live."

"I'll sleep once I've made her happy by going."

"Are you sure? She won't let it go if you say yes, then change your mind. She's had a tough afternoon."

His back grows rigid beneath my fingers. "Did something happen?"

"No. Nothing like that."

I reluctantly release him and move back, knowing we're not alone and that Addie is probably chomping at the bit to interrupt.

Oliver's arms tighten around me for a beat before he drops them to his side. "I'm coming to her class as long as that's okay with you."

"I never took you for a ballet lover, cousin. I actually remember you refusing to go to your mom's recitals more often than not," Addie says, poking at him from where she leans against the wall.

He scowls at her, scratching his jaw. "I knew that was your Jeep outside. Your front right tire is low, by the way."

"Tell Cooper about it. I've never put air in my own tires," she replies, tone thick with attitude.

"That's because you don't know how."

"And with a husband, why would I want to?"

"What if it popped on the highway? Do you know how to change a tire?" he asks.

"Not a fucking chance."

"Two older brothers and you don't know how to change a tire?"

"Leave her be," I say, drawing both their eyes.

Addie narrows hers on me, the black liner around them making the blue pop. "You've betrayed me, Avery. I thought after you'd ignored his crush for this long that you'd wind up with Jamie, at least."

I inhale sharply while Oliver tucks his finger through the back loop of my jeans. Tipping my head back, I watch the tick of his jaw, wondering—no, knowing—that he's annoyed at Adalyn's mention of me being with his brother.

Not prepared to let what I've just heard go, I step in front of him and palm his chest. "This is the second time I've heard about this crush. Want to explain it to me?"

"If he doesn't, I will," Adalyn sings.

Oliver stares her down. "Why don't you go check on Nova? I'm pretty sure she's eating all the cookies I brought."

"Fine. But I'll be back. Time to come clean, Olliepop."

I know she's wandered to another room when he drops those broody brown eyes of his and stares at me, his cheeks tinted pink. The prickly hair covering his jaw is more obvious up close, and I'm pretty into the addition. Oliver's a rugged guy, and a fit of facial hair fits him *really* well.

With the back of my finger, I brush the underside of his jaw, testing the feel of the hair there. The thrum of arousal growing between my legs is a distraction that I don't want right now, so I drop my hand instantly.

"If you had a crush on me, why didn't you say anything? Why didn't you reach out at all since I last visited?" I ask.

"You were dating that fucking tool that your dad set you up with, and I knew I was too damn young for you. There wasn't a point, princess. Not then."

"I was here only a few years afterward. We could have reconnected or something—I had no idea. If I did anything wrong, I'm sorry. I was so young then too."

He licks his bottom lip and shakes his head. "I don't wish anything happened differently anymore. Not now."

"I used to stalk you online," I admit blatantly. "If you had a crush on me back then, I had one on you after based off of only your internet profile."

"A silent stalker," he grunts, a smirk teasing his lips.

"Don't get arrogant about it. I doubt you don't know how good-looking you are."

"Doesn't hurt to hear it from you."

I roll my lips, dropping my stare to the floor before bringing it back up. "You could use a shower."

"Class is at seven, right?"

"Yes."

"I'll be back at six thirty, then."

I reach for his hand, taking it and linking our fingers for a moment. "There's a plate of leftovers in the microwave . . . if you want them. Have you eaten this afternoon?"

The warmth in his expression threatens to undo me. "No, princess. I haven't."

"Leftovers, then. You have an hour, Lieutenant."

When he dips his head to kiss me, I lean up on my toes, meeting him halfway. It's only a second, but my body doesn't understand that. It lights up at the first taste of his lips, my nipples pebbling in my bra and core turning molten.

"An hour," he breathes against my mouth.

Then he's stepping back into his shoes and disappearing, the promise of more time with him settling in my chest, turning me giddy with excitement.

27

Oliver

IT'S EASY TO LEARN THE IMPORTANT THINGS ABOUT A person when you dial in and pay attention to them. With Nova, I've found it impossible to ignore the subtle wrinkle that grows between her eyebrows when Avery mentions frozen yoghurt instead of ice cream or the pout that forms when she's told that she has to earn her way to a pet frog.

She might only be seven, but she's highly intelligent for her age. Her homework is harder than I remember it being when I was in the second grade, and she flies through it without asking for help with a single question. When Avery asks her to load the dishwasher after every meal, she doesn't complain before doing it. There are no arguments as Avery reminds her not to put the bowls on the bottom rack, only a slight nod and grin of thanks. She's proud of the night lights plugged into the outlets around her room and shows them off to me with innocent excitement.

Avery's raised her all on her own, if we're being honest, and she's done a phenomenal job. While there are still questions I want to ask about her life before she came to Vancouver, I'm happy soaking up these moments.

Watching Avery and Nova together, just the two of them existing doing regular things, makes me feel like I'm a real part of their lives. It's a front-row seat to the workings of the family I hope to join one day.

Leaning a hip against the counter, my offer to help scrub my dishes gets turned down for the third time, so I finally relent. Adalyn left as I was striding up the sidewalk, and with a flick of her hair over her shoulder, she slid into her Jeep.

She'll probably never notice that I filled her tire for her, but I wasn't going to let her drive home alone with the risk of it popping.

"Can we do my hair now, Mom? Auntie Addie never finished it," Nova says in between sips of her juice.

"Oh, shit—I mean, oh *no*." Avery wrings out the dishcloth and drops it into the empty sink. "Yeah, sweetie. Can you go get your hair basket from your room?"

"Okay, Mom."

I watch Nova skip out of the room, her ballet tights and bodysuit already on. I'm half a second from calling Adalyn and scolding her for not finishing her hair when Avery sighs, turning to rest her back against the counter.

"We're going to be late."

"No we're not. It's only a fifteen-minute drive to the studio from here. How long does it take to braid her hair?"

"I'm the world's slowest braider."

I chuckle and trap her against the counter with my body. Gripping the counter on either side of her, I say, "I'm fast at it."

"You know how to braid hair?"

"Your doubt in my abilities hurts, princess."

She leans back, head tilted. "You have one brother."

"Jamie liked his hair braided beneath his football helmet when he was fourteen. Mom taught me how to do it."

"You know, I think I actually might remember him talking about braiding his hair," she says with a soft laugh. "Well, knock yourself out, then. I've got to grab Nova's bag and make sure she actually packed it properly before we go."

"Before you do that," I mutter, resting my hand on her hip.

She inhales and waits with parted lips for my next words. "I wanted to ask if you'd go to dinner with me this weekend. Just us."

"Like a date?"

I lean down, tucking a strand of hair behind her ear. "It's a little overdue, but yes, a date."

Her pulse flutters, and I don't bother hiding my smile, knowing that I affect her the way she does me. Our eyes hold, neither of us wanting to be the one to look away. A small smile toys with her mouth, and my fingers itch to reach up and touch it.

"I need to find someone to watch Nova, but if I can, then I'd love to go on a date with you."

"You have at least six people who would offer to take her off your hands for one night."

"This all feels very high school, you know? I haven't been asked on a date in years," she admits.

I stand a bit taller. "Good. I don't like competition."

Her laugh comes out her nose. "Addie made this big deal about you being the grumpiest guy in the Bateman family, but I think you've been putting on a show for everyone. Am I right, *butternalle*?"

"Tell me what that name means, and I'll tell you anything you want to know."

She blows a raspberry and slips beneath my arm, escaping my hold. "Nope. Not yet."

"I'll get it out of you, Avery."

"Try harder, then."

"Brat," I grunt at the same time Nova comes back into the kitchen with an overflowing basket of hair accessories in her arms.

"Got them!" she shouts, grabbing a seat at the table.

Avery stares at me while addressing Nova, as if she's giving me a chance to change my mind. "Oliver's going to braid your hair for dance. Be nice to him in case he's been lying about his braiding skills."

Nova starts taking everything out of the basket and asks, "Really? Awesome."

I don't take back my offer. If I hadn't wanted to make it, I wouldn't have. Spending more time with Nova while proving to her mom that she can start to lean on me for things sounds like the perfect way to spend the next few minutes.

Once I've got myself and Nova situated at the table, Avery leaves us. Nova's fidgety on the chair I've shifted in front of me, her head tilting side to side every few seconds and legs swinging. She's nervous, and all I want to do is soothe her.

"Do you remember meeting my brother, Jamie, at Aunt Ava's house?"

She hums. "The guy with long, messy hair?"

"Yes. He also has a pretty big scar on his forehead."

"Yes! It's gross."

I snort a laugh and finish parting her hair straight down the middle. "Don't tell him that. He thinks he's a pretty boy."

"He was pretty," she says.

"Don't tell him that either. He'll try to be your favourite."

"He can't. You are, Ollie."

My fingers stall as I weave the first of three strands into the braid. "Thanks, peanut. You're my favourite too."

"Even more than Mom?" she asks, voice a gasped whisper.

I lean forward slightly and lower my voice to match hers. "Can you both be my favourites?"

"I don't know," she hums.

"Think on it while I finish your hair and tell you why I asked if you remembered Jamie." I reach for a tiny pink elastic from the table and wrap it around the end of the first braid. "He's a professional football player, and he still gets the jitters before every game. He'd tell you that if you were nervous for your first ballet class, that means all you want to do is be the best you can be."

She twists in the chair, staring back at me with wide, hope-lined eyes. "Do you get nervous, Ollie?"

"'Course I do, peanut. Every time a call comes through the

station, I get nervous. I want to make sure I can be my best every time I go out there, and sometimes I worry that I'll make a mistake."

A single mistake or lagged response can cost me and everyone involved everything. I have to keep my decisions instant but thought out and safe for everyone involved. My nerves look a lot more like fear now than they did years ago.

"I think you're the best firefighter ever! Thank you for braiding my hair," she says, pushing onto her knees to smack a kiss to my forehead before sitting back down flat.

My heart pumps harder than it does the minutes before arriving on a scene, and I sniff to try and disguise the swell of emotion I feel taking over my body.

There's a hand palming my shoulder when I take my next breath, and the scent of Avery's perfume swirls around me. I don't know what to say, or if I can even say anything at all to describe how I'm feeling, so I don't. And she doesn't force me to.

Glancing up, I watch as she nods, eyes watery and bright. It's enough of a statement without either of us speaking aloud.

She pulls an extra chair beside me and leans close to watch my fingers as I work on finishing the second braid. Her hand falls to my thigh, and I stare at it for a moment before getting back to work.

THE STUDIO IS full of moms and little kids Nova's age. They bounce around the room in a flurry of pink tutus and excited squeals while the instructor has them gather in a circle to stretch.

Nova's not shy around unfamiliar faces once she's been introduced to them, and she's already made friends with every single kid, her prior nerves be damned. My chest has been puffed for minutes now, and I don't dare try to deflate it.

The moms are all sitting on slightly cushioned chairs along

the wall, and Avery's been chatting with the same one since we got here. Tasha, I believe her name is. Her son, Jacob, has been following Nova around like a hound with a scent.

I'll be keeping an eye on him.

The dance instructor was my mom once upon a time but is now a woman named Lauren, whom she hand-picked years ago. She seems good enough but nowhere near as skilled as Mom. Nova would have loved being taught by her.

"So, which one is yours?" the mom on my left asks.

I brush my thumb over Avery's knuckles and rest our linked hands on my thigh before looking to see if the woman was speaking to me.

"Mine?" I ask.

She smiles, nodding encouragingly. "Yes. You're the only man here, so I'm assuming one of the students has to be your daughter."

"Right. Nova's mine," I tell her, searching for Nova in the line along the mirrored wall. Finding her instantly, I point her out before I realize what exactly I've just said. "She's not mine—well, not not mine. I'm not her father—he's not here right now. Nova's—"

Avery, having heard every fucking word I've blabbered, reaches across my lap and offers the mom the hand I'm not gripping for dear life.

"Hi, I'm Avery, Nova's mom, and this is Oliver, my boyfriend. Which one of these rug rats is yours?"

"Hope's my daughter. I'm Lillian. It's nice to meet the both of you."

They shake hands before I offer her mine, and the two women fall into easy conversation. Avery might have a tendency to be just as grumpy as me if she wants to, but she's also far more outgoing than I've ever been.

Maybe that's a skill she learned after becoming a mother, but either way, I'm grateful that she's able to jump in when I can't manage to wrangle a single sentence together.

Nova's busy chatting to the boy who can't seem to leave her alone for all of two seconds while the instructor tries to show them a few basic stretches, and with one quick look to the other side of the room, I find my mom watching from the doorway.

"I'll be right back," I tell Avery, giving her hand a squeeze before leaving her talking to Lillian.

Mom's backed out of the doorway and is waiting for me in the hall when I step out of the studio. Practically vibrating, she reaches for me and grips me tight.

"You're here, Oliver! With Avery and Nova. Oh, my heart is going to explode straight through my chest," she gushes, shaking me.

"It's not nice to shake people, Mom."

"Don't get all grunty with me, Oliver Bateman. This is important."

"It's just a ballet lesson."

"Just a ballet lesson?" She scoffs, shaking her head at me. "You're here for them. Like a dad would be."

I grow rigid, liking the sound of that and wishing it were closer to reality. "Slow down, Mom. Nova already has a dad."

"I'm sure there's plenty of room for another one in that little girl's life. What did you think was going to happen once you've fallen in love with Avery and have grown to love her daughter as well? That you'd just be a random male figure in her life? Is this a game to you, Oliver, or are you serious about them? It's easy to say you're ready for this, but it's far harder to prove it."

I reel back at her words, so damn stiff she could turn my arm to dust if she keeps squeezing it so hard. I've avoided thinking those things because I didn't want to move too fucking fast and scare Avery away. It's not easy falling for a woman who's tied to another man by a little girl who you can't help but want to bundle in your arms forever. Avery might be open to me right now, but I have no clue if she's ready for me to have a permanent spot in her daughter's life.

I'll never be Nova's father, but I'll love her like I am. And if that scares me, I can't begin to imagine how terrified it will make Avery feel when I find the nerve to tell her. I might as well be asking her to marry me with the commitment I'll be offering.

"Honey, you're pale," Mom murmurs, touching my cheek with the back of her hand. "Cold to the touch too. I've downright terrified you."

"It's still new," I mutter absently.

She strokes the side of my head in slow swipes of her hand. "Alright. I know it is. What you two need is time alone together. You've got to talk some things through and lay it all out on the line. There's no point in either of you continuing to grow your relationship if you don't set boundaries or come clean about what exactly it is you both want. And not just for the right now, but for ten years from now. This isn't the kind of casual dating you've done before. If you're going to pursue Avery, it should only be for keeps."

My nod is weak. "I was planning on taking her out this weekend. Saturday night."

"I'll speak with Avery and take Nova for the night."

She sighs at my lack of reaction to her offer and, despite being so much smaller than me, tucks me in for a tight hug.

"You've never done anything half-assed in your life, Oliver. We're the same, you and me, sweetheart. When we want something, we stop at nothing to get it, and that includes those we love. Don't let Avery be any different. Not again."

"Thank you, Mom," I whisper.

There's no point in explaining to her that I didn't love Avery the first time I let her get away. Things were different then. I was different.

Avery managed to shake a teenage Oliver, but I'm a man now, and I'll stop at nothing to call her mine forever.

28

Avery

"Be good, Nova. Don't fight when Gracie says it's bedtime, and listen to her rules. Remember that every house has their own rules, and it's rude not to obey them. If you need me at all, I'll be there as soon as possible. No matter what," I say, squeezing the life out of her.

She giggles, nodding along with every word I say. It's not her first sleepover, but it's her first one at Gracie and Tyler's, so my brain is working quickly to try and ease any worries she could have.

It's me with the worries, though, and we both know it.

"Okay, Mom," she says, patting my back.

"I'm serious. If you need me at all, you ask Gracie to call me."

"Okay."

"I'll take good care of your girl, Avery," Gracie says, waiting at the bottom of the porch steps.

"I know. I'm just . . ." Puffing out a breath, I let Nova out of my arms and swipe my palms down the front of my dress, my nerves springing back now that I've stopped worrying about her. "I haven't been on a date in a long time."

Gracie smiles softly, knowingly. "Well, you look gorgeous.

And because Oliver's my son, I know him well enough to tell you that he's just as nervous as you are."

I doubt that. All he told me in preparation for tonight was that we'd be eating somewhere nice. I took that and went out yesterday to buy this dress after realizing all of my old ones didn't fit anymore. It's a soft, navy satin material that's tight to my waist and hips and cups my tiny tits in a way that makes them look maybe half a size bigger. My plain black heels are old and worn but are also my comfiest pair.

After spending an hour curling my hair, I made sure to unplug the cord from the wall and sent a selfie of it and me to him with a message that I hoped made him smile when his shift ended.

Me: Proud of me yet? No fire today.

"Does Oliver even get nervous?" I ask Gracie.

Nova bounces down the stairs, her backpack weighing heavy on her shoulders with the amount of clothes she packed for a one-night stay.

"He said he gets nervous at work," Nova says.

I arch a brow. "When did he do that?"

"When he braided my hair. He said football makes Jamie nervous too."

"Oh," I whisper, remembering that night and the way I nearly burst into tears when Nova thanked him and kissed his forehead. "That was nice of him to share that with you."

"Yeah. I like him. He's really nice."

Gracie laughs softly and opens the back seat of her car. The booster seat already installed draws my attention. It's not the same one that Oliver transferred over the night she drove us home.

"Did you go out and buy a new booster seat, Gracie?"

"Who, me? Of course I did. My son needs his in the SUV, especially if you're going to be driving it. I hope it's an alright brand—things have changed since I had to have boosters for the boys. Tyler just went into the store and asked for the best one..." She takes Nova's backpack and sets it on the middle seat.

"Speaking of driving Oliver's SUV, have you heard anything from the insurance company on your car? Or the shop?"

Nova practically dives into the car and settles into the seat before doing the seat belt up herself. Gracie double-checks it before leaning back and looking at me.

I sigh. "They're still investigating. It's only been a few days, so I expect it'll be weeks before I know anything. My car's totalled, though. I've told the shop to junk it."

RIP, bumper stickers. You will be missed.

"The man responsible for this should have to pay out of pocket. Leaving a mother without a car and a way to get around? Absolutely ridiculous," she hisses.

"I'll make do. I didn't have a car when I first got to Canada either."

Gracie frowns, her eyes filling with guilt. "Things are very different now for you than they were then. Not a single one of us did right by you when you moved here—"

With a shake of my head, I cut her off before she can apologize further. "I didn't *let* anyone help me. Didn't want it. What were you supposed to do when I refused to answer everyone's calls and kept myself hidden? Even if you had forced my location out of my parents and shown up outside of my house, I still would have turned you away. I wanted to do everything on my own. It was a choice I made and am trying to learn from."

"I should have tried harder. I've always taught my boys to fight for what they believe in and those they care about, and I should have pushed. It makes me sick to think of everything you've had to do on your own and the toll it must have taken on you. Raising a child is hard enough with a million people in your corner helping every day, but with no one? Oh, honey. I'm just sorry we weren't there for you."

I shrug a shoulder, playing off the sudden ache in my chest at the reminder of long, sleepless nights and silent shower cries with a newborn tucked in a bouncer outside of the tub.

"You're all here now."

Her frown tugs up the slightest bit. "Yeah, sweetheart. We are. And I know Matt and Morgan were there for you as much as they could be. I'm just . . . It's menopause, I think. I'm a mess."

"They were the most supportive parents ever. The amount of money they spent flying here over the first few months after I had Nova could have probably bought them a second house in cash. I wasn't ever truly alone."

"Good. Good, Avery." She nods, swiping a thumb beneath her eyes. "I should get a move on before my son shows up and sees you in that dress. You look phenomenal. He's going to lose his mind."

"You think so? It's been a while since I've dressed up like this." Doubt seeps into my tone despite my best efforts to keep it hidden.

Gracie closes the back seat and holds me by the arms, her touch a comfort. "You're going to, as Jamie says, rock his shit, Avery."

My laugh comes from deep in my gut. I roll my glossy lips together and hug Oliver's mom, wishing for a heartbeat that it was my mom here instead.

"Thank you, Gracie. For this and for watching Nova. She's been so excited about the sleepover since I told her about it."

She pulls back but keeps me close with her hold on my elbows. "Anytime, sweetheart. I mean that. Anytime. Not only just when Oliver pulls you both out of the house, but if you're ever needing a break. You hear me?"

"I hear you, and I'll try."

"That's good enough for now. I'll get out of your hair. Don't even think of spam texting me for updates either. I'll send you pictures, I promise."

I nod, laughing softly at being called out. "Go before I haul my girl back into my arms and refuse to let her out of them again."

Gracie lets me go and strolls around the car before hopping in with a final wave. Nova blows me a kiss from the back seat, and I return the gesture as they pull onto the street and disappear.

I leave the curb and start up the sidewalk, but I'm stalling after I've stepped over two cracks. Oliver took his SUV this morning after I told him I didn't need it, and as he pulls up beside me, looking incredible with a pair of square-rimmed sunglasses on and his forearm straining with his grip on the steering wheel, I wonder if he should be allowed to drive it without me ever again.

The passenger window is down, and the clean smell of the interior mixed with his cologne nearly sends me into a spiral. Not only is his house impeccably clean, but his car doesn't even have a single crumb on the floor mats. Nova's habit of eating Froot Loops on the way to school will have to come to an end this week if he's going to insist I drive this monster around.

Maybe if I tell him how many times I've run over curbs or clunked into poles in parking lots, he'll change his mind.

"I'm gonna need you to go back inside before I crash. We need at least one vehicle, Avery," he rumbles, the sunglasses shielding what I know is blistering heat in his eyes.

My cheeks flame. "Something tells me you're too focused of a driver to crash into anything."

"Usually, yes. Now? Not a fucking chance." He shifts into park and then runs a hand over his mouth, attention solely on me. "I was supposed to walk up to the door and get you all proper. I've got flowers and everything."

I peek into the open window before glancing into the backseat. The two bouquets of flowers make my heart soar.

"Two?"

"One for each of my girls," he states easily. Like it's instinct for him to claim both of us as his.

"Well, bring them inside and help me put them into water so we can go. Nova just left with your mom, but she'll be happy to see them tomorrow."

"Yeah? She likes flowers too? I wasn't sure."

"I'm pretty sure she'd love anything you got her. But yes, she does like flowers."

His grin is blinding, heart stuttering. I feel the effect of his happiness like an arrow to the chest.

He's quick to step onto the street and grab the flowers from the back before coming toward me. I'm reaching up to pull his glasses off the moment he gets close enough, desperate to see behind them.

Even expecting the heat, it still shakes me to see it. He stares at me like a man desperate for something he's always dreamed of having. I never thought I'd be the recipient of such a look. Such a declaration.

"Sorry, were those in your way?" he teases lowly.

The lines are still slightly smudged between us, not quite as clear as I need them to be yet, but in this moment, I don't let that detail deter me. I lean up on my toes and kiss him anyway. He's waiting for it and presses his warm lips to mine with a fierceness that multiplies the butterflies in my stomach.

Grasping my hip, he pulls me in until we're flush and I can feel the hard press of his cock against my stomach. It makes my head swim, arousal hot in my blood.

"Are you hungry?" he mumbles against my mouth.

"Yes."

His chuckle is hot, breathy. "For food, princess."

I let my disappointment show with a deep frown when he ends the kiss and moves his hand from my hip to my back to lead us to the house.

"I could eat."

The bouquets in his hands are wrapped in white and pink paper that crinkles with every slight movement of his fingers, and I steal the biggest of the two, ripping at the paper to get a look inside.

"The boy who wrapped those is dying a little inside with how you just ruined all his hard work," he says.

"He did a great job." With the paper flayed and flopping in

the breeze, I smile at the first arrangement of flowers. "And so did you. I was expecting roses."

"Teenage crush, remember? I listened. You hate roses. Especially red ones."

I've always thought they were cheesy. A lame choice when it comes to men needing to show affection to a woman. They walk into a store and grab the first bundle they can find without putting any real thought into it. It's an empty, thoughtless gesture. One Chris made every single time we'd fight. He never cared when they wound up in the garbage the next morning.

The pink peonies in my hand tonight mean more than Oliver could ever know. They aren't anything loud, but instead, they're thoughtful. I remember explaining the rose trap to all of the guys when we were just kids. Oliver was always hiding somewhere or ignoring everyone back then; I never thought he'd been paying attention after all.

I tuck the bouquet into my chest, holding it tight. "Thank you. I love them."

His eyes crinkle before I lose sight of them, stepping onto the porch ahead of him. The door is still unlocked, so we walk right in.

"You can keep your shoes on. I just need a second," I tell him.

My heels clack on the floor, but his lack of footsteps has me sparing a look behind me. He's toeing off his black dress shoes, disregarding my comment.

I don't tease him for it because, again, he's being incredibly thoughtful. It's like he's cranked his gentlemanly dial up to a thousand in hopes of seeing me falling all over myself in front of him.

I'm nearly there already.

In the kitchen, I make quick work of snipping the stems of the flowers and adding my favourite plant food in two vases before filling them with water. The smaller bouquet, Nova's, is an arrangement of simple yellow daisies that I know she'll take one look at and squeal over.

Oliver joins me but stands back and watches me work in silence. His presence fills the kitchen, and I sneak another glance at him before shaking my head.

Black slacks, a navy blue button-up with the sleeves unbuttoned and folded three times, and a thick black belt make him look like a model from *GQ*. He's gelled back his hair and shaved away the scruff on his jaw. The flowers were a distraction earlier, keeping me from checking him out like this when he first stepped on the curb.

My pulse beats in double time before I drop my eyes back to the flowers I'm sticking into the vases.

"What?" he asks.

I wet my lips. "You look handsome."

"Do I?"

"You know you do."

His socks keep his steps silent, but I feel him once he's come close. He circles my wrist with one hand and holds my waist with the other as he stands behind me, my back to his chest.

The fabric of my dress is thin enough for his touch to seep through. I let my eyes flutter shut and lean into his hold, swearing I can feel his heart pounding against my back.

"You're breathtaking, Avery. Now and always."

His mouth moves to my throat, and I expose it to him with a tilt of my head. The first press of his lips to my pulse has my knees weak. The second makes me moan, the sound unfamiliar to my ears.

The vibration of his answering groan splatters against my throat before he's spinning me around and gripping my thighs to lift me onto the table.

I spread my legs on instinct, allowing him the room to move between them. He's so fucking close now, and I lock my ankles around his back, the top curve of his ass brushing my heels.

He presses his palms to the tops of my thighs and bends to level his face to mine. I arch my back, using my arms to prop myself up. One nod of my head and he's digging his teeth into his lip, a silent battle clashing in the brown of his eyes.

"Tell me if you need more time, Avery. Because if you don't, I'm going to spread you out on this table and make you come. I'm too hungry to wait for dinner. I need an appetizer first. Been waiting a long, long time for this one."

The deep, throaty tone of his voice is almost enough to take me there without anything else. My answer is instant, sure.

"I'm ready."

29

Oliver

The words are hardly out of her mouth when I unhook her legs from my waist and spread them wide on the table. Her dress rides up, bunching at her hips as she's left exposed by the new position.

She leans back on the table, elbows at her sides holding her up and allowing her to keep those pretty eyes on me. My favourite place for them.

"Keep your legs like that, princess," I murmur, touching the inside of her thighs with light pressure.

She's splayed out for me so perfectly, her yellow panties on full display, the wet spot on their centre turning them nearly see-through. They cling to her pussy as I lean closer, bracing my hands on her thighs again.

"Last chance," I warn, debating tearing her panties with my teeth.

She shudders a breath, nodding. Her dress is tight over her chest as it expands at a quick pace, but before I can tell her to pull her tits free of it, she's shrugging out of the straps and doing it herself.

Small and perky, her chest snares me, the two pink nipples hard like bullets amongst the creamy white skin. Her fingers hesitate to fall back down, palming her stomach instead, as if she's too nervous to relax.

With a groan, I lean over her chest and bring my mouth to her nipple, sucking it deep. Taking her hands in mine, I push them above her head, my cock throbbing in my slacks. Her skin tastes like candy, a lotion, maybe, but I can't get enough of it. I roll my tongue around her nipple and suck harder before shifting to the other, paying it the same dedicated attention.

Avery rocks up beneath me, her legs still spread but tense, the muscles tight when I release one hand and touch the taut skin. My patience is snapping, weeks of back and forth between us having me desperate to finally taste her where I'm aching to.

When I bring my hands to her wet panties, I rub my thumb over them, up and down, up and down, spreading the arousal pooling there. She gasps, eyes wild and bright as she watches. Her panties grow damper, my thumb slick, and I waste no more time.

I can tease her later. Once I've satiated the savage hunger inside of me with her cum on my tongue.

Slipping my thumb into my mouth, I suck it until it's clean and I need more. She reaches for me, gripping my shoulder as I tuck a finger along the edge of her panties and pull them to the side, baring her glistening pussy.

"Christ," I grunt, yanking her until her ass hangs off the edge of the table.

It's been a long while since I've done this, and never have I wanted to this badly. As I bury my head between her legs and draw a line up her slit with my tongue, I confirm that this is the only woman I should have been doing this to all along. Only ever her.

"Oh!" she cries, jerking beneath me as I explore, parting her and dipping my tongue inside her opening. "Oli—Oliver. That's *really* good. What . . . *fuck* . . ."

With a glance up her body, I tighten my stare on her bewildered expression. Something expands in my chest, making it difficult to gulp down full breaths. I don't fucking need to breathe right now, but I don't want to be forced to stop what I'm doing either.

Avery jerks her hips again, and I lean even further forward until I'm half on the table with her. I palm her tit while curling my fingers into her thigh, keeping her in place beneath me.

Alternating between rolling her clit beneath my tongue and feasting on the arousal she's gushing, I try to gauge what she likes most. She gives nothing away, appearing in awe of everything. Every lick and suck and nip creates the same moans and writhing motions.

Realization blinds me as I press my tongue flat against her clit and move it side to side. She snaps her hand down and grabs a fistful of my hair, pulling hard as she whines, rolling her hips. It's like she's never experienced this before. The sensations and pleasure I'm bringing her with my mouth alone.

"Have you ever had someone eat this perfect pussy, princess?" I ask roughly, driven by a blazing possessiveness that really fucking likes the idea of being the only one between these thighs.

Her cheeks are pink enough to show through her makeup. I run my finger through her soaked lips before gliding it inside her entrance, hoping to distract her, pull her out of her head.

Throat bobbing, she shakes her head just once. Her mouth is swollen, the deep cherry lip gloss she wore earlier long gone. I lick my lips and find the hint of the flavour there beneath her arousal and curse at how much I love the mix before I'm swiping my tongue over her clit again.

"It's intimate," she whimpers, sounding so fucking needy. So beautiful. "It's not something I expec—"

My growl hits her pussy at the same time I start to fuck her with my finger and then add a second. She stretches around them as she cries out, both hands using my hair as reins now.

"I could spend days right here. Could eat this pussy for every meal of every day and still not get enough. Fucking glad I'm the only one who's ever tasted you here because I'd commit murder over keeping it just for me. I'd find every single man who's tasted you before me and make them suffer for it. I'm the only one who gets to make this sweet cunt come. Right, princess?"

"Right! The only one. The only . . ." A moan interrupts her words, spurring me on.

"Need you to remember that, Avery. Remember how you come on my tongue and fingers. How you soak my face and cry my name while I fuck you with them," I hiss, pleasure blooming in my gut despite my cock being trapped in my slacks with no relief.

Even with her pupils blown, the blue is still so bright, and I fall into their trap, not letting my gaze sway from where I watch her. She pulls so hard on my hair I'm surprised it doesn't rip clean from my scalp as she snaps her legs around my head and squeezes, done with keeping them stretched out. I let her move, too lost in my own obsession with pleasing her to tell her to keep them spread.

"I'm going to come, Oliver," she says on a gasp, nodding to herself. "I'm going to *come*. Don't stop, or I swear—"

I answer by pounding my fingers inside of her at lightning speed and curling them to drag across the spot that has her dropping her head back and clenching down tight. She drips down my knuckles as I piston them deep, but I'm there to lick every drop before it's wasted on the floor.

When she comes, I'm grateful I'm already on my knees. It's easier to pray this way, and that's what she's owed. She blesses me with her cries, and I'm utterly transfixed. Trapped beneath the beauty of her parted mouth and pleasure-drunk eyes, I kneel on the ground and continue to touch her until she's pushing me back, too sensitive for more.

I feel weightless when she sits and guides my cheek to her thigh before soothing my sore scalp with gentle strokes of her fingers. My eyes droop shut, a sudden wave of exhaustion crashing into the bliss lulling me into a state of half-consciousness.

"You're good at that," she says after a few more moments of silence.

I hum in question, holding her leg to maintain contact.

"I'm . . . You were right. I've never done that before. It's embarrassing, so don't make a big deal out of it."

The insecure tone of her voice causes me to open my eyes, looking for hers in the light of the setting sun outside.

"It's embarrassing for them, not you," I grunt.

"I didn't push for it, though. Even with Chris, I never asked him to go down on me. He said he didn't like it, and that was that for me. The last thing I wanted was to have to beg for something like that in the bedroom, especially from him. That would have been far more mortifying than never having experienced it at all."

I sit forward and reach for her panties, still tucked to the side, and pull them back in place. Smoothing my thumb across the waistband, I kiss the inside of her thigh before doing the same to the other.

"You'll never have to beg me for anything, Avery. Not outside of the bedroom or inside of it. I promise you that. Chris was never deserving of you, but I hope to be."

"Oliver," she whispers, cupping the back of my head.

A smirk toys at the corner of my mouth. "Avery."

"I hope you know how worthy you are of everything you want for me. Happiness, love, success. I've always been the type of person who sets everyone else's well-being above mine, but you're the same way. There has to be a balance somewhere for us to find."

Her words are nails in the coffin I've willingly fallen inside of. I've already begun falling in love with her, and now, I wait for her to jump in after me.

"We need to find an even ground."

"Easier said than done, but we both deserve to be able to trust someone else to take care of us when we need them to."

"You're right." Climbing to my feet, I bend to bring our faces together. Her lips still taste like faintly like cherry when they meet mine in a soft kiss. She exhales into my mouth, and I swipe at hers with my tongue. "We need to go before we lose our reservation."

Avery stands on her feet and smooths her dress back down her thighs while I watch her brazenly. It's impossible to wish away my erection while standing this close to her.

"We could always just order in and stay home. Eat on the patio and watch the sunset. Maybe go for a swim later," she suggests, her voice dropping an octave at the last suggestion.

"We'll swim after I've taken you out."

"Promise?"

I grasp the material of her dress where it rests on her hip and nod, keeping a tight hold on my self-control before I rip it clean off. I'll have her again soon. And this time, I want her to soak my face before taking my cock eight inches deep in her perfect pussy.

"I promise, princess."

30

My legs are still jelly as we stare at the first course in front of us. I'm nursing the same glass of white wine I was a few minutes after Oliver ordered the bottle. It's my favourite kind, but I'm already buzzing, and the only thing alcohol will do is make me completely lose my inhibitions. I'm weak enough already after being eaten like dessert on my kitchen table.

The restaurant he chose for us is high-class. We're on the rooftop patio surrounded by lanterns and a garden of flowers that I've been wanting to go up to and explore. It's romantic, and I'm flattered that he wanted to take me somewhere like this.

The filet mignon on my plate smells really damn good, grilled to a perfect sear with a light-coloured juice leaking onto the plate around it. Six sprigs of asparagus are beside it, dusted with freshly grated Parmesan and paired with a hefty scoop of fluffy mashed potatoes. My stomach growls, but it's drowned out by the soft music playing.

"It seems the only meal we know how to eat together is one with steak," I joke while unrolling my fork and knife from their napkin blanket.

Oliver takes a gulp of his beer, a smirk tugging around the rim of the tall glass. "I'm a simple man."

"Are you? In what way?"

Patting his lips with his napkin, he keeps our eyes locked. "I know what I like. No use straying or trying to shake things up now. I'm content with my life now."

"Completely? Is anyone ever really one hundred percent content?"

"Are you hinting that you're not?"

I reach for my wine on instinct, needing something to soothe me. We've avoided heavy conversation so far here tonight, but we both knew it was coming. We need to dive deep before things can go any further between us.

And I really, really want them to.

"I always hoped that by the time I was in my thirties, I would be completely content. I'd have everything figured out. But a successful future seems easier to achieve the younger you are. Thirty years seems like plenty of time to get your life together the way you want it, but there are a million reasons for things to go belly up on you. If I'm being honest, I've never been perfectly content. And these past few years, well, I think I lost hope that I ever would be," I admit.

"Chris plays a part in that, I assume?"

My brows jump in confirmation. "I wish I could say he hasn't and that I haven't allowed him to have that power over me, but yes, he does play a part in it. I'm angry with him but also with myself. Everything that happened made me resent myself and turn against my own mind. How did I allow myself to get caught up in a man who never wanted a future with me past a couple of fun years? Or why didn't I leave him earlier? I know what a healthy relationship and marriage look like, like I'm sure you do, and while I was never married to him, I know what we had wasn't healthy.

"My experience with him did more damage than anything else

I've ever gone through. But I still don't regret it. I struggle with that."

Oliver's hand closes around mine on the table, a gentle comfort. It's hard to keep eye contact as I drop my insecurities on the table for him to poke and prod at, but the thought of looking away is just as unsettling.

"How are you supposed to regret something that gave you your daughter? You can want to go back and talk some sense into yourself without regretting what you gained from that relationship," he says gently, stroking my knuckles. "Chris hurt you. He skewed the way you see and react to care from others because he didn't show you hardly enough. Are those things supposed to make you happy, Avery?"

I swallow. "I feel guilty when I think back and wish things had been different. That's what eats me up inside. How is it fair to have been gifted something so precious with Nova while damning her father in my mind every day?"

"Chris might be her father, but that doesn't grant him the right to treat you poorly. He doesn't get immunity in my eyes. He lost you because he was a fucking idiot, and one day, he'll think back and be the one full of regret and guilt."

I flip my hand palm up and thread our fingers. Being the one to touch him instead of the other way around is freeing in a way. Like I'm finally allowing myself to open up to him fully.

"I'll get to the point where I'll look around and be content with the life I've built. It's taking a little longer than I'd hoped, but I know that time is coming," I say. "And you? What makes you content? Outside of your career, what makes you *happy*, Oliver?"

He hesitates for a moment, and I wonder if I've overstepped for all of a second before he speaks, voice low and steady.

"If you asked me two months ago, I'd have told you I was nowhere near being content, Avery."

"What's changed?"

His wide shoulders stretch and straighten, tugging at the dress shirt around them. My breath gets caught in my throat when he takes our threaded hands and lifts the back of mine to his lips, ghosting a kiss across it.

"You. Nova. Both of you," he states, not a single waver or hint of doubt in his voice. "I've spent my entire life around families. Around kids and love. I watched my closest friends fall in love and get married, have their own kids. I didn't know the extent of my loneliness until you moved in next door and the two of you filled my house with the laughter I hadn't noticed was missing and gave me a purpose for something more than just my job. Before you, I hadn't dared think I could have a family of my own or that I was even ready for one, but now . . . Now, I want the two of you to be my family."

"And you're ready for that?" I choke, my heartbeat racing, loud in my ears.

His slight grin is beautiful behind our hands. "Really fucking ready, princess."

"We'll still have to move slow around Nova. I've never—she's never been introduced to another man as someone important to us in that way. It was challenging explaining to her why Chris and I aren't together anymore, but she's been handling it alright . . . I think. It's been four years now, and she's strong. I'm just scared of overwhelming her," I ramble, moisture building on the back of my neck. Nerves twist and turn inside of me.

His smile doesn't fall. It grows at my word vomit, a playful gleam in his eyes. "Slow is fine. Nova's had a lot of changes in her life. I just want you to know where I stand. I'm not going anywhere. You and Nova are what I want, and that's not going to change, no matter how long it takes. I'm in no rush."

His words relax me. I drop my chin, rolling my lips to hide an oncoming smile. Resting our hands back on the table, he takes another drink of his beer.

"You didn't answer me before. What makes you happy?" I

ask, pulling my hand free only so we can eat before our dinner grows cold.

The steak cuts like butter, and the first taste of it on my tongue pulls a moan from me. Oliver stiffens across the table, fork and knife unmoving in his hands. His playfulness is shoved aside by the blazing heat of desire. I rub my thighs together beneath the table.

"Those moans of yours, for one," he mutters.

I bat his words aside. "I'm being serious."

"So am I." He resumes cutting his steak and clears his throat. "I go fishing with my brother and dad every few weekends. Sometimes we'll rent Jet Skis and take those out too."

"Jamie likes fishing?"

"He hates it. But Dad and I do, so he comes anyway. We didn't used to invite him, but he would get pissy, blubbering on about not being included in family activities."

I laugh at that, the idea of Jamie saying that not hard to believe. "You always did like silence. Is that why you go fishing?"

"That and spending the time with my dad. Sometimes I think he's trying to make up for lost days and weekends from when Jamie and I were kids and he was still in the league."

"Mine does that too. Or he used to when I still lived in Sweden. Once he retired, it was like he was trying to replace the time he lost."

"How was it there when he was playing? Having a parent in the NHL is hard on any family, but I'm sure the Swedish league is just as bad."

"Gone for practice, games, interviews, special occasions. The same. Mom travelled with the team, too, for a while, but she decided to stay home with me a couple years in."

"She was the team physio, right?" he asks before eating a bite of his steak.

"Yep. But she didn't want a nanny raising me, so she left and never looked back."

"When did you decide you wanted to open a flower shop?"

"I used to play in the flower fields by our house. There were all kinds of them everywhere, really. I used to pick bundles and bring them inside to decorate my room until there were bugs everywhere and Mom started getting all tense about it. There was a flower shop down the street from our house, and she started taking me there once a week instead. I'd choose a different arrangement every time, and I grew to love doing it. Having somewhere all my own where I can be surrounded by flowers all day, creating bundles for special occasions or sweet gestures, sounded like a dream to me." I push my hair over my shoulder. "I know it probably seems lame to you."

"No. It doesn't. You're doing what you love. That's not lame at all."

I want to tell him that that means more than I know how to explain, but I have a feeling he's already aware of that if his understanding smile is anything to go off.

"Do you have a list of what you still need done before you can open?" he asks, directing the conversation again.

For someone who isn't much of a talker normally, he sure seems to be chatty with me.

"More like scattered sticky notes all over the place."

"Can I see them?"

I shake my head. "I'm nearly done. Only should be a couple more weeks, and then I can start planning the opening."

"Avery, let me help you," he pleads.

I fill my mouth with a scoop of mashed potatoes to stall, but once they're gone, I sigh. "I've got a new light fixture that I need put in. It might turn out to be a big job, but the bathroom is in need of a sprucing up, and the painting is nearly done. Then I have to set up all the new shelves and put in my first orders of flowers. Planning the opening will come at the very end."

"Easy," he grunts.

"Easy? The first few things, maybe. But advertising myself is harder than you'd think."

He looks at me deadpan, one brow lifted slightly. "You're quite literally surrounded by celebrities. Use them."

"Oliver, I'm not going to use my friends that way. I don't want to have anything handed to me," I argue.

"It wouldn't be handed to you. You're the one who's done all the groundwork to get to this point. It's your shop, your money dumped into the place and effort spent working to get it ready. You'll be there every day. They wouldn't see it as being used either. They want to see you succeed."

It's hard to ignore the warmth in my chest at the reminder that I'm surrounded by so many people who care about me and would help with this if I asked. I've always known that if I just asked for help, I'd receive it from every one of the people in my life. But it's always seemed scarier than it should be.

Putting yourself out there and asking for help means admitting that you need it in the first place. Clearly, I struggle in that department.

"I'll talk to Adalyn. But that's it," I tell him sternly.

His expression evens out, but there's a nip in my gut that tells me he isn't going to let this be at just that. I let it go for now.

"Alright." He finishes his beer before starting on his water. "You called me your boyfriend the other day. Is that my title now?"

"I thought you missed that." He hasn't brought it up since ballet on Wednesday night.

"Not possible."

"You called Nova yours," I return.

"I want her to be."

I suck in a sharp breath, emotion welling up deep inside of me. It sounds good. *Right*. But it can't possibly be this easy.

"I'll prove it to you, Avery. I'm not giving you meaningless words or promises," he adds.

"How do you plan on proving something like that?"

His eyes smolder, the brown growing deeper and darker as he watches me. I lean forward as if he's yanked the cord tethered to the two of us.

"I'll start with tonight. Just you and me. And tomorrow, we'll go pick up our girl."

31

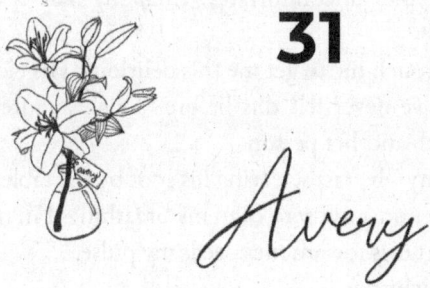

"Do you want anything to drink?" I ask a little over an hour later, the two of us standing in my kitchen after leaving the restaurant.

My stare drifts to the table as I roll my lip with my teeth and grow hot again beneath my dress. Dinner was amazing. The conversation was heavy and needed. But I can hardly stand the tension that's continued to fizzle between us. Being here in this room with him so soon after having his mouth between my legs is intoxicating.

I'm fidgeting, but not from nerves. From *excitement*.

He's being polite, a gentleman through and through. The bill was swept away and paid for, every door was held open for me, a spare coat from the back seat was drooped over my shoulders at the first sign of a shiver. He even offered to walk me to my door and go home without coming inside before I all but tugged him in after me.

Under normal circumstances, I'd preen under this sort of thoughtful affection. But right now, I want him to tuck that gentlemanly trait of his away for the next several hours.

I've had a taste of him, and now I'm lost to the thrill of it. I want it again. Feel like I could explode without another.

My panties are wet for the second time tonight. Even the soft material of my dress is too tight and stuffy. It scrapes against my chest and pointed nipples uncomfortably. Even my hair is too heavy on my head.

He hasn't had to touch me to get me this delirious. His closeness is all I needed. I've never felt this before. This . . . intense desire to simply be with another person.

"No. I'm not thirsty," he rasps, leaving his spot by the table.

I jerk my head in a nod and try to calm my breathing. I'm near panting. Every step he takes toward me speeds my pulse.

"Are you tired?" I whisper.

"No, Avery. I'm not tired. Or thirsty. Or hungry. I'm . . ." He sweeps a hand around the back of my neck and guides it back. "I'm trying not to maul you in your kitchen again."

"Maybe you could try another room instead. There's plenty."

His laugh is a puff of air on my nose. "Pick one."

"A room?"

"Yes, princess. Pick a room."

"My bedroom," I answer quickly.

Dipping low in front of me, he grasps both of my thighs in his big hands and lifts me off the ground. I gasp and curl them around his waist when he bounces me up his body, readjusting his hold to my ass.

He tosses me around like I weigh nothing, and it's so fucking hot that I can't help but press my middle to his abdomen, searching for some sort of pressure or relief. With my hands moving to hold his shoulders, I sigh in bliss, staring down into his blistering gaze.

"Kiss me," he orders gruffly.

We spin down the hall, and he takes the first step upstairs when I lower my lips and do as he demands. I'm in control in this position, and I make him work for every single lick of my mouth and moan I breathe for him. He may be carrying me, but I'm the one deciding how hard and fast we kiss. How long I keep our mouths pressed together before pulling back and making him chase me.

His fingers bite into the bottom swells of my ass as his grip turns punishing, and by the time he's ducking us through the doorway to my bedroom, I'm hoping there will be bruises there in the morning.

I fall to the bed with a squeal, bouncing on the edge with my legs parting in a silent order for him to stand between them. In another life, I might have been nervous about this. My first time with a man in four years should be daunting, but I'm buzzing with too much excitement to feel any of that.

"I want you naked, Avery. Not a fucking thing on you."

My lips curl as I lean back on my hands. "So take my clothes off, Lieutenant Bateman."

Lowering his hand, he hooks a finger beneath the strap of my dress and slowly slips it down my shoulder. He does the same to the other strap before guiding the top of my dress down, exposing my chest with a sharp tug.

I keep focused on his movements. He's so enthralled with his task that he continues his slow pace, eyes latched onto my breasts as they rise and fall with my deep breaths. Nipples hard and aching, I wait for his next move, my anticipation thrilling.

"Stand up for me."

I do, and the dress falls to a heap at my feet. After I've kicked it to the side and tossed my underwear out of sight, he loops a thick bicep behind my back and lifts me before tossing me further up the bed. I blink at him in surprise, scrambling with my hands to push myself up.

His expression is one of pure desire. The sensation of his eyes raking up and down my body has me dripping down my thighs before I'm reaching for him and clawing at his belt.

"Impatient girl," he scolds lightly, unbuckling the buckle too fucking slowly.

"Since when are you so playful?" I huff.

"Since I'm trying not to rush. I don't want this to be over too quickly."

"Why? Only have enough stamina for one round?"

Oliver smirks at that, not offering me anything more. He slides the belt out of the loops in his pants before untucking his shirt and starting on the buttons. It's a slow, agonizing torture. Each button that springs free reveals another inch of his chest until finally, his shirt hangs open.

The same thick abdominal muscles I've thought about a million times since seeing them in the backyard the first time make an appearance after weeks of being hidden away. I suck my lip into my mouth and palm my stomach, feeling the heat coming off my skin.

"Do you want to touch yourself, princess? Want to dip your fingers between your thighs and show me how ready you are to take my cock?"

"Will you finally fuck me if I do?"

"Try me."

Letting my head fall to the mattress, I stretch out my legs and slide my hand down my stomach to the slick lips of my pussy. I brush my thumb over my clit and find it swollen and so, so sensitive. A moan slips free as I rub the skin around it, teasing myself.

"I'm the only one who makes you come from now on. Stop touching your clit and slide a finger inside, Avery. Now," he says, sounding more beast than man.

My lashes flutter as I dip my chin and glide a finger deep inside myself. I'm not the least bit embarrassed by how easy it is to do so due to the amount of arousal I find waiting. How could I be when Oliver lunges between my legs before I've had a chance to pull my finger free?

He grabs my wrist and tugs. Another sensation of wet warmth envelops my fingers, this time from his mouth as he sucks them clean and groans.

"*Fuck*, you taste good."

My heart gallops. "Better try me again to make sure."

With a sharp nod, he shrugs out of his shirt and unzips his pants before lowering himself to the bed to use his mouth on me again. Three long, slow licks have me crying out and slamming my hands above my head to grip my pillow.

"Yeah, princess, this is good fucking pussy," he mumbles into my entrance before diving his tongue inside and sucking at the skin around it.

It's loud and messy. My arousal drips onto the bed, turning the blankets damp beneath me, but he doesn't stop. Doesn't pull away. Not until I thread my fingers into his hair and tug, dragging his eyes up my body to rest on mine.

"Inside," I whine.

Digging my heels into the mattress, I try to lift myself against his mouth, seeking more, more, more. It's not enough. Not his tongue or teeth or fingers.

He kisses every inch of my wet, puffy skin before flicking his eyes up and dragging his mouth up my stomach to my chest.

"Oliver," I breathe out, shaking my head. "Do whatever you want to my tits once you're inside of me. I need you now. No more waiting. I'm done with teasing."

"I should smack your ass for bossing me around, but I'm too much of a fucking fool for you to try. I'll give you anything you want, anytime you need it."

He steps off the bed to discard his pants and briefs. My eyes bulge, breath catching when I notice the cock between his legs. Eight inches is probably estimating down, not up.

I try not to gawk at him, but as I clench around air in my desperation for him to drive inside of me, I can't help it. Long, thick, and wet at the tip. He wraps a massive hand around it and pumps once before climbing back onto the bed, settling between my legs.

"I'll shoot right now if you don't stop," he warns.

His hand pushes my leg up toward me, bending it at the knee as he comes close. The hair on his thighs tickles, but instead of making me laugh, it only serves to make me hornier.

"Condom?" he asks.

I tense slightly. "Have you been with anyone recently?"

Almost like I've offended him with the question, he frowns. "No. I'm practically a virgin."

"I doubt that."

Fuck my jealousy, and fuck my insecurities. This is so not the time to be diving down the rabbit hole of who he's slept with and when. But we're adults. As awkward as it is, it's necessary, responsible.

I keep my knee bent at my side as he removes his hand from it and reaches up my body to touch my face instead. His knuckle traces the length of my jaw, and I sigh, softening again.

"Alright, maybe not a virgin. But I don't go out and pick up women at bars and rarely even leave the house outside of work. I keep to myself, and because of that, it's been a long time since I've slept with anyone. In my bed or outside of it until you," he says, eyes flicking between mine.

I like that answer because apparently, when it comes to Oliver Bateman, I'm a possessive little hoe.

"I haven't had sex in years. And I got the implant a few years after Nova was born. If you're okay without using a condom, so am I."

His throat strains with a swallow, affection bleeding in his stare. "Never not used one."

The answer confirms that it's what I want. I don't need any barriers between us tonight, not even the small one a condom would pose.

Nodding, I reach for him, stroking his shoulder and bicep. He grips his cock is a loose fist with one hand and gently spreads my pussy with the other. A finger breaches my entrance, moving slowly at first before speeding up when he adds a second, stretching me.

"I don't want to hurt you," he murmurs.

"You won't."

He searches my eyes for confirmation before releasing them

and staring between us. His fingers slide free before they're replaced with the head of his cock. I hold my breath as he runs it through my wetness, getting it slick and then pressing inside.

My gasp is loud in the quiet room, and he looks at me, pausing. "Don't stop. Please."

It's a stretch to fit him inside, but I tighten my grip on his arm and relax, allowing him to go deeper. An inch at a time, he fills me until I'm struggling to suck in air. There's no pain, only a tingle of discomfort when he bottoms out and holds himself there.

"Tight fit, princess. You okay?"

My nod is wild. "Move. Keep moving."

He doesn't need to hear another word. His retreat is slow and controlled, but his first thrust is quick. My head falls back at the power in the movement and the blast of pleasure it brings.

"Christ," he spits, eyes squeezed shut on the second snap of his hips. "You're squeezing me tight. Trying to keep me buried deep."

My vision blurs as I cry out, pleasure zapping all the way to my bones. I lift my hips to try and meet his thrusts, but I'm too drunk on bliss to keep up.

He pushes forward on his knees and palms my breast in a rough hand before tweaking my nipple. I whimper at the sensation and close my eyes.

"Eyes open. On me, Avery. I want to watch them as you come for me," he growls.

I snap them open without hesitation. The burn in my lower belly grows hotter and hotter with every hard thrust, pressure building. He doesn't look away from me as I writhe beneath him. His expression tightens when he shifts his hips and drives upward, the head of his cock hitting a place inside of me that has me flying.

"Oh, fuck!" I cry, my orgasm cresting in the blink of an eye. "Right there, right there!"

He pistons his hips and hits that spot over and over until I'm gasping for breath and come smacking back into my body.

"You've got one more for me," he grunts, hovering above me

now, lips on my neck and teeth raking my skin. "One more and I'll fuck my cum deep inside of you."

Something about his statement has me fluttering around his cock, already ready for another orgasm. It's never happened before. Two in one night like this. But I know he'll accomplish it. Even if we have to stay here in bed for hours.

"You want me to fill you full of cum? That why you just gripped me tight?"

"Yes," I whisper, curling a leg around his hips.

He reaches between us to hold my stomach and grinds against my clit. "You know what happens when you get full of cum, princess?"

Oh, God. I'm already close to coming again.

"I do. Fuck me, I do!"

"Tell me. Tell me what happens after I've filled you so full you drip," he demands in a voice so rough it scrapes down my bare skin.

I want more of that tone. Want it all over me.

Squeezing my walls, I roll my hips beneath him. My tongue feels weighed down as he sucks on the shell of my ear.

"I'll tell you what happens, Avery. You get pregnant. I fuck you so full of cum you'll have no choice but to get nice and round for me," he breathes out.

My second orgasm is stronger and bigger than the first. It's full and overwhelming. Time fades as I grip onto him for dear life and just let go, accepting the force of pleasure.

I feel him get there right after me. Hot pulses of cum fill me as he drops his forehead to my chest and grunts, every thrust accompanied by a grind of his hips.

"Do you feel it?" he groans.

"I feel it."

In more ways than one. Far beyond the sexual.

"I didn't mean anything by what I said before. About getting you pregnant. It had nothing to do with why I didn't use a condom or—"

I soothe him by gliding my fingers through his hair and scratching at his scalp as he relaxes on top of me. "I know."

My mind is at peace as we lie here, nothing but silence and the rapid thump of my heart against his cheek. And I think I could stay here forever, just like this.

It's not something that could really happen, but for tonight, I'll take what I can get.

32

Oliver

WAKING UP WITH AVERY IN MY ARMS THIS MORNING feels different than last time.

She's huddled onto my chest, breath spreading in warm puffs between my pecs and leg thrown over my waist. The light is bright in my room from the open curtains, and I take advantage of the opportunity to look at her.

Her lips are parted, no longer swollen from how long I kept them attached to mine long after we'd crawled under the blankets. Blonde hair frizzy and standing up every which way, she looks youthful. Unkempt yet as beautiful as I've ever seen her. Even when we were kids, I don't remember her hair being messy. It was always smooth and shiny.

"We don't want to play with a bunch of stinky boys," Tinsley sasses, shoving Noah aside when he hovers, not listening.

She's only ten, but she can be really mean when she's hungry. Noah's nine and always tries to skip out on our football games to sit and watch her. It's weird.

"Well, I don't want you to play with us either. You reek like perfume, Tiny," Maddox grumbles. "It was Oliver's idea for you to hang with us."

Noah glares at him and punches him in the gut. "Don't talk to her."

Cooper thinks he's too old to hang out with us because he's seventeen, so he's inside painting instead of in the yard. I don't think he's that old. Maddox is fifteen but always makes time for us. Especially when Avery's in town.

I scratch at the back of my neck and look at the blonde girl beside Tinsley. Avery Miller's fifteen too, but her age doesn't matter to me. I want to date her someday, even though she's older than me by four years.

"Don't start a fight," she tells the boys, sighing in annoyance at their behaviour.

I jump between Noah and Maddox and look at the older brother. "Listen to her, Dox."

He frowns at me. "You're supposed to be on my side."

"Well, I'm not."

"You're such a suck-up. She's going to notice your crush because you're so obvious," he whispers.

Noah leans close, his smirk making him look more his brother's age than his own. "A crush?"

"I'll tell Braxton you have a crush on her if you tell Avery about mine," I threaten Maddox, ignoring his brother.

Braxton is Maddox's best friend outside of our group of family friends, and I'm pretty sure he loves her already. He always chooses her before the rest of us. I hate her a little bit for it.

"There's no loyalty around here," he mutters.

Noah's gone when I turn around, but it only takes one look at Tinsley to find him back at her side like a creep. Maddox may be weirdly addicted to being near Braxton, but he has nothing on his brother with Tinsley. He's like a weirdo stalker.

Avery smiles at me when I look her way. She smooths a palm over her slicked-back hair and pulls at her ponytail so it swishes in the air. Her hair is so pretty, but I've never told her that. She's even prettier than her hair.

The prettiest girl I've ever seen.

I puff up my chest and head her way, but Maddox grips my shoulder and tugs me against him, keeping me away. Even when I stomp on his toes, he doesn't release me.

"You're eleven. Don't embarrass yourself."

Even though I want to spend time with her before she goes back to Sweden, I listen to him and leave her standing there with Tinsley.

Next time she comes to Vancouver, I'll talk to her. I can wait that long.

I blink out of the memory when lips press to my chest. Swallowing to bring moisture back to my dry mouth, I sit up in bed and drag her along my body until she's straddling my lap. Her cheeks are stained pink when she places her hands on my shoulders and smiles.

We're both naked, and every slight shift of her body atop mine has me biting back a curse.

"Good morning, *stilig*," she whispers, toying with the hairs at the back of my neck.

"Another Swedish name you don't plan on telling me the meaning of?"

"It means handsome, *butternalle*."

I scowl. "You get pleasure from teasing me, princess?"

"I get pleasure in plenty of ways," she purrs.

With a slow, upward thrust of my hips, I watch her mouth part on a silent moan as her bare pussy spreads over my shaft, enveloping it in warmth.

I grin and lean forward to chase her lips for a kiss. "Do you want some right now?"

She answers by reaching between us and scooting back just enough to expose the sight of her gripping my cock in her hand. I grunt at the sudden pressure and fight to keep still, allowing her to touch me how she wants to.

"Do you want pleasure, Oliver?" she asks, snapping her eyes upward.

The first stroke of her hand has my toes curling. And the second yanks a groan from my lips.

Her smug little grin is sexier than it should be. "I'll take that as a yes."

"You're a cruel woman."

"Should I stop?"

A second set of fingers wrap around the rest of my cock, and then she's stroking the full length of it. Slowly, teasing in a way that feels like half punishment and half reward. I palm her waist and urge her forward, desperate to get inside of her, but she shakes her head.

"I want to taste you first," she says.

My head falls back against the headboard with a whack. I squeeze my eyes shut as she moves down my legs and coats the head of my cock in warm air. Without her waist to hold on to, I grip the comforter on either side of my body.

"Open your eyes and watch me."

"If I open my eyes, the sight of you with your mouth around me will make me come in two seconds."

"Don't ruin my fun so soon, Ollie. Let me suck your cock with your attention on me." She swipes her tongue over the slit once. "Please?"

I snap them open and throb at what I see. Tits bare and ass in the air, she bends over my lap and looks up at me through her lashes. Her mouth is open, and her pink tongue hovers over my cock, waiting.

"Go on," I order, but my voice is soft.

She smiles before lowering her mouth over my tip and sucking gently. I huff a shaky exhale and watch, enamoured, as she creeps down another inch, drool dripping down between the fingers that grip my shaft.

"Fuck, you look pretty with my cock in your mouth," I whisper, collecting her hair from around her face as it drapes over my thighs.

She hums, and the vibrations hit my balls. Her hands start to move once she's gotten me wet, twisting and stroking while her mouth suctions the first few inches. A swipe of her tongue along the underside of the head has me one second from begging her to stop before I come.

"Don't make me come, princess. Only doing that in your pussy," I warn.

Amusement sparks in her eyes, but she doesn't push me this time. She releases me with a wet gasp and crawls back onto my lap before tucking my cock inside of her and bearing down.

It's a different sensation than her mouth, and it strips me of restraint. Next time, I'll let her ride me nice and slow, but not now.

"Hold on, princess. Need to fuck you raw."

She nods quickly and threads her fingers behind my neck before I start thrusting up into her. My pace is unrelenting, each snap of my hips loud and hard. But she moans and moans until the only thing I can hear is the sound of her pleasure in my ears.

I kiss her with the same desperation I feel kicking in my chest. A glimpse at an obsession that's been growing for her forever but can now be set free. It's alive inside of me, and I'm not stifling it again.

She palms my cheeks and holds my face in place, her movements just as frantic. It's relieving to know she wants me even half as bad as I want her. She knows about my schoolboy crush on her back then and hasn't let it change anything for her now. We're starting over together.

"Oliver," she whimpers, watching me through our kiss.

I hold her stare. "Avery."

Bliss fills her expression as she squeezes me tight, an orgasm sweeping through her just moments before mine hits. I keep buried to the hilt, shooting deep inside of her as she goes limp in my arms.

Pushing her hair out of her face, I kiss her forehead and then her nose before taking her lips again just once more. Her lips curl into a soft smile, and I know I'm fucked. If I wasn't already locked in her life forever before, I sure am now.

An episode of *Survivor* plays in the background as Avery curls up on the couch beside me beneath a fluffy pink blanket and calls her parents. The lingering smell of bacon fills the air from breakfast, and an empty coffee cup rests on the coffee table in front of her.

Hair wet from our shower and draped over her shoulder, she watches me with her lip between her teeth while the FaceTime call rings.

"They don't have to know you're even here. But if I don't call soon, they'll cancel all their plans for the next two weeks and book emergency flights," she says.

I hold her thigh over the blanket. "I know your parents, princess. Just because I haven't seen them in a while doesn't mean I've grown too scared of them to say hi."

"It's been a decade, not just a while. And they're not going to be happy with just a hi. I haven't told them about us yet, and one look at you here with me and they'll know. Well, at least Mom will."

"I want them to know."

She lets go of her lip and smiles. "Okay."

The ringing cuts off, and I watch the screen as it turns from black to a slightly fuzzy picture of her parents. They haven't changed much in the years since I've last seen them. Apart from the natural signs of aging, Matt looks eerily similar to the last time I saw him. His brown hair is short and wavy, and his wide jaw is sporting a silver-speckled beard that's trimmed neatly.

Morgan is like my mother. The only signs of aging on her features are the crinkles at her eyes and beside the corners of her mouth from years spent laughing. There's a wisdom to her that I can only hope to have one day.

It isn't wisdom in Matt's eyes when he notices me sitting

beside his daughter, though. It's protectiveness. Every inch of his expression puts his tense curiosity on display.

"*Varför är det en man i ditt vardagsrum?*" he asks sternly.

Avery rolls her eyes at him. "Don't try to intimidate him by not speaking English, Dad."

"I wasn't. Your accent is hardly noticeable now. I was testing you."

"I hadn't even spoken yet," she points out.

Matt frowns, clucking his tongue. "Too much time in Canada has taught you how to backtalk."

"I'm pretty sure that was you, actually. Now, say hello nicely. I've missed you."

He darts his eyes in my direction, and they tighten at the corners before going back to Avery and softening. "Hello, *mitt hjärta*. I missed you more."

The name is the same one she uses with Nova. My heart.

I squeeze Avery's thigh. "It's nice to see you again, Mr. Miller. You as well, Mrs. Miller."

"Oliver Bateman? Oh, you're a spitting image of your father now. He used to have the same scowl lines," Morgan says, smiling warmly. "It's been a long time since we've seen you."

"And I can't say I expected to see you in my daughter's living room this morning," Matt grumbles.

His wife pinches his chest. "Ignore him, Oliver. He hasn't had dinner yet, and he's just so old now that he gets a bit grumpy if he doesn't eat during seniors hour."

Avery snorts a laugh and sets her hand over mine, rubbing it gently. I thread our fingers and tug them into my lap as she looks over at me, eyes sparkling.

Speaking to her parents makes her happy, and I'm already half out of my mind thinking of how hard it would be to plan a trip back home for her so she can see them in person and how I could get it done no matter the difficulty.

"Why are you in my daughter's living room, Oliver Bateman?" Matt asks, kissing his wife on the cheek instead of feeding into her dig.

"Boyfriends usually hang out at their girlfriend's house during the day, Dad. Or have you forgotten how dating works?" Avery answers for me.

Matt full-on glares at me now, and I hold it, not giving an inch. I'm not a teenager he can intimidate, and I want him to see that. He's known me since the day I was born, even if he hasn't seen me in a decade.

"Boyfriend? Why?" he asks tightly.

"Why?" Avery echoes.

"Why do you need a boyfriend? My heart can't take it. It would be very thoughtful of you to break this relationship off before it grows any weaker. I'm too old and fragile for this type of news."

Morgan shakes her head at him, sighing. "And everyone always called me the dramatic one. You're worse than I ever was."

Avery strokes a finger along the back of my hand; whether it's meant to be a symbol of support or something subconscious doesn't matter.

"You have one of the healthiest hearts in Sweden, Dad. Save the dramatics for Nova," she says.

"And where is my precious granddaughter? Still sleeping?"

"She's at Oliver's parents' house."

"Did he make you send her away?" Matt asks, leaning closer to the camera until all that's visible are his narrowed eyes.

He's pulled away a moment later, and Morgan's holding him by the shoulder. "Just ignore him, sweetheart. I'm happy for you. Both of you. When did this happen?"

Her warm, motherly tone is comforting. At least one of Avery's parents isn't already planning a way to hide my body the next time they're here.

"A few weeks after I moved in. He's my neighbour," Avery explains with flushed skin. "We didn't get along at first."

"Why? Is he mean?" Matt asks before Morgan pins him with a glare.

"No, Dad. We just butted heads a bit. Miscommunication and all that."

Matt hums stiffly. "Miscommunication isn't exactly a good sign to a healthy relationship."

"Avery's covering for me with that. It wasn't miscommunication. I didn't recognize her at first, and by the time I did, I'd already been a grumpy ass to her and been marked off. It took a few weeks to make it up to her," I say, stepping in.

If he's going to write me off for my past actions, then I'm more than willing to put in the work to get back in his good graces. I've already done that with the most important Miller. I can do it again.

"The apple never falls far from the tree, does it?" Matt huffs in question. "First, your father with your mother, and now you with my daughter. You couldn't have fallen for one of the nicer boys, Avery? What about Jamieson?"

"Dad!" Avery scolds him before flashing me an apologetic look.

"My brother's not ready to be a father, Mr. Miller," I say.

I've put it all out there now, and by the gasp that explodes out of Morgan's mouth, she wasn't expecting my comment. Matt's not as obvious with his surprise, but he doesn't hide it well either.

"And you are? After only . . . what? A few weeks?"

"I wouldn't be here if I wasn't."

Avery's hand tightens in mine.

Her father opens his mouth to say something, but his wife cuts him off with a hand in the face. "I don't want to hear another word from you, Matthew. No more arguing. I'm so excited for the both of you and will be calling Gracie as soon as we get off the phone to scold her for not telling me about this sooner."

"Gracie and Tyler both knew?" Matt asks.

"Keep up, honey. Do you think Gracie took Nova for the

night without knowing all about what these two were up to? Not possible."

"She doesn't know everything," I say.

Morgan frowns. "More than us."

"I've been busy, Mom."

"I know. I know. I'm just being petty."

"It wasn't planned. Neither of us expected anything after meeting again the way we did. But I'm serious about Avery and Nova. I want to be a part of their lives for the rest of my life," I say past the nerves in my throat. "I'm up for the task of proving that to you."

Avery's attention has me looking away from the camera and toward her. Her mouth is tipped in a gentle smile that has me positive that I made the right call by being honest with her parents.

I smile back and pull our hands to my lips to kiss her knuckles. A heavy, comforting feeling of contentment falls over me as we sit here. We might not be alone, but that doesn't mean shit right now.

I'm starting to believe it never will.

33

Avery

I'M INCREDIBLY HORNY.

I'm not joking. It doesn't feel funny either. Not in the slightest.

There's something criminally sexy about a buff hulk of a man playing mermaids in the pool with your daughter while you get to lounge on a hot pink floatie and drink a bellini that he made you.

Nova squeals and screams as Oliver picks her up and tosses her into the water again. She surfaces with a grin so big it makes her eyes squint nearly closed before she swipes her hand through the water to splash him. The water hits me instead, and I gasp at the shock of cool water under the hot sun.

"Mermans aren't supposed to stand, Ollie!" she tells him when he starts to chase her around the pool.

"Why not? You're standing," he replies.

"Mer*maids* are different. We're special!"

"That doesn't seem fair."

"Too bad." She giggles and splashes him again seconds before she's yanked into his arms.

He holds her above his head, grip strong even as she wiggles and reaches for me on my floatie. I shake my head at her and lift my cup in the air. She doesn't have to know it's empty.

"Sorry, sweetie. You're on your own this time."

"Mom!"

"You heard her," Oliver says. Our eyes catch behind my dark sunglasses as he smirks and takes a step closer. Unease creeps in.

"Don't, Oliver," I warn, already dipping my free arm in the water to try to paddle further away from him.

"Don't what?"

"Don't dump her beside me."

"What do you mean? Like this?"

Nova falls into the pool with a splash that swells over my pool floatie and wets my entire body. Nova grips the side of my floatie to try and stay above the water, and it goes rolling, sending me falling in beside her with my mouth and eyes open.

Water fills my ears, but I shut my mouth and blow the rest of the air out of my lungs before I resurface. I wipe the water from my eyes before pinning Oliver in place with them, fire in my belly. My cup is gone, floating in the water, and I leave it.

"You're going to pay for that," I threaten, standing now.

My bikini's modest, with ultra-high-waisted bottoms and a top with thick straps and a wide chest, but the way he stares at me right now tells me I might as well be wearing nothing.

I lick my lips and arch a brow in a silent question. I'm egging him on, and I fucking love it. His reactions not only boost my ego, but they make me feel like a woman again and not just Nova's mom. I'm desired by someone, and not just by any man.

By Oliver.

His chest moves with his slow, even breaths, and the water dripping from the ends of his hair and down his chest is downright sinful.

"How do you plan on making me pay, princess?"

His pool is big. Huge, really. The water hits below my breasts and Nova's chin, and as I take a leap at him, he goes down beneath it like a dead weight.

My arms wrap around his shoulders as I fall onto him and

cling like a koala. He grips me back with an arm banded along my back as he pushes us up through the water until we break above it.

Nova's laugh is louder than I think I've ever heard it, at least in the last few years. Her cheeks are flushed from the afternoon in the sun, and I fight off happy tears, knowing how okay she is with Oliver being around.

Hell, the moment she saw the both of us outside of school this afternoon to pick her up, she ran out of her classroom so fast that she almost tripped on the laces she forgot to tie. Even ushering her inside the house for just long enough to get changed into her swimsuit and unpack her lunchbox was a struggle. All she wanted was to spend time with him.

Fuck, my eyes burn behind my sunglasses. Tipping my head back, I suck in a breath and smile.

The past two days have been something from a dream. I want to hope that they're a sneak peek into the future, but I don't want to jinx anything.

From our first real date to our night together and the morning waking up in my bed with him beside me, I've been walking on air. He even got my parents' approval. Or, well, my mother's. Dad will play it off for as long as he can, but he's sure to fall for Oliver too.

"She got you, Ollie!" she shouts with a poke to Oliver's chest.

"She did, peanut. But you know what happens now?"

"What?"

"We get payback. Mermaid attack!" he bellows.

In a blink, I'm in his arms and up in the air, the pool water beneath us. I flail my arms and play into the act as Nova cheers and jumps, egging Oliver on.

"Tickle her stomach, Nova. We have to torture her before tossing her overboard," he says.

Nova doesn't hesitate. She digs her fingers into my ribs and has me scream laughing in an instant. My cheeks burn alongside my abs, but all I can focus on is the mix of laughter coming from

Oliver and Nova. I add mine and prepare to be dunked under again.

This time, I plug my nose and close my mouth before falling beneath the water and flailing back to the surface with my feet planted beneath me.

"Okay, okay. No more dunking Mom," I beg once I've wiped my face free of water.

Neither of them replies.

Confusion sparks as I stare between them before realizing neither of them is looking at me. I follow Oliver's stare and stiffen, my well of happiness suddenly empty.

"What are you doing here, Chris?" I ask tightly.

He inspects me with a dirty glare from his place by the front fence, and I feel underdressed in my bathing suit. Still outside of the yard, he grabs hold of the silver top of the chain-link fence and leans against it.

"What the fuck is going on here?" he spits.

Oliver moves at my back, so close now I can feel the heat from his body. I want to be comforted by it, but the subtle shift of his position doesn't go unnoticed by Chris.

Nova wades to the edge of the pool and lifts herself up by the rim. "It's not the weekend yet, Daddy."

"Our custody arrangement was made loosely."

It's an innocent reply wrapped in a threat as clear as any I've ever heard. My back snaps straight as I stand beside my daughter.

"Why are you here?"

"I found one of Nova's library books at my house. Apparently, I should have called before coming by to drop it off."

"Which book?" Nova asks, curious now.

Chris nods back at his car. "It's in the car."

"Give me a second, and I'll walk you to the house so you can bring it inside," I say when it's the last thing I want to do.

He's as angry as ever. Only one comment he doesn't like away from exploding on me. I'm not going to let him ruin Nova's day when she's had such a great one.

We've never had a strict visiting schedule. Nova stays with him every second weekend because it's all the time he can spare to give her his full attention, but he's visited plenty of times outside of then. He just chose a really bad time to pop up. One where he's had to see both me and Nova laughing with another man.

Fuck.

"Not yet, Avery. I want you to introduce me to him."

I inhale deeply. "You've already met him, Chris."

Chris stares at Oliver, jaw pulsing. He reaches over the fence for the latch on the gate, and I rush for the ladder to climb out of the pool.

I don't glance back at Oliver, and embarrassment is a dark stain in my mind. "Don't come back here. This isn't my house."

"It's his?" he asks, opening the gate regardless of my plea. "If my daughter is here, then I'm plenty welcome to come as I please."

"Actually, no, you aren't."

I freeze on the top rung of the ladder, my neck slick with sweat. Oliver's deep, stern tone smacks Chris in the face, keeping him stuck just inside of the yard, expression twisted.

"You planning on keeping me out?" he asks.

The sound of water sloshing fills the yard, and a beat later, Oliver's laying a hand on my back. His touch is so soft I lean back into it despite the circumstances. I can't help it. My body seeks his comfort even when it's not smart to.

"Your daughter is watching you right now. Turn around and let them meet you out front," Oliver encourages, no room for argument in his tone.

"Not until you tell me why my family is hanging around you."

My family.

He's wrong. It's *my* family. Not his.

Oliver pauses, not answering. Waiting for me to make the next move. Nova beats me to it.

"Don't be mean, Dad. Ollie is nice," she says. Turning in the pool, she grabs the frog floatie that's hanging over the edge on a hook Oliver rigged to sit on the side. "Look what he got me! It's a frog."

I'm over and down the ladder quickly then. Eyes as hot as lava, Chris flings them at me, watching my every step. Nova meant well, but all she's done is prove that Oliver knows her well and that he's been doing thoughtful things for her. Both of which only serve to piss her father off more. His possessiveness was always my least favourite quality about him, but I hate it right now more than I ever have. I wish he could be something other than himself, just once.

"Let's go, Chris," I say, voice quiet. "You're making a scene in front of her."

When I risk setting a hand on his arm, he shrugs it off. "No. I'm not going anywhere until I know more about the guy you've been flaunting around our daughter without my permission!"

"Your permission?" I echo incredulously.

He ignores me. "Are you seeing him?"

"I am." More water splashes, but I don't look away from Chris. Don't back down. "Don't tell me you have a problem with me dating when you've been doing it for years now. How many women have you introduced to Nova now? Four?"

"Don't turn this around on me. I've always been honest with you about who I'm dating. But this? This is deception!"

"I didn't deceive you. It's only been a few weeks," I defend myself.

"A few weeks? He's been around Nova for a few weeks, and you didn't tell me? Oh, Avery, you've fucked up."

The hairs on my arms stand on end at his cruel tone. "What is that supposed to mean?"

A shake of his head. "I think we need to discuss our current custody agreement."

"Don't say shit like that, Chris. Especially not in front of Nova."

My throat is sticky, stomach turning.

He doesn't deserve more time with her than he already gets. Nova can't take the false hope that would come with hearing that her father wants to take her more often, only to flake and bail when it comes down to it. We've tried for more than every second weekend before, and he doesn't have the commitment in him to hold up his end. I'm not confusing her again.

I've worked too hard to pick up his slack all these years to let him do more damage simply because he's feeling threatened.

"Why can't Nova hear about it? She deserves to know the truth just as much as I do."

I ignore my fear and stay firm. "Don't do that. This isn't about her, and you know it. Don't bring her into this pissing contest of yours under the pretense of wanting more time with her."

"It's not a pissing contest!" he shouts, face red as he takes a menacing step toward me.

Oliver's between us before he can get any closer. "I highly suggest you don't yell in her face again and leave. Now."

"Mom?" Nova calls, standing at the bottom of the ladder with her feet in the thick grass.

My smile is wobbly when I say, "Why don't you get your towel and go inside to dry off, okay?"

"In Ollie's house?"

"Yeah, baby. Make sure to stand on the rug while you're still wet so you don't get drip on the floor."

"Don't go inside that house, Nova," Chris snaps at her.

I nudge Oliver out of the way and step into my ex's face. My chest pounds hard and fast with the adrenaline that comes whenever I stand up for my daughter. It's an instinct as natural as breathing.

"*Don't* talk to her like that. She can't go to our house because you're currently pitching a fit in front of the way out of here."

He takes a wide, dramatic step to the side, making more than enough room for us to leave the backyard.

"Nova. Home. Now," he commands sharply.

She scurries past us in a blur, her green-and-yellow towel wrapped around her neck. The first sniffle I hear... I need to find something to hold on to. Oliver would be my first option, but also the worst one. His closeness doesn't help like it usually does. Not right now.

I need Chris gone. Away from my safe place before it loses that quality.

"Follow her, then. We'll finish this discussion inside."

He juts his chin in the direction Nova took off in, and reluctantly, I force myself to leave him behind with Oliver. My man can handle himself, but fuck, if anyone could get him to decide I'm too much work and not enough reward, it would be Chris.

My priority is Nova, and right now, making sure she's okay is the only thing that matters. Even if that means I risk losing the second-best thing that's ever happened to me.

34

Oliver

THIS GUY IS A FUCKING LEECH THAT'S SUCKED THE light out of Avery right before my eyes.

He watches her chase after their daughter with a deep-rooted possession that has me bristling. His presence is all wrong. A stain on an otherwise perfect day.

I knew a conversation had to happen between Chris and me, but I wasn't expecting it to be today or in a situation where Nova was bound to get hurt. The last thing I want is to see that little girl with tears in her eyes. Her sniffle hurt to hear and called to a protectiveness that I now know has been dulled my entire time.

I've never felt it as strongly as I do right now. Like I could push myself over the edge of every one of my limits to make her smile again and would do everything to succeed. It's an instinct.

"You talk to the women in your life like that often, Chris?" I ask, stepping into his face to block his view of my girls.

I'd call them that to his face if I didn't think I'd be sporting cuts and bruises that I'd have to explain to Nova later.

"It's not any of your business."

"I'm making it my business. It has been for a while now, and you'd be smart to start accepting that it will be for the foreseeable future."

His laugh is short and angry. "Avery tell you that?"

"It's what I'm telling you. Don't think about her. Don't talk about her either."

"I wouldn't be so sure. We might be separated right now, but Avery knows she's mine. She likes to flex her muscles and keep us apart when she wants to prove a point, but it won't be long until she's calling me drunk in the middle of the night and asking me to come back home again."

Again. The word lingers longer than I want it to before I shake it away.

Chris' smirk is sleazy as fuck. "Didn't tell you about all those calls, did she? I'm not surprised. She always plays the embarrassment card the next morning."

"A drunk phone call in a moment of weakness is all you've got?"

"Did you need more?"

"I don't give a flying fuck how many times she's called you after a night of drinking. I can guarantee you it won't be happening again in this lifetime or the next. You're not going to scare me off. I'm not nervous that you'll somehow get her back. Avery's too smart to open that door for you again. You've got my word on that."

No number of drunk calls she's made in the past matters to me. I won't hold those against her, especially not when I know how much she's struggled.

Chris tenses his jaw but doesn't back down. Instead, choosing to dig deeper with his attempts to piss me off.

"She's mentioned you before. Years ago. Oliver, right? I recognize you now from all those times I've caught her scrolling through your social media pages. You're one of those kids from her childhood. The one she didn't give a shit about back then."

"Avery cared about all of us. You've never met the rest of her family, though, right?"

"You're not her family. She hardly mentioned any of you," he spits, eyes flashing.

"No? But she talked about me enough for you to know she doesn't give a shit? You don't have a clue what you're talking about. The first time we met, you swore you had no idea who I was."

He takes an arrogant step toward me and huffs, rage making his features spasm. "They're *mine*. Avery's trying to prove a point with this fucking house of hers and new life here without me. But Nova's my fucking daughter, and Avery's supposed to be with me. We'll raise her together."

"They're not possessions," I grit out, voice deep and rigid. "They're people, and I'm going to try not to stand between you and the relationship you have with Nova, but there's room in her life for me too, and I'm not going to waste my chance to be there for her the way you have."

"You don't know shit about me!"

"I've learned more about you in the past few minutes today than I'd have in years. You don't want Nova and Avery in your life because of genuine love or care, but only so you can say that you have them. You don't mind yelling at them or making your daughter cry with your angry words because you know it'll only take a weak apology for her to forgive you. You take advantage of their love and kindness and use cruel words and inconsiderate actions to wear them down until they don't know their own worth. They can and have done better than you. I'm here to prove that to them."

He snaps a hand out and grips my shirt. With a tug, he pulls at me, and I allow it, keeping my arms pinned at my sides.

"You don't know anything," he says coolly.

"You're wrong," I mutter, staying just as cold. "And I'm going to be here helping them realize that what they had before with you was nothing. That it isn't worth remembering. I'll give them everything they want and show them that they're so fucking much more than two trophies on a shelf. They're everything, Chris. Dammit, they're *every. Thing*. How have you not been able to see that?"

The fingers curled in my shirt relax before disappearing. I step back, and he does the same. The tight lines in his expression don't loosen despite the new distance.

"You won't stick around," he says.

"I'm not going anywhere."

"Avery wants to move back to Sweden one day."

"I'll go with her."

Shaking his head, he scoffs and looks out at the street. "I thought that at first too. Thought a lot of things."

"Like you were ready for a family when you weren't?"

"No. I knew I never wanted one of those. Nova was an accident. A mistake I made by not being responsible."

I flinch, physically repulsed by the words. "Don't call her that again. She can be unplanned, but never, *ever*, a mistake."

"I did what was expected of me. Stayed and took care of them. Avery decided that wasn't enough, but I never agreed to her finding someone else to take over my responsibilities when I'm capable of handling them myself."

"They aren't responsibilities. They're choices someone makes when it comes to caring for those they love."

"You don't love them."

It's easy to tell him otherwise and easier to admit it to myself.

"I do. I love the two of them more than I've ever loved anything. They're my family, and I'm not here out of obligation. I want to be here more than anything else. I chose them, Chris. And I'm not letting them go. Not right now with you spitting mad in my face, and not in twenty years. So, either get over the fact we'll be seeing a lot of one another or don't and continue having every meeting with them feel like this. Either way, I'll be here to put you in your place."

"She's hard to love, buddy. Expects someone who can move mountains with his bare hands and will turn up her nose at anything less than. I gave up trying to be the man of her dreams years ago."

It's comical. So much so that I toss my head back and laugh

beneath the weight of his poisonous stare. Never in my life have I heard anything so fucking wrong.

Laughter finally ceasing, I say, "Avery's so incredibly easy to love that I started falling for her when I was just a kid. The problem has never been her, buddy. It's all you. Always has been."

Chris is shit at hiding his emotions, and when his top lip curls, I swing out of the way before he can hit me with the fist he sloppily throws at me.

I take another step back to create more distance between us. "Collect yourself and get the fuck off my property. If you try to hit me again, I'll have the cops here before you can run off with your tail between your legs. Don't let your daughter watch you get driven away in the back of a squad car."

"Are you sure you wouldn't enjoy that? It would make it easier to take her from me," he hisses.

I swallow, a sudden sadness seeping into my blood. With a slow shake of my head, I stare past him at Avery's house, wishing I was there with her instead of here.

"She's not a possession. I don't want to keep you from her. If you can't see past your own selfishness when it comes to them, that's on you. I'm not fighting you. I'm fighting for them. And Nova deserves better than to witness her father make a fool of himself again."

"I won't let you turn them against me," he threatens.

Every word I've spoken has fallen on deaf ears. It becomes obvious that nothing I say will ever make a difference with him. He's stuck so far in his own habits of selfish manipulation that he can't see the truth right in front of him.

"Alright, Chris. Don't let me, then. It won't make an ounce of a difference once you've done it all on your own."

I leave him in my yard, deciding here and now not to give him another second of my time when I could be next door with my family. Nova has Avery, but who does Avery have?

"Tell her that we need to talk," he says from behind me. *"Alone."*

Closing my eyes, I halt. "If you want to speak with her, call tomorrow once you've both had time to cool down. I'm not your middleman."

"You know what? I'll talk to her right the fuck now."

I'm spinning and planting a hand on his chest before he makes it a single foot on her lawn. Anger bleeds into the calm façade I've slipped on.

"One more step."

"Until?" he goads.

"Do you have any idea how lucky you are? I've known several men get handed terrible custody agreements and take them on the chin because they didn't want to cause a stink with their kids. But you? You get served with a generous one and still take it for granted." I scrape a hand over my jaw, chuckling in disbelief. "Any judge worth a dime would take one look at you and know you deserve far less than one weekend every two weeks. Your threats would mean nothing to Avery with something written in ink."

"She won't take it to court," he snaps.

"Maybe not before, no. But now? You've just threatened her, Chris."

This time when I turn and leave, I let his next words drift away on the wind. He's not worth my time. Not worth anything when it comes to Nova and Avery.

His threats to Avery were worthless in my eyes, but to her, they might not mean the same thing.

They could mean everything.

35

Oliver

THE DOOR IS UNLOCKED, BUT I CALL FOR AVERY BEFORE stepping further than a couple of inches into the house. When she answers with a short and sharp "come in," I take my shoes off with a heavy stomach.

Once I've locked the door behind me and set my sneakers beside Nova's new bright orange Crocs on the rack against the wall, I'm following the sound of hushed voices. The hallway is short but feels miles long.

"Cotton candy or bubble gum?"

"Both? In a waffle bowl?" Nova's voice is dull, sad.

I clench my jaw and stop halfway down the hall. I'm close enough to see only one deep green wall and a sliver of the big white dresser through the cracked door to Nova's room, but nothing more. My breathing is tight and ragged, but I focus on getting myself to calm down before joining them. They don't need my anger right now.

"Sure, sweetheart. A waffle bowl. You can even get rainbow sprinkles and gummy frogs if you want," Avery says soothingly.

"I don't want gummy frogs today."

"Are you sure? They're your favourite."

"I just don't want them, Mom."

Invisible fists use my heart as a punching bag. Maybe I should go back outside and pummel the sorry fuck before he leaves—

"You can have anything you want, *mitt hjärta. Vad som helst.*"

"*Jag vill inte att Pappa ska skada Ollie.*"

The soft voice speaking my name amongst words I don't understand is enough to have me moving again. I knock my knuckles against the door and slowly push it the rest of the way open before they notice me.

"Ollie?" Nova sniffles, pushing herself from her stomach to sit amongst the pillows on her bed.

The sight of her puffy red eyes fucks me up inside. My previous protectiveness grows tenfold.

"How are you doing, peanut?" I ask, fighting past the thickness in my throat.

She shrugs. "Is my dad gone?"

I look at Avery where she sits on the floor beside the twin bed, her knees tucked to her chest and arm splayed over them. One hand is clutching Nova's on the bed, holding on so tight it's like she's scared someone will try to take her away.

She's still wearing her bathing suit, but Nova's buried in a sweatshirt I recognize the moment she shifts and the name stitched into the right corner becomes visible. Something settles inside of me. Slots itself into an empty crevasse left in my soul.

Avery sighs and presses her forehead to the edge of the mattress when she notices where my attention's gone. The action nips at my gut, telling me something's wrong, and I pay attention to the warning.

I trust myself completely. In my line of work, my gut instincts are all I have sometimes. And when this one demands I go to her, I don't ignore it.

"Your dad went home," I murmur.

Nova reaches for a fuzzy frog pillow from its spot along the inside edge of her bed and pulls it onto her lap. She picks at the material of it and rolls little bunches between her fingers.

"Okay."

"Can I talk to Oliver for a couple of minutes, sweetheart? Then we can go for ice cream? Maybe you'll be up for gummy frogs then," Avery suggests with a pat to Nova's thigh.

Nova blinks up at me, a small sparkle of hope in her eyes. "Can you come for ice cream too?"

"If you want me—"

"No. He can't. Not this time," Avery interrupts, answering for me.

The rambled denial is unexpected. But maybe I should have seen it coming.

Nova's voice takes on a different pitch than I'm used to. One that's angry and raw. Stubborn. "Why not? I want him to come!"

She's glaring at Avery now, her thin brows scrunched and lips downturned. I grapple with what the right thing to do is here and look at Avery for help or guidance, but a sullen, defeated expression is what I find instead.

Clearing my throat, I answer Nova so she doesn't have to. "I have to go to see my mom for a few hours, peanut. She needs my help, and moms always come before ice cream."

"But I want you to come with us," she persists.

"We'll get ice cream soon. When you're up for getting a sore tummy from all the gummy frogs, okay?"

"If I get frogs today, will you come?"

My heart splinters down the centre. "Not this time."

"Don't argue on this, Nova. Please," Avery pleads while pushing off the floor and gliding her hands down her ass to dust herself off. "I'll be right back, okay? Why don't you get dressed?"

"I am dressed."

"You can't wear that out, you'll trip on it. And it's not yours."

"It's not yours either! I found it on your bed."

It's hard not to beat my chest in satisfaction at that bit of knowledge. I'd give the both of them every sweatshirt and hoodie I own if they wanted me to. I've got so many of them that I didn't notice Avery stealing one and bringing it here.

"If you listen to your mom and change into something your size, you can keep that sweatshirt, okay?" I offer.

Her entire face lights up. "Really? It would be mine and not Mom's?"

"It would be yours."

"Okay!"

She bounds out of bed and rushes to her dresser before starting to search through her clothes. I follow Avery out of the room and watch as she shuts the door behind us.

In the hallway, the silence between us is louder, more obvious. My nerves are buzzing, that terrible fucking feeling growing in intensity.

"What did he say to you out there?" she asks on a weighted exhale, sounding as if she's been struggling to hold that question in.

"Nothing that matters."

"Don't try to placate me, Oliver. Tell me the truth. How bad was it?"

I reach for her, cupping her shoulders and holding her in place when she tries to start pacing. "Hey, princess. Take a breath with me. You're getting worked up, and he doesn't deserve this reaction from you."

Her eyes focus on me, the crinkle between her brows softening. "What did he say about me, Oliver?"

"It was all bullshit. Repeating it won't do anything but hurt you."

"Tell me. Tell me so I know what to prepare for once he makes good on his threat and tries to take my baby away from me."

My muscles harden to stone. "He's not taking Nova from you."

"You heard him. He thinks I've been sneaking around with you, and he . . . He wants to change our custody agreement. I won't give him more time with her. Not more than he already has," she rambles, face paling further with every word until she's as white as the paint on the walls.

"Avery," I murmur, reaching up to brush her cheek with my knuckle. The skin pinkens, but it's not enough to settle me. "He's not going to take any more time with her. I won't let that happen. *We* won't. He's just upset."

She shakes her head, forcing me to drop my hand too soon. Losing the heat from her skin feels wrong. Makes me colder than before I touched her.

"I have to fix this," she whispers vacantly.

Arms wrapping tightly around her middle, she licks her lips and jolts back a step away from me. I keep my feet planted to the floor, even as I scream at myself to move toward her.

"You will fix it, Avery. He's not a threat to you. I'm positive about that."

"I always knew he wouldn't let me be happy. He has a way of making everything about himself. It was all about Chris for years, and now that I've found someone who's made me happy for the first time in years, he's taking it all away from me," she says weakly.

"He isn't taking anything from you. Especially not Nova."

Her eyes are wet with tears when she asks on a breath, "What about you?"

"Never me," I declare.

Saying fuck you to the space she's placed between us, I move closer. She doesn't retreat, but the slight stiffening in her limbs is a sign as bad as any I've ever seen.

"He could fight me for custody. I have the financial resources for a legal battle, but when it comes to everything else? I'm not emotionally ready for that. Nova doesn't need to live through that either."

"Yes, you are. You're strong and you're brave and resilient. And I'm here. Just say the word and everything I have is yours. Every single thing already is, Avery. Let me be here for you. Share this weight with me. With my family and our friends."

It's desperate and not anything I anticipated to do in this lifetime, but I lay it out on the line for her without a single regret. There's no going back for me. Only forward, either with her or without.

"I'm no one's charity case. I don't need—"

"Don't say that you don't need help. I already know you don't *need* it. I'm saying you can have it if you *want* it. Not everything has to be about necessity and can be about what will make your life easier. Let me help you, baby. I really, really fucking want to."

She lifts her chin, something unsaid solidifying her resolve. "I'm not ready to accept it yet. I've got to try and settle this on my own first."

"How do you want to do that?"

"Chris needs to know that he can't come here and stomp all over me. He's not allowed to discard us and then come back whenever he pleases to snatch us back up and stuff us in his pocket."

"You're right."

"But I want to do it on my own. If I don't, he'll think he's won, and I won't give him that satisfaction."

I nod, but it's a slow, laggy movement. "Okay."

"It won't be for very long, but once I've taken care of Chris, we'll be able to come back together. You and me and Nova, we can be a family . . ."

I stop listening, not wanting to hear the rest of her sentence. It's obvious what she was about to say. What she wants.

"Oliver?"

"I don't want you to do this on your own. Without support again," I mutter.

"As soon as you've done it once, you can do it a million times."

Frustrated, I blow out a breath. "I'm not going to complicate anything for you while you do this. I don't understand why we need to wait to be together until you've, what? Taken him to court? Dealt with a lengthy legal process against him all on your own?" I ask, fighting tooth and nail to keep my voice even instead of booming with the fear and nervousness building in my chest.

"If that's what it takes. I don't know. You're just . . . you make me want to forget about everything else other than you, me, and Nova. A family like that can't thrive with someone like Chris constantly swinging threats and bringing chaos into our lives. I want to start a life without looking over my shoulder for him, Oliver. But I have to focus, and you're the biggest, greatest distraction I've ever known.

"You deserve better than the baggage I bring. I'm putting you first, the way you always fight to do for me. Please, let me."

"Nova is not baggage. Chris is your past, but he isn't baggage either," I argue, taking her cheeks in my hands and bringing our faces a breath apart. "I don't want to spend a single day without you at my side or waiting to come back home to you after work. Don't make this decision for the both of us."

Her smile is soft yet so fucking sad. "I'm a mom, Oliver. Making the tough decisions when no one else wants to and bearing the weight of them is my specialty."

"I love you," I say, the three words thick with clarity and vivid honesty.

I've never spoken them to a woman like this before, but nothing has ever been easier. It's been a long time coming.

She kisses me, lips tasting faintly like salt. "I love you too."

36

Avery

"Come in, sweetheart."

Ava Hutton opens the door for me and ushers me inside with a brush of her hand across my back.

Dressed in a pair of loose jeans and a Hutton hockey shirt, she glows in the afternoon light. A candle is burning on the entrance table, making the house smell like cake and berries as we walk through to the same kitchen where I had a near food fight with Oliver. I toss that thought off a cliff and inwardly scold myself for thinking about him again.

Another chance to torture myself is all it is.

I've already spent the past two days in a downward spiral with takeout dinners and horror film bingeing. Nova's enjoyed the lack of vegetables at dinner and a strict bedtime, but with every night I loosen the reins on my parenting, I only feel shittier. All of my hard work is so easily destroyed because I'm too busy overthinking and worrying. I fear the habits I've instilled in Nova are hanging on by a thread as I ignore mine.

I put on a brave face for everyone the way I always have, but for the first time in the past seven years, it's almost too hard to keep up the act. Every stressful night that's kept me up into the early mornings has taken its toll, and now I'm left weak and tired.

Overworked and drowning without a life raft because I've tossed it away when it was offered in a pair of safe, reliable hands. The same ones I miss feeling on my body and in my hair.

"Your text sounded urgent," Ava says, going right for the double-door fridge.

She grabs a jug of pink lemonade from the right side and turns to set it on the counter before meeting my eyes. I take a seat on one of the leather stools at the giant island and release a heavy breath. It does nothing to relax me.

She laughs lightly while collecting two glasses and filling them with the pink liquid. "Oh, you have a rant brewing, don't you?"

"You could say that."

"Well, let me have it," she encourages, tucking a brown curl behind her ear. The round diamonds in her ears glitter in the sun rays that stream in through the tall windows.

I take the glass of lemonade she hands to me and drink half of it before she's managed to pull the stool out from beside me. "It's more of a word vomit and favour than a rant, if you still don't mind listening."

"I've got three children, Avery. Word vomit is a staple in this house. And I'd accept any number of favours for you."

I crack a smile at that. "Right."

"I also lived with your mother during her rowdiest years, so trust me when I say that nothing you tell me today will be worse than what I've heard from her," she adds with a reminiscent smile.

"Do you miss her? And my dad?"

She wraps her hands around her cold glass and nods. "I've missed your mom from the moment she moved away. Time and age hasn't made that any easier. It was a lot easier to visit each other when we were younger, but you get Oakley on a plane now and he'll sit and grumble about the stiff seats for the majority of the flight. Hard to believe he used to spend a good chunk of the year in the air."

"He was spoiled with private team jets."

She blows out a breath. "That he was. I think he believes the kids moved all over the country on purpose just to torture him. He has to take a Xanax before every flight we take to Toronto."

"In his defense, that airport is a nightmare."

"A night terror, more like."

After taking another sip of my drink, I let the cool glass rest in my palms, hoping it will help settle my nerves. "I know that my parents kept a lot of details regarding me and my circumstances quiet, but Mom must have told you something more than she did everyone else."

Ava and my mom are best friends. Have been since they were teenagers, and while distance may have worn down that bond a bit, it's still there. I've overheard several of the calls between them and know that my mom must have confided in her with topics she'd never bring up to me or Dad.

Chris was a subject I didn't want anyone to know about, but Mom has a blabbermouth. She had to have told *someone* about him, and I'd bet it was Ava.

The woman beside me copies my actions and drinks from her glass before setting it aside and folding her hands on the table. When she looks at me this time, her eyes shine with an openness that settles me slightly.

"She told me everything," she admits. "All the way from the beginning."

The honest admission startles me. "Everything? As in, *everything*?"

"As in everything."

"So you knew where I was and didn't tell anyone?"

Her chin dips slightly. "Only Oakley. Your mom swore us to secrecy and begged neither of us to interfere with your wishes to be left alone."

Ashamed, I fight off a flinch. "When you say it like that, it sounds worse than I thought. It wasn't that I didn't want to be around any of you. The opposite, actually. If I had told everyone where I was, you would have taken me back in, and I didn't want the help I would have been offered. I didn't want to rely on it only to have it stripped away if I couldn't handle it here and wound up having to go back home away from you all again."

Ava reaches over and sets a hand over mine, squeezing softly. "And it was hard on you being so far away."

"You could say that," I say with a short, blunt laugh. "Having to watch all of my childhood friends grow up with one another while I was in a different country, unable to do the same, wasn't great. I was jealous all the time, wishing I could have been here for all the birthdays and Christmases. The graduations and hockey and football games. Noah's concerts and Addie's fashion shows."

"They would have loved for you to be here then, Avery."

"Yeah, I know."

It doesn't make me feel better knowing everyone missed me the way I missed them. Wishing to be with someone when there wasn't a way of making it happen doesn't help anyone. But the guilt I feel for wasting the past decade we could have all been together out of pride and embarrassment is the hardest pill of all. I'm unable to swallow it.

"In your text, you mentioned needing family lawyer recommendations," she says, leading the conversation in a different direction.

"If my mom told you everything, does that include my custody agreement with Chris?"

"No. I only know you two share custody with you as the primary caregiver."

"We've had a non-legally binding custody agreement since we split, but Chris . . . he found out about Oliver and threatened trying to take more time with her." I tighten my hold on my glass, leg beginning to bounce. "He can't handle more time with her. If he tries to do this, it will only be so he can prove a point."

Ava's brows draw together as her mouth tips down into a frown. "He's threatening custody because he's jealous of my nephew?"

"It's ridiculous, right?"

"Incredibly. Does he have any ground to stand on here if he

did pursue a more involved custody agreement? What is your current one?"

"He gets her every second weekend. No holidays after he forgot her fifth birthday and Santa was a no-show during the Christmas prior."

"I'm sorry, Avery," Ava whispers, disgust twisting her expression.

"Don't apologize. Nova has me."

"She does. And I have a few family lawyers I can reach out to. I've been a part of a few custody battles with the foster system, and it's not easy, especially when one of the two parents are not willing to compromise. But if he truly is just doing this out of spite, he'll be put in his place once you've shown how serious you are with legal aid at your side. He won't continue to wave threats around when nobody will listen to them."

"He's slimy. I want to believe it will be easy to prove that I'm the better choice for Nova if it comes to that, but I don't know if he'll somehow weasel his way into taking her from me. I've worked too hard to let him take her when the right place for her is at home with me. He doesn't know how to parent her, Ava. He's never had to. I've always been there to pick up his slack, and there's been so, so much of it," I say, feeling an overwhelming sense of defeat wriggling beneath my skin already.

It's premature and not the right time for it, but fuck. I won't let him have more time with Nova than he deserves only so he can disappoint her and wish he'd never attempted this only days afterward.

"He won't take her from you. You're her mother and an incredible one at that."

My throat is sticky when I blurt out, "What if it becomes a custody battle and Oliver doesn't want to stick around for it? What if he starts to believe I'm too much work. That *we're* too much work. I've already pushed him to sit on the sidelines and wait. Will he get pushed too far and leave?"

"Oh, honey. I don't think it's possible for you to push Oliver away."

I shake my head, immediately ignoring her attempt to placate me. "I did, though. Chris pushed all my buttons, and I shoved Oliver out the door the moment he tried to offer me his support."

"Has he told you that once you left Canada with your parents that final time when you were seventeen, he forbid anyone from speaking about you around him? Or that he yelled at his brother on his eighteenth birthday when he made a joke about him finally being old enough to fly to Sweden to ask you out?"

My stomach flutters. "He mentioned not asking about me."

"He did a lot more than that, sweetheart."

"That was all a long time ago."

"Are you trying to convince me of the relevance of that or yourself? Because I don't think time matters much at all. It's been over a decade since then, and right now, he's the one your daughter's father feels threatened by.

"Oliver can be his father's son when it comes to mood and demeanour, but oftentimes, he's more like his mother than I think anyone realizes. Once they set their mind to something, there's no going back. No second option. You've been the one thing Oliver's always wanted and wished he could have had. Now that you're here, I have a feeling he won't be letting go as easily as he did the first time."

"He told me he loved me," I whisper, her words sinking their claws into my heart.

Ava peels my fingers from around my glass and pulls them into hers before guiding them to rest on the countertop. "And he means it."

"Falling in love with him was the easiest thing I've ever done."

"That's how you know it's the forever kind. When loving someone feels natural. Like it was always meant to be that way," she says.

"I need to take care of Chris, Ava. I don't want him to be a hurdle I have to constantly jump over."

I refuse to fully integrate Oliver into my life until I have this mess sorted. If we're going to be a family, I want us to have a stronger foundation than I've allowed myself in my past relationship because this isn't going to be one I let wither away.

This one will be for keeps.

Forever.

37

Tyler

MY WIFE ALWAYS SAID SHE WANTED TWO BOYS, AND that's exactly what we got.

One loud and brash with a laugh you can hear from space and another that likes his privacy and scowls more than he smiles. Oliver was born looking exactly like me. Even down to the wrinkle between his barely there baby eyebrows.

He was the angel child, the one that set us up for failure once Jamie came along like a fucking terror from hell. Oliver didn't cry, slept through the night from three months old, and took to breastfeeding like a champ.

Jamie preferred screaming at night and forcing our hand to formula. He grew to be a sarcastic little shit who has no problem being the loudest one in the room. So similar to his mother, she took to him easier than I did. To this day, she's the one who understands him with little thought.

I love both of my sons equally and with a fierceness that was unheard of in my past. It terrified me how easy it was to attach myself to them and to witness the extent of the love I was capable of giving another person outside of Gracie.

And while all of that is true, Oliver will always be the son I was able to connect with the easiest.

From a very young age, he portrayed himself in a manner that I could relate to in a soul-deep way. If he wanted to be alone but didn't know how to ask for that little bit of support he needed, I was there to sit in a chair beside him and provide silent comfort. When he was struggling with expressing himself, I was the first one to knock on his door and offer advice that I wish I'd had growing up.

No matter the circumstances, I made sure I was available to him for every moment of disappointment or happiness that he didn't know how to handle.

My past is shaded in greys and blacks, but from the moment the boys were born, I worked to ensure both he and Jamie could look back and see theirs in a kaleidoscope of colours.

So, after I get home from a run on a Thursday afternoon and my gorgeous wife tells me that Oliver's shown up at home, I'm instantly on alert. I find him two minutes later, bent over the back of the couch in the basement rec room while staring at the shelves of old family photos on the wall in front of it, and hope to fuck I have advice at the ready.

Neither Gracie nor I come down here often anymore, if at all now that the boys are gone. I've all but forgotten about the open bins of old Vancouver Warriors shit in the corner of the room.

It's been tucked away for years now, too fucking many of them to admit without feeling like I'm one fast-food meal away from going into cardiac arrest. I'll never admit that I'm old and withered now, no longer a guy in prime health with an impressive career in the NHL and a row of trophies to prove it.

I spent a generous chunk of my life in the NHL, but that chapter's closed. Dad is my only title now. The only one that's ever mattered to me besides Husband.

"You didn't want to brood at your own house?" I ask.

Oliver doesn't react to the question, as if he already knew it was coming when he noticed me step into the room.

"I don't want to be there right now."

"Oh? Why not?"

He doesn't answer me, so I move to his side and set my hand on his shoulder before squeezing just once.

"Running from something?"

"Someone," he corrects me.

"You don't run from anything, Oliver. So what are you really doing here?"

"Avoiding doing something stupid and reckless."

My brows jump as I drop both my arms over the back of the couch and replicate his stance. "Since when are you either of those things?"

"Since I fell in love, apparently."

The admission is unexpected enough that I have to clear my throat to hide my surprise before speaking. "Love?"

"You and Mom. It wasn't easy, was it?"

"Do you want the answer your mother would give you or mine?"

"If I wanted hers, I'd be upstairs with her right now," he mutters.

I roll my lips to hide a smile at his bluntness and nod. "Alright. No, it wasn't easy. I was an asshole to her, and she overlooked that fact far too many times than I deserved and gave me a million chances when I should have only needed one. Your mother fought for me when I was too stuck in my head to see what was right in front of me. In a perfect world, I wouldn't have let myself believe I was unworthy of her and instead not wasted a single day with her fighting what had always been inevitable."

"Did she ever regret fighting so hard for you?"

"If she did, she never told me. Never acted like it either." I keep my eyes trained on him and watch as his frown deepens. "What's going on, Oliver?"

He pushes out a tight exhale and spins, leaning his back against the couch. Arms crossing, he tips his head back to stare at the ceiling.

"I've never had a problem fighting for anything, Dad. Not when it comes to those important to me. But being patient and waiting, that's where I struggle. And I'm struggling right now," he admits.

"You're talking about Avery?"

He jerks his head in what I take to be a nod. "Her ex is sniffing around and making a mess of things. She wants to handle it herself, and I'm worried that she doesn't think I'll stick around while she does."

"But you'd rather take care of it for her." I don't mention the sticking around part. We both know that isn't the problem here.

"Leaving her to deal with it alone doesn't feel right. Not when I'm the reason he's trying to throw his weight around."

"Do you doubt that she can handle her own problems without you? Because I'm pretty sure she's done just that for a long time now, son. You have to have faith in your girl."

He turns his head to glare at me. "I do have faith in her. It has nothing to do with that."

"Then what's wrong?"

"I don't want space from her," he grumbles.

My laugh escapes me before I can reel it back in. His glare intensifies when I don't immediately shut up. But how am I supposed to pretend that my son isn't as dramatic of a fucker as I am?

"You're here in the basement brooding like a heartbroken teen because you miss your girl?"

"Fuck off, Dad."

"I never thought I'd see the day."

He shoves his elbow into my ribs and takes a step away from me, scowl harsh. "I should have spoken to Mom instead."

"No, you shouldn't have because she'd be driving you to Avery's house right now at the first sight of you looking like a lovesick puppy. And that's not what you need to do."

"Are you going to tell me what I need to do, then?"

"Your uncle Oakley would call you an idiot for listening to a word of advice from me."

"Good thing he isn't here, then."

I snort. "Fair enough."

"She told me she wants to get Nova's father sorted out before we can focus on us again."

"Alright. So, let her."

"That's your advice?" he asks with a roll of his eyes.

"No, you shithead. It isn't. My advice is to use the time apart to prove to her that you're not going to bail out. You said you thought she was worrying about that, right?" His chin tips in answer. "So, make a statement and prove to her that you're serious about her and Nova."

I've never pictured my son taking in a daughter who wasn't his in blood, but it feels pretty damn right to think of him with Avery and Nova. Gracie's been raving about that girl since she met her, and I should have known from that very first moment that she was going to be family.

If there was ever a man who could take in a daughter and make her feel like the most precious person in the universe, it would be my son.

"And if she decides afterward that they'd be better off without me?"

"We don't make pointless metaphorical guesses in this house, Oliver. They're your family. No doubt about it."

※ ※ ※

AN HOUR LATER, Gracie slides onto my lap and winds her arms behind my neck, burying her fingers in my hair. With a soft, upward gaze, she drags her mouth across mine and hums.

"Did you ever think that there would come a day when Matthew Miller would demand a FaceTime call from Sweden so he can scold us for our son dating his daughter?"

I scowl at the mention of that fucker while she's on my lap and grip her thighs to pull her closer. "He can demand plenty of things right now, but that doesn't mean I'll give them to him."

"Don't be an ass, Ty," she coos.

"I could be way fucking worse, and you know it."

She smirks and tugs on my hair, shifting to settle herself higher on my thighs. Too high for a FaceTime call with Matt.

"Aren't you a little too old for the caveman act?"

I nip at her lips and soothe the sting with a kiss. "When it comes to you? Never, Gray."

Light beams in her bright blue eyes, making my pulse race. I stare at her and breathe softly, afraid that if I move even slightly, she'll slip free of my grasp.

It's been this way for years. From the moment I robbed heaven and stole an angel, I've been looking over my shoulder out of fear of someone taking her back. But somehow, she's still here two decades later, sitting on my lap with a smile on her face that I'd kill to keep from faltering.

"Call Matthew, Tyler. Then you can take me to our room."

"Oh, how you bribe me without fear, wife," I tease lowly.

"It's the only way to get you to do what I want."

"That's a lie. I'd do anything for you at any time."

She grins. "I know. It's just fun to rile you a little. Keeps you young."

I kiss her again, unable to help myself. She melts in my arms, kissing me back with ease and excitement.

Her hands shift and fall between us before I hear the sound of a dial tone and open my eyes to find her with her phone held beside my head.

I slap a hand down over her ass and narrow my eyes when she gasps at the sting.

"You didn't just spank me!"

"You kissed me to distract me so you could call that fuckface. So, yes, I did."

She laughs, holding the phone out so it catches both of our faces in the camera. "He's not a fuckface."

"Yes, he is. Especially if he has the nerve to fault our son for his relationship with his daughter."

"He can try, but it won't work," she says in an attempt to soothe me.

"He can try what?" the fuckface asks, appearing on the screen now.

"To blame Oliver for the relationship our children have entered into," I answer.

Matt glowers at me. "It is his fault! You should have seen the way he looked at her when they called us."

"And how was that? Like he loves her?" Gracie asks softly, yet with a hint of venom that makes my dick hard in an instant.

"Like he wants to bundle her up and keep her from me forever!"

"Oh, you're so dramatic," Morgan huffs, finally appearing once she takes the phone from her husband. "He's not taking the relationship well."

"Do you think there's something wrong with my son, Matthew?" I ask accusingly. "I assure you that there is not one person out there that's better for her than Oliver."

"I doubt it. She could have started dating an astronaut or something."

"You only want that so you could pray that he'd wind up lost in space and be gone forever," Morgan says.

Matt gapes at her in betrayal. "You think so low of me?"

"We know you better than you think," Gracie tells him.

I reach for the phone and take it from my wife. "I'm going to hang up the call now."

"This conversation is not over, Tyler! I swear, I'll send him to space myself—"

I hang up before he can finish his sentence and throw Gracie's phone onto the other side of the couch. She squeaks when I grip her by the thighs and stand, forcing her to hold on to me to keep from falling to the floor.

Heading in the direction of our bedroom, I ask, "Now that fuckface is gone, where were we?"

38

Oliver

AVERY SHOULD TAKE AWAY THE SPARE KEY TO THE SHOP she gave to my mother because it was entirely too easy to convince her to let me have it. One fast blink of my lashes and she was putty in my hands, offering it up with warm words of encouragement and a tight hug.

Tool boxes fall to the tile with clunks that make me flinch and rush to assess the potential damage they've caused. My squad watches as I shift each one and smooth a hand over the tiles beneath to make sure there are no dents or chunks taken out before pinning each and every one of them beneath a look that speaks to how on edge I am.

"Careful," I warn.

"You got it, Lieutenant," Hart calls, adjusting her baseball cap and the loose tool belt around her waist.

"You break it, you fix it. I appreciate you all coming to help me with this, but my fuse is short today."

"Just today? I thought you were going to start taking swings at Cap when he tossed you on desk duty last shift," Adams says, feeding into my displeasure with that reminder.

Desk duty has never been the end of the world. But to me, it feels like it more often than not. I'm too on edge riding the desk. I like to be out there saving lives, not locked inside while I watch my squad rush out in their turnouts with sirens blaring.

That's not to say I didn't deserve it. My attitude was piss-poor all last shift, and I'm positive it was the events of the day before that did my head in. Everything I was capable of doing before she came back into my life is impossible to accomplish now without her by my side. Her refusal to use my SUV instead of her rental is only another thing that I'm stressing over.

I've spent the last four days with my mind running fucking rampant with ways to convince her to let me help, but ever since speaking to my dad yesterday, I've shifted gears to what I can do to prove myself to her instead. And while finishing her shop up for her isn't the only thing I want to do, it's somewhere to start.

Mom told me she's taking Avery to meet with a lawyer today to finalize the terms of custody she's proposing to Chris. It was music to my ears. Pride flooded me at the strength and confidence it's taking for her to put her foot down with him.

Avery hasn't been to the shop in days, and I had Mom promise me that she'd try to keep her busy enough to avoid it for another three. By the time I'm off next shift, this place will be ready for her.

My squad didn't hesitate to offer me their help, and they'll never know how much that means to me.

"I'd take a swing at you, not Cap," I answer Adams.

He laughs brashly. "Yeah, yeah. Just tell us what you need."

"I ordered new countertops for the front desk and break room that should be arriving in a few minutes if one of you can help with the install. The flower cooler needs to be scrubbed clean before the new shelves go up, and there's some furniture in the back of my uncle's truck parked out front that's got to be brought inside, along with a new vanity for the bathroom."

"I've got the countertop. Do you want to wait to bring the stuff from the truck inside until after that's installed?" Patel asks, leaning back against the wall.

"If we bring it all in and set it along the one wall, it should be out of the way for the countertops. They're marble, so they weigh a shit ton. If you need an extra set of hands, just let me know," I answer.

Three more members of my squad volunteer to scrub up the cooler and bathroom and, without hesitation, head for the sink to fill the buckets I brought with soap and water.

Adams looks past me and stares questioningly at the guy that pulls the shop door open and steps inside. I extend my hand toward him once I read the business name on his shirt.

"Countertop guy?" Adams asks.

With a shake of my hand, the guy says, "Travis, but yes. You got an extra set of hands for me?"

"It's ready to go?" Patel asks before striding toward Travis and walking with him outside.

"It's you and me on lifting duty, then?" Adams knocks his shoulder against mine.

Hart steps up in front of us. "What do you want me on?"

"Avery likes you the most out of everyone. Are you up for a more personal job?"

"She doesn't like her most," Adams grunts.

Hart rolls her eyes at him. "Yes, she does. But your opinion doesn't matter, anyway. What do you need from me, Lieutenant?"

"Have you ever designed a kids' corner before?"

"No, but I'm up for the challenge. What do I need to know?"

I aim to dump the info on her quickly but wind up spending twenty minutes telling her about all things Nova. From her obsession with frogs, sprinkles on her pancakes, and ballet to her fear of the dark and courage to be the one to take care of the spiders that appear in the house. Some of the information isn't useful for the task I've given, but that isn't enough to stop me.

Even after Hart's started to grin at me, her head shaking slightly, I don't end my ramble. Only once I've momentarily run out of things to say do I finally trail off.

She dips out of the shop before I can dig back into my head

and find something else to say, but that doesn't mean I let it go. The opposite, actually.

I ignore the people moving around me and come up with another part of my plan, this one meant just for Nova.

"I'll be suing you for the injuries to my back after today, Bateman," Adams groans after we move the second pink armchair into position.

"If you think this is too much strain for your back, maybe it's time to consider retirement."

"I'll retire when I'm dead."

I make a deep, humoured noise in the back of my throat. "No point in retiring if you're already dead."

"I'm only a few years older than you, jackass."

"In mind or body?"

"Both."

"If you say so."

"I could bench-press you in my sleep," he boasts.

"You're talking out of your ass."

"I think I actually prefer when you don't speak. The days when you'd just grunt and mumble were some of the best of my life."

I adjust the placement of the glass-topped coffee table and grunt in reply before leaving him waiting for an answer. The shop smells like lemon cleaner, and while it isn't completely ready for any type of grand opening, it's close.

I left the last few tasks for Avery to complete. This is her space, and all the finishing touches and decisions should be hers to make.

The two armchairs and coffee table tucked in the corner and in front of a wall of shelving units were the only pieces of furniture outside of the several sets of shelves that I took a chance on filling the space with. They're the same pale shade of pink as the Swedish flowers she named the place after, and when Mom tested the comfortability of them at the shop this morning, she was quick to tell me to buy them before someone else did.

Now that they're here, I know I made the right decision.

Most of my squad has cleared out now, leaving just Adams and me waiting for Hart to finish setting up Nova's corner of the shop.

"What do you think, Oliver?" she asks, noticing I'm no longer bickering with Adams. "Think Nova will like it?"

"She will."

The round table Hart grabbed from the store earlier has been put together and painted with tiny frogs, a variation of Swedish flowers that I researched last night, ballet slippers, and scattered multicoloured sprinkles. It's not much—not yet—but it will be. For now, it's a piece of home brought here for Nova.

"You really love Avery's little girl, huh?"

It's Hart who asks the question, but Adams stares at me too, waiting for an answer.

"Yes." It doesn't feel sufficient enough.

Adams sits on one of the pink chairs and leans forward with his elbows on his knees. "Is there any update on the father?"

"Not yet."

They don't know much about it, and for now, I want to keep it that way. Avery doesn't need them knowing all the gritty details.

"My dad was a piece of shit. Sometimes they aren't worth a place in our lives," Hart says.

"It'll be Avery's choice and then Nova's. Whatever they choose, I'll be there for them."

She smiles up at me from the floor. "You're a good man."

"It feels like the bare minimum."

"That's because you're a stand-up guy. Grumpy as fuck sometimes, but you're good shit. Honest and honourable. Sometimes, even the bare minimum of qualities can be hard to find because everyone wants to be an asshole," Adams says.

"I don't want an award for being a decent person. I just want them."

"Swoon," Hart mumbles.

"Don't fawn over him, Hart. He's already too arrogant for his own good," he scolds her.

I cock a brow. "I thought I was a stand-up guy? Which is it?"

He stands and drags his big body toward me. With a deadpan expression, he tugs me into a hug.

"You've done good by them. I can't wait to spend more time getting to know your family, Lieutenant."

A surprising swell of emotion comes after his words register, and I clear my throat before returning the hug and slapping his back.

"Thank you."

"I still have hope Avery will be able to knock that grumpiness right out of you."

"You'd miss it," I say.

"Ain't that the sad truth. I'll see you in the morning for shift. Try not to get stuck on desk this time, yeah? Missed you calling the shots out there."

When he pulls back and pushes his hair out of his eyes, I jerk my chin in agreement. "I'll be fine."

"And for the love of God, make sure this is the last shift without Avery waiting for you at home. I can't take sad Oliver anymore," he adds.

"That's the plan."

"Great. If you need anything else, don't ask me. I need to sit in a hot bath until work tomorrow." He waves at Hart. "Finish with your arts and crafts and get home, rookie. You don't get points for coming into work exhausted."

She flips him off before collecting the paintbrushes on the table into a plastic cup. "See you tomorrow, sunshine."

Adams whistles while he leaves, and a minute later, Hart starts shoving all of her stuff into her purse. I take the paper plate with paint swirled over it and dump it into the garbage bag by the counter.

"They'll love this, Oliver. It was a nice gesture," she says.

"Hopefully. Anything less and I'll be figuring out something else to do."

"If you need any help with that, I'm up for the challenge."

"Thanks, rookie."

"Becs works. Even Rebecca."

"You'll be rookie for a long while still. Better to get used to it."

She huffs. "Right."

"I'll see you tomorrow morning."

"Good night, Lieutenant."

I hold the door open for her as she steps out onto the street and disappears into a tiny car. Once she's gone, I turn the lock on the door and survey the changes to the shop.

It's so close to the finish line.

I just hope I am too.

39

Avery

"Thank you, Gracie," I say, leaning my arms against the rim of the unrolled window.

The Range Rover is fancy enough that I feel bad touching it this way, but the position helps keep my back to the building behind me, a boundary held in place for a couple of minutes longer.

Gracie slips her designer sunglasses up into her hair and winks at me. "I'm always up to play driver for you, sweetheart."

"Can I just stand here for a second?"

"You can stand there for as long as you need. I'm in no rush."

I offer her a slight smile. The papers in my hand are thick and heavy. "What do you think he'll do when I tell him what I want?"

"Nothing that'll make you feel like you've made the right call, I'm sure. But you have, Avery. This is what's best for both you and Nova."

"I know that deep down. Nova needs stability and security in her life, not disappointment and uncertainty. But I also worry she'll be upset with me. What if he tries to turn her against me for this?"

"If he dared try to do that, he'd disappear off the face of the Earth. That's something else I'm sure of," she declares.

"I'm not sure if I should be flattered by the prospect of someone killing him for me."

"Nobody said anything about killing."

I breathe a laugh and pat my hands on the door. "You don't have to wait for me while I do this."

"I'm not going anywhere. I'll be here when you're done."

"Alright. Be right back," I say with a final calming inhale that doesn't help settle me in the slightest.

"Pin his ass to the wall, Avery. He deserves it."

I carry her words with me up Chris' sidewalk and into the entrance of his apartment building. With a jab of my finger to the number of his apartment on the keypad, I wait for him to buzz me in.

After the text I sent him an hour ago, he's expecting me. But even so, he keeps me waiting down in the entrance for three minutes before unlocking the door for me.

"Fucking asshole," I mutter.

There's no elevator in this place, so I take the stairs, climbing the two flights of them slower than ever as I repeat my speech in my mind another three times.

It's memorized, but I know the moment he opens his mouth and starts speaking, I'll forget every word I've rehearsed. His anger will trigger my fight or flight, but I'll stay and fight like I always do. Harder now than I ever did before.

The door to his apartment is already open when I hit the third floor and start down the hall. Arms crossed and his back leant against the doorframe, he keeps me in his sight and watches every step I take toward him.

In his usual jeans and hoodie, he looks lanky. The opposite of Oliver.

"Who drove you here?" is the first thing he asks me.

"Hello, Chris."

He moves aside to let me in before closing the door. "It's a nice car. Yours?"

"No. It's Oliver's mother's car."

"Of course it is."

I'm too busy taking in the sight of the home I haven't seen the inside of in years to respond to his goading words.

While the building itself is outdated, the owners have done a good job of keeping the apartments themselves updated. There's a small L-shaped kitchen with a single-doored white fridge and an oven to match, nice windows that overlook a man-made swamp, and a small but cozy living space that used to be covered head to toe in family photos but is now empty, bland.

Surrey holds a number of memories for me, majority of which were made here, in this apartment. But this isn't the place it was then, and it never will be again.

"Where do you keep all of Nova's things? Locked away in her room?" I ask bluntly.

"They make the place feel smaller. When she's not here, they're put away."

"Is that the real reason, or do you just not want those you invite over to know you have a daughter at all?"

His nostrils flare. "If you've already made your own conclusions, why bother asking?"

The papers in my hand grow heavier, every slight crinkle of them reminding me of why I came here. The forty-five-minute drive from Vancouver to Surrey isn't going to be wasted.

With one large step forward, I shove the papers into his chest and wait for him to reach for them before hissing, "This is our new custody agreement. Read it over and sign by every tabbed line. If you don't agree, we'll try mediation, and if that still doesn't work, we'll go to a judge next. But you will never, ever threaten me with our daughter again, Chris. Is that clear?"

"What the fuck are you talking about?" he asks, wide-eyed and lips pressing together.

He scrolls over the writing on the front page of the agreement at lightning speed, and I feel incredibly smug to have pulled a reaction from him with this. It's about time he's felt the hard smack of reality.

Welcome to the club, asshole.

"I didn't come here because I missed you and Surrey, Chris. It was to make sure you knew that I'm done with you thinking you still have any pull or say in my life. Everything you need to know from now on is in that agreement. Including the extent of the contact between you and me."

Or lack thereof. Unless we're speaking about Nova, there won't be a word coming from either of us.

He flips through the next page and then the next, only pausing his searching when he stumbles upon the exact section I was expecting him to pay more attention to than any other.

"You're not asking for child support?"

I keep my expression blank. "No. I would rather you use that money to take care of Nova while she's here. There's more outlined in the agreement involving holidays."

"You're going to share them with me now?"

I swallow down a laugh. "No. But you will get a set day following every holiday to spend time with her. There are conditions, though, considering how little you've cared about celebrating them in the past. First, you'll receive a list of gift ideas from me for both her birthday and Christmas and be expected to get her at least one of those items. If you can't afford something, I'll send you the money needed. And if you take that money and still don't follow through, all holiday celebrations will be stripped from you."

The hit to his pride is obvious in the tightening of his jaw and flushing of his cheeks. I enjoy every single moment of his suffering.

It's been a long time coming for all of this, and it feels so incredibly freeing to be laying it all out there with a legal team and family at my back. The repercussions of his lack of care and responsibility have weighed on me for years, but no more. That ends today. It's time to move on from him and the hold he's had on me and Nova.

"And second," I continue, spine straight, "if she declines celebrating with you, that's that. That counts for everything, even outside of holidays.

"Fuck up one too many times, and she'll decide you're not worth her time, Chris. And I'm going to be there supporting her every step of the way. This is serious. It's not a game where you can lose and come back over and over again to try to win. If you keep hurting her the way you have been, it will be game over. No more chances. You'll lose her forever, and I won't be here for you encouraging her to reconsider her decision."

Flipping through to the next and final page, he glances up at me and flicks his tongue to wet his lips. I cringe at the weird nervous habit of his and seriously consider what was wrong with me to think that this man was what I wanted, both emotionally and sexually.

"I'll need a lawyer of my own to look over this. If I decide it's all worth agreeing to," he grumbles.

"You can have two weeks."

"Fine."

"Are you still good to take her this weekend?"

"Am I allowed to?"

I slowly exhale, keeping calm. "Yes, you're allowed to see her. Every second weekend will still be yours, as long as there are no more early drop-offs. She was really fucking hurt when you discarded her as if she wasn't anything more than baggage last time. It's stuck with her."

"Something came up."

"Yeah, I bet. It doesn't matter now. Just be at the house on Saturday morning at nine. If you're late, you can wait another two weeks. I'm done with the babying. You're a grown man and a father to a seven-year-old girl who wants to spend time getting to know her father. I'm begging you to act like it and quit letting her down every chance you get. She won't be a little girl forever. You'll look back on these days years from now and wish you hadn't acted this way."

"And you and Oliver?" he asks after a beat of silence, avoiding my eyes and staring down at the papers in his hands. "That's for real? It's serious?"

My brain lags at the . . . sincerity in the question. The lack of judgment and fire in his tone is startling. Unexpected to the point of confusion.

"It's serious," I answer, keeping my tone strong yet still gentle. "He's not going anywhere. He'll be in our lives for . . . Well, for a long time, I hope."

It looks like it pains him to speak, but when he does, the jealousy I expect isn't there. "Okay. I'll see you Saturday."

"Yeah, maybe."

I take the break in arguing to head out, only lingering for long enough to blurt out the last thought in my head before I lose my confidence.

"For what it's worth, Chris, I really hope you get your shit together. For Nova. She deserves both of her parents in her life."

He doesn't have a chance to reply before I open the door and leave, feeling lighter than I did when I arrived. Hopeful, even. The remaining weight on my chest doesn't have anything to do with Chris and all to do with the man he was asking about.

It's been a brutal few days without him. My bed is cold and empty, and Nova's laugh is missing the special jingle it has when Oliver's helped pull it out of her.

I've swayed away from the takeout meals and have managed to pull myself together enough to use the air fryer, clear out the overflowing containers of leftovers from the fridge, and tuck Nova into bed on time. All of my wineglasses are washed and back in the cupboard, and when one of the local baseball teams came by asking for bottle donations, I let them load up the empty wine bottles into the truck they drove down the road.

The bill from the lawyer was hard to stomach, but paying it felt like an accomplishment. A step in the right direction.

There's only one more thing to do now. One more person to speak to and spill the contents of my mind and soul in front of. I thought I could wait until Oliver got off shift tomorrow, but as I pick up speed down the stairs, excited at the mere thought of seeing him right now, I doubt that I can.

Breaking free of the apartment building, I jog down the sidewalk and to Gracie. She looks up from her phone the moment I open the door and fling myself in beside her.

"Can you take me to the firehouse?"

40

TWELVE YEARS AGO

Matt

"*PAPPA, ÄR VI NÄSTAN FRAME?*"

"Are you suddenly ten years old again?" I ask, turning the steering wheel with a loose hold. "And you should try to focus on speaking English when we get to the house. Nobody will be able to understand you otherwise."

My daughter rolls her eyes at me in the rear-view mirror, and I chuckle at the attitude. It's a new trait of hers that's appeared over the past six months. I always thought teenagers stayed nice and sweet if they were angels as children, but apparently, that's a load of bullshit I told myself to soothe my worries.

At least she isn't as terrible as her mother was at eighteen. Lord help us all if that were the case.

"They could have taken Swedish lessons," she says.

Morgan twists to look into the back seat. "Don't start, Avery. You know that's not fair."

Our daughter reaches a hand up to fiddle with her nose ring. Fuck, I hate that thing. One tug from someone and it would rip right out. I'll never let Morgan forget that she was the one who snuck her out to get it done, knowing I wouldn't like it.

The black hair and makeup . . . fine. It makes her happy, and she's still my beautiful princess, no matter what she wears or does with her hair. But the piercing is a hazard that damn well keeps me up at night.

"Do you think they still remember me?" Avery asks, voice softer, almost embarrassed.

I snap my eyes to the mirror, but she's not looking into it this time. "Of course they do, *mitt hjärta*. Why would you even ask that?"

"We've been gone a year."

"A year is nothing. Not to family," Morgan murmurs, reaching back to hold Avery's knee.

"We don't really text that much," Avery adds.

I'm immediately pissed off. "Who? You and Maddox?"

She shrugs, staring out the window as the highway turns to gravel. "Him and Cooper. Oliver sometimes."

"Is that such a bad thing? You don't need to be texting boys, anyway. Especially not Maddox," I say.

My wife huffs. "Don't start, Matthew."

"Yeah, *Matthew*," Avery echoes.

"I'll pull the car over and let the two of you walk to the Huttons' if you'd like?"

Morgan pats my arm lovingly, but I read the threat in the action. "You know I don't walk on gravel. I'm in flip-flops."

"And what's your excuse?" I ask Avery, brows quirked.

"I don't walk in general."

I chuckle, flicking my blinker on before turning onto the Huttons' driveway. The over-the-top rocky road that leads to the giant ranch house was Oakley's attempt at giving them more privacy, as if living outside city limits doesn't already accomplish that.

"Back to the boys," I start, ignoring my wife's frustration with me. "From what I hear, Maddox is prepping for the NHL draft, and Cooper's buried his head in his paintings, prepping for school. It's not anything personal, baby girl. And I know if the girls were old enough to have phones, they'd be texting you like crazy."

I'll never forgive my friends for not having girls first like Morgan and me. Instead, they all decided to have boys as if they were wanting to punish me. Selfish pricks, each and every one of them.

Tinsley is the closest girl in age to Avery, but even then, there's still a five-year gap. No eighteen-year-old wants to chat with a thirteen-year-old. Instead, I'm left to suffer while she talks to the boys.

Tyler's son, especially. That fucker is only fourteen, but I've heard all about his little crush on my daughter. I should tell his father to take his phone away so he can't text her. Hell, he should lock him in his room until he grows out of this phase. Who gives a fourteen-year-old a phone, anyway?

Sure, that's when Avery got her first phone, but she's my baby girl. The rules are different for her.

"So, you're saying they're just too busy for me now. Nice. Thanks, Dad," Avery snaps, narrowing her blue eyes on mine in the mirror before crossing her arms and turning to face the window.

Morgan slaps my thigh, and I glance at her in disbelief.

"What did I do? That's not what I meant, Avery."

"It's what you said!" she shouts, threading her fingers in her black hair. "They're going to forget all about me because we're only here once a year!"

"Honey, nobody is going to forget about you. I think you're underestimating how much everyone loves you," Morgan soothes.

One look into the back seat as the gravel becomes pavement, and my heart seizes. Tears shine in her eyes, one slipping out to smudge her black eyeliner. She uses the tip of her thumb to carefully swipe it away, lips in a tight line.

I keep my apology tucked inside as I drive us past the cluster of vehicles on the driveway and then bring the rental car to a stop along the edge of it, out of the way. A burst of pride fills me when I see the familiar faces waiting outside the front door of the house.

"If everyone forgot about you, then why are they all outside waiting for us to arrive?" I ask.

She leans forward in her seat and looks out the windshield, tears drying quickly. A small smile tugs at her mouth before growing into a massive, teeth-sparkling grin.

Without another word, she whips the door open and takes off down the pavement, running as fast as possible in her untied Converse. Maddox is the first to hug her, and while Oakley and I thought—or hoped—that they'd wind up together when they were only kids, it's obvious now that that would never happen.

Not only is Maddox in love with someone else, but my little girl isn't into jocks. They make one hell of a pair of friends, though. And she needs that.

"Do you ever wish we had stayed in Canada?" Morgan asks, watching everyone welcome our daughter.

There's a sadness in her expression that worries me. I'd do anything to fix every single problem she's ever had. Exterminate everything that doesn't bring her happiness. I've spent a long damn time trying to do that, but there's still forever left.

"No. I don't. We did the right thing, Mo. And something tells me that she'll be coming back here sooner than we'd like her to."

Avery's passed from person to person, getting smothered in hugs and kisses on the head. Oakley ruffles her hair, and Jamie, Tyler's youngest son, stands on his tiptoes to plant his lips to her cheek. My attention is focused on Oliver, though.

He's the last one to speak to her, waiting patiently with his hands tucked into the pockets of his jeans. There's a glow in his eyes when he meets her gaze that's hardly noticeable. Invisible to everyone but me. My spine snaps straight up in my seat.

It seems I've underestimated this so-called *crush* Maddox told me about. No fourteen-year-old should look at someone like that. They shouldn't know how.

Fuck.

41

Oliver

I FINISH ROLLING THE HOSE SECONDS BEFORE ADAMS IS there, hauling it over his shoulder. The second is already laid out flat for me, and I drop to my haunches to start on it. Every two pushes, I look up at the clock on the wall and hope that it'll have jumped forward to tomorrow morning.

Only one more shift, and I'll be heading home to my girls. I'm done with the space, and I'm ready to tell Avery exactly that.

I'm here in her life to stay, and it's way too fucking late to go back now. There never was an opportunity for it in the first place. Not with us.

She's stuck with me now, and I'm prepared to tell her that. That there isn't any future for me that doesn't involve her sass and Nova's giggles. I'm ready to put it all on the line for her without a single doubt that this is the right choice.

My pulse is strong, excitement buzzing beneath my skin at the thought of holding her in my arms again and kissing her so hard she'll feel my mouth against hers long after we've pulled apart. She's etched her name in my ribs, but now I want to do the same to hers.

I finish the second hose and shift to start on the third one before I realize that Adams is back, watching with an all-too-knowing expression.

Dropping my attention back to the hose line, I grunt, "If you'd prefer to roll, just say so."

"Not a fucking chance. My back still hurts from the other day."

"Then stop watching me."

"But it's so fun watching you work for a change."

I shove the growing roll of hose hard and turn my head to blink at him. "For a change?"

"Been a minute since I've seen you sweat."

"There's already enough of my sweat on this floor."

"Yet, here you are. Rolling hose is for probies, Lieutenant. Why isn't Hart doing it?"

I'm growing breathless, and it's obvious in my weak reply. "Because she doesn't need to do it today. I've got it."

He bends to grip the second rolled hose and laughs. I ignore the noise and finish the third hose before shifting to the last one. By the time he's hauled the second one over his shoulder, I've double-checked the fourth for any kinks and started rolling.

"You've been in a better mood the past couple of days. Fixing up that shop helped, right?" he asks.

"I'm excited to get out of here and see my family, Brent."

He glances out of the engine bay, and his smirk grows so big it's goofy-looking. "I don't think you'll be waiting much longer."

The teasing tone is enough to encourage me to follow his line of sight, focusing on the woman on the other side of the windowed wall. My legs move of their own accord, forcing me to abandon my task.

"Don't worry, I'll finish up for you!" Adams calls, and I shove my hand behind me in a wave of acknowledgment.

The door to the office is the last boundary between us, and once I've torn it open, Avery turns to look at me. The rookie at the desk is quick to hop up out of his chair and leave as I quicken my pace.

With her soft blonde hair curled down her back and tucked behind her ear, she smiles wide. I wrap her in my arms and tug her close. Fully enveloped by my body, she laughs, and the blissful sound of it burrows itself into my soul.

Dragging my hand up her back, I cup her nape and gently guide her head back just enough for our eyes to meet. Electric blue, my favourite colour for as long as I can remember.

"What are you doing here?" I ask, unashamed of how deep my voice has gotten. How desperate I sound.

She presses her palms to my chest and, at a snail's pace, drifts them up to twine around my neck. On her tiptoes, she kisses my chin just once.

"I missed you."

"As simple as that? You missed me?"

"Do I need something more than that to want to visit you?"

My laugh is brash, filling the entrance to the station. "No, princess. You don't."

"I just couldn't wait until tomorrow. You're busy, so I won't stay long, but . . . I needed to come, even for a couple of minutes."

"Because you *missed* me?" I ask, pushing, digging further.

Humour lights more than just her eyes. Her entire expression has become brighter since the last time I saw her, like the clouds that used to veil her happiness have been lifted. She looks free, the way she did when we were just little kids.

"Missing you is just the beginning, *butternalle*." She leans further forward, using me to stabilize herself. Her lips taste like oranges when they touch mine. "My grumpy bear."

The name registers a moment too late. She's kissing me with a fierceness that sets fire to my blood before I can comment on the meaning of my nickname. Running my fingers through the hairs at the base of her neck, I slip my tongue into her mouth to remind her of my claim. Not just on these soft lips but over every inch of her. Mind, body, and soul, she's mine the way I've always been hers.

"Come with me," I whisper, dipping a hand to wrap around

hers. "I don't know how long we'll have, but I can't let you walk out of here without telling you what I need to."

She lets me pull us into the bunk room with a soft noise of agreement and waits with her hand in mine as I shut the door behind us and twist the lock.

"We could have ten minutes or two, but—"

My words die against her lips when she kisses me and strokes a finger along my jaw. "There's no rush. I'm not going anywhere other than back home to wait for you."

"Fuck, Avery," I breathe out. "If you say shit like that to me again, I'll lose my mind."

"I've already lost mine."

With a shake of my head, I grab her hands and hold them between us, letting them anchor my thoughts. If she keeps touching me freely, I'll have her beneath me on one of these beds before we've even started speaking.

"I love you, Avery Miller. But I also love your daughter. I've been struggling with how to describe to you just how much it means to me that you've let me into not only your life but into her life. The two of you . . . you've filled this aching, empty spot inside of my chest that I'd grown used to ignoring. I'm no longer lonely, my life dull and bland, because with the two of you, it's impossible for my cup to be anything short of overflowing.

"Our connection goes soul-deep, baby. You're mine on a molecular level. I'll never understand how it happened or why, but I do know that it means you're stuck with me for the rest of our lives."

"Oliver," she whispers, her nails tracing the undersides of my fingers.

"I have a few promises to make you."

"Promises?"

I hum, hovering my lips over hers but never quite touching them. "I've spent the past week kicking myself for not making these to you the very first night you fell asleep on my couch and I carried you to my bed because you deserve to hear them all.

There's never been a doubt in my mind that you were it for me, Avery, but I want you to know that until I can slip a ring on your finger, I'm completely fucking yours."

"I already believe you," she declares, cheeks flushed.

"Humour me, then. Please."

She grazes her teeth along her bottom lip before nodding. "Okay."

"I've said it before, but I know you're a woman who appreciates action more than words, so until I can make good on all of these promises, my words are all I have." I lift our hands and unlink our fingers before guiding hers to rest against my chest. My heart jumps against my sternum. "You've gone through too many experiences alone, struggled with hard decisions, and have carried enough weight on your shoulders to buckle a grown man's knees, but I promise from today on, that's going to change.

"I want to be by your side through every bad day and be there to witness your smile on the best ones. You no longer have to be both the good and bad guy. Choose one and give me the other. We do things together. And all that weight you've been carrying, baby, shrug it off and pass it over. I'm strong enough to handle the bulk of it while you get some rest. Then, we'll split it straight down the middle. There's no more suffering alone. Not anymore. We're a team."

A tear leaks from the corner of her eye, but I thumb it away before it falls down her cheek. With a shaky inhale, she curls her fingers in my shirt and grips it tight.

"That all sounds . . . It sounds perfect, Oliver. But what about Nova? Where does she fit into all of this? There isn't anything I want more than this. For you to make good on all of these promises to me, but with a daughter, it isn't going to be an easy road," she says cautiously, but there's an optimism there that I latch onto.

"I know I won't ever be Nova's father. I'd never overstep that boundary. Chris can have his title. What I want to be to her is whatever and anything she wants me to be. The one thing I can promise you right now is that I will love her with everything in me and will always only be one call away. From now on, she will always have my love, support, and care," I declare. "You asked me weeks ago if I knew what I wanted my life to look like in ten years, and baby, the only right answer to that question is you and Nova."

"And down the road, if Nova chose to think of you as another father figure? If that life you dream of becomes a reality?" Avery asks, her voice a near whisper.

"Then I'd be grateful she loves me even half as much as I love her."

With a blink, she leans her forward against my chin. "I love you, Oliver Bateman."

"I love you, Avery Miller. Soon to be Bateman."

"Soon to be? That's presumptuous of you. It's only been a couple of months," she teases, breath bathing my throat.

"It was always meant to be Bateman."

"My father wouldn't agree."

"Your father's always known I wanted you."

She leans back, eyes wide as they lock onto mine. "What? No, he hasn't."

"The summer you visited when you were eighteen, he called me out on it behind the Huttons' garden shed," I say.

"He never said anything. Neither of you did."

"I doubt he wanted you to know that he threatened to beat my fourteen-year-old ass if I even thought of looking at you again," I grunt.

She laughs, relenting. "Well, you didn't listen to him either way. You were always hanging around all of us."

"No. I didn't listen. And I still wouldn't."

"I wouldn't want you to."

"What is it you want me to do, Avery?" I ask lowly, curving a hand around her hip, loving the way she wiggles in my grip, pressing further into it.

Her stare flicks to the bunk bed closest to us. My cock throbs, stiffening in a matter of seconds. I swallow a groan.

"How much time do we have before—"

The fire alarm blares, cutting her off. She gasps at the noise, and the dispatcher's voice follows, explaining the call. My pulse spikes, and then I'm moving.

I kiss her too quickly, but she melts into me like I'm taking my time. It's painful to pull back, and I have to remind myself that tomorrow, there won't be anywhere for either of us to run.

"Go. Be a hero," she says with a shove to my chest.

Walking backward to the door, I point at her. "Tomorrow, princess."

"Tomorrow," she agrees, and the kiss she blows is the last thing I see before ducking out of the room.

It's the image that stays with me for the rest of the night.

EPILOGUE

Avery

NOVA PUSHES ME ALONG THE SIDEWALK, HER GIGGLES loud and proud for everyone to hear ten kilometres away. The blindfold Gracie helped her tie around my head is snug, making the world pitch-black. With my arms outstretched, I focus on not stumbling on the uneven concrete.

"Please don't make me trip," I plead with them both.

Nova giggles again and stops pushing so hard on my back. "Sorry, Mom."

"It's okay, sweetheart. I'm excited too."

"Me three, and I already know what's waiting for you," Gracie says.

"Oliver's here, right?"

I sound as shy as I do hopeful. After seeing him at the station yesterday, I've been antsy, to say the least. Sleep didn't come easy last night, and I tossed and turned for hours with his voice speaking soft promises to me in my mind.

Maybe I should have just gone over and barged into his house after watching his SUV pull up his driveway last night, but the anticipation almost makes this... sweeter.

Now, I'm just ready to take off down the sidewalk and run into his arms. He'll catch me. There's no doubt about it.

"He's here. About ready to crash through the door and grab you, from what I see," Gracie teases.

I make note of the tidbit of information and pay attention to anything else that can give away our location. A long sidewalk and noisy street that smells like freshly ground coffee...

"Is he done with his work now?" Nova asks, her Crocs making scuffing noises on the sidewalk.

"He's done, sweetie pie. I'm sure he won't leave the two of you alone now until he has to go back."

I don't make a habit of pulling Nova out of school early, but when I stepped onto the porch this morning to a box of Nova's favourite cookies and a bouquet of flowers so massive they were hardly contained in their crystal vase, I would have said yes to just about anything.

He didn't have to ask me to pull her out early, and I doubt he ever would. The moment I saw the handwritten note tucked into the flowers with all of the information for today, I made that choice all on my own.

I want her to be here for whatever it is he has planned, and she didn't have any arguments about a half day of school.

"Okay!" Nova squeaks. Her pace quickens.

A warm, dainty hand wraps around mine and leads me forward until we come to a stop. My heart jumps into my throat when I hear the sound of a door opening and feel the brush of wind on my face from its swing.

The scent of lemon hits me first. It's a gut feeling, a tingle at the back of my neck that tells me where we are. A sense of rightness fills me, and I smile without hesitation.

"Hi, Ollie!" Nova shrieks, hands falling from my back as her shoes scuff the ground again.

Oliver's low, gruff laugh brings goosebumps to my arms. "Hey, peanut. Thank you for getting your mom here for me."

"You're welcome," Nova says before a soft jingling fills the shop. "I made this for you, Ollie."

A pause. "For my keys?"

"Yep. Mom has some too. I made you a blue one!"

My throat tightens. Without looking, I know she's handed him the key chain she made last night before bed.

"I love it. Thank you, Nova."

"You're welcome!"

What do you say we take her blindfold off now? Then you can help me put this on my keys?"

"Can I?"

"'Course you can."

More shoe scuffing, and then I feel her behind me. I bend at the knees so she can reach the tie of the blindfold easier. She gives it a tug, and it falls to the floor.

Blinking at the sudden light in my eyes, I release a laugh. "Thank you, Nova."

"Look, Mom. Look!"

I search for Oliver first. He's already looking at me when I find him, his eyes bright and clear. There isn't a smirk or a scowl on his lips, but a smile. A wide, happy one that spears right through my chest.

"Princess," he murmurs.

"*Butternalle.*"

"Did you like the flowers?"

"There were no roses again," I tease.

"I'll tuck one inside next time if you're missing them that badly."

"Next time?"

He moves, coming closer to me. "I'd spend my last dollar buying flowers for you, Avery."

The declaration is spoken without hesitation, another promise that buries itself deep in my soul.

A sniffle comes from beside me, and I turn my head to look at Gracie. Her tear-streaked cheeks are alarming to me, but Oliver only shakes his head at her, humour lining his expression.

"Need a moment, Ma?" he asks her.

She rolls her eyes at him and pats at her cheeks with the back of her hand. "I'll be in the backroom to give you some time alone."

"There are tissues by the sink," Oliver teases before she steps into the other room with a light punch to his shoulder.

I watch her leave and then finally allow myself the time to look around the shop. Each new addition makes me feel one breath away from following after Gracie and bursting into tears.

It's far from what it was the last time I was here. A real flower shop is what it is now. One with life and colour and love embedded in the painted walls.

"Wow," I breathe.

"Do you like it?" Oliver asks softly.

"I love it. It's . . . beautiful. Perfect."

Everything from the new countertop installed, floor-to-ceiling shelving units built along the wall, and soft yellow curtains hung on the window was purchased with thought and care. I turn in a slow circle, taking in all of the new changes, when I see one that has me sucking in a breath.

Nova's Corner has been painted in colourful cursive on the wall above a small table and chairs decorated with matching doodles. Frogs, ballet slippers, tutus, flowers, and a plate of red Jell-O have been painted on the tabletop. The two chairs have small pink pillows on the seats to match the armchairs on the other side of the shop.

"Did you do this yourself?" I ask, dragging my palm over the back of a chair.

"I had help. Rebecca painted the table and helped pick out the furniture. All I wanted was for Nova to have someplace for herself here. I know that you'll want her here with you as much as possible, and this way, you can both have your own space. You can work, and she can draw or read or anything she wants to do. I hope I didn't overstep," he says, reaching up to rub at the back of his neck.

Emotion clogs my throat as I nod and give a weak smile. Happiness overflows inside of me to the point I'm struggling not to choke on it.

"It's perfect, Oliver. Honestly. So perfect."

His grin is beaming, as if maybe his happiness is as striking as mine.

The pile of large Styrofoam plates and handful of paint bottles on the table have me turning to where Oliver's watching me with Nova at his side.

"What are these for?"

The two of them come my way, and then Oliver's taking my hand and bringing it to his lips. I hold my breath, watching him kiss each of my knuckles before releasing my hand in exchange for my waist. He holds it with a steady, sure grip, each one of his fingertips searing through my shirt and into my skin.

"While I made some changes and fixes to this place, it's still yours. I tried to keep that clear throughout every change I made or item I brought in. But this is for you and Nova. I thought you could finish the walls off with your handprints. To mark it as yours."

There's no stopping my tears now. They spill out with a vengeance, and the second a sob slips up my throat, he's frowning, hands holding my cheeks.

A smaller body pushes between us, and two arms wind around my chest before Nova's pressing her face to my stomach. I watch through a blurry gaze as Oliver curls his other arm around her and tucks us both into him.

"It's okay, Mom. I want to do it. Do you?" Nova asks.

Oliver holds my gaze and swipes his thumb over my flushed skin. I lean into the touch and close my eyes for a breath, more tears dripping.

When I open them again, he's still watching, waiting for me to tell him I don't like his idea. But that's not why I'm crying.

"It's a perfect idea, Oliver," I say on a shaky exhale, still gathering my bearings and confidence. "But I don't only want two handprints on these walls."

"What?"

Nova tips her head back to look at me, appearing just as confused as him.

"If we're going to mark this place, I want to do it as a family. And there's another member of our family now," I say.

Before Nova can ask questions, I remove her arms from around me and gather her hands in mine. She watches with interest as I drop to my haunches in front of her.

"Nova, baby, how would you feel if I said I wanted Oliver to be my boyfriend?"

She shrugs a shoulder, grinning. "Cool!"

I laugh softly. "Do you know what that would mean?"

"Yeah. You kiss each other."

"We would, yes. But it also means that he'll be around a lot. He would stay at the house sometimes and be there for breakfast and supper. And he'd even take you to ballet with me and pick you up from school from time to time."

Her eyes grow wide as she whips around to stare up at him. "Really?"

"Yeah, peanut. I'll be around for as long as you want me to be."

"So always! Yay! This is awesome," Nova shouts, launching herself into his arms. He holds her with ease, smoothing down her hair instead of ruffling it the way she hates.

I take another long look at them, memorizing the sight and bliss it brings me before dropping my eyes to the table once again. Picking up the bottle of yellow paint, I pop the cap and squirt a huge circle of it onto the centre of a plate.

"We're putting it in writing," I declare. "No take backs. No running."

Oliver sets Nova down beside me at the table and takes a plate before squirting blue paint onto it.

"To always having prank wars and laughing with each other," he says.

Nova, having watched us, reaches for the pink paint. Oliver offers her a plate of her own, and she squirts way too much paint onto the plate. I don't mention it.

"What do you want from me and Oliver, sweetheart?"

"Like, as a present?" she asks, setting the paint bottle back on the table.

Oliver stares down at her intently. "As a promise. What could we do to make you happy?"

"Oh," she mutters. "Can we go swimming in the ocean together?"

"We can go every single day if that will make you happy," he swears.

"Okay. I want to have funny stories to tell my friends."

The reminder of that conversation about Chris is painful, but I take it on the chin, knowing it's better to be reminded than for her to trap it down and pretend her feelings don't exist. I know she'll make a million memories with Oliver, many of them funny enough to tell her friends about.

Our future is bright, and while she doesn't fully understand what's happening yet, she will. And I know Oliver will make it easy for her to love him the way he loves her.

"Press your palm into the paint, and then put your hand on the wall, sweetheart. Oliver and I will put our handprints beside yours," I tell her.

She nods eagerly and smooshes her hand into the pink paint. I reach over and help when she presses too hard and the paint squishes up between her fingers.

Giggling, she lets me guide her hand to the wall beside where *Nova's Corner* is written. I instruct her to spread her fingers, and when she presses her palm to the wall, I smile.

"Perfect, Nova," I praise.

She pulls her hand from the wall and cheers before saying, "Your turn, Mom!"

I coat my hand in yellow paint and hover it over the wall, her handprint on my left. With soft pressure, I let my handprint join hers.

Oliver kisses the top of my head and keeps close while coating his hand and pressing it to the wall on the opposite side of Nova's, sandwiching hers between ours.

One hand big, one tiny, and the last medium-sized.

A family, now written in stone.

EXTENDED EPILOGUE
ONE YEAR LATER

Oliver

"Good morning, wife."

"Good morning, husband."

I stretch my arm out around Avery's body and tug her closer. The California-king-sized bed is too fucking big. I'd have preferred to spend our first night as Mr. and Mrs. Bateman with her sleeping right on top of me, but no. She awed over the size of this thing and tried to roll away in her sleep before I woke to a dark room and brought her right back into my arms.

As fucking if.

"You're insatiable," she coos, wiggling her ass back on my cock.

I'm painfully hard, and the feel of her naked body against mine doesn't help me soften at all. I lost track of how many times I was inside of her last night and early this morning, but I know it doesn't matter.

I want her again already. Have wanted her every day for as long as I can remember, and as of last night, I finally made that feeling permanent.

The band of her wedding ring is cool against my fingers when she links hers through them and presses them to her pregnant belly. The slight swell there still feels surreal. Like a dream.

"Yeah, I am. Are you sore?"

"Mm, not at all."

"Good." Slipping our hands down her belly and between her thighs, I uncurl my fingers and stroke her pussy. She's wet, slick with the same arousal that's beating in my chest like a kick drum. "Lift your leg, baby."

She does as I say and tucks it over mine, opening herself up to me. I give my cock a hard stroke and guide it between her legs, nudging the tip at her opening.

"Mrs. Bateman," I grunt before gliding deep.

She moans, drooping her head back along the pillow and reaching behind her shoulder to hold me. "Mr. Bateman."

"That feel good? Nice and full?"

"Yes," she whispers.

I press my lips to her shoulder, over the bruise left by my mouth last night. There are several of them scattered all over her body, but I clearly focused more on the visible parts of her, where I knew everyone could see.

Thrusting up gently, I bring my hand to her chest and squeeze her nipple, her pleasure obvious in the tightening of her walls around me. She arches back and wiggles in my hold, backing her ass into my groin with a whine.

"You're just as gone for this dick as I am for this perfect pussy, aren't you, wife? You were missing me inside of you, even after only a few hours," I rasp.

She quivers at my words. I curse into her skin and drag my tongue over her skin, tasting her. She tastes more like me than she does herself, and that fact goes right to my cock. I'm a possessive fuck, and I've never felt that as strongly as I do right now.

"I'll give you what you need. Keep squeezing me so fucking tight and I'll fill this needy pussy with cum, princess. Have you so full you're dripping on the sheets and down your thighs. Then, I'll carry you into the bathroom and do it all over again. If you weren't already pregnant, I'd have you there by the end of our honeymoon."

"Oliver, fuck," she cries, meeting me stroke for stroke with desperate jerks of her hips.

I nip at her throat and hum as my groin tightens. "Yeah, baby. You have to soak this cock before I give you what you want."

"Yes!" she shouts, nodding furiously.

Her orgasm comes on swift and strong. She's sensitive, and I've had over a year to learn how to get her there the way she wants. I know her body as well as she does, and I'll never get bored of bringing her this pleasure.

I give in to my release and come with rough groans in her ear. Buried to the hilt, I don't move as I fill her full of cum, each pulse shooting deep. It's intoxicating, and once I'm done, I remain this way for seconds, minutes, maybe.

"Is the baby okay?" I murmur, smoothing my hand over her belly.

She laughs at me. "The baby is perfectly fine. Just like I say every single time we have sex."

"You can never be too safe."

"She's perfect, Oliver," she says, satiating me.

The announcement that she was pregnant came three months ago after only one spent trying. After the night of the grand opening of Linnea and Lillies ten months ago, she was adamant about being unsure whether she wanted another child, but when Adalyn gave birth to a tiny baby girl she and Cooper named Valerie, she changed her mind in an instant. Baby fever hit her hard, and I agreed with no hesitation.

Being the second father figure in Nova's life has filled me with more purpose than anything else ever has. I love my role in her life, and I knew without a doubt that I was ready for a baby. Especially with the love of my life.

I kiss her neck, over the red mark I left. "And you? Are you perfect?"

She rolls to face me, and I relax my hold until she's comfortable. "I'm even better than perfect. Happy and loved. Grateful."

"Me too, princess."

"I am hungry, though."

I tuck her hair behind her ear and kiss her, revelling in the soft feel of her mouth.

"Then let's get you something to eat."

She shoves away from me and throws herself over the bed toward where the room service menu rests on the nightstand. I chuckle and sit against the headboard, watching her.

Goosebumps cover her arms, and in a blink, she reaches over the edge of the bed and grabs my dress shirt before slipping it on. Leaving it open, she sits cross-legged beside me and starts flipping through the menu.

With her hair messy and skin flushed, I can't help but stare at her, enamoured with how beautiful she looks with no effort. My wife, my life. My future.

"You're staring at me. I can feel it," she notes, not lifting her eyes from the menu.

"You're too beautiful to look away from."

Her lips tug into a smirk. "If you want me to order you extra hash browns, just say so."

"I always want extra hash browns, but that's not why I said that, and you know it."

She glances at me, her smirk slowly morphing into a demure smile. "I love you, Oliver."

"I love you too, princess."

"Now, waffles or pancakes?" she asks, tugging her lip between her teeth as she reads the menu.

I don't have time to answer before there are three knocks on our hotel room door. With a curious expression, she peels her attention from the menu and glances at the door. I kiss her cheek and step off the bed to tug on some underwear.

"I'll check who it is. You can order the waffles," I say.

She tugs the duvet over her bare legs and does up the buttons on my shirt up before I leave her in bed.

"Tell them to go away," she calls. "Unless it's your mom."

"If anything was wrong with Nova, she'd call first, baby."

"Still."

I nod and unlock the secondary lock on the door before pulling it open. My brother's face isn't one I was expecting to see this morning.

"Did you miss the memo where it's the day after my wedding? You're not supposed to bug me today," I tell him.

The smell of booze wafts off him, turning my stomach. One up-and-down look at his clothes tells me he hasn't so much as changed out of the ones from last night. Hasn't showered either.

"Sorry, that rule doesn't apply to me. This is an emergency. Now, scoot and let me in," he says, trying to weasel his body between mine and the speck of a gap available from him to enter the suite.

I set a hand on his shoulder and give him a light shove backward. "What's wrong with you?"

"Oh, you know. Nothing much."

"Don't play with me today, Jamieson."

He peeks over my shoulder into the room before I shift and block his view.

"I don't want to talk about it in the hall, Oliver. Let me in so nobody else hears this," he pleads, dropping his voice.

"Keep your eyes off my wife," I warn before letting him in.

I shut the door after us, and he ignores my warning, heading directly for the bed, where Avery's sitting watching us. She quirks a brow at me, and I shrug, choking off a huff halfway up my throat.

Jamie tosses himself onto my side of the bed, and I snort.

"Wouldn't sit there if I were you. Honeymoon and all," I say.

It takes him a minute to clue in to what I mean, and when he does, he hops off the mattress with his nose crinkled. "Fuck off, Oliver. I knew it smelled like sex in here."

"I'm going to the bathroom while you boys talk," Avery mutters, her cheeks red and gaze fixed on me with a heat I want to feel closer up.

I track her every move. "We won't be long."

"We might be," Jamie says.

She slips from bed, and when he doesn't immediately look away from her, I snap, "Eyes off my wife, asshole."

He boasts a laugh but brings his eyes my way. "Call her your wife again. I don't think you've said it enough yet."

"I'll call her my wife anytime I want to. Now, tell me what it is you need to so I can get back in bed with her."

His humour fades instantly. "I'm engaged."

I stare at him, deadpan.

"I'm not lying. Hand to God."

"We're not religious."

"Okay, hand to the fucking sun, then. I don't know. I'm not lying."

"Since fucking when are you engaged? To who?" I ask, maybe a bit too sharply. My head's spinning.

"I met her a couple of weeks ago. Nice girl."

I blink, my jaw slackening. "A nice girl? She's a nice girl? You asked someone to marry you, and the best you can do is say she's a nice girl?"

"Okay, she's a nice, gorgeous girl. Better? Fuck, don't bust my balls right now."

"You came here, Jamie. I'll bust your balls if I fucking want to because what the fuck did you do? You're not the marriage type. And you're surely not the asking a nice girl to marry you out of the blue type. Has Mom met her? Dad? I damn well haven't. You've gotten one too many concussions. I knew you should have stopped playing football."

He shoves his hands out in front of him and shakes his head, face paling. "Slow down. First, I've only had three concussions. And second, no. Nobody's met her but me. But that doesn't mean anything. We're getting married, and that's that. I just wanted you to know before the news went live tomorrow."

I balk. "The news?"

"Yeah. I'm announcing it tomorrow. It's happening."

"No. It's not. Call it off right now. I'll have Dad come over, and we can talk about it together," I declare, already hunting for my phone.

He grabs my wrist and tugs. "No. You're not calling Dad. I'm not telling them yet."

"What?" I shout.

"Don't yell!"

I scrub a hand down my face. "You've lost your mind."

"No, I haven't. You and I both know if I tell them, they'll convince me not to do this the same way that you are right now."

"If you want me to do anything other than convince you not to do this, then you need to tell me everything. You might be able to bluff your ass off to anyone else, but I'm not falling for it. Tell me what the fuck is going on, Jamieson, or I swear I'm going to call Mom and Dad and get them to come here right now."

He pales even further, turning a ghostly shade of white. The bathroom door squeaks open as Avery slips out and comes to my side, worry shining in her eyes when I look down at her.

Jamieson collapses on the small couch across the room and swallows before speaking. "Fine. But nobody learns about this. Not even our parents."

"Fine."

The explanation that tumbles from his mouth has me joining him on the couch, a wild next three months on the horizon for the Bateman family.

At least I'll have my wife at my side for this ride and every other to come.

THE END.

Thank you for reading His Greatest Treasure! If you enjoyed it, please leave a review on Amazon and Goodreads.

The fifth and final book in the Greatest Love series is coming early 2025. Jamieson Bateman is about to sunshine the hell out of you.

To be kept up to date on all my releases, check out my website!
www.hannahcowanauthor.com
If you have not read all of the original love stories in my crazy fictional world, now is the time to do so!

While you're waiting for more of these characters, jump into my backlist or start from the beginning of the Greatest Love series with Maddox and Braxton!
Want to read about a group of best friend's in the small town of Cherry Peak? There might be a few familiar characters that pop up from time to time ;)

(Second generation) - Greatest Love series:

His Greatest Mistake – Maddox and Braxton (Hockey romance)
Her Greatest Adventure – Adalyn and Cooper (Brothers bff, age gap romance)
His Greatest Muse – Noah and Tinsley (Rockstar x boxer romance)
His Greatest Treasure – Oliver and Avery
Her Greatest ?? – Jamieson and ?? (Marriage of convenience romance)

Translations

Butternalle - Grumpy Bear

"*Du är dramatiskt igen.*" - You're being dramatic again.

"*Hej min älskade.*" - Hello, my love.

"*Mitt hjärta.*" - My heart

"*Lägg dig ner med mig, butternalle.*" - Lay with me, grumpy bear.

"*Vad som helst.*" - Anything.

"*Jag vill inte att Pappa ska skada Ollie.*" - I don't want daddy to hurt Ollie.

"*Varför är det en man i ditt vardagsrum?*" Why is there a man in your living room?

"*Stilig.*" - Handsome

Swift Hat Trick trilogy:

Lucky Hit — Oakley and Ava (Hockey romance)

Between Periods (Novella and BH prequel)

Blissful Hook — Tyler and Gracie (Hockey romance)

Craving The Player — Braden and Sierra #1 (Boxing romance)

Taming The Player — Braden and Sierra #2 (Boxing romance)

Overtime – Matt and Morgan

Vital Blindside — Adam and Scarlett (Single dad, female hockey player romance)

The Cherry Peak series:

Strung Along — Brody Steele and Annalise Heights (Country music star, pen pal romance)

Catching Sparks — Garrison Beckett and Poppy Huntsly (FWB, can't stand you to lovers romance)

Chasing Home — Johnny Mitchell and Aurora Bennett (Sunshine cowboy, black cat romance)

Acknowledgements

First and foremost, thank you to everyone who's been here from the very start to those who just found me with this release. Every time I wake up and get to do this for a living, I'm just so, so forever grateful. It's because of you that I'm here, and I'll never stop saying thank you.

To my amazing team of beautiful creative souls, thank you for everything you do with every release. The Books And Moods team for creating this fucking phenomenal cover and all the others in my backlist. Sandra for correcting me on all my silly and not-so-silly mistakes. Jordan for creating the stunning PR and interior artwork for this book and all the others in the series.

To Lauren-Brooke, thank you for keeping the wheels turning. I'm so grateful to call you not only my friend but a phenom assistant who I would have lost my mind without these past few months.

To Hayley, Becci, and Nicole, are you sick of being in my acknowledgments yet? Goddamn I love you, and I'm forever in your debt. Thank you for being not only my best friends but the ones I trust to give it to me straight every single time. In case you didn't hear me the first time, I love you.

To Sierra, yeah, you get your own paragraph at this point. It's been how many years now of you being not only my friend but one of my biggest supporters and cheerleaders, and an alpha reader to boot? You don't know how much I appreciate everything you do and have done for me, now and back when I was just a baby author struggling to get my name out there. You have my appreciation for. Ever. I love you.

To Courtney, Catherine, Christina—holy C's?—your voices

are so loud, and I just want to bawl my eyes out when I think about the fact you use them to speak love for me and my books. Thank you.

To Elin, thank you for lending me your mind and time when it came to everything Sweden in this book, from the translations to the snacks and treats. Thank you thank you.

And to all of my ARC readers and every person who's shouted about my books, thank you.